HIGH PRAISE FOR EDWARD LEE!

"The living legend of literary mayhem. Read him if you dare!"

—Richard Laymon, author of *Dark Mountain*

"Edward Lee's writing is fast and mean as a chain saw revved to full-tilt boogie."

—Jack Ketchum, author of *Old Flames*

"He demonstrates a perverse genius for showing us a Hell the likes of which few readers have ever seen."

—*Horror Reader*

"Edward Lee continues to push the boundaries of sex, violence and depravity in modern genre lit."

—*Rue Morgue*

"One of the genre's true originals."

—The Horror Fiction Review

"The hardest of the hardcore horror writers."

—*Cemetery Dance*

"Lee excels with his creativity and almost trademark depictions of violence and gruesomeness."

—*Horror World*

"A master of hardcore horror. His ability to make readers cringe is legendary."

—Hellnotes

The Scene of the Slaughter

It was the living room, if one could call it that: stained walls with holes the size of fists, dilapidated furniture and a collapsed couch, plus lots of plastic milk crates that the crackheads sat on when they came here to light up. The place smelled like urine and sweat—like any crackhouse—but there was something else more pungent in the air that Rosh knew had to be fresh blood. Garbage was piled in the corner, while several crack pipes lay on the ancient carpet, along with familiar one-by-one-inch plastic mini-baggies.

"Where's Cookie?" Captain Rosh whispered.

"In the bedroom. With the rest. That's where they all ran to."

Down a shabby hall with mold-stained carpet, then Rosh turned into a room where more photo flashes popped.

The sight made him feel kicked in the face.

"The tech says six bodies total," Stein advised.

"How the hell can he tell?" Rosh shot back.

It wasn't bodies as much as body parts that lay strewn about the reeking room. Arms and legs that appeared yanked from their sockets could be seen anywhere Rosh looked. Here the original color of the carpet was almost completely masked by still-wet blood.

Rosh counted six torsos, though he couldn't be sure because two of them looked pulled apart.

THE
GOLEM

EDWARD LEE

LEISURE BOOKS NEW YORK CITY

For Dave Boulter——Rest in peace.

A LEISURE BOOK®

April 2009

Published by

Dorchester Publishing Co., Inc.
200 Madison Avenue
New York, NY 10016

ISBN 10: 0-8439-5808-1
ISBN 13: 978-0-8439-5808-9
E-ISBN: 1-4285-0650-0

Visit us on the web at www.dorchesterpub.com.

ACKNOWLEDGMENTS

Wendy Brewer, Don D'Auria, James Barnhard of JRB Illustration, Tim McGinnis, Kathy Rosamilia, Liz Boulter, Mike McQuinn (for the tech stuff), Dave Barnett, Rich Chizmar, Ian Levy, Michael Ling, Dave Hardberger, SPC Andrew Myers, Rob Johns, Jim Argendeli, Chris Casmedes, Bob Strauss, William D. Gagliani, Jeff Burk, Bryan Smith, Mark Justice, Christine Morgan & Becca, Rudy, David, and Christian, Larry Roberts, Shane Staley, Jason Byars, Ken Arneson, peteboiler, Wetbones, Killa Klep, asimmons, Liquidnoose, Harvester, Jack Staynes, corpsegrinder, darvis, darkthrone, splatterhead, maladar, patronick, infnlfolowr, Mike Lombardo, Bloodhammer, bellamorte, Zombie905, Babaganoosh, boysnightout, worldspawn, jdamen, Specky, Bellamorte, everythinghorrordude, thereptilians, jonah. GNFNR, bsaenz24, reelsplatter, morleyisozzy. Folks at Phil's: Anda Norberg and Tim Shannon, Ashley and Jared, Alicia, Crystal and Becky, Suzanna, Tess. Charlie, Chris, and Sarah Meitz for the Austrian trek. Also, exponential thanks to Maharal Judah Loew for creating the Golem of Prague in 1580.

THE
GOLEM

PROLOGUE

August 1880

"You look like you've seen a ghost, lad," Captain Michael McQuinn said at the boat's broad wheel. He'd made the comment to his first mate, a work-weathered Bohemian named Poelzig who now stared listlessly out a starboard window in the small wheelhouse. All around them stretched the perfectly flat Chesapeake Bay.

"A ghost," muttered Poelzig. He dragged a callused hand across his forehead. "Didn't sleep much last night, Captain, nor did the wife. You?"

"Ah, I slept like a baby," McQuinn insisted in his Irish accent. He patted his hip flask with a smile. "Ain't nothin' to be restless about. We're both immigrants welcomed to this fine land, ay? Promised freedom and good, honest work. We ought to be grateful at all times . . ."

This much was true. McQuinn was an Irish Catholic, and Poelzig, a Jew from somewhere in Europe. Austria? *Who can tell after all them bloody wars?* McQuinn thought. Poelzig and his wife, Nanya, had fled Jewish persecution, while McQuinn had fled Dublin's tax collectors and more than one irate husband. But from what he could see thus far, America honored its promises.

Yes, *that* much was true, but what *wasn't* true was Captain McQuinn's remark about sleeping like a baby. He'd done anything but. They'd been on the bay two weeks now, starting in Baltimore Harbor, delivering goods first up the Patuxent River to Sandsgate, then across and up the Nanticoke, and next up the Wicomico to Salisbury. It seemed that with each off-loading of cargo at each port town, McQuinn felt more and more peculiar, and each night he slept less and less.

Poelzig was still tiredly staring off into space. "My God, last night I dreamt . . ."

McQuinn snapped his gaze to his sullen colleague. "Ya dreamt what, man?"

Poelzig shook his head. He was probably forty but right now looked eighty.

Gads! McQuinn didn't like it when he had to demonstrate his authority. Most of these river runs went like clockwork. So what was wrong now? "Somethin's been addlin' you since we left Baltimore," he snapped, "and more so after every stop. You and your missus ain't no good to me if ya ain't got your minds on your work. So. What is it? What's wrong?"

The otherwise confident first mate now seemed at a loss for words. He pointed behind him while keeping his eyes on McQuinn.

"What? The cargo house? Poelzig, we only have one more stop, then the route is done."

Poelzig's accent cracked. "The destination, sir, is what I and Nanya are troubled by."

For the Lord's sake! McQuinn snatched up the manifest orders and read the destination aloud: "Lowensport, Maryland, eleven miles east, northeast on the Brewer River. What's rubbin' ya the wrong way 'bout goin' there, man? It's just a mill-town's what I hear."

Poelzig cleared his throat. "More than that, sir."

"I scarcely heard'a the Brewer River 'fore this run, but the harbormaster tell me it's a deep trough all the way up'n free of snags. And don't forget, the *Wegener's* as tough a steamboat as they come. For God's sake, we ain't gonna sink."

Poelzig's somber face didn't change. "Lowensport itself's what I mean, sir."

McQuinn squinted, leaning forward. "Ain't you and your missus Jews?"

"We are, Captain, and proud of it."

"Well I don't know nothin' 'bout your faith, and precious little 'bout my own if you want the truth, and I don't got nothin' against any man fer what he believes." McQuinn emphasized his next words. "But the harbormaster tell me somethin' else, Poelzig. He tell me this little place called Lowensport was settled by Jews. *Your* people, Poelzig!"

"Not . . . our people, sir," Poelzig whispered sharply.

Can't figure none'a this, McQuinn thought. Best to just forget it. Why would two Jews have the frights over a town full of folks who believed the same thing? *It'd be like me bein' leery of steppin' into Mass.*

He lined his sight back on the bay, spotted the wide mouth of a river, then checked his maps. "Whatever it is that's got your ire up, ya can stow it for now, man, 'cause here's the Brewer River. Bet we're up to six knots an hour now, and goin' upriver'll likely only knock us back to three, so we should be dockin' in Lowensport not more than two hours after sundown. We'll spend the night there."

Poelzig suddenly tensed when he shot a gaze forward and saw the river's wide mouth. Then he went lax with a forlorn despair. "Captain, I and my wife implore you.

We cannot spend the night in Lowensport. Please, sir. Let's anchor here and finish the route tomorrow, in daylight."

Now McQuinn was getting mad. "We'd get back to Baltimore a day late, man! Are ya bonkers?"

"Please, sir. I and my wife cannot go there at night," Poelzig reasserted. "Because if you must, then I and Nanya will have to swim ashore now, and walk back to Baltimore, leaving the rest of the route to you by yourself."

McQuinn offered his first mate a chiseled stare. Was Poelzig threatening McQuinn with the outrageous implication? *I'm the captain of this boat and no first mate is directing my course, damn it!* But the harder he glared at Poelzig, the more forlorn the man became. "Poelzig. Are you tryin' to countermand my authority on this boat?"

"Not at all, sir. And you've been as fine a man as ever let me work for him," Poelzig said rather dolefully. "I am pleadin' with you, though. Let's *not* spend the night in Lowensport. Please."

McQuinn took a big sip off his flask, thinking. *I'm so mad I could throw the bloke* and *his pretty wife overboard right now, but . . .* But what? McQuinn let his temper idle, and then it occurred to him, *Poelzig's worked himself to the bone for me for months and never once has he asked for anything . . .*

"All right," McQuinn agreed. "I'll give you your way. I'll take us upriver a mile or two, then drop anchor. But I want that bin *full*, are ya hearin' me?"

Poelzig smiled for the first time since the trip started. "I hear you very well, Captain, and you have I and my wife's fondest thanks." And then he rushed out the back door and began to shout the news to Nanya in their own arcane language.

Jesus, Mary, and Joseph, McQuinn thought.

After anchoring, McQuinn halfheartedly raked for oysters off the stern while Poelzig lowered the crab traps and his wife methodically chopped the last of the wood for the tender. When McQuinn looked down the length of the boat, he felt the same pride he had on the day he'd taken it over. The *Wegener* was the last of its kind as far as shallow-draft riverboats went: a 100-foot-long sternwheeler that burned wood under its boiler instead of coal. Coal in some parts was too hard to come by. Sure, the coal-burners would move faster but their furnaces cost double. Wood-burners like the *Wegener,* however, could take plenty of freight up more narrow rivers, and when fuel ran short you merely dropped the brow, went ashore, and cut more. McQuinn had never seen such hardwood forests as those along the Chesapeake. Forward of the wood-tender, the furnace, and the great paddle wheel was the freighthouse on First Deck, and the quarters on Top Deck. There was no belowdeck for there was no hull; the boat was essentially a great rectangular platform that floated atop the water, which made it ideal for poorly charted rivers with unknown true depths and sandbars. McQuinn had never run aground, ever, not even at low tide; neither had he ever damaged the paddle wheel over snags. He loved navigating the water, and after so many years now, he could choose his own routes for much more pay than the younger captains who'd survived the War.

McQuinn tended the oyster rake—not much luck tonight—and alternately glanced over his shoulder with each great *thunk* of the ax. *Can't figure these Europeans out,* he puzzled. The man let his *wife* chop wood, but he had to admit it was much more pleasing to watch her wield the ax than Poelzig himself. Nanya was a unique woman, indeed, a head-turner if McQuinn ever saw one but proportioned so uncommonly.

Mother Mary, he thought, looking at her now. While he and Poelzig wore typical canvas overalls, long-sleeved cotton shirts, and Jefferson boots, Nanya wore identical boots, which came up just past the ankles, and a heavy cotton smock—nothing more. Her hard face remained pretty for its angles, and her roughly cut off-blonde hair looked appealing even in its unkemptness. Her body, though, was another thing. She stood tall or taller than most men—a large-framed woman, but with nary a pinch of fat on her. Instead, her body seemed sculpted from pale marble, her muscles so toned from ceaseless labor that she was likely as strong as McQuinn or Poelzig themselves. The word *statuesque* came to mind.

Thunk . . . thunk . . . thunk, went the ax in perfect rhythm, and each swipe caused the most precious jiggle of Nanya's unbridled and quite ample bosom.

McQuinn didn't feel he was lusting after another man's wife but instead admiring the bonnie physique. The woman raised and lowered the ax in a machinelike synchronicity, and with each drop of the blade—*thunk!*—he could actually feel the vibration through the boat's great platform. *Lord,* he thought next. The sun sank just behind her, silhouetting that coltish body through the baggy smock.

Thunk . . . thunk . . . thunk . . .

McQuinn had half a flask in him now, and he saw no harm in a complimentary comment. "Poelzig, my good man, I hope ya don't mind me pointin' out that that is one sure-fire woman you've got for a wife."

"Yes, it is quite true, sir," Poelzig said. He had his back to McQuinn as he tossed each log wedge into the tender.

McQuinn chuckled. "But I also got to say that if an Irishman was to let it be known he allowed his wife to chop wood, why, that same Irishman would be thrashed in the square."

Poelzig gave an odd chuckle himself. "But you see, sir, I would be thrashed worse for *not* allowing Nanya to chop wood."

McQuinn didn't understand. "Thrashed by who?"

Poelzig pointed. "By Nanya. She can fell a tree or cut a cord faster than near any man. Strong, she is. *Limber.* Her father—a useless cad—beat her every day as a child, until one day, when she was older, she beat *him* to within an inch of his sorry life."

McQuinn's eyes widened at the account.

"And that is why she insists on cutting all the wood, to keep strong, so that no man'll ever raise a hand to her again."

Thunk! went the ax, and the boat shuddered as one stout log section burst into two.

"My," McQuinn murmured. "That is indeed one strong lass . . ."

"And it's her desire to keep fit and never go to fat," Poelzig added, "so I'll never be of the mind to leave her."

McQuinn guffawed whiskey-breath. "Only a man off his head would leave a woman with a body like that. I can only imagine what she's like in—" But he severed his crassness before he could say the word *bed.*

Poelzig gave him a half smile and a nod.

They only kept a quarter-fire going in the furnace now,

since the boiler wasn't needed. The front trough was where they cooked, and it came equipped with a pot-hanger and grill. Poelzig "ah'd" when he hoisted up the wood-slat crab trap, and found it full with large, snapping crustaceans.

"Lord, man! The size of 'em!"

"Ja," the first mate agreed, and hauled the trap to the fat pot of water hanging over the fire. "One must be careful how he handles these, for they can be vicious." He opened the trap and plucked each of the shelled creatures up by a rear appendage and flung it into the pot.

"They're nearly as big as the brown crabs we had back in Ireland," McQuinn remarked. "Poelzig, do you have crabs where you come from?"

"Ne—er, no, sir." He pushed several of the more stubborn crabs back into the steaming water with the fire tongs. "None such as these, though we do have river crabs called *kraben*, but they're not nearly as sweet as these."

Nanya had finished chopping, and she smiled as her husband narrowly avoided being nicked by a crab's saw-toothed claw.

McQuinn rowed his long oyster rake again but pulled up nothing. "Blast it, I was hopin' for some oysters like we been gettin' all week, for they go mighty fine with these crabs."

Nanya said something to her husband in their language, then Poelzig took McQuinn's rake and handed it to her. "Nanya knows the ways of the water, long as she's been workin' it. In a river's mouth, the salinity's lower so the oysters grow closer to shore."

"Damned if I knew that," McQuinn said, but now his eyes were stuck back on the sturdy woman. "But—wait, lass! What are ya—"

Nanya had kicked off her boots, then splashed immediately into the water. She grinned at McQuinn as she turned on her back and began kicking, the rake across her breasts. When she shouted something else to Poelzig, the man heaved a large sack-net to her.

Blimey, McQuinn thought next. Nanya waded up till she was waist-deep and began to work the rake, but with each rearward stroke, the current lifted her smock over her bare bottom. McQuinn's cheeks billowed at the sight. Ten minutes later, she returned to the boat with a full sack.

"You Europeans have a sound touch with the fruits of these waterways, I surely must say." But then McQuinn almost fell backward when Poelzig helped his wife out of the water.

She stepped on deck, dripping. The water-logged blouse now adhered to the contours of her body, revealing every detail. *My eye-teeth are havin' a banquet today,* McQuinn thought. The woman—and Poelzig as well—seemed oblivious to the rousing effect of the drenched gown. Nanya sat at a deck table and immediately began opening the oysters with a knife.

"The *aperitiv,* Captain," Poelzig said. "In our language, we call these *ustrices.* And they're best raw, for they're known to make a man . . . well . . ."

Nanya giggled as she expertly shucked one oyster after the next.

McQuinn struggled to keep his eyes off the woman. "Since you've brought it to mind, Poelzig, what *is* your language?"

"We are Czech, Captain." And then the first mate loaded a tin plate with shucked oysters and passed them to McQuinn.

Czech. McQuinn had heard the word before, but knew nothing beyond that. He sucked several oysters down, and asked, "So *where* are you from in Europe, exactly?"

"A region known as Czechoslovak. It is a beautiful place illegally taken by lying monarchs of Austria—the Habsburgs." When Poelzig said this, Nanya grimaced and attempted, "They Habs ne Jude leek."

Poelzig smiled. "What my wife means, sir, is that the House of Habsburg doesn't like Jews. They promise religious tolerance in their constitution but then force us to live in ghettos. That is why we come here."

"That's right low-down of the blokes," McQuinn said, and it was something he could never figure himself. "As long as folks work hard and mind the law, what difference does it make how they choose to worship? Faithwise I couldn't tell ya the difference betwixt a Jew, a Prot, and a Catholic to save my neck."

Poelzig nodded. Then his wife said, "You more like *ustrices*, Captain, ano?" and piled more oysters on his plate.

McQuinn thought he understood, "Why, yes, you can bet I would." Then, to Poelzig, "Well, it seems your darlin' missus *can* speak a smidgen of English."

"She's learning, sir. A *good* learner, she is."

And a good-looker, McQuinn amended. He nearly moaned as Nanya leaned over to grab more oysters from the sack. The position caused her smock's neckline to plunge, revealing glistening bare breasts. To divert himself, he resumed the previous topic. "So, Czechs, ya say? Could ya name me a *city* so that I might have a better reference of your homeland?"

"Praha," Nanya intoned, but then Poelzig corrected, "The city we was born in, sir, is known to Americans as Prague."

Even with the whiskey buzzing in his head, the name piqued McQuinn. "You don't say . . . Well I'll be *blasted* if that ain't the—" He broke from his stance. "I'll be back in a wink. Just let me fetch the manifest . . ." He climbed the ladder to the wheelhouse and grabbed the book. When he returned astern, Poelzig was tonging out the cooked, bright-orange crabs from the water. The sun had crept fully away now; McQuinn lit a fish-oil lantern and eagerly opened the boat's cargo manifest.

"I knew I'd heard of that city before," he exclaimed. "Here. The city of origin for the Lowensport cargo is Prague." He looked up and found Poelzig undismayed.

"I and my wife are aware of that, sir. It was stamped on all of the shipping barrels. We're aware also that the people who now live in Lowensport emigrated from Prague."

McQuinn scratched his head. "Well if that ain't the most daft . . . I just don't see it, Poelzig. You're more than a tad unsettled by the prospect of goin' to Lowensport yet not only are the folk there of your own faith but they're from your own hometown! Why? What is it that's givin' ya the willies about meeting people from Prague who are Jews just like yourselves?"

Poelzig's voice rattled when he replied, "They're not Jews such as ourselves, Captain."

Nanya's eyes darkened and she hissed the word, "*Kischuph!*" and turned in a rush to glance fretfully over a rope rail.

These two I cannot reckon for the life of me, McQuinn thought. "Ya have my most steadfast apology if it was somethin' wrong I said."

"Not all at, sir." Poelzig set the steaming tray of crabs on the deck table. "Nanya is just a little more sensitive about some things. It's best understood to put it this way: Judaism comes in different forms just as Christianity does."

McQuinn belted a laugh. "I'll drink to that, Poelzig! Try bein' a Catholic in bleedin' Kentucky! Now I'm gettin' what it is you're sayin'."

Eventually Nanya returned, having shaken off her unease. She nudged her husband away from the table and began breaking the crabs open for them.

McQuinn offered them his flask. "Have a nip, the both of ya. It's struck me only now that I've yet to see either of ya imbibe."

"Thank you for your generosity, sir," Poelzig said, "but I and Nanya never partake in spirits, for reasons of our faith."

"Jews are forbidden to drink?" McQuinn asked in astoundment.

"It isn't that, sir, but most often choose not to. We believe that a fuzzy head prevents one from seeing En Soph."

"En Soph?"

"God," Poelzig translated.

McQuinn's brow rose. *If this be true, I'll definitely not be seein' God tonight.* He took another nip from his flask.

Nanya's eyes flicked to Poelzig's, and she whispered something.

"What's that yer missus is sayin'?" McQuinn chuckled. "Probably that the captain's your typical Irish drunk!"

"Of course not, sir. But my wife is curious, as am I, as to the actual contents of the Lowensport cargo. I'll tell her that it's none of our business."

This much was true; confidentiality of a buyer's merchandise came as part of any captain's job. Revealing the nature of freight could lead to theft. *But this pair here is certainly trustworthy*, McQuinn regarded. He knew that by now. "Well, I don't rightly see no harm; I believe it's little more than tools and such, and porcelain ware." He re-opened the manifest. "What exactly we're takin' to these folks in Lowensport on the morrow seems to be ten shipping barrels, one of which is full of marbles and another with *pewtery*, it says here. Barrels three and four . . . sharpening tools and sledge heads, and five and six, coal dust . . ."

"That would make sense," Poelzig said, "for Lowensport boasts a sawmill of some repute."

McQuinn frowned. "So they buy their tools from Prague and ship 'em all this way. Why spend such a sum when they could easily purchase the same manner of tools here?"

"*Sudeten* steel is much more superior, Captain, and worth the price. The ore comes from mountains within our homeland. A hammerhead forged from such ore will not even dent, and sharpening files last years."

McQuinn didn't object, though he was sure he'd place more faith in *Irish* steel. He squinted harder at the manifest. "And . . . hmm. It seems that the remaining four barrels contain crockery composite, though I'm not sure as what that is."

Com . . . posite, Captain?" Poelzig questioned.

"Kilning material, perhaps?" McQuinn noticed another word scribbled in the inventory, in parentheses. "There's another word, too, but it appears to be written in something other than English. Maybe *your* language, Poelzig. Here, have a look."

Poelzig followed McQuinn's finger on the parchment, and then gulped. "Written here is the Czech word *hilna*, Captain . . ."

Nanya clenched her husband's arm. "Ne!"

McQuinn couldn't help but notice the buxom woman's reaction. "Hilna? And what might that be?"

Poelzig's face looked rigid as stone. "The word means *clay*, sir. In other words, the cargo house contains four full barrels of clay . . ."

I'll never understand these foreigners, McQuinn complained to himself as he unlocked the cargo house on First Deck. *They acted as if their own graves had been trodden on*. What could it be about potter's clay from Europe that would cause such a shocked effect? Nevertheless, Poelzig had asked the captain's indulgence, and requested that they be allowed to actually see this clay.

"That would be outright irregular, Poelzig! That's paid-for merchandise, and we as well are being paid to deliver it—unmolested."

Poelzig paused to search for the proper words. "I and my wife, sir, would only like to *see* it. I can only equate it to—what's the word?—sentimentality, if you can understand."

McQuinn smirked. "Ya mean like seein' somethin' from your homeland, to warm your heart, somethin' like that?"

"Something like that, sir, yes. If part of the Blarney Castle from your own grand homeland of Ireland were to be moved to America, would you not want to see it for yourself?"

It was a strange parallel but . . . "Well, since ya put it that way, man, I suppose I would."

"I can only add that this cargo has a special meaning for any Czech Jew—"

"It's nothin' but a bunch of bloomin' *clay*, man!"

"Yes, sir, but to a Czech Jew, it's more than that. You

really wouldn't understand without *being* a Czech Jew yourself."

McQuinn looked back at both of them as the high summer moon glared down. Cicadas and peepers pumped a throbbing cacophony of sound all around them. McQuinn, even in his perplexity, let his gaze slide up Nanya's toned legs, robust curves and bosom, and just when he began to feel guilty, he noticed that those big, bottomless eyes of hers held wide on his in the most struggling hope.

"Oh, for the Lord's sake, come on!" he consented and dragged his keys from his pocket. Nanya beamed; Poelzig sighed relief. They grabbed lanterns and quickly followed McQuinn to the loading door of the cargo house.

McQuinn's key opened the clunky latch-lock, and an earthy redolence greeted them when they entered. Earthy and a bit foul. Their footsteps echoed; by now, the cargo house was three-fourths empty. In the back, in the lantern light, they could see the massive shipping barrels and their shining metal bands. *Can't believe I agreed to this*, McQuinn thought, hefting a crowbar and approaching one of the later-numbered barrels. Across the beige-wood staves, each barrel was stenciled with the words: VLTAVA HILNA. "Vltava?" McQuinn asked.

"The great river of Prague, sir," Poelzig replied. His words echoed. "It's where the clay is from, just as the legends say."

"Legends?" *This is daft.* McQuinn crowbarred the high quality lid off one barrel, then stepped back at the waft of unpleasant odor. "There's your clay, Poelzig. It stinks like an outhouse!"

But Poelzig and Nanya approached, silent and wide-eyed in awe. "You see, sir," Poelzig began, "if one believes the legends, the clay from this same river saved our people long ago, in the ghettos of Prague."

"The Jews, you mean?" McQuinn felt fuddled. "So would ya mind tellin' me how a bunch of vile-smellin' *clay* saved your people?"

Poelzig smiled thinly. "It's only *legend*, sir. But it's thought that clay from the Vltava is blessed, in a manner of speaking. At least . . ." Meanwhile, his wife seemed enraptured by the opened barrel. She was running her hands down the containers' wooden staves. Poelzig went on, "According to the old archives, you see, those pure of heart and devout to God receive *power* from this clay."

"Power from clay," McQuinn muttered and reclaimed his flask. "I gotta tell ya, man. I don't know *what* you're talkin' about."

"You'd have to be a Jew, sir—" Poelzig turned with a start when Nanya reached forward. She meant to touch the pallid clay in the barrel, but her husband snatched her hand back before she could. "But one must not touch it without the proper regard for it."

"Regard?" McQuinn snapped. "It's clay! Damn near the same as mud!"

Poelzig seemed amused by McQuinn's dismay. He replaced the lid and prized it back down. "Indeed, sir, the clay will empower the faithful, but for those untrained in the proper graces and disciplines, it can work the reverse. It can turn a white soul black. Good things can be made with this, but also bad." Poelzig chuckled. "That is, sir, *if* one believes the legends."

"All right, fine," came McQuinn's testy reply. "And now you've seen it, so let's be out of here." He ushered them back out to the port walkway. Something caused him to glance one more time at the barrels, after which he frowned and relocked the door.

"Thank you for indulging us, sir," Poelzig said. "I and my wife are most grateful."

"Good, then be gratefully off to your bunks for some shut-eye. We've a busy day on the morrow, and it starts at the crack'a dawn."

"Good night, sir," Poelzig said. Nanya bowed. Then they both glided up the steps to Top Deck. McQuinn watched their lanterns disappear.

What a pair, those two, McQuinn thought. He sipped from his flask. *Clay. From some stinking river in God knows where, and they're actin' like it's the Holy Grail.*

McQuinn slouched up to his own quarters, and soon fell asleep with the faint sounds of the river in his ears.

McQuinn turned fitfully on his bunk. Sleep claimed him like a bad flu; his head seemed to pound in step with his woozy dreams. First he dreamed of blackness, then of a slowly rising sound that eventually became the repeated thunks of an ax.

Thunk . . . thunk . . . thunk . . .

Next came words, exerted words but feminine and even impassioned:

"Goilem!"

Thunk!

"Kischuph!"

Thunk!

"Loew!"

Thunk!

Finally the dream image surfaced. McQuinn groaned in his sleep now, for he could see Nanya manically chopping more wood for the tender on the boat's back deck.

Jesus . . . So beautiful . . .

All that Nanya wore was the harsh moonlight. Her toned body tensed, her belly sucking in and breasts thrusting out, as she raised the ax in a high arc, paused, then—

Thunk!

—slammed the blade down so hard the boat shuddered. A fat log wedge flew apart.

The dream's eye crawled up the exquisite nude physique, across the sweat-misted white skin, the sleek straining muscles and the prettily angled face. Disheveled hair hung forward so that her eyes could only be seen through gaps. The eyes looked wide, yet somehow dead.

Then the dream's perspective pulled back on the strange face, and that's when McQuinn's eyes snapped open. Affrighted, he gasped when he saw the identical face looking down on him.

How in the blazes . . .

Nanya was straddled atop McQuinn, naked as the dream. She'd slipped in here as he dreamt, pulled his trousers down, and—

McQuinn didn't have to ponder long as to what was taking place now. His own body strained as she meticulously rode him, her excited breasts full, nipples erected as her top teeth clamped her lower lip. McQuinn felt as though she'd skewered herself on him.

Her dead eyes spiked him, and with each slow, straining stroke she gasped a word:

"Kischuph . . ."

McQuinn's hands sculpted up her thighs, then over her hips—

"Loew . . ."

He veed the gorged nipples between his fingers—

"Goilem . . ."

His senses finally roused. *What am I doing! This is another man's wife, but . . . But . . .*

But she'd already hijacked his morality. Could he be blamed? She'd begun the seduction herself as McQuinn slept unaware . . .

"For God's sake, woman! Have ya no respect for your husband?"

But even as some impulse directed him to push her off, she seemed to sense it, the dead eyes bearing down, and a wicked grin showing through the gaps of her hair. Suddenly she let the slow strokes turn manic, and she was riding him like an animal. The cot springs shimmied. McQuinn's body clenched as Nanya's sex spasmed to an excruciating tightness—

McQuinn's climax exploded.

Had he cried aloud? He hoped not! If Poelzig were to waken from the sounds and come in, what could McQuinn possibly say?

Nanya sighed, face strained up at the raftered ceiling. Light flickered to her side, and at first McQuinn feared that Peolzig had entered with a lantern, but then he remembered that he hadn't turned his off.

And that's when he noticed—

"What in bloomin' . . ." There was something on her belly, wasn't there? Daubs of some kind, or—no, circles. The crudest little circles forming a larger circle over her belly. It looked like something a child would finger paint. "What's this on ya, woman?" he asked. He counted exactly ten rings forming the outer circle, and an eleventh circle around her navel. When he touched one, his finger came away wet, tacky. It had a grit to it.

Then he sprang up. "You daft bitch! That's clay, ain't

it? You've been into that blammed clay!" He churned her off of him, hauled up his trousers, and ran out and down the steps with the lantern. Behind him, he thought he heard her giggling.

What am I gonna tell the buyer if she's messed with his goods?

McQuinn's feet thunked down hard on the wooden walkway. He cursed aloud when he saw the latch-lock on the cargo door gouged out—obviously the work of an ax.

"Poelzig!" he bellowed. "Get your arse down here right now!" McQuinn's voice boomed out across the water, such that several gulls squawked in surprise. He bulled into the cargo house, rushed back—

Thank God! came the relieving thought. Only one of the barrels was molested, its lid pried off. McQuinn held the lantern down to see several of the crazy woman's finger streaks in the surface of moist clay, but that was all. When he picked the lid up to replace it—

Thunk!

McQuinn shouted. The lid split and flew out of his hands, then—

Thunk!

Nanya brought the ax down again, missing the captain's arm by an inch. The blade buried itself in the barrel lip.

"You're bleedin' *nuts*, woman!" he yelled, then caromed around her as she struggled to dislodge the ax blade.

"Poelzig! Poelzig! Wake up, man!" Panic carried Mc-Quinn back up the side stairs, lantern rattling. He barged into the crew's quarters.

"Can ya not hear me, Poelzig! For God's sake, wake up! Your wife's gone mad!"

Poelzig did not wake up.

McQuinn raised the lantern when he saw the couple's cot empty. The floor was another story, though, for in the middle of it lay Poelzig, or at least what was left of him. Blood shined on most of the floor. Poelzig had been chopped in half, from his crotch to the top of his skull.

McQuinn stepped back, trying to think through his shock. *My gun—Damn it! It's in my quarters! I've got to—* But it was already too late.

Just as McQuinn turned to flee to his quarters and secure a mode of defense—

Thunk!

—the clay-dabbed madwoman buried the ax right in the middle of his face.

CHAPTER ONE

Somerset County, Maryland, The Present

I

Seth Kohn felt in a trance as he flipped through the wallet-sized snapshots. The Tahoe idled as he waited, the purr of its engine adding to the hypnotic effect. The first picture bid a smile; it showed a pretty yet overweight woman with long sable-dark hair. She was standing on the St. Petersburg pier, smiling insecurely back into the camera. Seth hadn't taken the picture himself; it was old, presumably taken by one of Judy's old boyfriends. She'd given it to him recently, though, instructing him, "Keep this in your wallet. It's one of my 'fattie' pictures. I think I weighed one eighty then."

"Why do you want *me* to have it?" he'd asked.

"So you can gauge me."

"*Gauge* you?"

She'd laughed, tossing her hair the way she always did. "Yeah. If I *ever* get that big again, lock me in a room for a year and don't give me anything but bread and water. *Whole wheat* bread."

She's a riot, he thought now. The next picture was taken only six months ago, of them together after one of their re-hab meetings. On cocaine, Judy Parker had gone from 180 to ninety-five in only a year. But in snapshot she couldn't have looked better: 120, bulge free, smiling in a clingy maroon twinset sundress, her hair a foot shorter than the "fattie" picture, but her eyes brighter than he'd ever seen them. *How did a nerd like me ever land a woman like this?* he wondered, and then he raised a brow when he looked at himself in the same picture. Tall, thin, and a bit stoop-shouldered, but just as bright eyed. He knew why they each looked so radiant. *We got our lives back . . . and didn't think we would.* Seth scrutinized his hair in the snapshot: dark, longish, and wavy. A year before it had been gray, from over a year of chronic alcoholism. He figured that the vanity of hair dye was a legitimate reward for getting through rehab without a drop of booze. One last glance at the photo and he muttered with some satisfaction, "For a geeky, stoop-shouldered, big-nosed, almost fifty-year-old computer nerd, I guess I'm not a half-bad-looking guy . . ."

The next photo paralyzed him. Were his hands suddenly shaking? The pic was a portrait shot of a peaches-and-cream blonde with a luscious smile.

Aw, Jesus. He knew he shouldn't keep it in his wallet, not after all this time.

Helene.

He quickly put the photos back in his wallet when he heard the thrashing footsteps.

Just as Judy opened the passenger door, Seth was caught by surprise: an old black step van with some kind of markings on it blew by, breaking up the green of the fields. Something or other Fruits & Vegetables, the markings had read. A half-second glimpse showed him two ungainly men with grizzly chins and missing teeth in their grins. Did one of them wink?

Maryland rednecks, I guess. County boys. Seth snorted a chuckle. *I sure hope Maryland rednecks aren't as pathetic as Florida rednecks . . .*

"Oh my God!" Judy exclaimed, sliding her rump into the seat and slamming the door. "Did those guys in the truck see?"

"See what?" Seth asked.

"See me peeing in the field!"

"Oh, I don't think so," Seth tried to comfort her. "The grass is too high."

Judy sighed and leaned back, refastening her seat belt. "I don't know if this is just new for me, or a new *low*."

Seth pulled off the gravelly shoulder and accelerated back down the road. "You mean to tell me you've never peed in the great outdoors before?"

Judy smirked, primping her dark hair. "No. I'm a *woman*. I don't have . . . one of those things. Guys got it easy as far as that goes. I'm an elegant, sophisticated woman, Seth."

"So when you were pissing like a racehorse back there in the grass, I guess you had your pinkies extended, right?"

"Of course!" But then she looked paranoically behind her. "I hope those two rednecks don't call the cops." She touched her chin. "What would the charge be? Unlawful public bladder-voiding? Tinkling on county property?"

"I wouldn't worry about it, honey, and come to think of it . . ." He pointed to the upcoming sign which announced, LOWENSPORT — 6 MILES. "It may actually be that we own the land you just . . . voided your bladder on."

"Good. That means we're almost there, right? Didn't you say the house was five miles *before* Lowensport?"

"Yep." Seth flipped down the dorky sunglass clip-ons over his glasses. He squeezed Judy's hand. "And thanks for being such a sport about all this."

Judy seemed distracted by the endless green fields sweeping past. "How am I a sport?"

"I know how you hate long drives. Tampa to Maryland can be done in a day and a half. I didn't mean for this to take three."

"Well, let's see, let's count them," Judy replied. "Sex once in Florence, South Carolina, twice at rest stops on the interstate, then once in Ashland, and twice today on the ferries from Virginia to Maryland." Judy brushed a shock of shining dark hair out of her face to grin. "That's six times in three days. You definitely know how to keep a woman pacified on a long drive."

"I'm flattered," Seth chuckled. "But you better make that seven times, because there were *three* rest stops. You forgot Tappahannock."

Judy paused, thinking. "That's right! The picnic table! How could I forget?"

Seth nodded.

"And since we're almost there, we should be christening the new house real soon . . ."

Seth exaggerated a groan. "Honey, I'm forty-nine. Give an old man a break."

"Old man, my ass." She laughed and let her gaze return to the window. The river couldn't be seen now, for all the grasslands. "So that's what switchgrass looks like," she remarked. The seemingly limitless expense of man-tall grass shined so deliriously green it made her eyes hurt. "That's pretty cool about all the tax breaks you'll get from that stuff."

"Oh, is that it? I didn't even know," Seth said and slowed on the road to look. "It looks just like . . . well, grass."

"It's a high-bulk biomass crop," Judy said. "By October,

it'll be ten feet tall. Then they cut it down and start all over again."

"It's for ethanol or something, right?"

"Chiefly, yeah, but other things, too, like hydrogen, methane, ammonia, and a form of synthesis gas that'll run an electric plant just as efficiently but much cleaner than coal-burning plants. Even better is that switchgrass grows on land where farm crops *don't* grow so detractors can't bitch about cutting into the food and feedstock supplies. Switchgrass is essentially junk that—thanks to the marvels of modern science—can get the U.S. off fossil fuels. It's carbon-neutral, and renews every year."

"It still must cost money to farm."

"Almost nothing compared to corn, soybeans, or any other food crop you can name. Switchgrass doesn't need fertilizer or pesticides, and it's the most drought-resistant plant that can be used to make money. Very recently it's become a wondercrop, especially for people concerned about pollution and greenhouse gases."

Seth found the subject mildly interesting but—"Look, I know you used to teach philosophy but how do you know so much about *switchgrass*, of all things?"

She snorted a chuckle. "I used to date a professor of agricultural science. The guy was *obsessed* with renewable energy sources."

Seth was instantly curious. "Yeah, but was he also obsessed with *you?*"

Judy hooted. "Are you kidding? First of all, it was back in my 'fattie' days, and secondly—I'm serious—this guy would read *Environment Times* like a regular man reads *Playboy.*"

"That is if regular men even *read* it at all." Seth *did*

have a subscription, and sometimes they even looked through it together. "So . . . how long did you date him?"

"Seth, please, I don't want to talk about him. He was a dolt."

"Ah, now I don't feel so bad."

"And anyway, we were talking about the switchgrass and the tax breaks you'll get from it."

Seth got back to the speed limit. "This year I need all the tax breaks I can get. But . . . I guess I'm being greedy, huh?"

"That's what I don't understand about you," she said, but in a jovial way. "You have almost a Christian-style guilt over success—and you're Jewish!"

Seth winked at her. "Yeah, but I'm damn glad air is free. My nose is *huge*."

She sluffed him off with a shake of the head. "When you work your butt off for twenty-five years and finally strike it big, you shouldn't feel guilty, you should feel proud."

He couldn't let it die just yet. "But pride's a sin, honey— for all you Christians, that is."

"So is sex out of wedlock, lover, for heebs and goys alike, and after doing it seven times during a three-day road trip, I think we're probably both on God's shit list."

Seth searched for a witticism but stalled. *Why did she have to mention wedlock?* he thought. He didn't even know why he'd be bothered by the prospect. Helene had been dead now for two years.

Judy gave him an astonished look, then nudged him hard on the arm. "It was a *joke*, Mr. Jokester! If I even *joke* about marriage, you clam up."

"No, no, that's not it—"

"Uh-hmm. Besides, I told you on our first date that I never want to get married." She rolled her window down, perhaps as a distraction, and let her hair fly in the breeze. "Let's not kid ourselves. As paranoid as you are, and as impulsive as I am, marriage would probably wreck our relationship."

"Come here!" he said quickly, and startled her by slipping his arm around her and pulling. "Here, right over here next to me—"

"I can't!" she squealed. "My seat belt's on!"

"Take it off, take it off," he urged. "Right now!"

Bewildered, she did so, and then Seth dragged her right over till she was half in his lap. He kissed her immediately, and hard, and even playfully slipped his hand down her blouse and into her bra. She just as playfully feigned resistance until the kiss grew more serious. The Tahoe began to weave on the old country road. When he broke the kiss off, he held her even tighter and whispered, "Listen to me, Judy. Are you listening?"

"Yes . . ."

"Nothing, and I mean *nothing* is going to wreck our relationship. No booze, no dope, no bullshit from our pasts. Nothing. Do you believe me?"

Suddenly a tear welled in her eye. "Yes, I do."

"Good." And then he kissed her again.

Eventually she laughed and pushed him back. "Maybe nothing will wreck our relationship but you're sure as hell going to wreck the car if you don't keep your eyes on the road!"

"I guess you're right."

"Let's just get to the house," she whispered. Judy's face was flushed now. "Then we can go for number eight . . ."

II

"Not bad," D-Man muttered just after they'd passed the forest green Chevy Tahoe. "See the knockers on her?"

"Did I?" Nutjob questioned. "And I also saw the pencil-neck she was with. Shit, man. We could go back there and take care of business. Who'd know? Wouldn't be the first time we left some bodies in the switchgrass."

The sun glared off D-Man's nearly bald head. "See, Nutjob, that's why you been in the joint three times and I never been." D-Man's muscles tensed when he jabbed a hard finger in his colleague's shoulder.

"Oww!"

"Lookin's one thing. But the only *business* we got's with Rosh. You wantin' to fuck with people just to get your whistle wet could blow the whole game for all of us. I ain't gonna lose this big-money gig 'cos of your redneckin' around. Ya hear me?"

"Yeah," Nutjob grumbled.

Nutjob drove and D-Man rode shotgun. The big black step van rattled down the road, bearings shrieking. It was Nutjob who had more missing teeth. His mud brown hair stuck to the sides of his possibly malformed head, and whenever he scratched his goatee, dandruff fell out. Hokey cobra tattoos wound up his forearms. The missing left ear-lobe, he claimed, could be attributed to a gang fight in Jessup Penitentiary. "I lost an earlobe," he claimed. "He lost an eyeball." In truth, though, the loss was due to some initial noncompliance on his part when a number of fellow cons had wanted to play the well-known prison game known as "Choo-Choo Train" and had decided Nutjob would be the caboose. "You bend over right now, bitch," a con named Barbell said after he spat the earlobe out in the shower, "else next thang get bit off'll be mo' than yo' earlobe." Nutbjob had taken the advice.

D-Man, however, had a different redneck look: brawny, serious, and, though not exactly clean, his unkemptness didn't come close to Nutjob's. They called him D-Man because he'd once driven a doughnut delivery truck until he'd gotten fired for falling asleep at the wheel and barreling off a bridge, consigning hundreds of honey-dipped, jelly-filled, and french crullers to the Brewer River. Since then he'd managed to ascend in the world of commerce, or *descend*, depending on one's viewpoint. His brawn and the almost-shaved head made him look like a trailer park version of Bruce Willis.

"Here we is," Nutjob announced after they'd hit downtown Somner's Cove and pulled into Crazy Alan's Crabhouse. They slowed around back, both quiet now, and kept their eyes peeled. Every other day they'd be hearing about new antidrug initiatives, and though D-Man wasn't exactly think tank material, he was smart enough to know that all it took was one rat to turn a sure thing into a twenty-five-year jolt with no parole. "Careful," he urged. "Get'cher speed down."

Nutjob sputtered. "Like what we got to worry about, man? You a 'fraidy-cat?"

"Just do what I tell ya or I punch your face inside-out," D-Man asserted.

The drab black van idled along the docks behind the crabhouse. Nutjob parked and shut the motor off. Stacks of crab traps sat in piles on some of the docks, but the boats had already come and gone. *Good sign*, D-Man thought. *But where's—*

"Hey, D-Man? Where the hell is—"

"He'll be here." D-Man smirked. Rosh was *always* here on time. D-Man wrung his hands a few times. "You get the stuff, I'll go look for him."

Nutjob climbed into the back as D-Man disembarked and cautiously walked down several of the sorting aisles where undocumented workers would separate the crabs into the various size categories before taking them into the restaurant. It was the crab boats themselves that made the pickups, from more maritime suppliers who passed off the shipments from one to another along the crabbing routes. Rosh never made the switch with D-Man in his own vehicle; he always had it here at the crabhouse, because the crabhouse was where the boats dropped off the base product. He tried the back door but it was locked.

This don't feel right, he thought, and quickened his pace back to the van. *Why do I got this funny feelin' today's the day I get busted?*

"Nutjob?" He could see the van's back doors hanging open, yet could hear no familiar voices. D-Man looked in the back, saw that the corn bushels remained untouched, and then looked on the other side of the van—and froze.

"Holy sh—"

Nutjob lay facedown on the bare dockwood, his hands lashed behind his back with yellow Flex Cuffs.

Tick!

"Don't move, redneck, or it's lights out."

D-Man's jaw jittered as he raised his meaty hands and felt the tip of a pistol barrel against his temple.

"I-I—".

"Yeah." A hard hand shoved him toward where Nutjob lay, then spun him around. A Somner's Cove cop he'd never seen before sneered back: slim, mustached, weasel-eyed. The nameplate over his badge read STEIN. "So you're the big bad D-Man, huh, punk? Drive any doughnuts in the river lately?"

"I-I—"

"Our intel's had the line on you and your scumbag buddy for a while." Stein kicked Nutjob over on his back. D-Man's partner looked teary-eyed.

"He come from out of nowhere, D-Man! He knows all about—"

"Be quiet," ordered the cop. "You sound like a woman, and—look at that. Nerves of steel." He pointed to Nutjob's crotch. He'd wet his pants.

A chuckle. "I'd say you guys *ain't* making it as bad-ass crack dealers. You should've stuck to delivering doughnuts."

Finally D-Man found some semblance of a tongue. "We're just deliverin' corn to the crabhouse, Officer."

Stein shoved him back to the rear of the van. "Let's check out your produce, huh? Haul out the last bushel in the corner."

How the hell does this guy know . . . D-Man's mind spun in a frenzy. *Someone dropped a dime on us, but . . . who? Rosh? Ain't no way!* After another hard shove in the middle of the back, D-Man kneed into the van and started moving the bushels aside. *And what the fuck am I gonna do now?* His hands shook when he grabbed the corner bushel.

"Oww!" D-Man wailed when Stein kicked him hard in the thigh.

"The *other* corner, tough guy."

D-Man was blubbering as bad as Nutjob when he hauled the bushel back.

"Now . . . let's see what we got here." Stein kept his pistol trained on D-Man, while his free hand threw the top ears out of the bushel.

At once, D-Man noticed the oddity. *What the . . .*

The cop had a clear plastic glove on his hand. He pulled out two large coffee cans from the bottom of the bushel. "You guys are real geniuses. Let me guess . . . Harvard?" Stein peeled off a plastic top to reveal hundreds of pieces of crack cocaine in the can.

D-Man was dragged back out, then slammed against the side of the van. "You pieces of shit sell that stuff to *kids*." And then *FFFwump!* D-Man doubled over from a fist to the solar plexus. "This town's got thirteen-year-olds turning *tricks* 'cos you pathetic walking garbage cans got 'em hooked."

"No, man, no," D-Man wheezed. "We're just makin' a drop, I swear. We, we, we—"

"Who's your point man?" Stein asked.

D-Man and Nutjob fell silent.

"Come on, boys. You better start talkin'."

"Look, Officer. We just make the switch, don't know who for," D-Man began to run his mouth. "We trade the crack for a couple pounds of blow, plus cash, once or twice a week."

"With who? Who's your point man?"

"It's someone different every time, man—er, Officer. It's someone here, at the crabhouse. Look, we'll cut ya in."

FFFwump!

This time it was not Stein's fist that smacked into D-Man's gut, it was the end of a blackjack. D-Man's cheeks ballooned, and he fell to his knees.

"You're lying," Stein said. He walked over to where Nutjob lay. "Don't fuck with me. Who's your point man, Nutjob?"

Nutjob whimpered. "I—aw, shit! I don't kn—"

FFFwap!

Stein smacked the blackjack right into Nutjob's crotch. Nutjob bellowed, face creased.

"Ain't got time for this. My coffee break's coming up."

D-Man remained bent over on his knees. His teeth clacked together when he felt the pistol barrel pressed against the top of his shaven head.

"Who's your point man? You've got to three."

"Aw, Jesus, man—"

"One."

"Please, look! My people'll *pay* ya!"

"Two."

"No, wait!"

"Two and a half!"

"D-Man!" Nutjob shrieked.

"Three—"

"Rosh!" D-Man and Nutjob yelled in unison. "It's Captain Rosh!"

Stein lowered the pistol. Meanwhile, both D-Man's and Nutjob's hearts hammered.

"Hmm. Well, you know? Let me think," Stein said. "That's good of you to say, but you know what? I already know that. And you know what I'm going to do in exchange for verifying this?" He nudged D-Man.

"Uh . . . let us go?"

"Close." Stein snickered. "I'm gonna kill ya both anyway." And then he put the gun back to D-Man's head, and—

"Noooooo! Holy Jesus don't kill me!" D-Man bawled.

—pulled the trigger.

CLICK!

The hammer fell on an empty chamber. D-Man dropped his face to the dock, his bladder emptying.

"Just kidding, guys," came Stein's next statement, and with it a long, rowdy laugh and footsteps. Lower lip hanging, D-Man looked up and saw Rosh coming down the walkway in his crisp police uniform, captain's bars shining. He began to clap, still honking laughter. "I'm impressed, boys! It took you a whole five minutes to give me up."

D-Man rose as if he'd just gotten off a bad roller coaster. He stared cockeyed. "What the *hell?*"

"D-Man, Nutjob, say hello to Charlie Stein. Charlie's my new partner."

Chuckling, Stein snipped Nutjob's Flex Cuffs with a wire cutter, then helped him up. "You can take a joke, right, buddy?" Then he squeezed Nutjob's cheek and gave it a pat. "We were just playin' around."

Nutjob looked appalled, cradling his crotch. "Playin' around? Ya blackjacked my nuts!"

Stein slapped him on the back. "Captain Rosh wanted to see if I can walk the walk, you know? I gotta look the part on the street, breaking bad and all that."

D-Man's heart was still fluttering like a hummingbird's wings, and Nutjob looked right at him, mouthed something inaudible, then fainted outright.

Rosh huffed a laugh. "Leave him be; he'll be all right. Poor boy's still shook up."

"Well, he's fuckin' got a right to be!" D-Man complained.

"Come on, come on." Rosh tapped on a back door and out walked several overalled workmen, all grinning. "Load up that corn, boys," Rosh said, and gave the coffee cans to Stein. "Stein, stash these and bring in D-Man's package. We'll be inside."

"Sure, Captain."

D-Man was still dizzy when he followed Rosh into the

crabhouse and around to the sunny front bar. "You scared the living shit out of us, man!"

"Relax. Can't ya take a joke?" The bar was empty. They pulled up two stools. "Hey, Jimmy! Couple beers, huh?"

"Sure, sure," said a redneck 'keep polishing a glass. He smiled, showing missing teeth.

D-Man tried to finally simmer down. Rosh was pulling something out of his pocket. He had short red hair and a pale complexion, which somehow made him look even less trustworthy. D-Man had been making pickups from him for over five years. "Demand's on the rise, my friend."

"My people can handle it. You bring all the pure blow you can, and we'll turn it into rock."

"Good, good."

The barkeep put down two beers. "I love it," he said. His voice sounded like a kazoo. "Captain of the police department sitting in my bar rapping with a drug dealer, and drinking in uniform to boot."

"And not just *drinking*, Jimmy." Rosh winked. "Drinking for *free*."

"Just what I need."

"Hey, Jimmy, how about disappearing for a few, huh? Got some private biz to talk with my pal here."

"Yeah, yeah," the man said, and walked away.

Stein entered with a small suitcase and set it down at D-Man's feet. "It all weighed up just right."

"Don't it always?" D-Man tried to sound authoritative, but fumbled when his voice cracked from the scare he was still getting over.

"It should work out to a thousand rocks per can." Stein slapped D-Man on the back. "Hey, you're not pissed about the fun and games earlier, are ya?"

"No," D-Man stretched the response. "I thought it was hilarious . . . fucker."

Rosh and Stein laughed hard.

"See ya in a few days, D-Man. I'd wait for you to count the drop but . . . I don't have till midnight."

Rosh and Stein laughed harder this time.

Fuckin' assholes . . . D-Man peeked into the case, saw several one-pound bags of cocaine and three $10,000 bands of century notes. But even with the bullshit he had to put up with sometimes, D-Man knew he was damn lucky to be involved with this. It beat working for a living, which was something he'd never been good at anyway.

"Solid?" Rosh asked.

D-Man nodded.

"And now I need a favor."

D-Man winced.

"A *five-grand* favor," Rosh appended, and slipped another stack of bills to D-Man. "Your man does good work, and we appreciate it."

"What's the favor?" D-Man sighed.

"We need another button job like last spring." Rosh lay down a mug shot and slid it over.

D-Man was still too wracked even to drink his beer. He peered at the arrest photo of a generic female crack addict: shabby red hair around a sucked-in face, hollow eyes, thin lips. "She's just a crack ho, ain't she? I think I seen her around."

"Name's Tracy Roberts, aka Cookie."

D-Man shrugged. "Why you want a button on her? She's just another skinny junkie."

"Yeah?" Rosh looked serious for the first time today.

"One of our stoolies told us she's talking about being an informant."

"Big deal. You're the cops."

"Not with *us*, D-Man. With the county."

"Oh."

Rosh tapped the money in D-Man's lap. "Tell your man. We need this bad. We need your *hitter*. She cribs at the address on the back."

D-Man flipped the photo. "It shouldn't be a problem."

Rosh smiled. He finished his beer. "Well, since you're not drinking this . . ." He started on D-Man's. He slapped D-Man on the back again, something D-Man hated. "You know something? I was reading in the paper today that last year's drought created a shortage in America's surplus food supply, and a lower surplus means it's less food aid that we can send to poor countries like Africa, where people starve to death every day."

D-Man frowned. "Yeah?"

"And I got to thinking." Now Rosh tapped the photo. "These crackheads? They don't weigh but ninety, a hundred pounds—any of them."

"It's 'cos they're junkies, Rosh. Junkies barely eat."

Rosh held up a quick finger. "Right! They barely eat, and that's my point. That's how I figure we're doing a lot of good."

Now D-Man's face twisted up. "Selling *crack?*"

"Yes, yes! See, the more kids we turn into crack addicts, the less food they'll consume over their short lifetimes. I figure if we work even harder, we can get that surplus back up, then start sending more food aid to Africa. And that's a good thing, isn't it?"

D-Man stared at Rosh's serious expression, but in an

instant the officer slapped his hands down hard on the bar and honked laughter.

D-Man shook his head. "You really are a ton of laughs today, Rosh, but I gotta split and change my pants. Thanks for making me piss them."

Rosh tugged on D-Man's sleeve before he could get up. "Let me ask you something, just between you and me."

D-Man groaned and sat back down. "Come on. What?"

"I know it's none of my business but . . . Are *you* the button?"

D-Man grew instantly out of sorts. "No, man."

"It can't be Nutjob; that redneck hammerhead couldn't turn on a light switch without fucking it up. So—come on. Who is it?"

"I couldn't tell ya if I knew. That's the deal."

"I know, but I'm . . . curious."

"And any fuckin' way, I *don't* know, so just drop it, all right?"

Rosh nodded, gave up. "Cool, cool. But whoever it is, tell him we need a real gore-house job like last time, okay? Gotta look like a crazy boyfriend thing or a drug gang."

D-Man repressed a hard gulp. "Yeah," he said, then he grabbed the suitcase and left as fast as he could.

III

"Oh, I love this!" Judy exclaimed from the passenger seat. She was clicking away on her notebook computer, trying to play her way through the next add-on level of the game. "Right now I'm crossing the Chyme Canal!"

"Don't fall," Seth warned as he drove. Since he and

Judy had become involved, she proved a wonderful level-tester for the new beta additions of the game. "If you land in *that* stuff, you better have an excess of Derm-Balm in your health packs."

"And the rope bridge!" she enthused. "What a neat touch! Was that your idea?"

"It certainly was."

"I love the way the rope kind of squishes whenever I grab it."

Seth chuckled. "That's because it's not rope. It's intestines."

Judy squealed.

I guess I'll keep quiet now, let her keep playing . . .

Even with all that had happened—good and bad—Seth Kohn managed to keep his head straight. Seeing Virginia, for instance, for the first time since the death of his wife, Helene, hadn't leveled the impact he'd feared. He still missed her—and still loved her—but now he knew that what he had with Judy was the best possible alternative. *Helene would've wanted it, too,* he felt sure, *and I'd want it for her if I'd been the one who'd died.* The only problem was the lingering guilt that he couldn't shake, when, in the grimmest hours, he wished he *had* died in her place, for he always felt he deserved it.

Providence works in strange ways, he reflected, watching acre after acre of switchgrass passing by outside the window. *Or is it God?*

He and Judy had left Tampa three days ago—they'd left it for good—and taken 95 all the way to Virginia. Was it sentiment that urged him to lengthen the trip by cutting across southern Virginia, not only to spend a moment at Helene's grave, but to ride the ferries again? *Sentiment, or the house?* But he knew that both were synoymous. Indeed,

Judy was a sport, for she knew the real reason he'd needed to do this.

Had that been the reason she'd seduced him on both ferries?

It doesn't matter. It's part of a dream come true. Mine and Helene's, but Helene's not here anymore. So now it's mine and Judy's . . .

The house was the keystone of the dream—the Lowen House—but it had been a different house of sorts that had *empowered* that dream, a scary off-the-wall computer game called *House of Flesh*. Instead of typical spaceship corridors, warlock castles, or terrorist strongholds, this game's concept invited the player into an utterly new graphical environment: an *organic* domain. Footpaths of skin wended through grasslands of human hair; labyrinthine forests stood thick with trees of columns of muscle sprouting polyp-laden branches; cottages made of human (and inhuman) bones offered havens where the player could seek first aid . . . unless said cottage had been previously infected by enemy Fungiforms. These interways existed between the game's major features: the Organa-Planes. Each Plane was a level, and each level offered a different organic motif, such as the Dermatropolis, Tumor Town, Viralville, and Bronchiburg. Sublevels offered still more diversity from typical "shooting" games: Cardiac Cove, Adipose Abbey, the Synaptic Suburbs, the Labyrinth of Leprosy, etc., all of which had been created by a diabolical alien preceptor known as the Red Watcher; hence the game's none-too-thick plot: the Red Watcher dares the human race to send its most resourceful soldier (Sergeant Jake Breaker) into the fleshy conundrum in a fight for his life. Unique enemies wait in eager droves (Corpusculars, Mucoid Men, the flying Oculari, and the stomach-acid-belching Vomitor) to stop their earthy invader in his tracks. Armed with his cache of weapons (a scalpel, a bone-saw, Bacticide Bombs, and his helium-cadmium Surgical Laser), Breaker charges into the organic fray. Should he manage to survive all of the deadly levels, he must then proceed into the cadaverous maw of the House of Flesh itself where he will come face-to-face with the Red Watcher in the final clash of vein-popping and disease-flinging combat. The ultimate object? Breaker must kill the Red Watcher, or else the earth will be destroyed!

That was the idea, anyway. Seth had scripted and coded the game himself, and after bringing on several friends who were skilled in computer-generated graphics, they'd completed their beta version of the game and started submitting it to production companies. All along Seth knew that the premise (aliens coming to destroy the earth and only one bad-boy human can stop them) was about as new as the Gutenberg Bible, but he also knew that originality and new concepts weren't welcome in the gaming industry any more than they were in Hollywood. Fans typically preferred familiarity, just with new trimmings. So that's what Seth had developed, but he'd gone to great pains to make the graphical eye candy exceptional. At best he'd suspected that *House of Flesh* might prove an interesting variation for fans while they waited for the next *Doom* clone or *Resident Evil* sequel. He even thought he might make a little money, but that's where he'd been wrong. He made a *lot* of money.

Since *House of Flesh* had hit the marketplace six months ago, it had been the country's number-one-selling computer game, and it looked like it would remain so for some time. Foreign versions would ship to a dozen countries this week, while movie contracts, action-figure deals, and comic book rights had already been signed. In less time than he could even contemplate, Seth Kohn had become phenomenally wealthy.

And here I am now, he thought, still almost in a daze, *driving to my new house . . .*

The place he'd bought was known as the Lowen House, built in the mid-1800s. He'd seen it only that one time over two years ago, and that had been enough, but his inspector had assured him that the house was as solid as the day it had been erected. Something about the wood it was made from. Larch, but Seth had never heard of it. And the natural wood sealant they'd used in the old days, a bodily secretion from something called a Laccifer bug. He didn't know from trees or Laccifer bugs; he only knew how to write programming code. The purchase had included a strip of land over six square miles that began a mile or so shy of the house and extended northeast nearly five more miles, to the town limits of some burg called Lowensport. The area, Maryland's southern eastern shore, had been economically depressed for a decade, hence the house and all that land had come cheap—less than a quarter million—but Seth had put four times that in the refurbishments and interior decor. He'd actually been quite picky about the details.

"Damn it!" Judy railed. "I'm getting swiped by something that looks like a big eyeball with metallic bat wings!" She manically flicked her button, firing a salvo of the game's bizarre weapons.

"The eyeball with wings is called an Oculari," Seth said.

"My God! And it's got a saw blade for a beak!"

"Um-hmm. And guess what it's going to cut with that saw?"

More frantic clicking and sonic reports. "Holy shit! It's cutting down the rope bridge!"

"Don't use your Surgical Laser; the Oculari will reflect the beam with its wings," Seth amusedly advised. "Try your Ultrasound Nozzle. It'll—"

The computer emitted a deep *buzz*, then a *splat!* "It worked!" Judy celebrated. "But—No . . ."

After some alien squawking, there was a *snap!* then a viscid *splash!*

Judy dejectedly closed up the portable computer.

"What happened?"

"Another one of those eyeball things cut the ropes," she said. "I fell into the chyme."

"That's what happens when you grapple with a diabolic alien design," Seth said, chuckling. "I appreciate your vigor, Judy, but you'll have plenty of time to test the new levels for me once we get to the house."

"The Lowen *House*," she said, as if enjoying the sound of the word. "So I presume the man who built it was named Lowen, and he founded Lowen*sport*, right?"

"That's what the Realtor said."

"So is Lowensport the nearest town, or Somner's Cove?" She diddled with her plastic cigarette which, so far, had kept her smoke-free for months. Seth had opted for cold turkey.

"Somner's Cove's five miles south and Lowensport's five miles north, I think."

"I hope Lowensport's in better shape than Somner's Cove," she remarked. They'd passed through it after getting off the ferry. "It looked kind of seedy."

"One of my quadratic techs at Empyreal grew up there. Said Somner's Cove's like a lot of small towns. There's a good section and a bad section. The bad section's full of bars and drugs."

"We'll never be going there," Judy asserted.

"As for Lowensport, your guess is as good as mine. All that matters is we're five miles from any towns *or* neighbors. And Salisbury's only a forty-minute drive when you start teaching again."

"Not when, if. My past might be too checkered to get hired anywhere," she muttered.

"You'll get hired somewhere," he assured her. "You'll see."

She made no reply, obviously not comfortable with the subject, but then something up ahead caught her eye. "What's this? Workmen?"

"Can't be any of the contractors I hired," Seth replied, noticing the vehicles. "Not this far away from the house."

They slowed by a gaggle of vehicles with state crests. One flatbed truck contained pyramids of stacked PVC pipe; another was a trencher with a digging blade up front that looked like a giant chain saw. But the blade was raised, the vehicle static. Close to a dozen workmen stood around, looking down with puzzled expressions.

"Looks like they stopped work for some reason," Judy said.

"Yeah, but—oh, I know what they're doing," Seth remembered the notice from the comptroller's office and the state department of agriculture he'd received weeks before. "I get the tax breaks for letting the government harvest the switchgrass. What those guys are doing is laying an irrigation line out to all the fields, and some of it's on my land."

Judy craned her neck as they passed. "Looks like they're

at a complete standstill. Maybe they hit a rock, or a gas line."

"Couldn't be a gas line 'cos there are none. In this neck of the woods everyone uses heating oil in the winter. And it couldn't be a domestic water line, either, because there aren't any."

Judy gave him a stalled look. "Uh, the Lowen House *does* have running water, right?"

"Well, sure," Seth said with an odd smile. "Just no domestic water lines."

"What!"

"Hey, honey, this ain't the big city. Our house has filtered and conditioned well water, and we've got a septic tank and leech field for, uh—"

"Wells? Septic tanks?" She seemed astonished. "I didn't know they had those things anymore."

"Remote houses do. Public works isn't going to spend all that time and money running water and sewer lines to one house. We're out in the boonies now, baby. That's how it is."

"I can hack it," she eventually conceded, but then snapped her eyes to him. "But . . . you don't mean there's an outhouse, do you?"

Seth laughed hard. "For a college professor you sure don't know much about how the world works. We have regular toilets, showers, and running water just like everyone else in twenty-first-century America. It'll be fun . . . and don't worry, you won't miss any of your TV shows. We've got satellite with something like five hundred channels and DSL Internet."

Judy seemed more content now. "Sorry, I keep forgetting, I'm the one who wanted you to move here more than you even did. The farther I am away from that damn Godiva shop at International Mall, the happier—and thinner—I'll be. I'm so sick of big cities . . ."

"It's the change we both wanted—"

"And needed, but . . . Where *is* the place?" She squinted at the map. "We should be there now."

Seth's hand clenched her thigh. "Honey, we are."

The road opened to an unpaved court, and before it sat a wide, two-story house that at first appeared black.

"Wow." Judy leaned forward to peer. "It's different from the pictures you showed me. It looks old, but in a good way. I expected something more run-down."

"There'll be nothing run-down about it when you consider the cost of the interior renovations. Three cheers for *House of Flesh*. But there was no reason to do anything on the outside except reshingle the roof. Putting siding up over the natural exterior seemed stupid. If I did that, it'd look like a regular house. And besides, it wouldn't . . ." His words fell off.

"It wouldn't be the same image that you shared with your wife." Judy knew.

Seth faltered. What could he say?

Judy hugged him. "I've told you a million times, I'm not jealous of Helene. I think it's wonderful that this was the dream house you two wanted."

"It's *our* dream house, too," he said in a lower voice. "Yours and mine."

"It looks unique the way it is . . ."

"And the lancet doorways are original. Kind of European, which seemed odd since I think this area was populated by loggers and woodsmen back in the old days."

"The windows and shutters are pretty cool, too," Judy

noticed, for they were in a similar but narrower lancet configuration. "It's like part mansard house and part beam house."

They spotted myriad tire tracks in the front grass, no doubt from the private contractors Seth had hired for the refurbishments, but the last of them had finished days ago. He presumed the movers had come and gone as well. Only one vehicle sat parked in the court—an old blue Pontiac two-door. Seth slowed to a stop, and just sat a moment to let the overall image of the place sink in.

A wide roof with a very low angle seemed to press down on the dark wood of the house. Most of the outer structure was built from rafters. If anything the house seemed a trifle too low for two stories. The high-impact windows had to be custom-made for the lancet frames, and Seth had re-placed the old slat-style shingles with composite shingles that looked similar. When he shut off the Tahoe, a twinge throbbed in his gut—part excitement, but part something else. *Yes, sir, it really is a long way from Tampa now . . .* Judy was beaming as she gazed at the edifice.

"I think that's the Realtor's car there," he said. "Same one he was driving more than two years ago when I got him to show us the place." Seth tensed when he'd said that. The "us" meant him and Helene, not him and Judy. *I'm overreacting!* he yelled at himself. *She didn't even catch it.*

In fact, she was already out of the car, slowly approach-ing the house in something like awe. It pleased Seth very much to see that she had no reservations about this ap-preciable change in their lives.

She was practically jumping up and down. "Come on! I've *got* to see the inside!"

"You go on ahead," he said. "I need to talk to the Real-tor but I'll be right there."

She jogged toward the dark, squat house.

"Perfect timing, Mr. Kohn," said the awkward man who limped forward. This was Mr. Croter, who wore a threadbare light-blue suit that must've been twenty years old. Worse than his attire, though, was the Elvis-like hairstyle shining with tonic. A few missing teeth showed when he smiled and shook hands.

"How are you, Mr. Croter? I take it all the work's finished?"

"Inside and out, and I just know you'll approve."

"Thanks for supervising the work," Seth added. "With my company and all, plus the sheer turmoil of moving, it was impossible for me to get up here earlier."

"It was a pleasure." Croter chuckled. "And so were those generous checks you kept sending. By the way, I've read about you recently. Congratulations on your success. My son is crazy about your *House of Flesh* game."

"I'm glad to hear it, and I'm happy to say it's still the top-selling game in America."

For a moment, Croter seemed sheepish. "Actually, Mr. Kohn, I hate to ask but . . ."

"But what?"

Croter slipped a copy of the game out of his briefcase along with a silver pen, and reluctantly asked, "Marc, my son, he'd have a fit if I didn't get your autograph. Would you mind terribly . . ."

"I'd love to," Seth said, grinning. It was something he'd done a lot lately, yet the notion was still weird to him. Only *famous* people signed autographs. He quickly signed the box with an inscription, then returned it. *But I guess I better start coming to grips with the fact that, in my field, I am famous . . .*

"Wonderful, wonderful. Thank you so much. It's quite a treat for an area like this to have a celebrity moving in."

"I don't know about the celebrity part," Seth chuckled, "but thanks."

"I'm dying to show you the interior." Croter squinted toward the porch, where Judy approached the front door. "Oh, I see your wife's changed her hair color. It looks very nice."

Damn, Seth thought. "That's my girlfriend, Judy Parker. My wife—the woman you met a long time ago . . . died."

Croter faltered. "Oh, Mr. Kohn, I'm terribly sorry—"

"It's all right," Seth cut him off. "Let's go—" But before he could say the word "inside," dust rose around the court as a white car pulled in.

"Who's this?" Seth murmured.

"Looks like a state seal on the car."

From the vehicle a stocky, short-haired man disembarked. He wore a white button-down shirt and tie with jeans and work boots. Gravel popped as he came up to them.

"Either of you Mr. Seth Kohn?" he asked.

"That's me."

"I'm Ernest Hovis from the Maryland Department of Agriculture. I've got a crew about a mile south; we've been laying the irrigation lines as per your agreement with the tax office, and—"

"Yes, my girlfriend and I noticed on the way up, but it looked like they'd stopped working," Seth said.

"Well . . ." Hovis's face took an expression that was a meld of amusement and confusion. "They stopped working, all right. They ran into . . . an obstruction."

"That's what we figured," Seth told him. "What, a bunch of big rocks or roots?"

Hovis paused. "Uh, no . . ."

"Well what was it?" Croter urged.

Hovis cast the odd expression directly at Seth. "I don't know how to tell you this, Mr. Kohn, but the digging crew ran into a boat."

"A *boat?*" Seth asked in disbelief.

"Yes, sir. There's a boat buried on your property."

Seth's eyes turned to slits. "A . . . boat. You mean a rowboat, right, or a canoe?"

Hovis smiled in his own befuddlement. "We haven't been able to dig much out yet, Mr. Kohn, but it appears to be a steamboat of considerable size."

Seth stared. "A steamboat. You're kidding me, right?"

"No, sir. It's a steamboat. Buried on your land. And probably over a hundred years old."

CHAPTER TWO

July 1880

I

Moonlight frosted the cemetery as the two men dug. Their shovels bit into the earth, the gritty sound maintaining a steady synchroneity which Czanek found aggravating. He kept looking over his shoulder.

Jihome's shovel sunk deep. "What's troubling you?"

Czanek paused. "The sound. The Sibley camp's not much more than a mile away," came the younger man's whispered accent. "It's feasible we could be overheard."

Jihome scoffed, lifting out another shovelful. "There's no quiet way to be about this, so just be about it and have faith."

Have faith, Czanek thought of the irony. *Have faith digging up bodies . . .*

All that lit their travails was the moon; they didn't dare light a lamp. When Jihome sunk his blade again, he touched wood. "The ignorant roughs of the camp have little regard for their dead."

"In what way?" Czanek asked.

"Their sin of sloth compels them to dig as shallowly as possible . . . but that's a good thing for us, is it not?"

Czanek looked paranoically over his shoulder again. "Sooner I'm gone from this ghastly place, the better."

"Set yourself at ease, brother." He stopped digging a

moment and smiled. "Our redeemer will protect us, for it is written in the Sefer."

Would he? Czanek hoped so. Lower deeds such as this he understood to be necessary—and even holy, considering. *The Conner clan'd kill us sure if they caught us . . .*

"See? Barely a foot of earth over these coffins." Jihome smiled in the moon. "How's yours coming?"

Czanek peered at his work; he'd nearly dug a foot himself. There were no tombstones here, just patches of tabby inscribed with the names and dates of the interred. Tabby was crude concrete that was poured into a shallow hole at the head of the grave, and the inscriptions, such as these, were often forged by a bereaved finger. Czanek focused until the moonlight let him read the plot he was exhuming. ELSBETH CONNER, MAR. 1860–JULY 1880. She'd been buried only yesterday, a wench and a thief. Jihome's plot was that of another surly goy, one Walter Caudil, a whoremonger. He, too, had been buried yesterday.

The Gaon had instructed them quite concisely. "You must open their graves before they've had much chance to rot, for their corruption is what we need . . ."

Czanek got down to the woman's coffin top, and began to clear it off. Jihome had already pried up the lid on the one called Caudil.

"Here we are," Jihome said. He leaned on his shovel for a rest, looking down at the dour corpse. "The scum looks quite at home down there. And thank our redeemer there's not much odor yet." He began to tamp his pipe.

"I'm right behind you," Czanek said, and shovel-bladed the lid out of its seat. The creaking sound unnerved him, but when the moonlight fell on the contents of the flimsy pine casket, his fear about being detected fell to the wayside.

This one's something . . . Czanek scarcely remembered her when she'd been alive; Conner and all his dirty charcoaling clan kept their contact with Lowensporters to a minimum. But . . .

Jihome's match flared as he attempted to light his pipe; meanwhile, Czanek found his gaze so taken by the comeliness of the corpse that he lowered himself into the grave. *Why oughtn't I?* came the crudely immediate thought. The girl's blonde tousles glimmered, the dead bosom still ample beneath the cotton gown.

Czanek ripped the gown open.

"What are ya doin'?" Jihome scolded.

Czanek looked up in objection. "She's a goy harlot, who mocked us all with the rest of her filthy clan. I see no reason why we shouldn't indulge ourselves—there's hardly even a stink yet."

Jihome shook his head. "The Gaon said nothing of it."

"And didn't forbid it, neither," Czanek almost raised his voice in the deepening night. He kept glancing to the dead woman's bared breasts, the plump flesh like dough freshly made at the baker's. Czanek tore the gown open more, to reveal the tight stomach and—

Jihome slapped Czanek's hat off. "You'll do as I say lest it'll be noted to the Gaon. We'll take no liberties such as what you're thinkin', unless we're told it's right."

Czanek simmered, and sat back at the grave's edge. "But they've done likewise to us, many times."

"With no proof, man. Like the Gaon spake. We obey the *law* . . . "

Blast it, Czanek thought. *It's only fitting we do to the Conners as the Conners've done to us. The fight started with them . . .*

Jihome climbed down into the man's grave, with a look

of disapproval. "We do as we're told, by the Gaon, for the Gaon knows best. Now unless you want a thrashin', check the bitch for valuables and her foul mouth for gold."

"Yes," Czanek obeyed. He stooped, and at least was able to treat his hands to the feel of her body, but the flimsy garment contained nothing of value, nor did she wear any jewelry. This was not surprising, for Conner's clan of thieves were piss-poor. Two fingers gritty with grave dirt pried open her mouth, but no gold sparkled. His hands slid across the vile woman's breasts . . .

"Here ya go, Czanek. A gift from our friend here," Jihome said, and threw something small.

Czanek caught it out of reflex, then paled: a set of shabby wooden dentures still moist from the dead rogue's spit. "You're a right bastard, Jihome!" He flung the dirty thing away.

Jihome gave a hearty laugh.

"And now your laughin' will awaken all the Conners in the camp, man!"

"Calm yourself," Jihome said, but then in an instant he and Czanek went rigid.

Their eyes shot wide in the moonlight.

Footsteps were approaching.

Polten and Corton each raped the woman twice, in the dark alley behind the row houses. It had been the mutton-chopped Polten who'd knocked her out when she'd turned the corner off the main street. The darkness hid their deeds well. Both men were charcoalers for the Conner clan.

"We had a right good time with this'un, huh?" Corton commented as he refastened his sturdy tent-canvas trousers.

Polten leaned against the wall, a sated smile on his

scarred face. "Yeah. And ya know what Lowen's Jews call us, Corton? They call us *goyim*. It means 'dirty animal' or somethin' like that." He nudged the unconscious woman with a booted foot. "So let's just hope our goyim jism puts a baby in this'un's belly."

Polten liked the idea. "If'n she only had some money on her, though."

"Ain't lookin' like anyone's about here," the other man observed and pointed a thumb to the dark window. "Whoever lives here's probably at that weird chapel'a theirs. Synagogue or whatever the hail they call it. The night's young, ain't it?"

Ain't no reason not to go in through this window, Polten reasoned. Rumor was the Jews had lots of silver and gold they'd brought with them from Europe somewhere. "Wouldn't even really be stealin', I don't reckon."

"You kiddin' me? They stolt our land, then somehow wrangle a deed for all of it. It's more ours than theirs, ya ask me."

"Yeah . . ."

Never mind that the Jewish population of Lowensport had properly *paid* for the land. Polten and Corton would have none of that.

Corton got his knife blade under the window, but just as he would force it open—

"Get back!" Polten whispered.

Lantern light suddenly bloomed in the window, the owner no doubt having just arrived home.

"Who's—"

"Shh! Quiet . . ."

Several more oil lanterns were lit. Polten and Corton each edged an eye in the window.

Two women, older, in dark frocks and white bonnets.

They chatted in their own language as they stoked a pile of glowing embers in a wide fireplace equipped with cooking brackets. High on the wall, an emblem caught both Corton's and Polten's eyes: a fancifully painted board showing a pyramidal configuration sitting atop another such configuration, only the latter was upside down.

"What'cha reckon's that there drawin' on the wall?" Corton whispered.

Two pyramids, Polten mused. *One right-side up, one upside down.* They were joined at the base. And what had been drawn within each of them? "Don't rightly know. Some Jew design I guess."

"But I thought the sign for the Jews were that six-pointed star we always see 'em wearin'. And then—" Corton thought on. "And what they done drawn in *them* things looks like faces, don't it?"

"Looks like it."

"But why's the faces so dark?"

Something about the image gave Polten a quick shiver. But, yes, he was sure the Jewish sign was the six-pointed star.

"And, ya know," Corton whispered further, "I keep hearin' ever now'n then that Lowen's people ain't really Jews at all, they was just born Jews, wherever they come from in Europe."

Polten looked at him. "I've heard similar."

"They ain't Jews, they'se just actin' like it."

Actin', Polten considered. But—*Shit. What I care* what *they believe?*

Now one of the women went to some cupboards and slid out a pair of large Dutch ovens.

"They're cookin'," Polten said. "Must be fixin' ta kettle-bake some corn bread."

Corton's eyes thinned. "Yeah, but ain't it an odd time'a night to be doin' that?"

"It surely is, but . . ." Polten squinted deeper into the room. "There ain't no men in there. Why not we go inside like we planned, thrash these two biddies, and see what we can pinch?"

Corton thought well of the idea. *Or maybe just say to hell with it, huh? Kill 'em, then spread them fireplace coals and burn the whole place down. Who'd know?*

Before either of them could embark on that endeavor, Polten elbowed his colleague hard. "Look, there!" he whispered. "What's that? Is that a—?"

Corton had already seen it. The woman near the cupboard was placing something into one of the Dutch ovens, and Corton gulped when he realized what it was.

A dog's head.

"What they hell're those women *doin'*, Corton?"

Next, the woman placed a second dog's head in the other Dutch oven. Then she calmly carried both ovens to the fireplace and sat them in the bed of coals. With a small shovel, she dispersed more coals on the ovens' tops.

"They're cookin' *dog heads*, man!"

"I ain't never heard'a such a thing," Polten admitted. He'd eaten dog, sure—ribs and loins and backstrap. But never the *head*.

"Must be some Jew thing," Corton ventured. "Or somethin' they do in Europe or wherever in blazes they come from."

"Don't much care what they cook." Corton got his blade back under the window. "We go in quick, kill 'em, then search the place, okay?"

He began to jiggle the knife but suddenly got the impression that Polten was no longer by his side. "Come on, get'cher knife out'n help me with this window . . ."

Polten made no response. When Corton glared over his shoulder, his jaw dropped.

Corton had been garrotted and hung up on a nail on an opposite wall. Even in moonlight, his face could be seen swelling. His fingers fruitlessly tried to dig under the garrotte to relieve the pressure, while his feet kicked a foot above the ground.

"What in blue bl—"

Corton's knife was cracked out of his hand as shadows converged. Before he could bellow, his elbows were chicken-winged behind his back and—

WHAP!

—his teeth were knocked out with a club. Meanwhile, more clubs pummeled Polten's groin as he hung helpless against the wall. As Corton was mauled by the barely seen crowd of men, he detected only glimpses of things through his dizzied vision. Other figures farther down unlashed and revived the woman they'd raped, and hustled her away. The figures who continued to bludgeon Corton's groin appeared to be wearing dark hoods and cloaks. Then—

WHAP!

—a similar bludgeon ruptured Corton's testicles in his trousers.

The explosion of pain shut down Corton's ability to even think, not that he could've thought much longer anyway. Hands nearly bodiless leapt from the dark cloaks to beat him in snatches. Corton's knife was retrieved and, first, rammed through his trousers into his anus, then dragged hard upward between the crushed testes. Blood poured like an open spigot.

Before Corton died he was fairly sure he saw his innards pulled out of his abdomen and slathered in his face . . .

The four figures glided slowly down the cobbled street. Angles of moonlight edged over slanted roofs, and wood smoke tinged the air. The men of this select group, each in hoods and cloaks, said nothing as they proceeded from door to door, passing dimly lit windows and empty wooden porches. Save for the mill, the town was sealed up, as it had been for some time now due to the evil deeds of the persecutors.

Evil for evil, one of the figures thought.

Beyond the foremost rows of houses, the river's formidable current could be heard, along with the mill's great buzzing steam-pistoned saws.

The four figures glided on, one of them swaying a thurible of incense. All of the men prayed silently to themselves.

The queue stopped before the next house. One figure mounted the steps and knocked on the door, which creaked open in a moment.

"The time has come," spoke the figure, "as the Gaon has spoken. Through the power of our redeemer we must deliver ourselves from the hands of our persecutors just as Moses delivered the Tribes from the slavery of the pharaoh."

A hand emerged from the doorway and offered a block of some kind, wrapped in burlap. The block was perhaps half the size of a brick.

The figure nodded, then returned to his cloaked companions.

Through the course of the night, this holy gathering would stop at every house in town to collect from each a portion of the material—some wrapped in burlap, others in jars or tobacco tins.

Each portion was actually a piece of a substance called, in their native tongue, *hilna*, which was also known as clay.

Czanek shivered, knowing he might have to fight. Jihome, too, considered the grim possibility. The footsteps drew closer to the graves they'd just unearthed, and if indeed it was any of Conner's rogues come to put upon them, Jihome and Czanek both knew they didn't stand much of a chance.

The moon backlit the encroaching figure; Czanek couldn't see its face but he could see something weighing in the shape's hand, possibly a weapon.

Czanek's heart began to slam in his chest.

"Ah, brethren," floated the familiar voice. "Hard work solicits grand rewards." And then came a chuckle.

Czanek collapsed in relief, while Jihome gasped, wiping fear's sweat from his brow. "Great ha'olam, Gaon! I and Czanek was nearly affrighted to death! We thought you was surely one of Conner's cutthroats."

The Gaon's chuckle fluttered deeper. "Soon, men, by the grace of our most divine melech, that swamp rat Conner and his rabble of scum will be no more." Then the chuckle faded. "Hear me, faithful servants, when I say to you, *yehiyeh tov.*"

"Amen," the other men whispered.

The Gaon's boots scuffed lightly when he neared the opened graves. Approval sparkled in his eyes, which first found the man, but then held longer on the woman's corpse.

"A lissome harlot, I see, quite fetching. Have you men of scripture not made recompense?"

Czanek and Jihome looked at each other, but finally it was Jihome who spoke up, "Great rabbi, we haven't, for I feared it would be against our laws."

The Gaon held some silence during another step that brought his face finally into the full moonlight. The face, lined by wisdom and grace, looked displeased, and his voice fell still darker. "Stalwart men that you are, you've failed to *perceive* your lessons. An eye for an eye, brothers, and an evil for an evil. You'll need to think harder during prayers."

"Yes, Gaon!" Jihome and Czanek shot back.

"When our own Sheila Harav, surely the fairest and most innocent of Lowensport's girls, died of the grippe last autumn"—the Gaon's hand clenched into a fist—"it was Conner and his treacherous scum who dug her up not a full night in the grave and ravaged her lifeless body for mere sport, was it not?"

"It was, Gaon!"

"So now . . ." The Gaon pointed down, with wrath in his glare. "Lift that bitch's corpse up from her grave and place her evil body on the soil . . ."

Czanek's former fear transposed at once to excitation. He nearly giggled when he hauled the dead woman out of the box.

". . . so that we may have our way of recompense with her sullied loins, as demanded by our redeemer, our shepherd, our melech, through the grace of the Eleventh Sefriot . . ."

And so the recompense ensued, beginning with the Gaon himself, then Jihome, then Czanek.

When they were finished, the Gaon smiled as a father might at children who made him proud. Then he used his boots to push the dead woman back into the hole.

"Your toil deserves such a prize, and now your toil is nearly over. Here. Take the bread." At last he unwrapped the parcel he'd brought, producing two loaves of fresh bread. He gave a loaf to each man.

But neither ate the bread.

"As is written, brothers, the offering must be sanctified. You know what to do."

Czanek placed his loaf into the coffin with the woman's corpse; Jihome placed his in the man's.

"Devout servants, both of you," the Gaon bid. "May the melech bless us all."

"Amen."

Czanek and Jihome took up their shovels, and began to heave the dirt back into the graves.

The Gaon walked away in the dark. "We shall regather here after the next sunset and dig this soiled bitch up, so that the melech's will shall be served."

II

The Present

"Well if that isn't the damnedest thing," Seth said.

"A steamboat," Judy giggled next to him.

"In the ground."

After Hovis's bizarre announcement at the house, he, Judy, and Mr. Croter had followed him to the site. The irrigation team had already shut down for the day, but now they'd been replaced by an excavation crew from the state. It hadn't taken long for them to uncover what looked to be the boat's wheelhouse and, more distantly, the corroded struts of a sizable paddle wheel.

Seth shook his head. "Our first day at the new house and, wham, guess what? There's a steamboat on my land. Why on earth would somebody bury a friggin' *steamboat?*"

"It was probably *nature* that buried the steamboat, Seth," Judy said. "I'll bet the boat sunk."

"How could it sink? The river's almost a mile south," Croter, the Realtor, asked.

"Actually, Mr. Kohn's friend is right," Hovis came back. "The river's not here *now,* but it used to be."

Seth gaped at him.

Judy piped up with one of her typical displays of across-the-board knowledge. "Riverboats sunk a dime a dozen in the 1800s, either due to poor construction or misuse. The captains got paid extra for getting to their destinations as fast as possible. The boilers could explode, or they could melt from stoking the furnaces too hot. Something like four thousand people died in steamboat sinkings in the 1800s."

Seth frowned. "How do you know so much about steamboats?"

"I used to date a history prof. He had a thing for the steamboat era in America." She laughed. "Unfortunately I *didn't* have a thing for him. Dumped him after the second date."

"Good," Seth said. "Now I'm not jealous. But that still doesn't explain why this boat is buried on my land."

"An earthquake or a flood is my guess," Judy said. "Flash floods and avalanches have frequently been known to reroute rivers."

"Right again," Hovis informed. "According to the state authorities I talked to earlier, there *was* an earthquake here, in August 1880. This boat may have sunk simply from that, or perhaps it sunk previously from some other reason. If we can find the name of the boat, we'd know a lot more."

Seth rubbed his face, still confused. "But this is dry land! Are you telling me this used to be a river?"

"That's exactly what I'm telling you, Mr. Kohn." He unfolded a small map of the area, then directed with a finger. "You can see here that the Brewer River runs fairly straight from the Chesapeake Bay to well past Lowensport."

Croter looked closer. "Almost a perfectly straight line."

"Yes, but from the end of the ice age up until August 1880—" Hovis made an S-shape over the river with his finger—"it was shaped like that. The earthquake redirected the river's flow. Meanwhile, the boat sunk as the water drained in this turn of the S, and probably was upheaved by silt during the tremor. Either that, or the riverbeds folded up on it." Hovis shrugged, and even smiled at the oddity. "I'd never heard of such a thing, but the experts tell me it happened more than a few times in smaller rivers like the Brewer."

"It *is* a pretty bizarre circumstance," Croter said.

The clatter of tools and chugging of motors rose. They all gazed back at the excavators. Smaller power-hoes carefully scooped up earth, revealing more of the ship's body. The wheelhouse looked amazingly intact for such an event, and even some of the glass in the portholes remained unbroken.

"I wonder how deep it goes," Seth ventured.

"Steamboats had very shallow hulls," Judy offered, "but they were usually double-storied abovedeck. What we're looking at now is the boat's cockpit, and behind it are probably crew quarters and maybe a small galley."

Seth considered the information, then realized a second level had yet to be uncovered. "Then what's below that?"

"The cargo house. That's what all these boats were used for, Seth—to haul goods from one place to another." Judy pointed behind her. "And between that paddle wheel and the cargo house would be the boiler and furnace."

Hauling goods, Seth thought. "Then this thing might still contain the cargo it was hauling when it sunk."

"It's a good bet, Mr. Kohn," Croter said. "And judging from its position, it was probably making a delivery to Lowensport."

Hovis agreed. "There's never been another river port east of here."

"Interesting," Seth muttered.

"And what's even more interesting—for you, I mean— is that anything of value on this boat is legally yours, un- less the heirs to the property itself can be traced." Hovis seemed doubtful. "I wouldn't worry about that."

Judy grabbed his arm with exaggerated excitement. "Long-lost treasure!"

Seth laughed. "There's probably nothing on this heap besides a bunch of mummified corn bushels and sacks of flour that are hard as cement."

"Maybe, maybe not," Croter said. "You'll have to wait and see."

"If there are serviceable antiques, jewelry, or even doc- uments on this boat, you may have hit the jackpot," Ho- vis added.

Seth didn't even pause to think about it. "I already hit the jackpot in my career"—he put his arm around Judy— "and with my girlfriend. I don't really care what's on the boat." He took one more look at the excavated wheel- house. "But it *is* interesting."

"We'll keep you informed, though," Hovis said, and suddenly one of the workmen interrupted him.

"Hey, Mr. Hovis! Looks like we found the name of the boat."

They all walked to the other side of the digging, where the port side of the wheelhouse had been dug down nearly to its floor. The worker was wiping at the sheen of old, dried silt that browned the sideboards above several more intact portholes.

Hundred-plus-year-old letters could faintly be seen. WEGENER, it read.

The oddity of an old riverboat buried on his land scarcely affected Seth. If anything, the discovery came as an annoying distraction. Aside from pictures Croter had previously emailed him, Seth hadn't seen the inside of his new house yet. Croter had taken them back up to show them in.

"It's an interesting idea you had, Mr. Kohn," the Realtor said, looking for the keys in his pocket, "maintaining the genuine appearance of the exterior while completely modernizing the inside."

"I just can't wait to see it," Judy said, but she still seemed dumbstruck by the dark, rough-surfaced outer walls. "You can tell how sturdy it is just by looking at it."

"Sturdy isn't the word," Croter said. "The exterior's made of larch rafters, a very dense wood. A superior insulator, and highly resistant to termites and deterioration." He finally found the key, but wrapped a knuckle on the wall beside the front door. "All these switchgrass fields around us were once a considerable woodland. Larch and oak, but mainly larch. The man who built this house, Gavriel Lowen, made a fortune from those woodlands."

"The lumber industry?" Seth speculated.

"No, actually he built a sawmill and became the area's

leading supplier of railroad ties. Larch is the best wood for that—they still use it today. He and his people were immigrants from Czechoslovakia, and they weren't content to be charcoalers like the local populace. He simply identified an industrial need and he did it. He became a tycoon in his day. Making railroad ties."

"Gavriel Lowen," Judy repeated the name.

"He built the entire town of Lowensport several miles west of here, and he built this house for himself and his family." Croter knocked on the wood again. "This is a mortise house, by the way. No nails in the outer frame at all."

"No nails?" Seth questioned. "Then how did—"

Judy answered. "Instead of nailing the framework and rafters together, they'd hand-drill holes into every joist, and then hammer wooden pegs into them. The pegs were from green wood, so when they dried out, they swelled. It essentially welded all the joists together."

Croter nodded. "They don't make houses like this anymore. In fact, the Lowen House is the only house of its kind in the area, and one of the oldest surviving single dwellings in the county. There are several streets of rowhouses in Lowensport itself, all built the same way."

The Lowen House, Seth thought. *It's my house now, but I guess the Lowen House is what it'll always be called.* "I don't understand how I got the property so reasonably. I would've thought that a house like this would be of great value to a historical society or something."

"You'd think so," Croter agreed, "but I suppose in this day and age, people don't much care about their history anymore." He was about to open the front door but then caught himself and stepped aside. "Ladies first, of course."

"Seth, you have the honors," Judy said. "It's your house."

"It's *our* house and like the man said, ladies first."

Smiling, Judy touched the knob, but something above it her caught her eye. "What's . . . that?"

Seth noted the sullen knocker mounted in the heavy door's center stile, a queer oval of tarnished bronze depicting a morose half-formed face. Just two eyes, no mouth or nose, no other features. *Must've been there since the house was built.* "It's the ugliest door knocker I've ever seen," he announced. "First thing we buy when we go to Home Depot is a new one."

Judy didn't even get both feet in before she went slack in awe. The foyer opened to a long living room and several open side rooms, all of which were appointed in a toned down art deco style, similar to the condo in Tampa. Soft, neutral tones made the room spill out into the others, fringed with more vibrant trim. A massive sectional couch wrapped around an equally massive plasma television.

"Oh, Seth, this is so cool!" Judy reveled.

"Very neutral and low-key." Seth chuckled. "Like our personalities."

"It's just like our old place. And the dichotomy of style is so clever."

Seth was thrilled she liked the appointment, but . . . "Dichotomy of style?"

"Yes! The modernism of the interior disguised by the nineteenth century look on the outside!"

"I . . . hadn't thought of that," he admitted.

Judy's approval followed her throughout the first floor: the cute breakfast nook that would capitalize on natural morning light from another set of lancet windows, a moddish kitchen with every new convenience, and a library fitted with neat bookshelves of chrome wire framework and black panels. "Plenty of room there for all your text-books," Seth noted. "And we each have offices upstairs." Sprawling through the entire first floor was a sea-foam green carpet, save for the exotic kitchen floored by black and white checkerboard tile. Boxes of their personal effects had been left neatly stacked by the movers.

"I love it!" Judy squealed, then quickly hugged and kissed him.

"The contractors went to great pains to turn your instructions into reality, Mr. Kohn," Croter said. "This truly is a unique house. There's nothing else like it in the county, I can tell you that."

"Check out the upstairs, honey," Seth told Judy. "Mr. Croter and I have some paperwork to go over, then I'll be right up."

Judy traipsed excitedly up the double-landing stairs.

Signing the final documents only took a few minutes. "And if you ever decide to refinish the basement," Croter reminded, "just call me, and I'll get some men right on it."

"The basement—wow, I forgot we even had one."

"It's just an old-fashioned fruit cellar—rafter walls, dirt floor. In the old days, though, that was the closest they had to a refrigerator."

Seth nodded through little interest. Even though he had the money now, why waste it on that? "Where's this mill you mentioned? Is it nearby?"

"Oh, yes. Gavriel Lowen's original sawmill is located just off the town square in Lowensport, right on the river. Believe it or not, this house used to be near the river, too—"

"But the earthquake took care of that, I take it."

"Yes. And as for the sawmill, there's only remnants of

the foundation there now. I doubt that the people of Lowensport will ever sell the land, or build on it, even though it's some impressive waterfront property."

"Why not?"

"It's important from a historical standpoint."

"Oh, right. The mill that made Gavriel Lowen's fortune."

"Exactly, and an example of good old ingenuity. And not to sound too morbid, but it's also the final resting place, so to speak, of Lowen himself."

Seth didn't get it. "You mean he was buried at the *mill?*"

Croter put his papers away and closed his briefcase. "Well, in a sense. He was *murdered* there."

"You're kidding."

"I'm afraid not. Lowen's success as a businessman generated quite a lot of sour grapes among the true locals of the area. They were a motley bunch known as the Conner clan. Even though Lowen owned the land free and clear, the Conners regarded it as their own—they were Americans, Lowen and his people weren't."

"Czech immigrants, you said."

"Yes, not to mention they were Jews. Back then Jews were persecuted in this country just like they were in most countries, and as was common in those times, there were ongoing feuds, which got quite ugly." Croter flinched from some sudden unease. "Anyway, in late July 1880, Lowen was abducted by Conner's men."

Croter seemed finished with the story, as though he cared not to go on, but Seth was already piqued.

"And?" Seth goaded.

"He was tied up in the mill, beaten, and then Conner's men dynamited the place with him in it; at the same time, the rest of Conner's clan went on a house-to-house murder spree. Every man, woman, and child was shot dead. The women were raped first, and there was talk of some of the older children being raped as well. Only babies and very young children were spared. But by the end of the night, Gavriel Lowen and the entire adult population of Lowensport were dead. All because they were Jews."

"Sort of like a night of the long knives," Seth said, irked. "But what did you mean when you said that Lowen was buried at the mill 'in a sense'?"

Croter hesitated. "It's pretty grim, Mr. Kohn, but since you asked . . . there really wasn't much left of Gavriel Lowen to bury. He was tied to a box of dynamite, and then the box was set off by a fuse."

"Oops," Seth remarked for lack of anything else. "That'll do it."

"According to the lore only his head was found. It was buried on the site."

"I hope at least Conner and his people were eventually brought to justice."

Croter seemed either weary or unnerved by the story now. "Not by the law, if that's what you mean. The marshal and his deputies back then were quite anti-Semitic themselves."

"So what happened?"

Croter grabbed his case and headed for the door. Only now did Seth notice the Star of David around the Realtor's neck.

"Over the course of the next week," Croter finished, "every single member of the Conner clan—over a hundred of them—were slaughtered most viciously. Not merely shot, mind you—they were mangled, decapitated, or torn limb from limb."

Seth squinted at the other man. "But . . . how on earth . . . If every adult in Lowensport had been murdered, who wiped out Conner's clan afterward?"

"No one knows," Croter said, then quickly turned and left.

III

"Somner's Cove Unit Two, do you copy?"

Rosh frowned at the darkened dashboard. He grabbed the girl by the hair and lifted her face out of his lap.

"Hey, don't you want me to—"

Rosh sputtered, keying the mike. "This is Somner's Cove Unit Two, go ahead."

"Meet officers at 12404 Pine Drive for multiple Signal sixty-four."

You've got to be shitting me! Rosh yelled in thought. "Roger, I'm ten-eight to Pine Drive now," he said and then hung up the mike.

The glassy-eye girl peered at him. "What's a multiple Signal sixty-four?"

The cop hastened to buckle his pants, redon his drill sergeant–style police hat, and start the car. "It's a multiple murder." He leaned across her and popped open the door. "Now get out. I've got to go."

Her lip trembled in defiance. "Gimme my rock first."

"You didn't finish, honey. So get out."

"Bullshit! It ain't my fault you got called! Gimme my rock!"

Rosh would've liked to crack her right across the face with his nightstick, but that wasn't his style. It was easier just to give it to her. "Okay." He flicked the tiny baggie out the door like someone tossing a cigarette butt. "Now get out."

The girl slipped out and slammed the door.

Rosh flipped on the cruiser's lights and hit the red and blues, then burned rubber out of the alley. The darkness of the ill-lit roads seemed to swallow him. He sped down Main Street and then Cove, past the monolithic subsidized housing projects where so many of his customers dwelled. *Keep cracking up, scumbags,* he thought. *You keep buying, we'll keep supplying.* As the middleman in this covert operation, Rosh felt perfectly safe. He made the transfers and delivered the crack to the bagmen, while they took all the risk. It was good money. *By the time I'm eligible for Social Security there won't be Social Security,* he reasoned. If he didn't do it, somebody else would. *Business is business. It's not my fault people are stupid enough to experiment with drugs. They should know better.*

The shabby house looked like a light show when he parked the cruiser. Three other cars were there, along with ambulances. Cops and EMTs swarmed the perimeter. Rosh disembarked to immediately stop one cop, Eliot, who seemed to be staggering out the front door.

"What the fuck's wrong with you?" Rosh demanded. "You sick?"

The younger officer looked back woozily, his face sheet-white. "Oh . . . Captain Rosh. Jeez . . ."

Rosh smirked. Appearances were important. "Straighten up, private. You're a *cop*. Christ, you look like you're about to throw up."

"I . . . already did, sir. In—in the house."

Rosh brushed past, caught Stein at the door. "What gives, man? This looks more like a hostage situation than a homicide."

Even Stein looked a bit shaken. He lowered his voice. "It's the gig we gave to D-Man and Nutjob."

"The dispatcher said *multiple* homicide. All I paid 'em to do was Cookie."

"Yeah? Well, you got a little extra bang for your buck." Stein showed him into the house, which was packed with cops and evidence techs. Flash units on cameras snapped repeatedly, the sudden bursts of light causing Rosh to flinch.

"In here."

It was the living room, if one could call it that: stained walls with holes the size of fists, dilapidated furniture and a collapsed couch, plus lots of plastic milk crates that the crackheads sat on when they came here to light up. The place smelled like urine and sweat—like any crackhouse—but there was something else more pungent in the air that Rosh knew had to be fresh blood. Garbage was piled in the corner, while several crack pipes lay on the ancient carpet, along with familiar one-by-one-inch plastic mini-baggies.

"Where the fuck is Cookie?" Rosh whispered.

"In the bedroom. With the rest. That's where they all ran to."

Down a shabby hall with mold-stained carpet, then Rosh turned into a room where more photo flashes popped . . .

Oh, for fuck's sake! The sight made him feel kicked in the face.

"The tech says six bodies total," Stein advised.

"How the *hell* can he tell?" Rosh shot back.

It wasn't bodies as much as body *parts* that lay strewn about the reeking room. Arms and legs that appeared yanked from their sockets could be seen anywhere Rosh looked. Here the original color of the carpet was almost completely masked by still-wet blood.

Rosh counted six torsos, though he couldn't be sure because two of them looked pulled apart. Another's belly gaped raggedly, showing glistening loops, and another showed a rib cage that looked dragged open. Rosh stared at the unbeating heart.

Yet even amid all this gore, he got past the initial shock quite quickly. Business, indeed, was business. *This roomful of dead losers don't mean shit to me. I paid those two rednecks to do a job and they damn well better have done it.* Rosh scrutinized each severed head.

Stein nudged him. "On the dresser."

Rosh hadn't caught it. Atop an old dresser with opened drawers full of trash sat the head he was looking for. The head lay on its side, rheumy eyes still open, lips curiously pursed as if in contemplation. It was beyond doubt the head of Tracy "Cookie" Roberts.

Good job. Rosh wanted to clap out loud that this informant-to-be was no longer a threat to them . . . but that might be inappropriate. *But I wonder . . .* "Hey, Cristo?" he asked the county evidence tech who was placing a severed arm into a large bag. He wore plastic booties and a hairnet. "The head on the dresser. Any idea which torso is hers?"

Cristo appeared unfazed by any of the horror that lay about him. "Oh, the redhead." He pointed to a torso in the middle of the room. "Probably that one there's my guess, but I can't be sure right now, not in this mess of a jig-saw puzzle."

Rosh got it at once. Cookie was a redhead and the torso had red pubic hair. *Wow*, he thought. *That's some primo work.*

"What's, uh, what's the thing hanging out of her, uh, you know—"

Cristo smirked. "Her *vagina*, Captain?"

"Yeah."

"It's her uterus and complete ovarian process."

Rosh raised his brows. "How could, uh, how could—"

"How could her uterus and ovarian process wind up *outside* her vagina, Captain?"

"Well, yeah."

Cristo got back to his arm. "I got no idea. A hook, maybe."

"A *hook?*"

"Yeah. When I worked in Seattle we had a chick who got iced by her boyfriend on one of the waterfront piers. He stuck a gaff pole up her and pulled stuff out."

"My, what an . . . awful world." Rosh was about to leave until he saw something else, and his heart leapt in more exuberance that he was forced to conceal. On a bed mattress that now looked tie-dyed with blood and various other bodily stains lay another head, that of an African-American male in his midtwenties. He had a silly earring of a tiny gold dolphin and, unbelievably, on his head was a New York Yankees ball cap.

"I'd recognize that head anywhere," Rosh announced. "That's Caddy 'Kapp' Robinson!"

"You're shitting me," Stein said, squinting.

"His and his brother's faces are on the station wall. Damn, Sergeant Stein, don't you ever look at our local wanted posts? Caddy always wears a Yankees hat, and his brother Jary always wears Red Sox."

"You know . . ." Stein squinted harder. "I think you're right."

"I know I am. One half of the Cracksonville Boyz, man. Big *big* crack dealers." He pulled Stein out of the house and back outside to the car.

"Don't look quite so happy," Stein whispered when they could no longer be heard.

"Hey, I'm a constable of the law and I'm merely overjoyed that a despicable drug dealer will no longer be able to corrupt our youth with the far-reaching evil of narcotics."

Stein smirked. "You're overjoyed because the Cracksonville Boyz are our only competition."

"Well . . ." Rosh cut a grin. "No shit! Talk about a *bonus!* We paid the Two Stooges to whack Cookie and they also wind up whacking one of the scumbags who's cutting hard into our profits. God *bless* those guys!"

"Yeah, but—Jesus." Stein let out a breath. "They didn't have to do quite so good a job, did they? I've never seen so many chopped-up people at one time in my life."

Rosh chuckled and popped a Certs in his mouth. "Oh, I'm singin' the blues, Stein. I'm *weeping.* Christ, a couple of junkies get buttoned and you're acting like it's a human tragedy. Fuck. I *love* it. I *love* seeing dead crackheads, man. A day like today, Stein—" He slapped Stein on the back and laughed. "It's a Good To Be Alive day."

"You really are fucked up."

Rosh snapped a hard stare on his subordinate.

"I'm sorry," Stein apologized. "You really are fucked up, *Captain.*"

"Better!" Rosh grinned. "I was beginning to think you were losing your manners!" He looked at his watch. "Hey, McDonald's is still open, isn't it? I could go for a double fish. You ever had a double fish?"

Stein's face seemed to lengthen in astonishment. "We just walk out of a slaughterhouse and you're *hungry?*"

"That's a big ten-four, good buddy!"

"Hey, Captain?" came an interrupting voice. They turned to see Cristo approaching, snapping off his evidence gloves.

"There he is, the Gore House Trooper," Rosh chuckled. "Bet'cha wish you wore hip-waders tonight, huh?"

Cristo sighed. "You're a real odd guy, you know that, Captain?"

Rosh mocked offense. "I'm not *odd*, Cristo. I think of myself as *unrepresentative*, which means extraordinary."

"Fine, but—" Cristo seemed irked by something.

"What is it? You find a gaff pole in there?" Rosh laughed.

Cristo cleared his throat. "Remember that sixty-four we had last spring, the crackwhore that someone stashed behind the Chinese restaurant?"

"Oh, sure," Rosh said but thought, *You're damn right I remember. I'm the one who paid for the hit.*

"Yeah, that one was kind of over the top, too," Stein said. "Didn't the chick have her arms cut off?"

"Not both arms—one arm and one leg," Cristo embellished. "And they weren't cut off; the M.E. said they were *torqued* off. And this crew in here . . ." He gestured toward the house. "Looks like the same thing. There's no hack marks on the necks or joints."

Rosh raised a dramatic finger. "And the diligent crime-scene investigator is perplexed because he can't for the life of him deduce how a human being could be strong enough to torque heads off of necks and limbs out of sockets. Well, then, let me alight you to the fact that rival drug dealers are known to frequently bestow such gestures upon their enemies. You tie one arm to a tree and the other to the back bumper and step on the gas. Presto. Instant dismemberment."

Cristo frowned. "I'm aware of that, Captain, but that's not what I'm talking about. I mean, on that sixty-four last spring, I did a lot of the pre-post work on the dead girl—"

"The dead girl's *pieces*, you mean," Rosh said and cracked a chuckle.

Cristo all but groaned. "Yes, sir, and do you remember the details of prelim?"

Rosh stalled. "I . . . regret . . . that the everyday pressures and responsibilities of being a police captain have left my overstrained mind unable to recall such minutia."

"I found a *perimortal residuum* on the body parts, Captain."

"A perimortal residuum—hmm. What the *fuck* is that?"

"A foreign substance left on the body—a residue—at the time of death," Cristo defined. "It was like soot or something but lighter, or . . . I thought it was dust."

Rosh crossed his arms. "Cristo, could you please get to the point? I'm dying to pick up a double fish before McDonald's closes. You ever have a double fish? They're *great*."

Cristo shook his head. "The M.E. authorized me to send a sample to the lab in Germantown—"

"The *perimortal residuum*." Rosh stretched the term for effect.

"By the time the lab sent the results back it was several months later, and the homicide had already been cold-cased but, you know, I swear that same type of residue is on a lot of the body parts in the house."

"Fascinating," Rosh said dully. "But in your probably incorrect implication that the guy who killed the girl last spring is the same guy who killed all the losers in this house, you *haven't told us what the residue was!*"

"Oh, right," Cristo admitted. "The lab in Germantown said it was clay."

CHAPTER THREE

July 1880

I

"Step into the Circle of Ten Circles and see how the flame brightens as you near . . ."

The Gaon stood solemnly as two disciples stepped within. There were ten torches, one for each circle, and one circle for each of the Ten Hells.

The Gaon was already beginning to feel ecstatic.

Only faith can save us now, my holiest melech, our black redeemer.

His heavy thoughts drifted further.

Empower us tonight, I beg thee.

Ten small circles of stones had been arranged to form the great circle, while the holy Eleventh circle formed the center. All of the stones were slick with the freshly spilled blood of dogs or jackals. The torches crackled, heating even the hot night. *It will be much hotter very soon.*

The Gaon contemplated the Zemu'im, the Secret Discipline from the time of Adam, and all three of them had followed it to the letter: the Drinking of the Blood, the Fast of Eleven Days, the Burning of the Oils and the Myrrh.

"Gaon," cried Ahron, coughing at a draft of torch smoke, "I fear—"

"Have *faith!*" the Gaon snapped back, his voice amplified from an impossible echo. "My brothers, we are all believers—hence we must *believe*, we must believe to the *end . . .* "

"Yes, Gaon," both Ahron and the third, Eli, intoned.

And there the three men stood, dark in their canvas cloaks, within the outer margin of the ten circles. The Gaon knew his attendants were afraid. Only he himself was not.

"What you see with your human eyes you must see instead with the eyes of your neptesh."

"I know, I know, my Gaon, but—"

The Gaon smiled. "Then you now know the power of S'mol, our holy melech, to be great. What will happen here tonight will seem beyond the realm of things possible, as this crowded circle of anointed stones—a paltry boundary—will stretch out to the illimitability of our redeemer himself."

"Yes, Gaon!" Ahron shouted, now joyous.

At their feet lay the wider Eleventh circle, which none had yet entered.

"And now bring in our fodder."

Ahron and Eli left the scarlet circumference; moments later they dragged in two dirty, naked men—two of Conner's despicable clan. They'd been bound and gagged but were very much alive, their eyes propped open by fear, their bodies trembling.

"Do we have enough for two, Brother Eli?"

"Yes, I pray we do, Gaon. Just barely, but—yes, enough. We must pack them thinly."

"So be it."

Ahron's eyes now fixed on the two quivering men. So great was their fear that their hearts could be heard.

"More is on your mind, Ahron." The Gaon could see. "Speak."

"But . . . but . . . must we kill these men? Questions would surely be asked. Conner would level suspicion against us. Would we not be safer to exhume a pair of corpses?"

"Have faith," the Gaon repeated. "These men are heathen thieves who sully our women and ravage our land."

"They are rapists, Ahron," Eli asserted, "and it is our women, even our *children* they've raped. The Zemu'im allows us, my brother."

"Good, good, Eli," the Gaon praised. "You haven't forgotten the Word as Brother Ahron has. The Zemu'im and the Calling of the Seals not only allow it, they *demand* it. Evil for evil."

Ahron gulped. "Yes, Gaon."

"Now we will close our eyes, and embodied in faith, we step together into the Eleventh circle, and you will drag these two filthy animals with you."

The act was done. Now they stood within the wider circle in the center. Conner's men squirmed at their feet.

"And when we open our eyes, we *know* the Circle of Ten Circles will have increased to eleven times its former circumference . . ."

A breath caught in Eli's chest. Ahron gasped. Now the torches guttering in each circle of stones seemed a hundred feet away.

"And we bow our heads now and hold our eyes fast to the ground . . ."

The Gaon recited more of the arcane Calling of the Seals. But Ahron only half listened to the holy words because . . . there was something *else* he heard in the newfound distance.

Footsteps?

"And when we look up again, we do so in the assurance of S'mol's immeasurable power founded by the Secrets God has whispered of but once . . ."

Ahron cried aloud now.

The torches within the circle were now easily a hundred yards away.

It was as though the world they lived in had been taken away. Where they should've seen Rabbi Jacob beyond, and the great larch forest, they saw only the queerest, pink-tinged darkness.

Howls and a hideous scrabbling, even in the now-great distance of the circle's border, could be heard rising.

And footsteps—yes, footsteps—were approaching.

Ahron noticed several figures. They came from beyond the perimeter, and when he counted, he saw that there were ten such figures.

"The torches are burning blue, Gaon!" Eli cried.

The Gaon nodded. "As we always knew they would . . ." He sighed a vast thanks for the powers granted him, now proven. Suddenly it was very hot.

Ever so slowly, the figures drew closer, and as they did so, the glow of the torch fires grew a deeper and deeper blue.

The Gaon thrust his fist straight out; in it was a knife. Like a divining rod, his hand began to edge toward Eli, but just as Eli reached out to take the knife, the Gaon's fist snapped around.

To Ahron.

"Take the knife, Brother Ahron," the Gaon's voice echoed deeply now, "and cut the flesh off of these two rogues."

Ahron's word droned as his heart raced. "Yes, my Gaon."

And then he took the knife, fell to his knees, and began to cut.

Only yards away from them now, the figures from the abyss stopped. Only the predominant one continued on, its ghastly face intent, its body like blackened cinders. It held out its abominable hands as if expectant of an offering. The Gaon looked at the two squirming men, then raised the two loaves of corrupted bread, and handed them to the glorious thing before him.

The figure seemed pleased, accepting the loaves. It leaned forward and began to whisper into the Gaon's ear.

Jacob was the only rabbi who remained outside of the Ten Circles, to stand watch with a rifle in the event that Conner's men noticed what was taking place . . . though he never once thought that would happen. He knew that the melech would keep them away. The sight was spectacular: the way the torches glowed blue, obscuring the activities within.

Jacob had *faith*.

He could hear the Gaon's voice uttering the intercessions of the Calling of the Seals.

Great glory, he thought and could've cried in joy.

Even yards away, though, Jacob could feel the rising heat. Suddenly—

POOF!

—the torches fanned outward, creating a dome of fire atop the Ten Circles.

Flames shot high. Glittering smoke mushroomed overhead.

Jacob stood and watched.

And prayed.

His faith never swayed.

It was Eli who first emerged, dragging one of the filthy corpses from the inferno. Then Ahron did the same. The dome of blue fire roared now, surely hot enough to incinerate any who stood inside. It illuminated the fallow field around them.

No one spoke.

Their eyes held on the blaze. A minute. Two. Three. Ahron's nervousness returned, while Eli's expression tightened in concern. *Where is he?* Jacob wondered, and perhaps even his own faith had begun to bend.

The heat blasted their faces; they all had to step back, lest they be singed. It was Eli who said, *"To je spatne,"* and then Ahron exclaimed, "He hasn't come out!"

When Jacob resolved to enter the blaze, his heart froze— *Great S'Mol!*

—and the Gaon came out just as the arch of blue flame collapsed. "My great brothers in faith—all of us," the Gaon said, and then Jacob rushed forward and embraced their leader. The man had been inside an inferno for many minutes, yet—Jacob could discern—his hair remained unsinged. Even his clothes remained cool.

The fire began to die.

A strange tranquility swept across the Gaon's face. His hand extended to the pair of pitiful corpses at their feet.

"It is done!" Jacob celebrated.

The two men were far less than human now, their flesh having been crudely cut off, their faces flensed. Only the scalps remained, keeping intact the long dirty hair. The upthrust rib cages glistened scarlet, and beneath them no organ remained. All those hanks of muscle and all those innards could now be smelled burning under the waning flames. In particular, the aroma of roasting livers hung heavy.

Jacob made hand signals toward the woods, and a horse-drawn wagon arrived swiftly. The corpses were loaded, and the wagon was off.

The Gaon addressed his brethren with a smile. "The time for our vengeance draws ever closer . . ." The men walked in silence back to town.

II

The Present

Seth awoke feeling different—better—than he could ever recall. He smiled even before his eyes opened, and in that moment of cerebral gray area between sleep and the waking state, he feared that the joy in his heart was corrupt, some cruel dream, and he would groan out of bed to find himself sitting in the middle of an alcoholic's going-nowhere-but-down life. Instead, he awoke, blinked, and thought, *It's all true.*

He was out of the city for good, gone from all its awful memories of loss and three-day hangovers. He finally had his house out in the country, and he was a self-made millionaire . . .

And I'm still in love, he added, a state he thought he'd never regain after Helene's death.

Frantic clicking and squeals grew more precise as he came fully awake. Judy sat naked at the desk by the window, her fingers a blur as she shot her way through the next level of the game.

"Damn—oh! Gotcha!" she exclaimed amid the reports of the Surgical Laser.

Seth watched in secret from bed. Just the image of

her there, the smooth white skin and shiny black hair, the curves of her nude shoulders and back, got him half aroused. *But half's about all I can muster right now,* he admitted. In the three days they'd been here, their sex life had exploded. *Three times a day—not bad for pushing fifty. And last night . . . Jeez. She rode me like I was a mechanical bull . . .*

"Oh, you bugger!" she shrieked after a sudden wet sucking sound. Obviously she'd just lost a confrontation with a Cancer Vamp. "And I forgot to save when I got out of the Cove of Diverticulum . . ."

"Sounds like you're halfway through the Gastric Colonnade," Seth said, leaning up from bed.

Her breasts jiggled when she quickly turned. "Oh, sorry! Didn't mean to wake you up. I get too caught up in this."

"Well, that's a good thing."

She grinned, her hair half over her face, then turned back to the game. "I never thought that game-testing would be this fun. These Cancer Vamps are bad enough, but I can never kill that damn Vomitor before he gets me."

"Ten blasts of the Laser or a full-charge burst from the Ultrasound," Seth tipped her off. "The thing about the Vomitor is you need *lots* of Neutralizer Tabs in your health pack."

"But there aren't any!"

"Check the Polyps; open them with your Scalpel. Some of them contain goodies."

"*Now* you tell me!"

An alarm beeped downstairs; Judy bobbed up. "Coffee's ready. I'll be right back." And in a nude flash she whisked out of the room.

God, I'm lucky . . . Seth rose and pulled on a robe. He glanced around with a satisfied smile. The entire house stood in perfect order now, most of the boxes unpacked and everything in its place. Their routine was already forming; Seth was back to work on the *House of Flesh* sequel, and when Judy wasn't testing the add-on levels for the first game, she spent several hours per day in her own office, sprucing up her job applications.

Seth stretched, let his back crack, then walked to the open window. The switchgrass fields stretched as far as he could see. *We wanted seclusion, we got it.* They hadn't even been into town yet, whichever town that might be: Somner's Cove or Lowensport. *Hopefully there are some good restaurants somewhere, and a movie theater would be nice.* Suddenly the room filled with the luxurious aroma of fresh-brewed coffee. Judy padded over and gave him a cup, then slipped an arm around him and gazed out the window.

"Uh . . . I know you've got that 'nudist' streak, which is fine with me," Seth stumbled. "But do you really want to stand buck naked in front of an open window?"

"*Yes.* And I'm not a nudist—that's so gauche."

"That's right. I forgot, it's not nudism anymore, it's naturalism—"

"No, no, no, I've told you a million times," she giddily complained. "It's *naturism.* Naturalism is a literary movement that allegorizes the principles of natural science, best exemplified by authors like Emile Zola, Henrik Ibsen, and Theodore Dreiser."

"Boy, when I get a word wrong I get it *wrong,*" Seth admitted, letting his hand idle over her hip. He was constantly amused by her unabashed indoor nudity.

"And I'm not much of a true naturist, anyway," she went on. "I've never even been to a camp."

"So you're a *closet* naturist, huh? Only in the house."

"Yeah. I guess that's pretty lightweight." She put her coffee down and leaned fully out the window.

"Oh, great," he protested. "Now you're showing your boobs to the whole world!"

"Don't be such a prude, Seth. There's no neighbors for five miles in either direction—you said so yourself."

"Sure, but—"

"So no one can see me."

Seth just let his eyes drink her up. Even though she complained about gaining weight, he found her proportions perfect. Her skin glowed, and when she inclined herself farther out the window, she rose on her tiptoes, which flexed her calves in toned, sexy lines. Her bottom constricted, showing adorable dimples.

"Look at all that switchgrass," she mused. "It's hypnotic the way it sweeps back and forth, mile after mile."

"The county said there's almost fifty square miles of the stuff."

"And six of them belong to you."

"It's all that grows here now."

"Because this is all deforested woodlands. The soil's too depleted of nutrients. If they tried to grow corn here, they'd have to use so much fertilizer it wouldn't be cost effective. You're a Greenie by default, I guess. Until they perfected the gasification methods, switchgrass was a worthless nuisance. Now it's a prime biomass crop. Fifteen-hundred gallons of ethanol per acre, for instance." Her face took on a studied expression. "Let's see, fifty square miles . . . Each square mile is six hundred forty acres, so that equals thirty-two thousand acres . . . times fifteen hundred—let's see . . . that's forty-eight *million* gallons of ethanol per year, just from here."

Seth frowned at her mental prowess. "I can't believe you figured all that out in your head in two seconds." Then he paused and thought about it. "But, wow, you're right. That *does* sound like a lot of ethanol."

"And it grows back every year. Kind of like having an oil pool that refills itself every season."

Seth shook his head, "How do you know so much about—Oh, that's right. You used to sleep with an agro professor."

She smirked back over her shoulder. "I never said I slept with him. I said I *dated* him."

He came up behind her and rubbed both hips. "Oh, so you mean you never—"

"Seth, do you really want to know how many times I had sex with that guy?"

Seth thought about it. "Hmm, well, actually maybe I really *don't* want to know."

"Zero!" she answered. "And I never slept with the history prof, either. Honestly, those guys were less interesting than unflavored yogurt."

"Ah, good . . ." He kept toying with her hips.

She was still leaning out and staring off. "I just can't believe this view."

"Neither can I—and by the way, I'm not looking at the fields."

"Oh, and look at that," she said and pointed aside.

Seth stuck his head out. She was pointing to a path of some sort that seemed to cut through the switchgrass in a perfectly straight line.

"It looks like it goes on for *miles*," he remarked.

She mocked shock. "Maybe it's a crop circle . . . only straight!"

"Yeah, or maybe it's a path. An access for the switch-grass farmers."

"I guess you're right." But now she was squinting in a more severe angle, leaning out even farther.

"Honey, do you really have to lean out that far? Somebody could drive by."

She scoffed. "No one's going to drive by, for goodness' sake. I don't think we've seen a single car since we moved in."

Seth couldn't help it. He caught himself staring unreluctantly at her perfect breasts as they depended from her chest. "What are you looking at now?"

"That's really weird, Seth."

"What?"

"Look. I think it really *is* a crop circle."

Seth rolled his eyes. "If there's aliens out there, you're giving them a terrific show." He looked out again, and let his eyes follow her finger.

She's right. Farther east, he spied a distinct area of space that seemed to be clear of the ubiquitous grass. "What could that be?"

"And there's another one."

Seth had to squint but, yes, he spotted another small clearing even deeper in the field. "Can't imagine what they are, but . . . probably not crop circles. That farther one doesn't seem to even be a circle, it's square."

"Seth, spaceships don't *have* to be circular," she joked, but had already lost interest. Now she placed both hands on the window sill and pushed herself up till her feet came off the floor.

"Ah-ha, now I see that my 'naturist' girlfriend is no

longer content with merely displaying her bare breasts to the whole world. Now she's got to show her, uh . . ."

"Pubies?" The tuft of dark hair showed fully over the sill. "And you're right, Seth, I'm showing the *whole world*. Look at all those cars out there," she mocked. "They've been driving back and forth all day long, hundreds of them—"

Car springs creaked. When they both looked down they easily noted the mail truck which had just stopped at the box. The mailman froze at the shock of the sight.

"Shit!" Judy yelped and pulled back.

Seth laughed outright. "No cars, huh? No one can see, huh? Well, it looks like my little nudist has learned her lesson the hard way."

"Naturist!" Judy yelled over her embarrassment and yanked on her robe.

"Whatever, and I hate to tell you this, but you really are a great big phony."

"What?"

"Your face is beet red," Seth chuckled. "A true exhibitionist is *never* embarrassed."

"Kiss my ass!"

Seth grinned. He looked out the window and saw the mailman drive away. "But it's a good thing in the long run. Mailmen work hard, and they probably don't get a lot of job satisfaction."

"What are you talking about?" she griped.

"But that guy there? You just made his day."

Later they had a light breakfast, then puttered about the house, looking for finishing touches. Seth had dressed but Judy remained barefoot in her robe. He frowned at the picture of herself she'd put on the refrigerator; it was from five years ago, when she'd been overweight.

"Is this really necessary now?"

Judy looked over. "Of course it is, it's motivation."

"Honey, you weigh a hundred and twenty pounds. It's your ideal weight. You're gorgeous and slim."

"Thanks for the gorgeous part, but *slim* is an overstatement. I weighed one-fifteen two months ago."

"That's because you're getting healthier after your ordeal, and I'm healthier after mine." He supposed he *could* understand her compulsion, considering the *way* she'd lost weight. But Seth was a positivist, at least about her. "Whatever you say," he conceded.

"You want to go to town today?"

"Let's wait and see. I'm kind of in my creative groove so I'm itching to get some work done."

Judy made a sultry smile. "Yeah, and you were definitely in your creative groove last night."

"You sure that wasn't more you than me?"

"It takes two."

Seth smiled. "Be right back, I'm going to get the mail."

He went out the front porch to suddenly be swept by the hot sun glowing over the fields beyond. He crunched down the driveway—not gravel but, he later learned, crushed oyster shells. In the old days most of the minor roads nearby were paved with this, for Somner's Cove had possessed an enormous oyster bed, and was also the state's leading supplier of crabs. Seth thought he liked the old-time look of the drive but supposed he'd eventually have it blacktopped.

He retrieved the mail but barely looked at it; instead, his brain was ticking away with new ideas and level layout for the *House of Flesh* sequel. *I need a bonus level that's trickier than anything to date, plus a new monster . . .* He was halfway back to the porch when the sound of a car pulling up on the crunchy drive made him stop.

A modest older model sedan, dark enough to be black, parked behind Seth and Judy's Tahoe.

"Mr. Seth Kohn, I take it?" shot a spirited voice from a man getting out. He was slim, medium height. Eyes that seemed enthusiastic and young were set in a fortyish face, and he had curly hair not quite long enough to be called unruly that seemed to struggle between blond and brown.

"That's me."

The man approached quickly with a toothy smile, extending his head. "My name's Asher Lowen, Mr. Kohn. We're neighbors, in a sense; I live up the road in Lowensport."

Seth shook a soft hand with a strong grip. "Pleased to meet you," Seth said, noting, first, the man's black yarmulke, then attire that seemed too conservative for midsummer: black slacks, shiny black wing tips, and a neat white dress shirt. Seth wore khaki shorts and a Tampa Bay Rays T-shirt.

"And this is my wife, Lydia. Lydia, this is Mr. Kohn."

Another figure was approaching more slowly than Lowen had—a woman, slightly taller than her husband, with long black hair dusted by gray, a face whose whiteness was more lustrous than pallid, and a heavy bosom. Seth nearly raised a brow at her ruffly ankle dress—also black—and the sleeves buttoned at the wrists. *She must be cooking like a Hot Pocket in that get-up*, he thought, but smiled and said, "Very nice to make your acquaintance, Mrs. Lowen."

"Likewise," she replied, thin lips barely moving, and

then she offered a basket of fresh fruit, cheese, and some jarred goods. "This is for you."

"Why, thank you, Mr. and Mrs. Lowen—"

"Please, Seth," the man said. "Formalities are hardly necessary among neighbors."

"Of course . . . Asher, Lydia. And, really, this is very kind of you." Seth paused. "And this is very interesting. Your name is Lowen, you live in Lowensport, and I've just moved into a place known as the Lowen House. Any connection?"

"Quite a connection, Seth." The question brightened Asher's already blazing eyes. "The man who built our town and also your house was Rabbi Gavriel Loew."

"Gavriel Loew," Seth repeated.

"He changed his name to Lowen in 1840 when he and his assembly emigrated here to flee anti-Semitic persecution in Europe. Unfortunately more persecution awaited; he changed his name to sound less Jewish, but to no avail. But I'm happy to add that Gavriel Lowen was my great-great-great-grandfather."

"How do you like that?" Seth said. "But now I feel guilty."

"What on earth for?"

"The house I'm living in was built by your direct relative. How come *you* don't live here?"

"Oh, our place is in town, with our people," Lowen replied.

His people? Seth thought the choice of words bizarre, but then he figured, "You mean a congregation—er, I should say a kahal?"

"Yes, Seth. You might say that everyone in Lowensport is a member of the kahal, our true assembly of worshipers."

"So you're a rabbi, too?"

"Indeed I am. And in fact nearly everyone living in Lowensport has a blood relative that links to Gavriel's original settlers."

"That's wonderful. Talk about close-knit." But then Seth could've slapped himself. "Forgive me! Please come inside for some coffee. I'd like you to meet my girlfriend." Immediately after the offer, though, Seth ground his teeth. *God, I hope she's got her clothes on!*

"Thanks so much, Seth, but it'll have to be another time." Lowen glanced at his watch. "We've got to get back to town, for—" He glanced urgently to his sullen wife. "What, dear?"

"Bible study," she said, nearly inaudibly.

"Yes, and then the community pie sale and then town council meeting tonight."

"Busy schedule," Seth remarked.

"Always busy, Seth," Lowen said. "But one can never be *too* busy, can they, when serving God?"

Seth almost balked. "I suppose you're right."

Lowen gave Seth a business card; Seth did likewise. "Please give me a ring soon. I'd be thrilled to show you around our wonderful town personally."

"I'll do that, Asher. Thank you."

"And please bring Judy. We'd love to meet her as well."

Seth opened his mouth, then paused. "How did you know my girlfriend's name is Judy?"

"The paper, of course, but—oh, you've only been here a few days so I don't suppose you've had time to subscribe to any yet." His gaze went to Lydia. "Dear, get the paper for Seth."

"No, please, I don't want to take your newspaper. I'll get one in town."

"Nonsense. It's the Somner's Cove edition, which we

don't read much, anyway." Asher laughed. "As for your names being in it, all I can say is welcome to Small Town America. It's not the big city by any means. The papers have little to write about locally, so with a little research into public records and such, I'm afraid we all lose some of our privacy—"

Great, Seth thought and pursed his lips.

"—but I'm sure it's something you're used to," Lowen added.

"I'm not sure what you mean."

"Please, Seth!" Lowen exclaimed amused. "You're so humble!"

Seth was confused, until Lowen's nearly silent wife handed him a copy of the *Somerset County Herald.* Seth could've quailed. *I should've known . . .*

A lower headline on the front page read: BESTSELLING GAME DESIGNER MOVES INTO HISTORIC LOWENSPORT MANSION.

I'll be damned, he thought but kept his air of cordiality. "I appreciate it, Asher. It looks like I'm in for some amusing reading."

"Yes, yes, enjoy it." Lowen hurried his wife back to the car. "And, again, welcome!"

Seth held up the basket. "Thanks again. We'll see you very soon."

After a parting smile, Lowen and his wife drove off.

Damn nice guy, Seth thought. *Wife's a little odd, but . . .* He took the basket, mail, and newspaper back to the house. Inside, he could hear the shower going upstairs. *Can't wait to hear her bitch about this,* he thought, skimming the article. Sure enough, both of their names were mentioned in the article, but most of it was about Seth's success as a game designer. Then there was a paragraph about the Lowen House, which cited the date of its completion as 1844. Several other short pieces on the bottom of the page were about the upcoming switchgrass harvest and the completion of a large biomass gasifier nearby. Evidently the process and harvesting was seen as a much-needed boon to the region's otherwise faltering economy. Then Seth turned the paper over to view the top of the front page—and sighed.

CIVIL WAR–ERA STEAMBOAT UNEARTHED ON CELEBRITY'S LAND, read the headline.

III

"Shouldn't be too hard if the workers stop at five like yesterday," D-Man estimated. He watched through binoculars at the work crew and equipment near the road. Looked like six or eight men, and some guy in a white shirt who must be the boss. Even half a mile away, he could hear the engine noise of the trenching machine and backhoe.

"Yeah, but what if we get seen?" Nutjob asked a question more insightful than was typical for him. He'd parked the black step van in a clearing within the woodline. "Cops, man, or say someone drivin' sees us and calls the cops."

D-Man shook his head. "Dog shit for brains! We *sell* drugs to the cops! That's why the cops *protect* us! And we ain't gonna *get* seen anyway, 'cos you're gonna hide the van in the switchgrass.

"Oh, yeah, well . . ." Nutjob went back to rolling a joint.

Redneck, D-Man dismissed. He focused the binoculars. "And speakin' of cops, Rosh called me today."

"Yeah? Next swap ain't for a couple days I thought."

"This is somethin' else. Says he might have another job for us soon."

Nutjob's face drooped. "Shit, man. Not another button job like Pine Drive." Suddenly, even in his pot buzz, he looked fearful. "That thing scares the shit outta me, man. I don't wanna do them jobs no more."

"Neither do I," D-Man agreed, and then he jabbed his finger hard into Nutjob's arm.

"Oww!"

"But we'll keep doin' 'em any time we're told 'cos it's all part of the gig, and I don't wanna work for seven bucks an hour moppin' floors. Do you?"

"No, but—"

"And anyhow, the way Rosh sounded was this wasn't another button job, just a disposal."

Nutjob relaxed again. "Well, that's different. I can dig that." Nutjob paused for a long moment, then cracked a laugh. "Get it? *Dig* that?"

D-Man frowned. "Shut up, you pothead psycho." He brought the binoculars back to his eyes.

He'd already figured it out. All they'd need were some hand trucks. *And there's only supposed to be four, so they'll all fit in the van just fine.* By now, he could even see the top of the exposed steamboat in the cleared pit.

We'll just wait till it's dark, he reasoned, *then haul the stuff out and split.*

Nutjob's mush-brain sparked with yet another constructive thought. "Hey, what if the shit ain't even on the boat?"

"Well, if it ain't then it ain't our problem."

"And what if they put a night watchman on it?"

"They didn't last night, and if they do . . ." D-Man shrugged. "We'll jack him out, kill him if we gotta."

"Yeah," Nutjob consented. He took another drag off the joint and coughed.

Asshole ought to stick to beer, D-Man thought, *like me. That pot shit's turnin' him into a moron*—But the thought severed when D-Man noticed something else in the binoculars. He focused closer. "Only thing we gotta worry about is the owner."

"What owner?"

"Jesus Christ, don't you listen to *anything* anyone tells ya? Like the man told us, the owner might be able to file some sorta claim on whatever's in the boat."

"Who's the ow—Oh, the guy in the green truck."

"Yeah," D-Man snapped. "His name's Seth Kohn, like the man said, and, shit, Nutjob, did you only *pretend* to read the story in the paper?"

"The rich guy, right," Nutjob muttered.

"Yeah. He's the dude just moved into the Lowen House, with that chick we saw with the Rebel Yell tits. He's all we gotta worry about. If he gets to the shit before we do, we're fucked."

Miraculously, another insightful thought entered Nutjob's head. Perhaps the marijuana actually made him *more* intuitive. "But why would he want it? The dude's a millionaire. Why would he care about a bunch of *clay?*"

D-Man kept watching. "We both better hope he doesn't . . ."

IV

•

"Give me a minute," she said frustratedly. "Damn! I can't decide what to wear." She stood nude before the mirror, holding up two different sundresses.

Seth sat on the bed, waiting. "We're not going to the Four Seasons, Judy. We're going to a hole in the ground." Seth could've gulped at the erotic sight. Even after a year of living with her, any time he saw her naked was as exciting as the first time. "But, by all means, take your time."

She grinned as if sensing his gaze on her. "Don't get any ideas, or we'll never get down there."

They'd decided to drive down to the excavation to see how it was progressing. Earlier, she'd read the articles in the paper, with a bit more amusement than Seth. "Yeah, in all the hubbub of unpacking I forgot all about it," she'd remarked.

"Me, too. And that *is* a pretty hard thing to forget: a steamboat buried on our land for over a century. I guess the main reason I forgot about it is I don't really care."

"Oh, come on. It's exciting." Now she was holding up two more sundresses in the mirror.

So is your body, he thought.

"But it was a trip that our names were in the articles."

"My name's on the deed," Seth had said, "but I wonder how they got your name."

"Research is easy these days. The car's registered in both our names, and you already got the tags transferred. Anybody's name can be searched on just about every department of motor vehicles Web site in the country."

Seth smirked. "It just seems like an invasion of privacy."

"It is, I guess, but the article raves about you, and that'll increase sales of *House of Flesh*."

"I didn't think of that."

"All they said about me was I used to teach at FSU." She paused for a momentary fret. "I'm glad this reporter didn't run court dockets."

"Oh, yeah, your dope bust and my DUI." Seth laughed sardonically. "I'm sure Rabbi Lowen would've been *really* impressed with that."

"It was very hospitable of him to come out and bring that goodie basket."

"Yes, it was. I figure we'll go to Lowensport in the next couple of days and take him and his wife to dinner."

"Good idea. But what was he like?"

"Nice guy, seems very sincere. He was dressed weird, though. Looked kind of Quaker or Amish . . . except Quakers and Amish don't wear yarmulkes. His wife seemed odd, maybe. Barely said a word."

"Countrified folk. They still exist, you know."

She finally decided on what to wear: jean shorts and an FSU T-shirt.

"Aw, shucks, the nudie show's over, huh?"

"There'll be another one tonight." She giggled, stepping into frilled panties and then the shorts. She pulled the T-shirt on.

"Uh, no bra today?" Seth asked.

"Come on, it's July."

"I'm not too keen about all those workmen ogling your boobs. The mailman already got the show of the day."

"All *right!*" she humored him, then put a bra on. "Now let's go. I'm dying to see how far down they've dug."

They tramped downstairs. Judy grabbed her camera, while Seth hunted for his cell phone and keys, but at the same time, they stopped and glanced at the window. Outside, a deep roar rose.

"What's that?" Judy asked. "The garbage truck?"

"Sounds like it," Seth said but then his cell phone rang. Judy went to the window as Seth answered.

"Hello?"

"Mr. Kohn? This is Hovis from the state department of agriculture—"

"Oh, wow. We were actually just about to drive down to the excavation—"

Judy interrupted with an astonished look. "Seth, there's a giant-ass truck parking in the front yard!"

"Don't bother, Mr. Kohn," Hovis said over the line. "We just pulled up. Come on outside."

Seth hung up. *What the hell?*

He followed Judy out to the porch, where they both stood in a mild shock. A large truck, indeed, a flatbed, chugged to a stop in the yard, followed by several pickups full of workmen. Hovis's state vehicle pulled in last.

"Are those—"

"Barrels, it looks like," Seth observed, because that's what was stacked there.

Nearly a dozen old wooden barrels.

Before Seth and Judy even had time to walk down, a group of hardy workmen were rolling the barrels down ramps off the truck and setting them up in the yard.

Hovis waved and came over, bearing his clipboard. "Good afternoon, folks. Just wanted to let you know that the steamboat, the *Wegener*, has been fully excavated."

"What—what—what—" Seth pointed to the barrels being placed in his yard. "What's all *that?*"

Hovis seemed as though nothing was out of the ordinary. "That, Mr. Kohn, is the entire contents of the cargo hold of the *Wegener*. Shipping barrels. Ten of them."

"Why—why—why . . . are you leaving them in my yard?"

Hovis was scribbling on his clipboard. "Because it's

technically your property. My superior's explained the details, and based on the common laws of lost property, any such *private* property not reclaimed by the original owner, if said property is lost or abandoned on privately owned land, transfers ownership *to* the owner of the land."

Judy, intrigued, approached the increasing congestion of barrels. Seth, though, was less intrigued. "Ten barrels? I don't want them, Mr. Hovis."

"Well, they're legally yours. The state is obliged only to deliver them to you, since they were found in the hold of a state-owned vessel. So . . ." Hovis offered a look that said, *Oh, well,* then continued, "If you want the barrels disposed of, you'll have to hire a private hauler yourself."

Seth remained dumbfounded at the sight of workmen quickly milling back and forth and propping the barrels up in his yard.

"The boat itself is a different story," Hovis went on with little interest. "It was owned by the state, by what was, in 1880, the Baltimore Harbor Authority. And that means it's *still* owned by the state. The Maryland Historical Commission wants the boat for its artifacts, mainly the nautical instruments in the wheelhouse, the anchors, and the furnace. But the material *inside* the boat"—Hovis extended his hands to the ten stained and moldy barrels— "is yours."

Thanks a lot, Seth thought.

Judy rushed back over, brimming. "They're all ours, Seth! This is so cool!"

"I'm glad you think so," Seth sputtered. "We've got ten friggin' *barrels* in our front yard. It'll be a major pain in the ass getting rid of them."

"Get *rid* of them? Are you nuts?"

"We don't know what's in the barrels, Mr. Kohn,"

Hovis stepped in. "Could be nothing of value, or it could be—"

"Stuff worth a fortune to museums or collectors!" Judy exclaimed. "That's not a bunch of junk in the yard, Seth. It's a bunch of *history*."

Hovis smiled. "I wouldn't count on gold bullion or long-lost jewels, but you never know."

Seth winced. The workmen were already packing up to leave. "The barrels are probably full of rotten flour, rotten wheat, and rotten foodstuffs."

"Probably," Judy said, then tugged his arm. "But maybe not!"

I can't leave this pile of shit in my yard! Seth railed to himself.

"How about the basement?" Judy suggested. "We'll put the barrels in the basement and go through them one by one."

Seth stalked to the closest barrel. He gave it a nudge but it didn't move. "I'm a game designer, not a forklift. These things weigh a ton!"

"They're standardized shipping barrels," Hovis informed him. "Around three hundred pounds apiece for wet volume. Dry volume? Depends on what's inside."

Seth's shoulders slumped. He gave Hovis a helpless look. "I don't suppose your men could move these things down into our basement . . ."

"Oh, my men could do it easily, Mr. Kohn, but they're state employees on the state time clock." Then he raised his brows at Seth.

"How about you take them *off* the state clock for a few minutes?" Seth proposed, "and I pay a hundred bucks per man?"

"Hmm . . ."

"It took your guys ten minutes to unload them; it wouldn't take them another fifteen to roll them all down into my basement."

"A hundred a man, you say?"

"Plus a hundred for you, of course."

Hovis turned, and whistled. "Fellas! We're not quite done for the day . . ."

Seth, Judy, and Hovis stood aside and watched the workmen hand-truck the barrels across the yard to the basement. The basement doors were a double trapdoor style, as was the fashion in the old days. Some of the men began lowering the barrels down the stairs. *At least Judy's excited about all this*, Seth reasoned, *and I guess it'll give her something to do for the next week*. As little as he cared himself, though, he was becoming mildly curious as to the barrels' contents.

Judy knocked on a barrel, surprised by its solidity. "It's amazing how well they held up. They must've been wet for a long time."

"Actually, no," Hovis said. "Believe it or not the cargo house was intact. The doors held against the silt, and most of the windows even held. The expert I talked to said the bend of the river probably drained immediately after the quake, so instead of being submerged it went down to the river bottom as the water level lowered."

Seth couldn't figure it. "Then how did the boat get buried at all?"

"Seismic shift," Judy said, half listening. "It happens sometimes. The earthquake severs the natural flow of the river, the bend in the river that the boat happens to be in drains, then the afterquake hits and sort of folds both shorelines of the river in on itself. The boat's in the middle, and after the shift it's buried in silt and mud."

Hovis nodded. "That's pretty much what our experts said. So you're an expert on earthquake phenomenon, I take it."

"No, I just dated some guy who taught seismology . . ." Seth rolled his eyes.

"But anyway . . ." Judy ran her hand over a barrel's lid. "It is conceivable that the barrels wouldn't deteriorate very much since they'd been sitting in a relatively dry compartment all these decades."

Hovis remembered something. "Oh, but there was one barrel that seemed to be damaged, and I don't think my men have taken it down yet." He looked around. "This one right here."

He took them over, and Seth noticed the one lidless barrel. It didn't seem to have been a crowbar that had unseated the lid; instead, a wedge had been cut into the barrel's rim, some of its slaves split, yet nothing of its contents seemed to have spilled out.

"That looks like an *ax* mark," Seth said at once.

"We think that's what it is, too," Hovis remarked.

"Yeah, but what's *in* it?" Judy slid her opened palm against the top of whatever it was that filled the barrel.

"Maybe lime," Seth offered, "but it turned to cement from the moisture?" He looked at it himself. "Or mud. That must be it. With no lid, the mud from the riverbed poured in and filled it."

Hovis shook his head. "The cargo house stood up to the pressure, Mr. Kohn. Very little mud ever got inside. If the barrel had been covered with mud, then *all* the barrels would've been covered. We never found an intact freight manifest and there's no known record of what the ship was hauling. But there are departure records from the Baltimore Harbor Museum that were accessible. All we know is that the *Wegener* was traveling to Lowensport when the earthquake hit, and we also know that the barrels came from Prague."

"The Czech Republic," Seth muttered. "Honey, what do you think that stuff is?"

Judy suddenly sucked a breath into her lungs, then put her hands over her eyes. "I'm having a psychic vision! I know what's in the barrel! It's—it's—it's . . . clay!"

"Clay?" Seth said.

Hovis looked atilt. "You didn't really have a psychic vision, did you?"

Judy laughed. "No. I merely read the label on the barrel." She pointed to paint-stenciled letters across the barrel's darkened middle bulge.

Hovis looked, then mouthed the strange word, "Hilna?"

What a joker, Seth thought. "Judy happens to speak Czech, along with several other languages."

"And *hilna*, Mr. Hovis, is Czech for clay," she beamed.

Hovis seemed impressed, but Seth was more fuddled than anything. "I can't imagine why somebody in Lowensport would be having *clay* shipped to them by steamboat."

"Kilning, pottery, brick-making," Judy said.

"Oh."

"And here—" She rubbed at the side of one of another barrel. "Marmorovy," she pronounced the hard-to-see word on the marking label.

"I have a feeling that word *doesn't* mean gold bricks," Seth said.

"It means *marbles*," Judy said, then pointed to another

barrel. The label read NADOBI. "*Nadobi* means dinner plates." She scanned the rest. "More of these are clay, but a few of the labels I can't make out." She grinned at Seth. "I can't *wait* to open them and find out what's inside."

Good, Seth thought, *'cos you're doing it, not me. I've got work to do!* He wrote checks for all the men as the last of the barrels was taken down to the basement.

Hovis took the checks. "Mr. Kohn, thank you very much. It you don't mind, I'll give you a call sometime. I'd like to know what's in them myself."

"No problem."

"Oh, Mr. Hovis," Judy said, "I wanted to ask you." She pointed across the road, to the opening of the path they'd noticed from the bedroom window. "What exactly is that there? A walkway of some kind?"

"It's a serviceway," Hovis said. "Every square mile of the switchgrass fields are gridded with these serviceways— if you flew a plane over the area, you'd be able to see the lines of each square mile very easily. They're all ten feet wide, so men and equipment have access to the irrigation valves and can check crop quality in different areas."

"Sure, that makes perfect sense," she agreed. "We thought it was something like that. But we also noticed a circular clearing about a half a mile east of here—"

"And then a square one even farther out."

Hovis nodded. "Oh, there are a number of clearings like that, and most of them are graveyards."

"Graveyards," Seth repeated.

"How wonderfully creepy!" Judy enthused.

"Some of them are very old," Hovis went on. "And if you want to go look at them, be very careful. There aren't any serviceways leading to most of them, just barely visible footpaths. And if you ever do that, or if you ever walk along any of the serivceways, it's a good idea to wear boots."

"Ticks?" Judy figured.

"Tick *and* snakes."

"We won't be doing any of that, Mr. Hovis," Seth assured.

"Copperheads are fairly abundant in Maryland," the man continued, "and we've even got some rattlers, but they all stay mainly in woodlands. But out there in the switchgrass, there's a lot of hognose and black snakes."

"Not poisonous," Judy knew, "but they can still bite the hell out of you and give you tetanus."

"Exactly."

"Like I said," Seth repeated. "We *won't* be taking any nature walks through the switchgrass."

"Oh, you can, just be careful."

The workmen had finished and were heading back to their vehicles. "Have a good day, both of you," Hovis told them.

"You, too," Judy said.

Just then something obvious occurred to Seth. "Oh, wait. Mr. Hovis? I never even thought to ask you. What happened to the *crew* of the steamboat?"

Hovis's face set with something unpleasant. "I didn't think it necessary to include the grim detail, Mr. Kohn, but during the excavation, we found the *Wegener*'s crew— or, I should say, their skeletons."

Seth and Judy looked at each other.

"The captain of the boat was an Irishman named Michael McQuinn, and he had two deckhands, Czech immigrants."

"That's too bad," Seth said. "They never got off the ship."

Hovis seemed reluctant to continue. "From what we could see, at least two of them died *before* the earthquake."

"How could you know that?" Judy asked.

"Because they appear to have both been killed with an ax . . . probably the same ax that was used to hack the lid off that barrel of clay," Hovis went on. "And the third skeleton was found inside the door of the cargo house, both of its hands gripping an ax . . ."

CHAPTER FOUR

July 1880

I

Henry Bozman's head thunked in pain as he regained consciousness. *What the damn hail?* He blinked dizziness from his eyes, looked around.

Where in blazes am I? I ain't never seen this room.

No, he hadn't, for he'd never been in the home of the founder of Lowensport, Rabbi Gavriel Lowen.

The night before he'd set fire to one of the docks near the mill, and tonight he'd meant to do the same to another, but—

They musta caught me, he realized.

Candlelight wavered over the wood-slat walls; logs crackled with flames in a great, wide fireplace whose log bed was nearly as long as the wall. No one else seemed to be in the room.

To hail with this, Bozman finally surfaced from his trauma, but when he tried to get up, he couldn't.

He'd been tied to the chair.

Eventually his eyes noticed a Dutch oven hanging atop the burning logs.

A door clicked, then a shadow crossed the room. Bozman couldn't see the figure.

"Where am I?"

The silence seemed to echo, then the figure said,

"You're in a very special place. Few gentiles *ever* receive the opportunity to enter here."

"Untie me! Ya got no right!"

"I have every right by every law ever written," the figure said, and then stepped forward.

I knew it, Bozman thought.

Gavriel Lowen.

"Your name is Henry Bozman, and you work for Conner as a charcoaler. You've done murder for him as well—"

"I ain't done no such thing!" Bozman lied.

"—and just last night you burned one of our docks."

"You're accusing me falsely, only 'cos Jews don't like Christians!"

"I suppose that is why your venerable Mr. Conner refused my offer, because I don't like Christians." Lowen chuckled.

"What offer?"

"I offered jobs to Conner and all of his clan, to fell trees for my mill. My mill generates much more profit than simple charcoaling. I offered twenty-eight dollars per month, per man."

Even in his predicament, Bozman jolted. *All's Conner pays me is twenty* . . . "And he turned it down?"

"He turned it down, Mr. Bozman, because he said he'd rather starve than work for *Jews.*"

Aw, he's probably lying, Bozman had to reason.

"Which brings us to our next problem: *you.*"

"Untie me now, damn it! This ain't legal. I know the sheriff in the next town, and, God damn it, I served in the War."

"You deserted in the War, Mr. Bozman." Another chuckle. "Not what anyone would call a national hero, hmm?"

How could this Jew know that? Bozman simmered. "You don't know what you're jabberin' about, and I didn't burn no dock last night."

"Ah, but the Zemu'im tells me you did."

"The *what?*"

"Certain formulae buried in the secrets of the Calling of the Seals . . . they never lie." Lowen swung the Dutch oven out of the fire and opened its lid with tongs. Steam drifted up, along with a meaty odor. Lowen closed his eyes and inhaled some steam. When his eyes reopened, he looked blankly at Bozman. "Yes, Henry Bozman. You deserted Company K in 1862 along with your cohorts William Tull and Thomas Parker. While real men died fighting the Confederate scourge you took up with Conner and his clan—"

Bozman stared. *How could he know?*

"—and you've raped three Lowensport women, the third, Jana Zlato, not even a woman at all, but a child of eleven."

Bozman gulped.

"And last night you set fire to our dock with a can of slurry that you stole from our lampmaker, Silah Srenc."

Bozman shivered. His nose began to run. "How could you know all'a that just from breathin' steam?"

"I know it because the Zemu'im of the great Kischuph tells me it is so."

"The hail you talkin' about! It's *deviltry* you's talkin' about, ain't it? Jew black magic!"

Lowen seemed more and more amused. "No, Mr. Bozman. It's simply *faith*, and I suspect that faith is something your spirit sorely lacks."

Bozman was getting sick, but in his contempt he tensed against his bonds and confessed, "All right! So what? I done all'a what you said'n more! And it's only proper 'cos it's you Jews who're makin' money off'a *our* land!"

"I *bought* this land, Mr. Bozman."

"Aw, I don't give a hoot 'bout whatever deal you cut with the county! And you're killin' our people!"

Lowen smiled, half his face divided by shadows. "Really now . . ."

"Polten and Corton! They was good men, and we found their bodies in the woods just yesterday!"

"You may have, but they were not *good* men. They were not even *men* at all, but scoundrels, scum. Like yourself, they were deserters and rapists."

"So you admit it!"

"I never lie, Mr. Bozman," came another chuckle.

"And two more'a our men have disappeared to boot! Nickerson and Lem Yerby! You killed them, too, didn't ya?"

"How sure are you of this claim? In fact"—Lowen came around behind Bozman—"I'll take you to them now."

"They're—they're *here?*"

"They are my guests."

In his terror, Bozman hadn't noticed that the chair he'd been tied to was a wheelchair. Lowen released the stops and pushed it toward the six-paneled door he'd entered from. The wheels shimmied and keened. As he rolled past the roaring fireplace, Bozman was able to glimpse, only for a second, the contents of the Dutch oven: the steaming head of a mongrel dog.

The rich, meaty odor sickened Bozman all the more, but his attention snapped alert when he was pushed into a dark, narrow room lit by oil lamps and candles. Bozman guessed his daze hadn't quite worn off yet, for the candle flames seemed to flicker with a slight bluish tint.

The wheelchair stopped.

What Bozman noticed first was an odd framing of stained glass the size of a typical portrait. Two triangles joined at the base so that the bottom triangle was upside down. A weird foreign letter existed at the top and bottom points, and in the center of each triangle was a face. The glass that composed these faces was crystalline black, save for the eyes, which shined blue.

Something about the look of the two faces made Bozman's skin crawl.

"So you see, I haven't lied, Mr. Bozman. Your friends are indeed here, Hiram Nickerson and Lemuel Yerby . . ."

The dark scene riveted Bozman's gaze. Lying atop a pair of wooden tables were two things that were no longer men at all. *The bastards done hacked all the flesh off 'em!* Bozman's head began to reel.

The little bit of muscle that remained stuck to the bones seemed partially burned. And while the flesh of their faces had been scraped off, their scalps and hair had been left, and so had their genitals. But what Bozman could understand least was what the two others in the room—two of Lowen's Jews—were doing.

Several buckets sat on shelves and it was into the buckets that the hands of these two other rabbis delved. Wet sounds crackled when each man removed handfuls of what appeared to be mud.

Then they commenced to pack the mud over the flesh-stripped bones of the two corpses.

Lowen seemed concerned; he approached the two others and the ghastly act on the tables. "Ahron, are you certain there's enough?"

One of the others smiled in the tinted dark. "More

than enough, Gaon—we've been packing it very thinly. It looks now that we shall have a little bit extra."

"Glorious," whispered Lowen.

And the other man: "With the extra we can repack the joints more thickly."

Lowen sighed as if in bliss. He whispered something in a language Bozman didn't know, then uttered, "S'mol is with us, the melech and deliverer of the Eleventh Sefriot . . ."

"Amen," the other two replied with bowed heads, and then they returned to their evil work.

Bozman began to sob, for whatever this devilish act was, he could only suspect the same was about to befall him.

"What in the name of Heaven—"

"Not Heaven, Mr. Bozman, but the Ten Hells to mirror the Ten Emanations . . ."

Bozman could at least be happy that he would not, as feared, suffer the same fate. Instead, Lowen pushed the wheelchair back out to the first room—

"Nooooo!" bellowed Bozman.

—and then right into the great roaring fireplace. Bozman went face-first into the flames.

II

The Present

"What do you guys want?" the auburn-haired woman said with an insulted smirk.

WHACK!

Rosh slapped her right across the face.

The woman squealed; she covered her face with her hands.

In the driver's seat, Rosh wagged a reprimanding finger. "Manners, please, Carrie. Not 'what do you *guys* want.' It's 'what do you *officers* want.'" Rosh glanced back to Stein, who sat in the cruiser's rear seat. "Can you believe the rudeness of people today?"

"Sure can't, Captain."

"Hopefully by the end of our little interview with Carrie, she'll learn better manners."

Carrie's hands slid down her cheeks, revealing teary eyes and a sharp pink slapmark. "My name's not Carrie."

"Really?" Rosh acted dismayed. "You're not Carrie Whitaker, alias Lazy?"

She paused. "No . . ."

Rosh held up a fax and read off it, "Whitaker, Carrie, aka 'Lazy.' Twenty-five years old, auburn hair, brown eyes. Wanted on three counts of escape, suspected drug trafficking, multiple open warrants, and first-degree armed robbery in Jacksonville, Florida." He showed her the picture on the fax. "Isn't that you, Carrie, in that picture right there? Robbing a Circle K store in Florida with a handgun?"

Carrie looked fretfully at the picture. "No . . ."

"Sergeant Stein?" Rosh showed him the picture. "Doesn't that look like our friend here?"

"Sure does, Captain."

"And the fella in the background in the baggy pants and Red Sox hat—doesn't that look like Jary Robinson, aka Jary 'Kapp,' brother of Caddy 'Kapp' Robinson?"

"By golly, it does, Captain."

Suddenly Carrie looked very sick.

Rosh nodded and crossed his arms. "So. Carrie. We can do this the easy way, or the hard way. We know that you're the top-shelf gal for the Robinson Brothers"— Rosh sighed—"aka the Cracksonville Boyz. Damn, Stein, I'm getting tired of all these aka's!"

"I hear ya, Captain."

Rosh looked back at the whimpering girl. *Damn good-looking in a hard-knock kind of way . . .* A pert bosom pushed against the trashy, ice-pink halter. "We know that you make the runs with the Robinson Brothers every month. That's all I want to know, Carrie. I need you to tell me about the Robinson Brothers . . . and, remember, there's an easy way and a hard way. Jive me, and you get the hard way. But if you level with me, we'll let you go."

Even in her sobbing defeat she managed some cynicism. "You guys got me cold. You'll never let me go . . ."

Rosh shrugged. "You're small potatoes, Carrie."

"Hey, Captain," Stein objected. "Words hurt. How would you feel if someone called you *small potatoes?*" And then Stein laughed.

"I'm sorry, Carrie," Rosh mocked. "I meant no offense. I hope that doesn't topple your self-esteem or cause you mental anguish. I want Jary 'Kapp' Robinson. Give him to me, and you walk."

Carrie sniffled, puffy eyed. "I—I don't know where he is—"

"Sergeant Stein?"

In a split second, Stein got a leather cord around her neck and was quickly cranking it down, tourniquet-style, with his nightstick. Carrie's tongue shot out and her back arched out of the seat. Muffled gagging sounds could be heard in her throat.

"This, Carrie, is the hard way," Rosh pointed out. When

her face began to darken and swell, he flicked a finger to Stein, who relieved the pressure.

Carrie fell back lax in the seat, breath whistling as she inhaled.

"Calm down, Carrie." Rosh eyed her bosom again. "Got anything to say now?"

She hacked, then burst into tears. "All right! I make the runs with them every month. We rip off a car in Jacksonville and drive the crack up here—"

"Good, good! Now we're getting somewhere! But I hope you have more to tell us. And *don't* tell us Jary left town because we know he's not stupid enough to do that with all the heat on since his brother got whacked. You *do* know that Jary's brother was murdered the other night on Pine Drive, don't you?"

She nodded.

"Does Jary know?"

"Yes," she croaked. "He . . . was there . . ."

Rosh, astonished, looked back to Stein. "Carrie? You're saying that Jary Kapp was *in* the Pine Drive house when his brother and those other people got hit?"

She nodded again, sniffling.

"Gee, Sergeant Stein, what do you think the next question should be?"

"I don't know, Captain, I'm pretty slow, me being only a sergeant, but you might want to ask her if Jary saw the killers."

"Brilliant!" Rosh exclaimed. "So how about it, Carrie? Did Jary tell you if he saw the guys who did the job?"

"Not guys," she croaked. "He said it was just one—"

"Wow, that's some handiwork. Only *one guy* killed all those people?"

"Jary was scared shitless when he got back to the crib," she said, and seemed terrified at the recollection. "And Jary—you don't know him—but he's *never* been scared of anything in his life."

"Go on, go on."

"He walked in the front room when he heard the racket, took one look at what was happening, and got out a back window."

"His lucky day!"

"He only got one look, but . . . he said it wasn't even a guy."

Rosh and Stein both popped their brows. "The hitter was a *woman?*" Rosh asked.

"No." She swallowed hard. "He said the hitter was . . . was a *thing.*"

Rosh contemplated that, making a face. "A *thing?* Hmm. Stein? Wasn't there a comic book character called The Thing?"

"Sure was, Captain. In the *Fantastic Four.*"

"That's it!" Rosh looked back at Carrie with concern in his eyes. "Was *that* who the hitter was, Carrie? Was it The Thing?"

Strings of snot dangled from Carrie's nose when she looked up in complete confusion. "What? What are you *talking* about?"

Rosh laughed. "Just kidding, Carrie. The truth of the matter is we don't care *who* killed that house full of garbage, but I just think it's interesting that Jary witnessed it. Carrie? We'd like very much to speak with Jary. Do you think you could help us with that . . . remembering, of course, that there's an easy way and a hard way to answer any question."

Very slowly, Carrie nodded. "Blue house on Chesapeake," she droned. "That's the crib we hole up in whenever we drive up from Florida. One of Jary's bagmen lives there with his grandmother."

"Ah! That's great. But would you happen to have an *address* for that residence, Carrie?"

Carrie gave him the address.

"You're a peach." Rosh picked up a newspaper folded between the seat. "Before we let you go, Carrie, I want to know what you think about this, 'cos it *really* ticks me off." He opened the paper. "I read the paper a lot, and it says here that Congress won't allow any further U.S. oil exploration in the Gulf of Mexico."

Carrie gave him a twisted look. "Huh?"

"It's true, it's right here. America's in the middle of an oil crisis, we're getting more and more dependent on foreign oil, even as OPEC keeps jacking the price. If we drilled for more oil in the Gulf of Mexico, we could relieve a lot of that dependency and keep more money in our economy."

Carrie slumped, still sobbing. "I don't care! You said you'd let me go . . ."

"Oh, we will, but seriously, this really irks me." He flapped the paper. "I want the best for America and I'm sure you do, too. But it says here the reason Congress won't let U.S. oil companies drill for more oil in the Gulf is because of the potential environmental hazard, even though America has the best track record for clean drilling. This is the point. We can't drill there, but because it's in international waters, anyone else *can*. Are you following me, Carrie?"

"I don't know what you're talking about," she groaned.

"*We* can't but anyone else in the world can!" Rosh

smacked his hand against the wheel. "*China's* drilling in the Gulf, and so is *Russia!* Even *Germany* and *France—France!*—and even, even *Denmark!* Does that make *no sense at all?* We can't drill there, but they can? It's outrageous!"

Carrie looked fearfully into the back. "What—what's he talking about?"

"Don't have a clue," Stein said. "He goes on these rants sometimes, the economy and stuff."

Rosh seemed suddenly pointed. "I'm just concerned about the way the U.S. Congress pursues its energy policy. Doesn't make a lick of sense."

Carrie was shaking in the seat. "Are you . . . going to let me go, like you said?"

"Of course! Thanks for your cooperation, Carrie." Rosh waved a dismissive hand. "You can go—"

Stein tightened the tourniquet in an instant.

"—*after* we kill your white-trash ass," Rosh finished.

Carrie's eyes bulged in the certainty of death. Her back arched up again, and her face darkened. Stein cranked the cord harder and harder. With each twist of the nightstick, the leather creaked and sunk deeper and deeper into the meat of Carrie's neck. Her tongue stuck straight out.

She began to convulse in her death throes, veins in her neck bulging like baby snakes beneath her skin. Her face went from pink to red to maroon, and then the whites of her eyes hemorrhaged.

Then she slumped in the seat.

"Hold it another minute or two," Rosh ordered. "Gotta make sure she's dead."

Stein gave the nightstick one last twist.

Rosh put an ear to her heart. "Good job. She's officially punched out."

As Stein uncranked the tourniquet, Rosh—without even thinking—pulled up Carrie's halter and began to fondle her breasts.

"Jesus!" Stein outraged. "You're feelin' up a *dead girl!*"

Rosh scowled. "What's the harm? It's not like she can complain."

Stein snorted. "You really are a sick pup."

Rosh jerked his stare back to Stein and pointed.

Stein sighed. "You really are a sick pup, *Captain.*"

"Good!" Rosh started the car. "Now call D-Man and Nutjob and tell those two scumbags we got a body for them to bury . . ."

III

Seth rushed to the Eyeball, hit the spacebar, then watched the hideously veined eyelid flick open with a wet click. The Heart Valve Door pumped open and Seth side-arrowed through, then clamored up the Bone Ladder. He sliced open a Water Cyst with his Scalpel, acquired the much-needed complement of Antigen Armor and a Platelet Sphere, which upped his Hemo supply to one hundred percent. Now all he had to do was make it across the Stomach Acid Channels and assault the dreaded Meatmen . . .

"Not bad," he said aloud to himself. He rubbed his eyes and pushed his chair back from the shimmering LCD screen. The second beta level of *House of Flesh II* seemed to be diverse without being too hard, and graphics rich without being distracting. He saved the programming index changes and turned off his computer. *Pretty fair for a half-day's work,* he figured.

The cool house stood comfortably silent around him.

I'd say the AC's working just fine, he thought when the temp gauge on the office window registered ninety-nine degrees outside. Downstairs, he made two big iced teas, went out into the stifling air, and tromped down the double-doored stairs to the basement, where Judy had been toiling most of the day.

Ovenlike heat hit him at once, but in the immediate distraction he barely reacted to it. *Oh my God . . .* The distraction was Judy herself. To help deal with the heat, she'd put on an old bikini.

"Iced tea!" she exclaimed. She set a crowbar down on one of the age-stained barrels. "What a thoughtful boyfriend!" She snatched a big glass, then chugged half of it. Seth stared in awe at her body as she leaned back to drink, hand on a hip. Every inch of exposed skin gleamed so intensely with sweat it could've been suntan oil, while the bikini itself, normally powder blue, looked almost navy from being thoroughly drenched.

"You're sexy as hell in that bikini and all dripping with sweat like that."

"I'm glad you think so"—she finished all the tea, then held the ice-filled glass to her forehead—"because I don't feel very sexy right now. I feel like a sweathog. I'll bet it's one hundred ten degrees in here. I thought fruit cellars were supposed to be *cooler* than the outside."

"Not in Maryland, not in July—here, take this, you need it more than me," he said and gave her the second glass. "And let's go back up. You could get heatstroke or something down here."

"Gimme a break, I'm a Florida girl. I like it *hot.*"

He was about to complain further but was taken aback when he saw that she'd managed to pry off nearly all the barrel tops.

"Prying one-hundred-thirty-year-old barrel tops off is good exercise," she joked, "and they didn't come off easy. It really gave my arms a workout."

"That's well and good but it's not your arms that are foremost on my mind. It's the rest of your body."

"You're sounding pretty feisty today." She giggled. "We live here now, you know. We could do something really off the wall, like have sex on top of a bunch of barrels from Prague."

"Don't tempt me," he said and walked to the ten barrels. They occupied more than half the basement, along with some yard tools, a lawn mower—which Judy had insisted on; "I'll mow the lawn so I don't get fat!"—and a can of gasoline. The basement itself was not brick or rock as one might expect but, like the rest of the house, walled by larch beams. The beams, however, stood upright rather than lying stacked as they were upstairs. Simple, hard-packed dirt composed the floor. Seth lifted a barrel lid and saw more old clay, then another and found the same. "Where's the one with the dishes?"

She pointed. "And they're *more* than dishes."

"Really? Valuable?"

"Nope. They're *broken* dishes," she said.

Seth looked inside and found a barrel full of shards and packing straw. "Great. What about the marbles? Old marbles might be valuable to collectors."

"Oh, sure they are . . . when they're not broken."

Seth lifted another lid, on the barrel marked MAR-MOROVY, and discovered it full nearly to the brim with thousands of marbles split down the middle.

"I'm sure over a century of hot summers and freezing winters caused all those marbles to crack at their chrysalises," she said. "Oh, and two of the barrels have tools in them."

Seth looked. One was full of sharpening files that were so corroded by rust they snapped like pencils. From the other he hefted out something that looked like a brick of rust. It had a hole in the middle.

"Hammer heads," Judy identified.

Ruined by rust. "*I'm* a hammer head paying to have this crap moved down here. So is there anything interesting in *any* of these barrels I just paid hundreds of dollars for?"

"Zilch. Oh, but we do have two barrels of *uhliprach*." She pranced in her flipflops to a barrel in the corner.

Seth looked in quizzically and saw only black powder. "What the hell is that?"

"Coal dust."

"Why on earth would anybody buy coal dust from Czechoslovakia?"

"Coal was in its infancy back then," she said. "It was hard to get, so it only went to the highest bidder: the cities. Rural burgs like Lowensport weren't priorities for power. The only thing available to lower population centers was coal dust. They added water and a small amount of methyl alcohol to turn it into slurry fuel. It burned very slowly; they used it for lamp oil."

Seth laughed humorously. "Broken dishes, broken marbles, rusted hammerheads and files, coal dust, and clay. That's all we've got?"

"That's it."

"Ten barrels of nothin'."

"Maybe not." She walked quickly to the barrel of dust and hammered the lid back on. "This one's probably the lightest."

"What?" Seth questioned.

"The barrels full of clay are too heavy. I don't know how those workmen got them in here so fast."

"They're strapping young men, unlike me, and would you mind telling me what you're talking about?"

Her stomach muscles tightened when she pushed against the barrel. The barrel moved. "Oh, yeah. I used to go out with this guy who wrote books about eighteenth and nineteenth century craftwork. Americana mostly, but foreign stuff is even better. You want to talk about a collector's market, try a Franklin Stove or an original stone-sled or wheelbarrow. Early American cabinetry, too, is worth a lot, especially if the designer's name is on it."

"There's no original cabinetry in the house," Seth reminded, more taken by the image of her body than the prospect of valuables.

"No," she chided, "but you've got ten very old barrels that were probably made in Prague and mostly in good condition. Cooperage, honey. Cooperage."

"Cooperage?"

"The art of making barrels. My point: collectors buy old barrels, especially if they have authentic markings on them."

Seth eyed the dust barrel. "Ah, so . . . we're going to tip this over on its side to see if there's writing on the bottom?"

"Writing, or engraving, or a brandmark," she defined, and grabbed the barrel's rim and pushed with a groan.

"Let me do it," Seth said, trying to assert his masculinity. He nudged her aside, grabbed the rim himself and, forcing himself *not* to grunt, shimmied around and lowered the barrel until it sat on its side. He winced when he leaned back up.

Judy excitedly knelt and examined the barrel's bottom. "Seth!" she squealed. "You're not gonna believe this!"

"Markings?"

She stood back up and smiled. "No markings."

"Real funny, baby. But I guess that settles it. These barrels are worthless."

"Not necessarily. I'll e-mail that guy I used to date and ask him—"

Seth groaned. "Please. Don't bother. I'm insecure enough."

Judy laughed. "I only had sex with him once, if you must know, and it was so bad I had to use my vibrator when I got home."

Seth felt a little better by the information.

"And, Seth, cooperage was one of the most important crafts as well as one of the first. It dates back to the Bronze Age. Some of the very first tools made of metal were slatcutters—froes, they were called—for barrel-making. It goes all the way back to the Alpine Valley civilizations five thousand years ago."

Seth shook his head. "You really do defy the clichés."

"What?"

"Egghead chicks are supposed to be mousy and dull. They're *not* supposed to have hot bods."

"Not that hot," she said, looking down at herself, fists to hips. "And I've definitely got some cellulite behind my thighs." Her lips pursed. "I'm almost forty. It's inevitable."

He stared outright at her gleaming physique. "Judy. You're *beautiful*. You don't have any cellulite. Yeah, you're almost forty but you look thirty. Your body's excellent. No, it's better than excellent."

"Then that would be *preeminent*."

Seth rolled his eyes. "All right! *Preeminent!* Your body's hotter than a rock in a campfire—"

"How sweet!"

"—so stop all this talk about being fat!"

"Oh, I know I'm not fat now, but I used to be," she said, and now she was errantly rubbing an ice cube from the glass all around her abdomen. "Ooo, that's nice in this heat."

Seth grew half frenzied. "Stop it, you're killing me. You know I've got that wet-skin thing."

She grinned at him and pulled her top up. She rose a moment on her tiptoes when she ran the cube around a nipple. "That wet-skin *thing* is actually a wet-skin *paraphilia*, more commonly known as a fetish, and that particular fetish, I believe, is called swetanoglia."

Seth sat down on the barrel they'd placed on its side, then put his face in his hands. "My God. Is there anything you *don't* know? You speak Czech, Greek, Latin, and Hebrew—"

"*And* Old Norse *and* Scythian," she added.

"You know about switchgrass, ethanol, and biomass, earthquakes, steamboats, fetishes, *cooperage*, lamp oil made out of coal dust—"

"Slurry fuel."

"—*and* you're a professor of theology."

"Theology and theosophy," she corrected yet again.

"You make me feel like a moron."

"No need to. I just read a lot," she said.

The ice had erected her nipples to pinpoints off which the water dripped. Then she lowered the quickly dissipating cube and traced it back and forth across the waist of her bikini bottoms.

Oh, man, Seth thought.

She took two cubes in each hand and circled them round her abdomen. The rush of melted ice ran in rivulets down her skin.

"You trying to drive me nuts?"

She shot a sly grin. "That ruffles your feathers, huh?"

"Yeah."

She kept doing it, bringing the cubes back to her breasts. Now water dripped off her nipples like a leaky faucet.

Can't stand it anymore, Seth resolved. He jumped up abruptly, then rushed into her, embraced her, and slid his arms tight around. He kissed her at once, at the same time sliding his hands up and down her slick back. She embraced him as well, and when her hand cupped his crotch, he became fully aroused. Seth flung her top across the room, then pulled her bikini bottoms down to the bottom of her rump. She squealed in his mouth when he rubbed several ice cubes around her buttocks, then up and down her back.

"We're gonna do it right here," he breathed.

Her hand struggled with his belt, and she panted, "Yes, yes, right in the dirt . . ." But just as she started to lower herself, she bolted back upright and pushed him back.

"What's wrong?"

"Nothing, but—"

"Come on! You can't tease a guy like that!"

"Seth. *Look*," she said and pointed behind him.

Flustered, he turned around.

"Holy crap . . ."

What neither of them had noticed was this: when Seth had risen from the barrel, it had begun to roll. It rolled right into the larch timbers of the wall.

And now some of the stulls pushed back at an even angle.

"That barrel's not heavy enough to dislodge heavy wooden beams sunk in the ground!" Seth exclaimed.

"Maybe they're not *all* sunk into the ground," Judy said with an edge of mystery and scurried over. "Grab the flashlight . . ."

So much for getting laid in the basement, Seth resigned. The blaze of sunlight from the open basement doors didn't reach back far enough. He grabbed the flashlight and returned.

Judy pushed on the dislodged beams, and three of them swung back farther, as if on a hinge.

"Judy, is that—"

"It's a door, Seth. A hidden door." And then she went in. Seth followed.

It's a hidden door, all right, he saw and came up right behind her. He waved the flashlight's heavy beam to reveal the details of a long, narrow, low-ceilinged room walled by still more dark rafters.

"Gavriel Lowen's hidden stash?" Seth joked.

"He *was* very successful," Judy said, looking around. "Which explains the hidden room."

"In what way?"

She smirked at him. "A successful mill owner, who manufactured railroad ties? He was very rich. Rich men need a safe place to store their valuables."

"Yeah, but I don't see any—"

The flashlight fell on the only thing that occupied the room. It was a cabinet that had been mounted to the wooden back wall.

Judy grinned in the light-wedged dark. She touched one of the cabinet's knobs. "Maybe *this* is where Gavriel Lowen kept his riches . . ."

Something primal in Seth upped his heart-rate, and

then it came right back down when he reminded himself
that riches were something he didn't need at all. *It wouldn't
matter if all those barrels out there were full of gold, and the
same goes for this cabinet. I don't need any of it . . .*

Judy opened the cabinet. There were three shelves. Seth
let the light shine inside, then something shined back.

"Even as negligent a Jew as I've been, I know what that
it. It's a menorah," he observed.

"Yep."

Cobwebs covered the eight-branched candelabrum,
and off of each cup hung stalactites of very old wax.

"Looks like gold," Seth said.

Judy pulled it out of its froth of webs, checked the bottom of the base for markings, and tapped on it. "Nope.
Brass. But the date on the bottom says 1810, Schecktel
Metalworks." Judy nodded, her bare breasts gleaming in
the flashlight glare. "This is worth money."

From the second shelf Judy withdrew a well-veneered
wooden bowl, and placed it under the light. Engraved in
the bottom was a—

"Star of David," he said.

"And, more accurately, the Magen David, the shield of
the king of Israel." She put it back inside, then her brow
furrowed. "Now what the heck is *this?*"

She pulled out something that looked like a black
carrot.

"I got no idea," Seth said with a chuckle.

She tapped it, sniffed it. "Some kind of root, I guess,
but I'm not aware of any Jewish rites that used roots."

Seth shrugged, looked deeper into the cabinet. "Looks
like only one more thing inside." He reached in to remove a finely crafted wooden box that looked like cedar.
It was about eight inches long, one inch wide, and one

inch high. There seemed to be no lid, but a crescent-shaped aperture at one end.

"You know what that is, too, right?" she asked.

"Uh . . . no . . ."

"It's a mezuzah vessel."

"Really? I thought mezuzahs were gold and tiny," Seth reflected. "You wear them around your neck."

Judy took it from him, ran her finger over the aperture. "It's only very recent that people would wear them around their necks. In the old days they were this size and almost always made of wood. They were hung on doors. But the actual mezuzah is the piece of paper inside, which has a calligraphied prayer on it."

Seth felt more inept than ever.

"Come on!" she blurted and moved toward the hidden door.

Seth's eyes went wide. "Oh, it's time to have sex in the basement now?"

"No, silly! Let's go upstairs and see what the prayer says!"

IV

"At least he didn't seem too pissed off," D-Man said, stepping behind the shovel blade to dig deeper. "Wasn't our fault the dude got those guys to move the barrels to his house."

"Damn straight," Nutjob agreed, wielding the other shovel. "Not our fault."

"We'll see what he wants next but a'course, I think I can guess." He looked down at the hole. "Won't be as nutty as this, though."

"Yeah. Go figure. We done some off-the-wall shit in the past but this takes the pie."

D-Man frowned. "Cake, moron! This takes the *cake*."

Nutjob smirked. "Cake, pie? Don't see what difference it makes."

They were digging just in the fringe of woods off one of the back roads. From the fields behind, peepers chirruped en mass, a throbbing sound like electronic music. The moon hung high and bright, which afforded them sufficient light for this very arcane job: burying a body that—they'd been told—would have to be dug back up later.

Strange, D-Man thought, and lifted out another shovelful of dirt.

"But it sure was a funny correspondence, wasn't it?" Nutjob chuckled. "The man calls us and tells us to find a body to bury, then five minutes later Rosh calls us and tells us he's *got* a body he wants us to get rid of."

D-Man stopped midstroke, thought a second, then glared. "A funny *correspondence*? You jack-head! It ain't a correspondence! It's a coincidence!"

Nutjob's bottom lip hung low as his brain registered the word. "Oh."

"Jack-head. But you're right, even though ya got the word wrong. First, the man, then Rosh. Like killin' two bears with one stone."

"Yeah, man. Two bears . . ."

When the hole was deep enough, they slid the flimsy plywood coffin out of the step van. Inside the homemade box lay a roughly attractive female corpse with mussed-up auburn hair. She had once answered to the name of Carrie "Lazy" Whittaker. She was naked now. But when Rosh had delivered her earlier in the day, she'd been wearing a radiant pink halter top and jeans. The why's and how's of her current nudity were best left unsaid.

"Guess I'll screw the lid on." Nutjob took the initiative, but then D-Man slapped the back of his head.

"Don't ya listen to nothin'? There's somethin' we gotta do first."

"Oh . . . yeah." Nutjob picked up the towel-wrapped bundle off the van floor and put it in the coffin with the dead girl. Her skin looked bluish in the moonlight.

D-Man smoked a cigarette while Nutjob screwed the lid on, and when the job was done, both men dropped the coffin in the hole and filled the dirt back in.

Nutjob began to tamp the earth down with a booted foot, until—

"Oww!"

—D-Man slapped him in the head again.

"Are ya stupid?"

"Uh . . ."

D-Man shook his head. "Don't pack the dirt down! It'll just make it harder tomorrow night when we gotta dig it back up again."

"Oh. Yeah."

"Now let's get outta here. Tomorrow'll be one hell of a busy day . . ." They got in the big van and drove off.

The towel-wrapped bundle contained several loaves of bread.

CHAPTER FIVE

July 1880

I

"It's damn near August, Mr. Conner," Norris said after his first sip of the whiskey that tasted more like varnish. He pointed to the calendar tacked to the wood-slat wall. "Then it'll be September, and then . . . Winter comes fast in these parts."

Conner slammed his mug down on the table. What splashed out was a cheap ale the saloon keeper made himself with whatever grain might be available. "Think I don't know that?" he growled more than answered. "Think I like half my men livin' in goddamn Sibley tents leftover from the War?"

"They're gettin' a bit uneasy is all I'm saying. You, me, and the other foremen and senior cutters—sure, we got houses to live in with woodstoves. But the rest'a the men . . . They don't wanna do another winter like they *been* doin'."

The cramped saloon had no name; in fact, neither did the town that existed north of Lowensport, not that one would even call it a town. It was a dilapidated hodgepodge of dirt-floor hovels built with splitting-froes instead of saws. Some dwellings were so ramshackle that their collapsed roofs had been haphazardly replaced by canvas. And just beyond the unnamed town sat the Sibley camp, rows and rows of tents that housed the roughened workers known as the Conner clan.

Norris, Conner's closest subordinate, seemed ill at ease to continue. "And there's rumors, too, Mr. Conner."

Conner's scarred face jerked up. "Yeah?"

"Yes, sir. That Lowen offered you'n all our men jobs cuttin' down trees for him . . . fer almost thirty dollars a month . . ."

Conner's close-set eyes seemed to burn under the stained leather hat. "I ain't workin' for kikes and neither are you! Shit, they ain't even from America! You wanna take a job from the same bastard who took our land from us? Do ya?"

"No, Mr. Conner, but the men—they don't wanna freeze again this winter. We lost six, seven women last year, and a coupl'a men. With Lowen's mill we could build ourselves a real town'n have real money. We make less'n less from charcoalin' each year, and they say there ain't gonna be a need for it real soon, what with coal."

"Lowen's mill," Conner croaked in disgust. "You just don't get it, do ya? That's *our* mill. And all these trees? They're *our* trees, and *we* should be makin' the profit, not a bunch'a heebs from God knows where across the ocean." He grimaced at the barkeeper for another ale. "Just be patient, and before winter Lowen and his shifty kikes'll be gone, and it'll be *us* livin' in that town'a his, *and* runnin' that mill."

"We been patient, Mr. Conner. And we ain't killin' 'em fast enough—"

"We're gonna kill *all* of 'em. I told ya long ago, I got a plan."

Norris bottomed out his drink. "It's just my job to tell ya, Mr. Conner, but the men? They're startin' to think there really *ain't* no plan. In the meantime, it's *our* men who're startin' to disappear. Polten, Corton, Yerby, Fitch, Nickerson, and—"

Conner pointed a dirty finger. "It's your job to tell me? Well, it's your damn job to tell the men. I *do* gota plan, and it'll work." He leaned over, quieter. "I used to do it in the War. I was a lieutenant."

"I thought you deserted . . ."

"Yeah, but *before* that, I mean. South Carolina and Georgia, mainly. We'd wipe out whole towns overnight, kill *everybody*. Then we'd bury 'em all and move on. And ya know what? No one ever asked a single question 'cos there weren't no one left alive to tell the tale."

"Mr. Conner, we ain't got enough guns to do that, and you know it . . ."

Conner grabbed Norris by the collar, yanked him close. "I been keepin' it to myself 'cos it's gotta be a secret for now, damn you." He shoved Norris back in his seat.

Norris glared. "Keepin' *what* a secret, sir?"

When the barkeep disappeared into the back room, Conner thunked a pistol down on the table. "See that?"

"Why, yeah."

The big, clunky cap-and-ball pistol shined at its edges. "It's a Beals-Remington .36. They ain't been used in ages, but they still work just fine. There's an armory in Baltimore that's sellin' 'em. They found a bunch of 'em, brand-new, still packed in their grease."

Something like hope began to flicker in Norris's eyes. "That's dandy, sir, but we'd need twenty or thirty of 'em to do a job like what you're talkin'."

"I got fifty comin'," Conner whispered.

Norris's mouth fell open.

"And powder'n balls. We should have 'em on the last

day of the month. But keep that to yourself. I don't want nobody jackin' the shipment, ya hear?"

Norris nodded, speechless.

Conner finished the rest of the bitter ale, then got up. "Just keep the men simmered down a few more days." He smiled with corroded teeth. "Pretty soon, Norris . . . we'll all be sittin' pretty." Then Conner walked out of the bar into the sultry night.

"Bonnie!" Conner's voice cracked when he came home to his wood-slat shack. Where was she? *Damn woman*, he thought. *A man's wife needs to be waitin' at the door when her man's comin' home from the fields.* Normally, she was, preparing dinner in the middle room, which housed the kitchen, the woodstove, and their bed. Conner smelled meat cooking, but there was no sign of his typically attendant wife.

First thing a man needs to see when he walks into his home is his damn wife . . . And not only was there no supper on the table, but the table hadn't even been set. Conner fumed.

It had been at least a month since he'd thrashed her. *Too nice—that's what I am*, his thoughts sputtered. *Guess I'll have to get back to beatin' her weekly. It's the only way to keep 'em cowed.* Conner heard something from the washing room in back. *Bitch is probably back there nippin' at my corn liquor.* But then his anger peaked when he looked to the woodstove. There in the skillet lay two once-fat deer loins, now shriveled and burned.

"God damn!" his voice boomed through the small house. "Ya've ruined good meat! Bonnie! Get'cher ass out here NOW!"

No voice replied from the hall, no footsteps.

Conner took his belt off, wrapped it around his knuckles, and stalked into the hall.

The hall stood dark but he could see lantern light flickering from the washing room. Conner would never consciously admit it, but the prospect of beating his wife made him aroused. He tromped down the hall, boots raising dust from the dirt floor, and he barged into the room—

Before he could shout, the scene he was looking at stopped him cold. "Bon—" The lantern light threw jagged shadows.

On the floor lay two bare arms that had obviously been wrenched from their sockets, and Conner didn't have to be told whose arms they were.

He squinted through the light-diced shadows. On the floor something moved rapidly; it appeared to be a figure lying atop another figure. And when Conner's brain finally allowed him to reckon exactly *what* he was seeing, he whimpered almost like a dog, then turned around and bolted out of the house.

What he'd seen was this: his armless wife convulsing naked in the dirt, raw sockets where her arms used to be. She was being fastidiously raped, but her rapist was something far less than a man.

His terror propelled him across the road to the nearest house, where Jake Howeth lived with his wife and sixteen-year-old son.

"Jake!" he yelled. "There's somethin'—some *thing*—just kilt Bonnie!" But before he could slam open Howeth's front door, more lantern light caught his eye, from the window. Conner's hands shook when he peered in . . .

Jake's son lay in a great circle of blood on the floor,

both legs pulled off; and Howeth's wife lay headless and sprawled nude in the other corner. Some dark, vile liquid had oozed from the dead woman's sex.

My God, Conner's thoughts croaked. *Another one . . .*

He saw the thing in better light than the one in his own house: a hideous figure with scarcely more girth than a skeleton, but a nauseating brownish-gray color. In fact, Conner thought of just that, a skeleton caked with mud. But this skeleton stood nimbly, one thin foot pressed against Jake Howeth's chest, while its skeletal hand ringed Howeth's wrist and pulled upward. With seemingly no effort, the thing tore Howeth's arm off his shoulder. Then, with a wet, grisly smacking sound, it pulled off Howeth's other arm.

Conner could do nothing but stare at this evil impossibility. It was almost with nonchalance, then, that the atrocious stick figure hoisted Howeth's armless body off the floor. Howeth still had legs, and those legs trembled as blood gushed, but the man was still alive, if only just barely. A muffled scream resounded when the thing pushed Howeth's head into the woodstove and held it there a few moments, to let it simmer.

Conner wasn't sure if he would pass out or simply be sick right there by the window. It occurred to him to brandish his pistol and go inside to confront the abomination . . . but that idea waned the second it entered his head. Instead, Conner remained half paralyzed before the window.

That's when the thing turned very quickly and looked right at him: black sockets for eyes, and a thin face whose flesh had been replaced by clay. Disarrayed hair stuck out from its head as though the only flesh that hadn't been stripped off the thing had been the scalp. Conner made out letters written across the thing's chest. The letters spelled this word: S'MOL.

Then, with lips like a knife-cut in meat . . . the thing smiled.

Conner turned, screamed, and ran and ran and ran.

II

The Present

Last night Seth and Judy had managed to remove the parchment from the mezuzah from its wooden casing. Seth had been sure it would've been written in Hebrew—something Judy could read—but instead:

"I should've known," she'd said after examining it. "It's Aramaic, and I don't know it."

Seth had jokingly put a hand to his ear. "Is that the earth I hear cracking open? Finally! There's something my super-smart girlfriend doesn't know!"

Judy had smiled snidely. "Oh, and you know *how* many languages?"

Seth had paused, "Uh, well, let's see, FORTRAN, COBOL, SPL-1 Cold Fusion."

"*Computer* languages don't count," she complained, but then laughed. "Seth, you're actually much smarter than me."

"Really?" he'd replied, astonished.

"I know a lot of things," she'd gone on, "because I used to teach college, used to be around a lot of academicians, and I happen to remember a lot of what I read and hear. You, on the other hand, are an aesthetic architect."

"Aesthetic architect, huh?" Seth had mulled the term over. "Whatever that means, I like the sound of it."

"You don't build houses or offices," she'd continued, "you build fantasy worlds with your mind. Me? I just have a great memory."

At that Seth had pulled her right up to him and peeled off her robe. "You have more than a great memory," he said, already anxious for her. "You have a great body."

Judy had hissed at the sudden feel of his hands running over her skin, and that's when they had forgotten all about the parchment they'd found in the basement. They'd made love until they were both exhausted, and then had fallen asleep.

Judy tended to rise earlier than Seth. The next morning she eagerly leaned over by the bed and shook him awake.

"What, what?" he grumbled. "It's early . . ."

"It's almost eleven! You need to get up."

He leaned up and looked at her, the sudden image jolting him. "Now that's even better than waking up to a beautiful sunrise."

"What is?"

"You. Standing there naked."

She laughed and kissed him, then waved something in his face. "I just thought of something. You need to scan this."

Seth blinked sleep out of his eyes. "What is it?"

"The mezuzah parchment."

"But I thought you didn't know Aramaic."

"I don't, but if you scan it, I can find out what it says."

Seth groaned, then put his legs out to sit on the bedside. "Oh, one of those translator programs. I heard they're not very accurate."

"No, no, I used to—"

"Let me guess!" he complained. "You used to date a guy who knows Aramaic!"

"Don't be ridiculous. I used to have a teaching assistant—a *woman*—who knows it. Her name's Wanda. I can e-mail the scan to her and she can translate it."

"Oh. All right. Let me get my gears turning." He rubbed his eyes, then looked up to find Judy's bare abdomen only inches away from his face. It was impulse that brought his hands to her hips and pulled. He began to kiss her belly. Then his fingers brushed up over her private hair, and he started to lick a line from her navel straight down. She moaned, moving closer, but then she flinched.

"Save it for later. We can't now," she whispered.

"Why not?"

She shimmied out of his clutches, then thrust the parchment toward him. "Because you have to scan this, and then we have to *go*."

"Go where?" he complained.

"To Lowensport. While you were in bed sleeping the day away, the rabbi called."

"Asher?"

"Yes. He invited us for coffee at noon and I accepted. So come on!"

"Talk about a picture-postcard town," Judy said from the passenger side, watching the clean, rustic row houses pass by. The Tahoe's tires crunched lightly over what was presumably the main drag, yet another road topped by crushed oyster shells. The sidewalks were darker. "Cobblestones," Judy said. "Probably used to be ballast." Every building seemed a row house style, all painted a deep pine-green with white trim. What Seth and Judy noticed at once was the architectural similarity between these houses and the Lowen House; they all had the same mansard-type roofs, lancet windows and doors. "I guess these are all original dwellings," Judy observed, "only they've been painted."

"I'll bet they were built the same time our house was built," Seth added, "and they're all made from the same larch beams. That's what I call getting your money's worth out of building material." Along the way, they noticed very few passersby: a woman walking a dog here, an aproned shopkeeper sweeping a sidewalk there. Very few cars were in evidence as well, but those they did see, though older models, were all clean and in good repair. "It's almost like we're driving into a different era," Seth mentioned. "A little slice of the past, American Gothic and all that."

Judy smiled in agreement. "There are still horse-posts in front of the row houses, and look, there's a cobbler's shop. When was the last time you saw that?"

"Never."

"Bakery," Judy read off the glass shopfronts. "Clothier, Kosher butcher's, and, look, a book *shoppe*, not a Barnes & Noble."

Seth pointed toward the corner. "No Seven-Eleven, either. But they've got Sidney's General Store."

"I love it."

"I guess some communities make an effort to hang on to as much of their past as possible," Seth said, but then they both laughed when they passed a Starbucks. "Make that, *almost* as much as possible."

As they proceeded, their angle allowed the sun to flash between two distant trees; Judy caught the glimmer at Seth's throat: his Star of David. "You're wearing your Star," she remarked. "Haven't seen you with that on in a while." Judy's cross caught some momentary sun as well.

Without forethought, Seth's finger touched the star. "Actually I barely remember deciding to wear it."

"Want to make a good show for the rabbi," Judy joked.

"I guess." He shrugged. "I don't *know* why I decided to wear it today."

"And I guess I'd be lying if I said I wore my cross out of any sense of devout faith . . . since I haven't been to church in years."

"Let's hope that *some* faith is better than *none*," Seth muttered, though it still puzzled him that he didn't remember putting the star on.

"This must be the town square," Judy said when oyster shells gave over to asphalt, and the row houses went from two-story to three.

"What address did Asher give you?"

"He didn't, he just said come to the town square and someone would be waiting."

They parked in a public lot but when Seth tried to put money in a meter, he realized they hadn't been functional for years. *More keeping of the old to ward off the new.*

Judy seemed awestruck the instant she got out of the vehicle.

"What are you looking at?" Seth asked.

At the corner a lone road descended between more row houses and ended at a massive series of docks beyond which they could see the shining river.

"I never imagined the Brewer River was that big," Seth said. "I'd never heard of it before."

"It looks almost a mile wide."

Midsquare was a longer, one level building, and a sign that read: HOUSE OF HOPE. A woman in a long dark ankle dress trimmed flowers in window planters outside.

"I guess that's the synagogue," Seth presumed.

"Yeah, but a pretty modest one."

Just then two women in their late teens, and a boy in the same age group, came across the building's long porch, nodded to the flower woman, and entered the double lancet doors. All three youths wore shorts and T-shirts.

"Must be a youth-group meeting," Judy said.

"Guess so." Seth squinted to the west, spotted an oddly vacant tract of land right on the riverfront that still had some foundation beams showing in the ground, and some crumbling stonework. "And that must be where the sawmill was." He grinned. "You like creepy stories. Mr. Croter told me that the man who built this whole town—*and* our house—was murdered in that mill in 1880. Gavriel Lowen. Some local loggers tied him to a box of dynamite."

Judy looked appalled. "I'd call that overkill, huh? Why did they kill him?"

"Because he was a Jew. The locals were anti-Semites. And they slaughtered the entire population of Lowensport, except for babies."

"That's taking Manifest Destiny a bit far, I'd say."

Seth lowered his voice, hoping to sound spooky. "But then someone slaughtered all the loggers later . . . and no one knows who . . ."

"What a charming story, Seth. Thank you *so much* for sharing it with me . . ."

Seth laughed, but then turned at the sound of footsteps.

"That must be Rabbi Lowen," Judy said.

"He likes to be called Asher, but, no, that's not him."

A thin man in black slacks, a white shirt, and a yarmulke approached with a wide smile. "And you can only be Seth Kohn," came a hearty greeting and handshake.

"I'm Rabbi Toz, but please call me Ahron. It's so good that you could come."

Seth introduced Judy as the middle-aged man led them quickly across the square to a row house unit a story higher than the rest. Inside they found a tranquil sitting room heavily draped, richly carpeted, and darkly paneled. Another yarmulked man in the same conservative attire turned with a great white smile.

"And this," Ahron said, "is our resident prayer councilor and coffee pourer, Rabbi Morecz," and then he introduced Seth and Judy. "But please call him Eli."

"Toz, Morecz," Judy commented. "They sound like Czech names."

"And that they are, Judy," the second rabbi said. "Just about everyone in Lowensport has ancestors who came here from Prague. Some changed their names, some didn't."

"I think Asher told me," Seth spoke up, "that his predecessors were named Loew, but they changed it to sound less Jewish."

"That is a fact, Seth." Eli poured coffee from a silver service while Ahron took Seth and Judy to a plush scarlet couch and low table. "Asher, Ahron, and myself, all have great-great-great-grandfathers who helped build this town. And they were all close friends."

"We're a very close town," Ahron said. "Though we welcome *all* to our town, we try to, um, well . . ."

"It's okay to keep the riffraff out," Seth said.

"You found the words I was looking for," Ahron laughed. At the same time, another door opened and in walked a handsome fortyish blond man with a radiant smile.

"How are you, Asher?" Seth greeted. "Thanks for the invite."

"It's my pleasure," said the enthused rabbi, who then was introduced to Judy with a vigorous handshake. "Welcome, both of you, to my home."

"Thanks very much for having us," Judy replied. "And that goodie basket was wonderful."

"I'm glad you liked it. It was my wife's selection," Asher told them, and served the coffee on the table. "And here she is now. Lydia, you remember Seth. This is his friend, Judy."

The dark-haired, dark-eyed, and darkly attired woman merely smiled and set down a silver tray of appetizers.

"She makes the best blintzes I've ever had," Asher bragged.

"*Tesi me, Pani Lowen,*" Lydia said in Czech.

Judy's eyes alighted. "*Srdecne vas vitame.*"

"How wonderful!" Asher announced. "You speak our native language?"

"She speaks so many languages," Seth laughed, "it makes me feel stupid."

"Not that many," Judy said.

"Yeah, not that many, just Greek, Latin, Czech, Hebrew—"

Now Asher seemed doubly amazed. "Hebrew as well."

"Well, only phonetic Hebrew," she admitted, "but I can't write it well in the original glyphic alphabet."

"Still, you're quite a scholar. Hmm, let me see—I'm a bit rusty myself, but . . . *Mah ha'miktzoah shelach?*"

"*Ani Morah,*" Judy responded. "*Ani me'od ohevet et zeh.*"

"How commendable! Where do you teach?"

"Well, I *used* to teach at FSU," she hedged, "but now that Seth and I have moved here, I'm applying in Salisbury."

"Wonderful, wonderful." Asher's enthusiasm kept brimming. "They say there's too many lawyers in the world—

and I'm inclined to agree—but there can never be too many teachers." Asher paused, then looked closer at Seth. "I just now noticed your Star of David. It's enlightening to find people that still wear them—and your cross, too, Judy. In a sense, faith is relative; the common denominator is what matters most. But I sometimes find myself more and more disheartened as I get older."

"Why is that?" Judy asked, errantly fingering her cross at her throat.

"Because faith is waning—there can be no doubt," the rabbi said.

Only now did Seth see that Ahron, Eli, and Lydia had disappeared.

Asher continued. "The more any culture tries to progress, the less of its *genuine* culture—its *spiritual* base—survives. These days I see more iPods and camera phones than I see *any* symbol of faith."

"Good old technology," Seth said.

"The new idolatry," Judy remarked. "The new Golden Calf."

"How true, Judy." Asher finally sat down opposite them, one hand in the other. He seemed intensely serious now. "That's what my people and I have tried to do here in Lowensport. Secure our culture at its roots, and those roots are *crucially* faith-based. Our town may seem odd to you, unadorned, and, well, unexciting." He made a fist. "But it's that same *cruciality* that helps remind us of our heritage, and the reason our people came to America in the first place—and your ascendants, too, Seth, and perhaps Judy's as well. They came here to preserve their *faith*."

"Now you're making me feel guilty," Seth half laughed. "I haven't actually prayed in a long time."

"Prayer is simply conversation with God, Seth. Sometimes we stop talking, but when we're ready to talk again, God's always ready to listen." Asher stiffened a moment, then blurted, "No more religious pep talks, sorry. Here!" He slid the tray forward. "Try the blintzes."

Judy's smile beamed through the awkward prequel; she helped herself. "To be honest, Asher, a little pep talking would probably do Seth and me some good."

Seth couldn't shake the odd feeling in his gut— something like remorse—but he knew it wasn't the same as his remorse for Helene. "It's funny, but Judy mentioned it when we were driving up."

"And what's that, Seth?" Asher asked.

"My Star of David. She said she hadn't seen me wear it in a long time, and she was right. I haven't. I don't really know why I put it on. I don't really . . . I don't really know what it means anymore."

Asher nodded. "All too often when we think we've lost faith, we've merely lost sight of God because we've *let* God pass us by on whatever this road is we call Life. We're humans, Seth. We err, usually by temptation, and by the same distractions we dismiss as progress. But what we must *always* remember when we lose sight of God is this: we can always regain that sight simply by desiring to, in our hearts. We just have to get back on that road." He waved a finger and smiled. "And God's a pretty easygoing guy. Sometimes he'll even slow down a little, to let us catch back up."

"That's a promising way of putting it," Seth said.

"Everything that faith's about is just that: promise." Asher leaned over closer. "Anytime you feel like talking about it, let me know. I'd like to help you remember what that Star of David means." Then the rabbi leaned back abruptly and laughed. "I mean, I *am* a rabbi! It's my job!"

They all laughed at that, and after Seth ate a blintze, he mentioned, "Where exactly is your synagogue or schule? That building across the square?"

"The House of Hope," Judy added. "It didn't really look like a synagogue."

"It's what I was saying before," Asher answered, "about preserving one's spiritual culture by honoring its roots. In worse times, during the centuries of persecution, Jews had no obvious synagogues to worship in. They had to be hidden, they had to be secret, or else they'd be burned down. So the faithful would hold services in basements, or even deep in the woods, in caves. Our synagogue, for instance, is right here in this house, and in Gavriel Lowen's time"—Asher smiled right at Seth—"it was in *your* house."

Seth's brow creased. "Then . . . what's the House of Hope?"

Asher had another blintze and explained, "We call it a youth-guidance center but that's a rather soft way of putting it. It's a drug rehab center, and—there? See? What we were talking about before. There are many ways to lose sight of God, and there's nothing that the devil likes more. Drugs truly are the great corruptor of our youth, the most devious evil, and very much indeed wielded by the beast." He shook his head in a lamentation. "The drug problem around here is *horrendous*."

Surprise focused Judy's attention. "That's quite a shock, Asher. If any town looks like it doesn't have a drug problem, it's *this* town."

"Oh, I don't mean here in Lowensport," the man clarified. "There *are* no drugs here. Our in-patients all come from Somner's Cove. We have a few alcohol abusers and one or two addicted to heroin, but almost all of it's cocaine—crack. Horrific stuff. We only have twenty-five beds, but when we get the money we'll be able to expand. We take whatever overflow we can, since the Somner's Cove facilities are always full to maximum capacity. We're legally a Yeshiva, the Jewish version of a parochial facility; because we're considered a faith-based clinic, we can't get federal assistance. It can get discouraging, though. We've barely got a fifty-percent success rate."

Judy sat up straighter. "That's phenomenal. The national average is ten percent for crack." She paused, then shrugged. "I ought to know. I . . . had some problems with that myself."

Asher nodded, probably trying to conceal surprise. "I wouldn't have guessed, but it is very true. The deviousness of drugs is all-pervading, while the cliché is that it's limited to lower-economic social levels."

Seth spoke up without any reservations. "Judy and I actually *met* in a rehab center. Drugs nearly destroyed her, and alcohol nearly destroyed me."

"Ah, then what wonderful proof of the human spirit—backed by God's love, of course—persevering over the most negative odds," Asher said.

Seth hoped that this sudden confession on his part wasn't putting the rabbi on the spot. Somehow, though, he knew it wasn't. "Before I met Judy, I was married—my wife's name was Helene—and it's ironic that she was the one who actually brought the Lowen House to my attention."

Asher sat focused in his seat. "I'm afraid I don't understand. I thought you were originally from Florida."

"Helene had relatives in Virginia," Judy informed him. "She and Seth drove up here to visit them, and—well, Seth, it's best that you tell the story."

Seth sighed. "Yes, we stopped to see her relatives, then planned to drive up to D.C. for some sightseeing, so we crossed over on the ferries and got off in Somner's Cove. We were trying to get on the interstate north but took a wrong turn and wound up driving past the Lowen House. Helene spotted it first, and we were so taken by it that I called the Realtor on the for-sale sign, and he showed it to us. The price was right but I couldn't afford a house at the time; I'd actually just lost my job with a computer game company that went bankrupt. I'd taken out several bank loans because I wanted to develop my game; I built the entire thing myself and used the bank loans to pay my graphic engineers and system techs to give the game the look I needed, then I sent the whole thing off to a distributor and kept my fingers crossed. This was two years ago. So, anyway, after I submitted the game, that's when Helene and I came up this way and saw the Lowen House. It was almost a joke. I said, 'One day, if I'm ever rich, I'm going to buy this house.'"

"What an ironic connection," Asher said. "Yet, I fear your reference to Helene in the past tense can only mean . . ."

Seth's throat locked up, so Judy answered for him. "Helene was killed in a car accident several weeks later, after they returned to Tampa. It just so happens that on the same day she was killed, the distribution company bought Seth's computer game."

Seth finally got his voice back. "After that—Aw, Asher, I don't want to bore you with the story."

Asher's eyes shined. "But I *want* to hear your story, Seth, and yours, too, Judy, if you like to share them. Sometimes a neutral ear can be quite therapeutic."

Seth nodded. "The game paid a very large signing bonus, and there were lots of offers for subsidiary rights pouring in, but I was barely aware of it. After Helene was killed, I . . ."

"Took solace in the bottle. I understand. All too often we only learn too late that there is no such solace."

Seth gave a humorless laugh. "Within a month I was a total wreck, a total clinical alcoholic. I would pass out in bars, in parking lots, several times I woke up in my car on the shoulder of some road I'd never been on before."

"Loss is sometimes unreckonable," Asher said. "Many of the patients in our clinic took to drugs due to some similar loss, and next thing they know, they're hooked."

"Yeah, well I was *very much* hooked, and you're right. I didn't know how to deal with the loss, I didn't understand it, but the thing that was the hardest were the details of Helene's death. That's what pushed me over the edge." He held Judy's hand, tried to continue, then just looked down and shook his head.

"Seth blames himself for Helene's death," Judy continued for him. "She was driving back from the mall one day, so Seth called her on his cell phone and asked her to stop and get him a pack of cigarettes. She turned around to go to the convenience store, then—"

"That's when she got broadsided," Seth choked the words out. *Don't fall apart!* he pleaded with himself . . . but already he was feeling better in this recital of his life's worst event. "And of all things, it was a drunk driver."

Asher calmly sat back, crossed his arms. "What's just as common as alcohol abuse, and drug addiction, is our inability to separate happenstance from providence or even bad luck. Hopefully by now, Seth, you know that it's folly to blame yourself for an *accident*. And we mustn't blame God, either, because it actually has nothing to *do* with God. It has only to do with human error. God is the spiritual hallmark in our lives, not a physical one. He gives us proximity to him through the love and wisdom of his emanations. He doesn't divert drunk drivers, or stop wars, or allay sickness and poverty by a sweep of his hand." Asher raised a finger. "Now, he *could* do those things if he wanted to, but then that defeats his purpose. We need to do those things ourselves, and we're just not there yet. It's important that you perceive this, Seth. Blaming yourself for your wife's death only offends her memory."

Seth dragged his eyes up and looked at the man. He gulped. "I never thought of it that way before."

"Of course not!" Asher said and laughed, "because it's too easy not to! Why? Because we're humans! We screw up! And the only way to alleviate our error is to try as hard as we can to keep our lives in the light of God."

Seth suddenly felt limp as putty. He nearly sobbed outright when he realized that the rabbi's words had unloosed a terrible burden from him.

Judy sensed that Seth was still too choked up to continue, so she diverted, "And Seth's not the only one who screwed up. I was a professor at an esteemed college. I had the career I'd always wanted, and the self-satisfaction, too. I was successful and well-liked by my peers. But one time I went on a date with this guy in the political science department. I was overweight at the time—I always had been—but this guy told me he lost forty pounds effortlessly—with cocaine. To this day I don't understand how someone with my education could've been stupid enough to fall for it. I believed everything he told me—I guess only because I needed to believe it. 'Oh, don't worry, it's not addictive, that's just propaganda,' and 'once or twice a week is perfectly safe,' and 'I've been doing it for years, Judy, and I'm not an addict. I haven't lost my job and my friends and my home.' Stuff like that."

"I hear almost identical stories right across the street at House of Hope," Asher said.

Judy wasn't surprised. "Before I know it I'm so habituated to cocaine that I'm not even myself anymore. The other teachers in my department can tell that something's wrong, but I *can't*. My lessons slide, students start dropping my classes, several filed complaints." Judy had to look at the wall to go on. "The dean's office ordered me to take a leave of absence and get treatment, but in the meantime powdered cocaine stopped working. It wasn't enough of a kick. So instead of going to treatment, I go to a crack dealer. That was the beginning of the end, but the end came pretty quickly. I . . . got arrested, the college fired me, and . . ." Judy's monologue faltered. "Well, to make a short story long, I eventually *did* get treatment, and that's how I met Seth. We both checked into the same rehab center." Judy laughed to buff off some of the grim edge. "That guy I dated was right about one thing, though. I did lose weight, though I wouldn't recommend this *particular* diet."

They all laughed lightly at the remark.

"And the best part is," Asher said, "you've both survived the odds, proof of your own free will overcoming the error we're all subjected to. Just as it says in the Bible, you've dressed yourselves in the *new* self, and discarded the worldly clothes of the old with nothing more or less than the free will granted to all of us through the wisdom of En Soph,"

"En Soph?" Seth questioned.

"One of the Jewish names for God," Judy said. "There's Yahweh, of course, and Elohim and Hayyim."

"It's remarkable that you know that," Asher said.

Judy shrugged. "I was a theology professor."

"Judy knows more about Judaism than I do," Seth chuckled, "and she's a Christian."

"Yeah," Judy said, "I'm Seth's *goyle*friend."

Asher had to stifle amusement. "You really are something, Judy." He turned to Seth. "Now, Seth, I did read the article about you in the paper, but I'll admit I don't know much about this career of yours. A video game developer?"

"That's essentially what I do, but I also devise the creative elements of the game."

"And this *House of Flesh* . . . it's science fiction, right? It's not . . ."

Seth laughed, now that he felt fully unwound. "No, no, Asher, I know the title *sounds* like something X-rated but it's just a sci-fi fantasy scenario."

"You must've outdone yourself, based on the game's success."

"In truth I just got lucky. I gave an old concept a new look, and fans took to it."

"Seth can be a little too humble sometimes," Judy said. "The first run outsold any game in history."

"That's quite an accomplishment," Asher said.

"And I'm his level tester," she added. "The game's really big now on multiplayer mode, which means people all over the country can play against each other on the Internet."

"Judy, I'll be honest," Asher remarked. "We here in Lowensport don't know the difference between the Internet and a hairnet. We don't even have computers. But I'm very happy for your success."

"Thanks, Asher," Seth said. "It's a lot of fun developing, but like I said, I just got lucky."

A door swung opened, and Eli appeared. "Anyone for more coffee or blintzes?"

They all declined, but for the moment that the door was opened, Seth and Judy noticed something on the wall of the other room: a diagram with two pyramid shapes joined at the base and a face in each pyramid. The top face was light, the bottom dark. Seth had no idea what it was but Judy seemed to recognize it at once.

"Asher," she said, intrigued. "You're a Kabbalist."

"Why, yes." Again, the rabbi was surprised by her knowledge. "Does it show?"

"I saw the Head of Zohar in the other room. Can't believe I didn't figure it out before that. No visible synagogue, and your reference earlier to emanations."

"I'm very impressed by your learning. Genuine Kabbala is barely known these days."

"Well, I was a theology professor but I also taught a course on theosophy."

Asher seemed enthused. "Now there's a word you hear these days even less than Kabbala. The study of the mystical elements of God."

"It was a terrific course but not too many applicants," Judy said. "But you'll be happy to know that the very first leg of the class covered Kabbalism."

Seth felt remiss. "I've heard of Kabbala but I really don't know what it is."

Asher looked at him. "You have to understand what it *isn't* first, Seth. It isn't magic, or shamanism, or anything like the current rage of Kabbala popping up in California. It's not esoteric or mystical, and it's not a denomination, it's simply a deeper and more subjective interpretation of Judaism."

Judy added, "True Kabbala is an oral tradition, right? Said to be the first religion, taught to the angels by God himself?"

"Exactly," Asher agreed, "and then taught to Adam by the angels—"

"Via the Ten Sefers, or books, reflecting the ten ideal numbers—"

"—and the Ten Emanations of God," Asher clarified.

"I must plead ignorance again," Seth said. "Some Jew I am, huh?"

"All that matters is faith, Seth," Asher said. "The Kabbala isn't for every Jew in the same way that, say, Jesuitism isn't for every Catholic. It's merely a deeper than usual study of the earliest tenets of Judaism."

Seth pointed to the door. "What was that diagram in the other room?"

Asher's eyes beamed at Judy. "Judy? I'd be interested in hearing your answer."

"The Magical Head of Zohar," she replied. "The top—or bright—face represents man in God's image enlightened by the Ten Emanations, and the bottom—or dark—face is the . . ." She chewed her lip. "Oh, I can't quite remember the name."

"The Neptesh," the rabbi responded. "Man's cruder soul, struggling to be worthy of the Emanations and their light."

"The more the pyramid shapes draw together the more enlightened the Neptesh becomes," Judy carried on, "and when they draw in to even angles, the shapes become the Star of David."

"Very good, very good," Asher complimented. "The Head of Zohar is our symbol just as Judy's cross is the symbol of a Christian."

Seth slumped. "Every day I learn more and more, which only reminds me of how little I actually know."

"Don't feel bad, Seth," the rabbi laughed. "Very few people know anything about genuine Kabbala. But it's the heart of my faith, and of everyone else in Lowensport."

"Was Gavriel Lowen a Kabbalist, too?" Seth asked. "Your great-great-grandfather?"

"Great-great-*great*-grandfather." Asher smiled. "And, yes. He probably led the very first Kabbala kahal in America." Asher gestured a small portrait on the wall, depicting a stern-faced man with a beard and no mustache. "That's him there. He was a great man . . . but met a tragic end."

Oh, right," Seth recalled. "The Realtor who sold me the house mentioned that."

"Persecution is everywhere, like any other evil." Asher looked at his watch and quickly raised his brows. "My, I've lost track of time. I'd love to chat longer but Lydia and I have to have some face time over at the clinic."

"We've got to be going, too, Asher," Seth said and stood up with Judy. "But thanks so much for having us. You're a very inspiring man."

"Why, thank you!"

They all shook hands. "Why don't you and Lydia come to dinner at our house some time?" Judy asked.

"Yeah," Seth said. "In your great-great-*great*-grandfather's house?"

"What a wonderful idea. We will, very soon." Asher showed them to the door. "And next time you're up our way, please stop by. My door is always open to you. And, Judy, based on your experience and the wonderful example of your own victory, perhaps I could impose on you to give a little talk to our residents at the House of Hope."

"It's no imposition at all, I'd be delighted."

They were about to leave but Seth stalled at the door. "Asher, you take donations, right?"

The rabbi didn't seem to understand. "Donations? For what?"

"For your rehab center."

"Oh, Seth, I didn't bring it up to needle you for a donation—"

"I know, Asher. But you must take donations."

"Honestly, we never have. It's all run by volunteers and any surplus in the community coffers, but I suppose—"

"We'd like to make a donation," Seth said and wrote off a quick check. "Please take this."

"Why, thank you." Asher nearly choked when he looked at the check. "Seth, I-I don't know what to say."

"No need to say anything. It's just a little something to help out."

"Well, well," Asher gulped. "Thank you *so much*."

"Sure, and thank you. We'll call you soon about coming up for dinner."

Seth felt vibrant when they left. "What a great guy. And you're right, he's very inspiring."

"Rabbis are supposed to be," Judy said. "How much did you give him?"

"Thirty grand."

"Seth!"

Seth shrugged. "It's because of guys like him that you and I are still walking and talking."

"I know but . . . That was very generous."

"I'm just grateful that I have anything to give." He took her hand as they headed for the car. Some passersby, mostly couples, were seen strolling the sidewalks, the men dressed like Asher, and women in dark conservative dresses akin to Lydia Lowen's. Those who took note of Seth and Judy smiled warmly and waved. At the end of a side street, the river gleamed, and seagulls floated in the air. "But now I think it's time to spend a little more money," Seth suggested. "Let's find a good restaurant."

III

"Where you at?" Rosh asked into his "special occasion" cell phone, a simple TracPhone with a calling card and no server to subscribe to. "I need to rap with ya."

"Rap, huh?" replied D-Man's fuzzy voice. "Can't wait. I need to rap with you, too. We're near the clearing—you know the little place at the edge of the woods, near . . . you know."

Rosh thought he did. His curiosity twisted. "Isn't that where you guys bury—"

"Yeah, we bury people here—usually for you, R—"

"Don't *ever* use my name—or *anyone's* name—over the phone," Rosh ordered. "Ever."

"Yeah, I know . . ."

"What's that?" Rosh snapped.

"Yeah, I know . . . *sir.*"

"Good, and don't forget that shit. We're in town now, but sit tight. We'll be there in fifteen minutes."

"We'll be here," D-Man's voice fuzzed out.

What the fuck are those two idiots doing up there? Rosh snapped his phone closed and grimaced at the scene.

The SWAT men were packing up, the responding patrol cars already pulling away from the teetering house whose roof looked sucked in. *Another day, another crackhouse,* the corrupt captain mused. *Just . . . not the right one . . .*

The sun set quickly, as if escaping; it left Rosh to stand in orange-tinted darkness. Stein came out of the house and walked over.

"Can't believe it," Rosh complained. "Lazy gave us bad info. How do you like that for audacity—lying to *cops*."

"Actually, Captain, she wasn't lying "

Rosh felt a surge of expectant joy. "You're not telling me you *found* Jary Kapp on the second sweep of the house?"

"No," Stein said with little interest. "All I said was Lazy wasn't lying. Jary ain't inside but he *was*." Stein flapped something against Rosh's chest.

A Boston Red Sox hat.

"You're right," Rosh admitted. "His brother wore Yankees but Jary always wears Red Sox."

"Thought you'd like the souvenir," Stein commented with a snide smile.

"Yeah, thanks a fuckin' lot. Now come on. You drive."

They got into the car and pulled off.

"Jary ain't stupid, Captain," Stein observed. "He knows there's a dragnet on for his ass, so he's not holing up in the same place for long."

"Probably stays in a different hideout each night. Fucker must think he's Bin Laden."

Stein lit a cigarette at the wheel. "We'll probably get him when he tries to get back to Florida."

"Probably's not good enough, Stein." Rosh dug his own fingers hard into his thigh. "I *want* him."

"You gonna tell me where we're going?" Stein asked.

"That clearing where the Two Stooges bury the scumbags we contract."

"What for?"

"I just want to . . . ask them something. D-Man said he needs to talk to us, too."

"Next switch is two days from now. Maybe he's got it early."

"Maybe," Rosh muttered, and watched the moon follow them along the top of the endless switchgrass.

Both men made sour expressions when they pulled into the clearing behind the familiar black step van. A gas lantern hung on a pole, lighting the macabre scene: D-Man and Nutjob both digging a hole.

"I thought those assholes only did button jobs and disposals for us," Rosh said.

Stein shut the cruiser off. "I guess we're not their only business. That's the American way, right? Isn't that what you're always talking about?" Stein grinned over. "Free enterprise?"

"Shut up . . ."

The cops walked over and looked down. The two ragtag rednecks continued to dig.

"Who the hell else is hiring you?" Rosh asked.

"No one," D-Man huffed. "Just you."

"Then who the fuck are you burying?"

Nutjob sniggered as he hoisted up another shovelful of earth. "We ain't buryin', Captain. We're *diggin' up*."

Now they'd managed to expose the top of a makeshift coffin a foot below the surface. Nutjob stepped down into the hole, and with a hammer claw began to pry off the lid.

D-Man forearmed sweat off his brow.

"Holy *shit*, she stinks!" Nutjob yelled after fully opening the lid. He jumped back out and fanned his face.

"You expect her to smell like English Leather, dimwit?" D-Man said. "She's been dead in the ground a day."

Rosh and Stein stared down in disbelief. The wan lantern light revealed the nude corpse within the box: a pallid yet shapely dead woman in her twenties. Pert-breasted, auburn-haired.

"Carrie Whittaker." Stein's voice ground like sandpaper.

"Aka Lazy," Rosh finished. His gaze spun to D-Man. "What the fuck's going on? We paid you to bury this bitch."

"Yeah. And we buried her," D-Man said, and swigged a can of beer. "And now we done dug her up. But don't worry, we're gonna bury her again." He flicked a finger at Nutjob, a signal.

"Shit," the other lout complained. Then he held his nose and got back in the hole.

Rosh could only stare stupefied. He'd only now noticed that something had been buried *with* the corpse: a towel-wrapped bundle. Nutjob hacked at the smell, removed the bundle, put back the lid, then jumped back out.

And next?

He and D-Man began to fill the hole back in.

Stein continued to stare while Rosh leaned over the bundle and, using thumb and forefinger as tweezers, unwrapped it to reveal—

"Three loaves of pumpernickel," Stein observed.

Rosh straightened up, rubbed his temples. He looked back at the two grave diggers, sighed, and said, "Sergeant Stein?"

"Yes, Captain?"

"Is it me, or is this the most fucked-up thing we've ever seen?"

"It is, sir, *the most* fucked-up thing we've ever seen . . ."

D-Man and Nutjob chuckled and kept shoveling the dirt in. When they were finished they wiped off their hands and stamped the dirt down.

"D-Man?" the captain queried next. He tried to regulate his tone of voice. "Why did you. Just dig up. The girl we paid you. To bury yesterday?"

"To get the bread out," the brawny man answered. "We put it there yesterday before we buried her. But now we need it."

Rosh rubbed his face and sighed again. "D-Man? Why. Do you. Need fucking pumpernickel. From a FUCKING COFFIN WITH A DEAD CRACKHEAD IN IT?!"

"Best not to ask," D-Man said and swigged more beer. "We don't really even know ourselves. We do what our boss tells us . . . just like you."

Spittle flew from Rosh's lips when he yelled. "I want to know why you buried that girl with three loaves of bread and then dug her back up!"

The rocketing exclamation caused several night birds to flutter out of the trees behind them.

"Calm down, man. I told ya. It's best not to ask."

"Yeah, Captain," Nutjob augmented. "Ain't ya ever heard the saying 'Curiosity killed the clown'?"

D-Man gaped. "It's *cat*, dickbrain! *Cat!*"

"Oh."

D-Man bare-handed the beer can to a ball of aluminum. "It's just some jive, Captain. We don't ask why, ain't no reason to. They're into some weird shit is all."

"Weird shit? Yeah, I'll say!" Rosh yelled, pointing to the bread.

"It's just superstitious stuff, you know, from Europe or some shit. Good luck or somethin'." D-Man worked a kink out of his back and cracked it like a walnut. "Oh, yeah, what I needed to tell ya is the next switch-off'll be two days late."

"Bullshit!" Rosh yelled. Between the exhumation, the bread, and now *this* bit of news, Rosh felt on the verge of a conniption. "I got bagmen and point guys wanting to give me money every fucking day! They can't sell enough of the shit! It's *business*, D-Man! I told 'em day after tomorrow so it's gotta BE day after tomorrow!"

D-Man looked annoyed by the outburst. "Relax! It's gonna be late. You don't like it"—D-Man handed Rosh his TracPhone—"call up your own self and say so . . . which you *won't* do 'cos he's the guy who bankrolled the whole operation and got you started."

Rosh looked at the phone, then gave it back. "All right. Two days late. Fuck! Any idea why?"

"No." D-Man stomped dirt off his soles. "We do what we're told, Captain. Me, you. 'Cos it's the boss who's paddin' our wallets."

"He's right, Captain," Stein said. "Can't fight the system. So what? Let the crackheads go into withdrawal a few days. It'll keep them humble."

Rosh finally simmered down. "Yeah, okay. You're right."

When Nutjob was scratching dandruff out of his goatee,

D-Man put the shovels in the van, and then tossed in the loaves of bread. "We're done here. What was it you wanted to tell us?"

The sound of crickets began to rise with the moon. Rosh handed D-Man a photo of Jary "Kapp" Robinson. "This is the brother of one of the dudes you waxed the other night on Pine Drive—Jary Kapp."

D-Man nodded at the picture. "No problem. Same deal, five grand and it's done. Just tell us where to find him."

Stein's glance to Rosh looked less than hopeful. "We don't know where he is, he's laying low."

"And we figure you must have plenty of stoolies on the street, just like we do," Rosh added. "Ours either aren't talking or don't know."

Nutjob was inspecting his finger after picking his nose. D-Man opened another beer. "We don't have people on the street, man. We're just deliverymen. *You're* the ones with the informants."

Rosh's lips pursed in frustration. "I don't want this guy buttoned, I want him alive."

"And you don't know where he is so you can't give us a loke," D-Man finally deduced.

"Yeah. So I guess ya can't do it, huh?"

D-Man and Nutjob traded a silent glance.

"What?" Rosh said. "What's that—that, you know? That *look?* Stein, what would you call that?"

"I don't know, Captain. I guess it would be a *sinister* look."

D-Man whipped his phone back out. "Gimme a minute, I'll see what I can do." And then he walked out of earshot.

Nutjob said nothing. He turned off the lantern and stowed it in the back of the van. Rosh and Stein followed him.

"Nutjob, what gives?" Stein asked. "You either got informants on the street or you don't."

"We don't, man. But . . . there might be another way. We done it before. Best to not ask details."

More fucked-up stuff, Rosh thought, aggravated. *Yeah, curiosity kills the clown.* If there was one thing he had a lot of, it was curiosity.

D-Man came over, frowning when he noticed Nutjob huffing more pot. "About that job you want? Boss says we can do it. But it's ten grand, not five. You want the dude alive, it's riskier."

No point bellyaching, Rosh realized. "Okay, but how are you gonna do it if you don't know where Jary is?"

"That's the hitch. We can do it, but we gotta have something that belongs to the dude," D-Man told him. "A watch, a shirt, a shoe—"

Rosh nearly snapped. "Or, let me guess! A piece of hair or a fingernail?"

"Either of those'll do—"

"Oh, man, come on! Is *that* what this is? Voodoo or some shit like that?"

D-Man hesitated. "Yeah, I guess. Sort of. You want the job done, that's what we need. Why you gotta bitch about everything?"

Now Rosh was a mess. "Great. That's just great. And even if I believed in bullshit like that—which I don't— shit, we don't have anything of his—"

"Yeah, we do, Captain." It was Stein, coming back from the cruiser. "Will this work?" He gave D-Man the Red Sox hat.

"Good thinking!" Rosh said.

"If it's the dude's, then it'll be fine," D-Man said. "And the ten grand? It's up front."

Rosh frowned at him. "You think I carry that kind of cash around in my pocket?"

"Yeah."

Rosh gave him a band of hundred-dollar bills.

"Solid," D-Man said. "We'll call ya when we got the guy."

Rosh was waylaid. "Just like that? You're shitting me. Because of a fucking *hat*?"

"Yeah," D-Man said, and then he and Nutjob got in the van and drove off.

Rosh and Stein traded glances, in a look that was not sinister but very nearly fearful.

IV

"Well, I'd say our first excursion to Lowensport *and* Somner's Cove was a success," Seth remarked when he pulled the Tahoe into the front drive. The cloudless sky full of moonlight cut their house into a crisp silhouette.

"Two completely different places," Judy said, "but both unique in their own way. And those steamed crabs in Somner's Cove were delicious."

"Crazy Alan's Crabhouse." Seth chuckled. "I wonder if there really is a guy named Crazy Alan . . ." Seth put his arm around her, and went in the house. They'd had a massive crab dinner in Somner's Cove, then killed some time driving through town and along the bayfront roads, some still paved with oyster shells like so many roads in the area. It had been stunning scenery when the sun had set. When they'd headed back, though, Seth forgot which road he needed, and they wound up having to drive through a surprisingly large slum that seemed pushed aside from the town's better environs. *I guess every place has its underbelly,* Seth reasoned. Judy had remained silent: young men who could only be drug dealers dawdled on every corner. *She could do without reminders like this,* he thought, and, next, around another corner, a drunk stumbled out of a ramshackle saloon and collapsed on the sidewalk. *And I guess I could do without that . . .* Seth drove out as fast as he could.

Judy's demeanor changed the instant they returned to the house. Seth hoped she felt as revived as he did. Their talk with Asher Lowen had left them both brimming with . . . something. "The effect of confession," Judy had commented later. "Because that's what we did, we confessed to him."

"Not quite but, yeah, I do feel a whole lot better now, better than I have in a long time," Seth had replied. He hadn't mentioned his drunk driving charge, though, where he'd crossed the center line and crashed into a guardrail, missing a minivan full of children by less than a yard. "I just didn't have it in me to tell him about my crash."

"And I wasn't too hip to the idea of telling him just how low drugs took me in the end."

Seth nodded. "It wouldn't have mattered, though—I'm sure of it. We could've told him all of that, and he'd still understand."

Back inside, Seth instinctively went to his office to check email, but before he knew it Judy came right up behind him and ran her hands up inside his shirt. "Oh, so you're putting the make on me?" he joked.

"Yeah," she whispered. "Got a problem with that?"

"Not in the least . . ."

"Why don't you check my emails, too," she said against

his neck, "while I check . . ." Now her hand slipped lower, fingers teasing into his pants.

Just the sensation of her hands made Seth reel in arousal. He logged on to her account, thought, *To hell with email*, and turned around to find her already stripped down to panties and bra. "This has just got to go," he muttered, about to unfasten her bra, when—

"Oh, look," she said, viewing the screen over his shoulder. "I've got one. Let me check it real quick." She nudged around him to lean over the keyboard.

Seth could've howled. "You really love teasing me, don't you?"

"It's not teasing, it's stoking," she laughed. "I'm *stoking* you up."

He was about to make some brazen comment but his voice fell short when the image of her hit him full-force: barely dressed, lustrous skin glowing, bent over the keyboard. Seth couldn't help it; he went right up behind her, rubbed his groin against her rump, and slid his hands around to shuck her breasts right out of the bra. She tensed, inhaled through her teeth when his fingers went to the nipples. "Can't you *wait*? I've got an email—"

"The email can wait, but I've got something that can't," he told her. He could feel her nipples swell between his fingers. "Besides, you started it . . ."

Judy giggled, hitting the print button, then she turned around and sat right up on the desk. Seth grew weak-kneed at this new, sultrier image: Judy sitting there with her thighs parted, the bare breasts inflamed. "We can do it now." She giggled some more. "Or . . ."

"Or, what?"

"Or we can check the translation!" she exclaimed and

hopped off the desk. Her breasts swayed when she scurried to the printer.

"Translation?" Seth said through a smirk. *Does she do this on purpose, or is she just scatterbrained?*

"From my friend Wanda," she reminded. "She translated the Aramaic prayer we found in the mezuzah."

Oh . . . that, Seth thought as his arousal foundered.

She excitedly retrieved the paper and read it under the lamp. Suddenly her enthusiasm seemed to degrade in notches, replaced either by confusion or solemnity.

"Not quite what I expected," she muttered. "I thought it would be some sort of baruch—"

"A Jewish blessing, you mean."

"Yeah, like a house blessing or something like that, but . . ." She shook her head at the sheet.

"So I guess you really like teasing me *and* keeping me in suspense," Seth complained.

All her previous sexual fire was gone. "Sorry, it's—The house wasn't *blessed* by a rabbi, it was, well, sort of exorcized."

"Oh, come on!"

"Wanda says that there were many Jewish exorcism rites that involve a bowl of holy water. Well, we found a bowl, didn't we? I'm *sure* that's what the bowl was for. Wanda also said that *specific* rites frequently included a mandrake root . . ."

The comment kept Seth's bombast in check. "There was a root, too, in the hidden room. It looked like a rotten carrot or something."

"Um-hmm. And there was always a menorah, and we found one of those."

"What's the translation?" Seth insisted now.

"Oh, right, right, I'll read it," Judy said. Then she began to recite, "'I adjure you En Soph, hear us as we beg. S'mol and all his retinue—avaunt! Holy Angels, hear us as we beg. S'mol and all his retinue—avaunt! and be banished from this house forever by the power of You who are forever, and may it be that anything tainted by S'mol and all his retinue that may be so interred—be barred from ever coming within. I adjure you, En soph, hear our prayer.'"

Seth had no conception. "Avaunt?"

"It means be gone," she defined. "And S'mol is a Hebrew reference to Lucifer. This is really strange, Seth."

"Yeah, I'd say so. You're telling me our house has been *exorcized*—"

"Not in the popular sense. Wanda says this is a fairly traditional *warding* rite."

"Huh?"

"Typically we think of exorcism as a ritual that casts evil spirits out of living persons who're victims of possession. But this is a bit different. It's beseeching En Soph—God—to cast out anything evil in the house." She held up a finger to emphasize. "But what do you make of this clause? '. . . anything tainted by S'mol and all his retinue that may be so interred—be barred from ever coming within.'"

Seth figured the obvious. "Coming within must mean coming inside."

"I'd think so, but you missed something." She looked at him to gauge his reaction. ". . . that anything tainted by S'mol and his retinue that may be so *interred* . . ."

The hint snapped like a wine stem in Seth's head. "Anything interred—anything *buried*."

"Buried in the house," Judy added.

Oh, for crap's sake! "You're not thinking—"

"I don't know," she said. "Somebody at one time thought there was something bad buried in this house."

Now all Seth could see in his head was the basement's *dirt* floor. "Croter said Gavriel Lowen died in August 1880—"

"This prayer is dated *September* 1880. I'll bet—"

"No, no, Gavriel *wasn't* buried here. I mean, Christ, they tied him to a box of *dynamite* and set it off, at the mill. Croter told me—and, well, I didn't think you needed *all* the gruesome details, but Gavriel's body was blown to bits. The only thing they found was his *head*, and they didn't bury the head here, they buried it at the mill."

"That's a gory detail, all right. So who *is* buried in the basement?"

Neither of them spoke for a few moments, then Seth broke from his contemplations. "There's probably *no one* buried there but even if there is . . . it's none of our business. And *this*"—he picked up the original Aramaic scroll they'd found in the mezuzah vessel—"belongs where we found it." He carefully slid the scroll back into the ornate box.

"Getting spiritual all of a sudden?"

Seth didn't say anything, but then looked at her. "Aren't you coming with me?"

"You're asking me if I want to go down into the basement in the middle of the night to put a prayer of exorcism back in its cabinet in a hidden room in a basement where there might be someone buried? Three guesses and the first one should be *no!*"

Seth smiled, grabbed a flashlight, and headed for the door. "I hope Gavriel Lowen's head isn't flying around down there on bat wings."

"Seth!"

"I'll leave the door open so he can fly up here and say hi to you. You know, I'll bet he's got vampire fangs—"

"Shut up, Seth!"

Seth chuckled and left the room. Judy pulled on a robe and ran after him.

Outside, Seth lifted the cellar doors, then let the strong flashlight lead them down into cool, earth-scented murk. "This sucks," Judy pointed out. The flashlight diced her face into wedges of black and white, her frown apparent.

"I never knew you were afraid of the dark," Seth chuckled.

"I'm only afraid of the dark when I'm in a basement that might have dead people buried in it."

It took Seth several moments to find the disguised entrance to the auxiliary room; he pushed open the three larch stulls, and entered. *Warmer in here, for some reason,* he thought.

"See? Nothing to it," he told Judy when he put the wooden mezuzah vessel back into the prayer cabinet. His eyes paused on the desiccated root. "Mandrake, your friend said?"

"Yes. For thousands of years it's been thought to possess supernatural attributes. Sometimes the roots can be sort of star-shaped, and resemble human forms—"

Seth picked it up.

"—and it's also poisonous."

Seth put it down.

"I think it's safe to say its lost its potency after being in here for over a hundred years."

Seth eyed the menorah and the wooden bowl, then closed the cabinet. "Well, no gibbering ghosts."

"You sound disappointed." Judy had shuffled to the

other end of the narrow room. "Nothing over here, in all this space—" But then something pricked her attention. "What the—Seth, shine the light over here."

Seth did so and found Judy down on one knee now. Evidently she'd scuffed against something in the dirt with her bare foot, and now she clawed her fingers into the earth. "I think there—Seth, there's something here." She kept digging. "It feels like—"

When Seth moved closer, the flashlight's angle changed.

And Judy screamed.

The atmosphere only made the scream more effective. Seth's hair stood on end when he rushed over. "What!"

Judy sprang up, pressed her back to the wall, and shrieked, "There's a skeleton in the dirt!"

Seth faltered, then frowned. *Even if there really is . . . there's nothing to be scared of.* He knelt, noticed the obtrusion, and touched it, digging around with his fingers. Then: "Wow."

"What!"

"You're right," he said and gently unearthed a skeletal hand. Seth was almost surprised by the indifference with which he held this severed body part that had clearly been buried for over a century. "It's . . . someone's hand, but—" He examined it more closely in the light. "Judy, look at this, this is—"

"For shit's sake, Seth! I *don't* want to look at it!"

"Would you get a grip on yourself? You're a college professor, for God's sake. You're an *objective* person. You must know there's nothing to be afraid of."

Judy calmed down in the darkness. "I know. It's just . . . not my idea of fun, finding a friggin' skeleton hand in our basement."

"Well . . ." He scratched at the object's surface. It was

nothing more than that: a withered hand but—"I don't know what this stuff is around the bones . . ."

"Mummified flesh would be my guess," she snapped and finally approached to stoop next to him.

"But it's *gray*."

"Mummified corpses are routinely brown or yellow, at least the ones I've seen in exhibits or arc departments. And it should be leathery."

Seth pressed the long thin hand closer to her. "It's not leathery at all"—he scratched the surface with a fingernail—"it's like baked-on mud or something."

Judy's puzzlement now overwhelmed her former distress. "It looks more like clay."

"Clay? Well, now that you mention it . . ."

Now she actually took the hand from him and looked closer. "Yeah, that's exactly what it looks and feels like, dried clay, almost like earthenware. But why would clay be surrounding a skeleton hand?"

Seth took it back. "I don't believe in ghosts or zombies, but one thing I *do* believe in is respect for the dead." He put the hand back in the shallow hole. "We're getting all worked up for *what?* We stumbled upon a grave, probably one of Gavriel Lowen's family members. It's not a big deal."

"I know," Judy agreed. She unconsciously rubbed her tiny cross between thumb and index finger. "It's just creepy. At least I wish we'd found it during the day."

"Or not at all." Seth patted the dirt back down over the hand once it was reburied. He looked at her, feeling odd. *We've just desecrated a grave . . .* "Do you . . . know any prayers for something like this?"

"Uh . . ." She thought back. "I think I can fudge one. God, have mercy upon this person so interred, and pardon this person of all transgressions. Shelter this soul in the shadow of thy wings, and make known to this person the path of everlasting life."

"Amen," Seth said, then helped her up. "That was perfect. Now let's get out of here and never come in again."

Judy nodded quickly and followed him out.

A hole in the outside of the moveable stulls allowed Seth to insert a finger and pull the makeshift door closed. "Hurry!" Judy said, still a bit squeamish.

"What, you don't want to make love down here like we almost did yesterday?"

"No!"

He grinned over the flashlight. "You sure?"

Judy ran for the steps.

Seth headed out himself but stopped after a final sweep over the basement with the flash. "Wait, wait!" he called out.

"What!"

"Doesn't something seem—" Seth squinted behind the flashlight's glare, roving it over the lawn mower, gas cans, and yard tools, among which stood the mass of barrels.

"Oh, Seth, would you come on?"

"Seriously. Look. What seems different?"

Judy reluctantly returned, gazing at the barrels. "My God, you're right." She began to count them in her head. Eventually she looked over at him. "Seth, weren't there a total of ten barrels taken off the boat?"

"Yeah. Ten."

Judy gulped. "Now there's only *six* . . . "

CHAPTER SIX

July 1880

I

"Just feels . . . off tonight, don't it?"

"Off?" Mears hesitated. *Off*, he thought. *Shit*. He could guess what Bullis was driving at, but . . . "More than *off*, Bullis. Just . . . somethin' ain't right, and ain't been fer a spell."

Bullis walked beside him, let his whiskey-roughened voice flutter lower. "Somethin' in the air . . ."

Both men, two of Conner's charcoalers, had been dispatched tonight by Conner himself, to investigate a small circular clearing a half mile or so deep in the scrubland. All this land around them, nearest the river, had once been tall with trees. A low yellow moon followed the men as they penetrated deeper. Conner's orders had been precise: "Bunch'a our men out trappin' a few nights ago *saw* somethin' at that clearing. The Jews was burnin' somethin', and a couple'a fellas said they saw the fires turn blue . . ." Neither Bullis nor Mears had liked the sound of that. "I need you men ta git yer balls up and go out there, see what Lowen'n his people've been up to." Conner had cleared his throat, as if uneasy. "I just *know* it's more'a their black magic . . ."

So here they were now, Bullis and Mears marching through the scrub by the sickly light of the moon. *Black magic,* Mears thought. He didn't think he believed in such things, but now with ten, twelve men missing, and a half a dozen dead just in the last week? *Lowen's on to us. He knows we been killin' his folk, so now he's killin' ours . . .* The disappearances were unsettling enough, but now, after what Conner claimed to have witnessed . . .

Their Jefferson boots crunched over thatch and dried weeds. "You believe it, Mears?" Bullis finally asked.

Mears didn't answer.

"Shit, I know Conner drinks now'n again, but I ain't never knowed him to make up fancy."

"Neither've I."

"And you heard what he said—black magic . . ."

They each flinched at an owl's hoot, then flinched again when a night bird—or a bat—flapped by.

It weren't no man that killed my family, men! Conner had grimly explained this morning. *Nor Jake Howeth's! I seen it with my own eyes!*

It, Bullis had thought.

And the devilish thing were fuckin' my Bonnie when she was dead. Then I run ta Howeth's and there was another one. Two'a these things Lowen and his Jews called up. Demons, they was. MONSTERS . . .

Monsters, Bullis thought now. Indeed, a night or two before several other men claimed to have seen a clearing, with a fire inside. *And the flame was blue . . .*

Bullis remained consciously unaware of this fact: as he and Mears approached the clearing, fragments of prayers sifted through his mind.

"And Conner ain't tolt us this plan of his, so's now I'm beginnin' to wonder—"

"If'n he's got a plan at all," Mears finished.

"Ain't no way we kin kill all'a Lowen's Jews, and that's

just what we'd have to do to end this'n stake our claim to the land."

"Looks like this's the place," Mears said when the scrub broke into a wide circle. Mears raised the flickering lantern, then peered. "The hell'n tarnations . . ."

There been a fire, all right. Bullis' boots crunched over char.

"Looks like somethin' in the middle, burnt black like it was in a oven," Mears observed, then both men stooped. Mears lowered the light—

—then they both gagged.

Maggots squirmed in and out of clumps of what at first appeared to be burnt meat. Chunks and strips. Blackened belt buckles showed in the cindery mass and one Bullis recognized, crossed metal cannon barrels with a "4" in the middle. "Lem Yerby was in the fourth Pennsylvania Artillery," he muttered. "And I'll bet the rest is Nickerson . . ."

Mears's face twisted when he looked closer at the charred and spoiling mess. He poked through the chunks with his knife; neither men needed to be told what had happened.

The Jews stripped 'em'n cut all the flesh off their bones . . . Why?

"Let's hightail out'a this devil-blasted place," came Bullis's parched suggestion.

"I'm right behind ya, but, shit, wait—"

"What fer?" Bullis almost yelled.

"I gotta hang a piss." Mears stepped away to relieve himself.

Mears had the lantern, leaving Bullis to stand at the path entrance in darkness. Was his heart missing beats? He didn't have a gun but he sure as hell had a buck-skinner

knife, and he'd skinned more than bucks with it during the
War. He waited a minute, then another, then turned in the
dark and frowned.

"Hurry up, man! Did ya drink the whole goddamn
river?"

Mears was still relieving himself, loudly, the lantern
light swaying. "In a place like this . . . I wouldn't be usin'
God's name in vain."

Bullis considered the point, but then a single thrash resounded and—

"Mears!"

—the lantern went out.

Bullis's instinct was to run away, but a few feet into the
path, he gritted his teeth, stopped, then shucked his
knife. *Cain't leave him . . .* His boots took him much more
slowly back to where Mears had been pissing.

"Mears! What's wrong?"

The only reply was a fast, wet gargling sound, and then
a grisly *pop!*

Bullis's eyes peeled when a cloud passed the moon and
brightened the clearing. He could see Mears lying there,
unmoving, and he could also see—

What in the . . .

Mears lay plainly visible . . . and plainly dismembered,
one leg and one arm gone. Black blood shined. However,
there was no sign of the assailant. Knife in hand, Bullis
knelt at the dead man. Mears's head looked . . . wrong,
and when Bullis touched it, he found the top wet. It took
a moment to realize his friend had been scalped.

Indians? *Naw, they all been cleared out years ago.* But
next, he noticed a clump of some sort at Mears's dead
mouth, and remembered the gargling sound. The oil lamp
lay on its side. Bullis quickly relit the wick . . . and looked,

and knew at once what had become of Mears' scalp: it had been forced into his throat until he'd strangled.

Conner's previous words whispered around his head. *Demons, they was. Monsters . . .*

Bullis turned and raised the lamp . . . and came face-to-face with something worse than any demon or monster he could ever imagine.

II

The Present

Seth's heart raced with the flux of the dream. Leaping to avoid deadly viral sacs, he dropped to one knee and fired a remote-controlled Stent into the mass of arterial plaque that blocked this final leg of Cardiac Cove. Wet crinkling resounded as the Stent expanded and opened a way, but then Seth's eyes bulged when he saw what waited on the other side: a gaggle of Corpusculars, two iridescent Nerve Men, and swarms of Peptidal Mites. First Seth unloaded Aspirator Pellets, but barely had time to watch the weapon siphon plasmotic effluents from the Corpusculars' nuclei, then—*BAM!*—his Calcium Carbonate Grenade neutralized the Mites. *FWWWAMP!* He discharged his last two Ultrasound charges at the Nerve Men. These latter enemies convulsed in a macabre dance of death as the sonic impacts short-circuited their synaptic ganglia. Seth spun, noticed the trio of Vomitors coming up from behind, then cut loose three Metastatic Lances. The Vomitors raged, then quickly died when the fast-acting cancers spread throughout the appalling forms and reduced them to shivering tumors. Seth charged through the Stentway just in time. *I made it,* he thought, ducking into an ossuary fissure. He dumped his last Platelets and Hemo vials to up his Health points, then strengthened his armor with more T-Cells and Macrophage Boosters. Bone Saw at the ready, he cut the Sutures of the hidden gash, pushed through, and was at last at the threshold of the House of Flesh itself, the domain of the nefarious Red Watcher.

Blood and lymphatic fluid cascaded down the stairwell of skin-covered bones. His surgical scrub boots squished as he ascended, and atop the organic stairs stood a single ominous Eyeball Switch. When Seth hit the Enter key, the eyeball opened, showing red where only white should be. He revved his saw, then proceeded through the throbbing, wet corridor. Flaps of meat hung like cobwebs; trails of blood vessels beat in the walls. At the end of the egress he could see a bright red light, and a moment after that a figure stepped into it. Seth could make out no details of the sharply backlit figure, save for the voluptuous curves that told him it was female.

He faltered in the dream, thinking, *Wait a minute. I invented this game. There's no female enemy on the last level . . .*

Ah, but then, it was a dream, wasn't it?

He toggled back to his Surgical Stapler, took a breath, then stepped forward.

Whatever it is, I've got to kill it; otherwise I'll never get to the Red Watcher.

The curvaceous figure made no hostile moves—it just stood there, as if waiting for him. Had his dream placed Judy in its midst? *Don't let it trick you,* he warned himself. Perhaps one of the game's enemies had mutated itself. When he took a few more steps, the figure sighed in a sound that seemed wanton, then held out its arms as if awaiting an embrace.

"Come to me, please," the sultry voice fluttered. "I've waited so long . . ." And then it quickly stepped into the egress and began to run toward Seth.

Don't let it trick you! he yelled at himself again, then ripstitched a salvo of staples. The figure shrieked, twitched, then collapsed to the spongy floor. Seth flicked on the lamp strapped to his forehead—

—and wilted.

"Seth," the figure sputtered, drooling blood. "How could you do this to me?"

All he could do was stare down at the nude figure. No, it wasn't Judy at all. It was Helene.

"You've killed me again," she croaked, shuddered one more time, then died.

Oh my God . . . But his nemesis's ruse worked. Seth was so distracted by the appearance of Helene that he'd let his guard down. Meat Men dropped down from dilated pores overhead, pummeled Seth to the floor, and mauled him outright. He could see their evil, swollen faces like masks of molded fat. They were grinning at him. Then one grabbed Seth's Surgical Stapler and—

rat-tat-tat-tat-tat!

—emptied it right into Seth's face. His Health points plummeted to zero, then his vision turned scarlet. PLAYER DESTROYED, flashed the screen.

Seth woke with a jolt, like someone falling asleep at the wheel and waking just in time to see the grill of a dump truck in the windshield. He felt part sickened and part enraged at the cruel trick his own subconscious had played on him. The clock read just past nine A.M.

What a shitty dream . . .

The other half of the wide bed was empty. He was about to call out for Judy but then heard the shower crank off. She came, drying off with a towel. She looked right at Seth and sighed in some undefined frustration. "Hi."

"What's wrong?" he asked. "You look—"

"I'm sure I look like I feel—in other words, like shit." She sat at the bed's edge, in the block of sunlight pouring in through the window. She seemed flustered as she toweled her hair. "I had an *awful* nightmare . . ."

"You're kidding me. So did I," Seth said and sat up next to her. He began to rub her back but could tell at once she wasn't in the mood. "I dreamed I was in the House of Flesh. I was kicking ass all the way up to the last level, but then I encountered an enemy that's not part of the game—Helene." Seth frowned at the recollection. "It really pissed me off."

"Mine did, too. I dreamed . . ." But then the rest never formed. "Forget it. It was disgusting."

"I guess we're both a little shaken up," he reasoned.

"Yeah, it's hard to rest easy knowing someone broke in the basement yesterday when we were out."

"It's my fault for not putting a lock on those doors, but that's first on my list today," he said, then checked his emails on the upstairs computer. *Why on earth would somebody steal four barrels of old clay?* they'd both asked each other a dozen times. *At least the rest of the house is alarmed.* "I'll call the local cops today and report the theft."

"Whoever stole the barrels," Judy suggested, "probably read about the buried boat in the paper, then took a bunch of random barrels thinking there must be valuable relics in some of them."

"The joke's on them," Seth chuckled.

Judy was still perturbed by her nightmare, whatever it had entailed. Her nude body glowed in the sunlight when she walked to the closet and put on shorts, sandals, and a tank top. "I have a splitting headache. Let's go for a long walk. Fresh air and sunshine'll do me some good."

"Damn it, I can't," Seth said, immediately catching the urgent email. "Stuey, my three-D tech, just found a big glitch in one of the bit-map streams. We've got four new enemies in the sequel; all the streams are running in reverse. Plus I've got to lock those basement doors and call the cops."

"Okay, I'll stick around to help."

"No," he insisted. "Go take that walk, you'll feel better. I'll call you on your cell later and join you."

"Thanks," she said and kissed him. "Sorry I'm so out of it today."

"You'll be fine," he assured. "Enjoy your walk."

She smiled meekly and left. Her mood disconcerted him as he dressed and went downstairs. *She's definitely not herself today.* After pouring coffee, he dug around in some storage boxes, then found some chains and a padlock. His own nightmare had spoiled his mood, too, but when he went outside, the gorgeous, hot day revived him. He hoped it would have the same effect on Judy. When he checked the basement, he counted exactly six barrels, four less than when the workmen had put them down here, but the same number they'd counted last night. *At least no one stole any more during the night*, he thought, but then jokingly wished they'd stolen them *all* because they were all probably valueless. He double-checked the hidden door to make sure it remained fully closed and unnoticeable. Then he went back up and chained and locked the basement doors.

That should do it, he thought.

III

Judy felt punctured as she embarked on her walk. The burglary bothered her, yes, but it was the harrowing nightmare that troubled her most. *After all this time, all this success . . . what an awful thing to dream . . .*

She'd decided to meander down the serviceway that cut into the switchgrass fields, remembering the peculiar clearings she'd spied from the bedroom window. The sun warmed her face and shined in her hair, but with each breath of the fresh, grassy air, she only felt more haunted—haunted by her past, the traumas of which she'd believed were far behind her. *Not far enough, evidently.* The nightmare had *stunk*, and it had even left a taste in her mouth as disgusting as its details. She'd dreamed of the final week of her downward spiral, when she'd already abandoned powdered cocaine for the black bliss of crack. By then she'd lost her job, her car, and her bank account, and had already been served a foreclosure notice by the bank that gave her the loan for her condo. *Everything up in smoke.*

She'd prostituted herself exactly six times for crack money, looking for johns in some of Tampa's sleaziest bars. Most of the tricks had been turned in the cars of the denizens she'd cleverly solicited. After her rehab she'd gratefully forgotten the most morbid details, but last night's dream had rammed them all back into her head like a blow from a baseball bat: the sights and the smells, the nauseating sounds and revolting tastes. Worst of all was the nightmare's viewpoint, which replayed all her deeds like a film she couldn't close her eyes to. Judy had woken up as if shocked by a light socket, then had run to the bathroom to be sick.

The lowest of the low, she thought now. *That was me. College professor to crackwhore, all in less than a year. Thank God for Seth. I never would've made it through rehab without him.*

She continued down the wide cutaway, the walls of grass on either side over six feet high. A strange rustling hush followed her, like a camouflaged voyeur. On that last night, she'd never felt less than human: a ninety-pound stick figure dead behind the eyes, with a brilliant brain that had once craved knowledge but now only craved a diabolical narcotic. Her sixth customer hadn't really been a john, it had been a Tampa undercover cop. The *Tribune* had been thorough enough to publish not only the shocking story of the crash her life had taken but also her sunken-eyed mugshot. Her family had never spoken to her again.

Why now? Why is this all coming back now? Her aimless footsteps took her deeper into the field; when she turned around, she couldn't see where she'd entered. *Snap out of this! It's all in the past! I have everything in the world to be happy about now!*

Just a bad day, perhaps, and now that she thought of it she hadn't really had one since she'd met Seth. *You fucked up, so now get over it and thank God you got your life back!*

Judy stopped when she noticed a perpendicular path—much more narrow than this serviceway—cutting east. *One of those clearings?* she wondered when she squinted down. Finally her curiosity sidetracked her morose mood; she turned and entered the path.

Watch for snakes, she recalled the remarks of the man from the state. This new path was barely shoulder width. Did ticks live in switchgrass? No, she didn't think so. Fifty yards later, the path discharged her into a circular clearing of mostly bare, rocky earth, little more than ten yards wide. *What is this place?* she wondered. Mr. Hovis had mentioned irrigation valves but there was no sign of that here. He also mentioned graveyards, but no tombstones could be seen. Just—

Something odd, she noticed now. Within the clearing's circular boundary she noticed another smaller circle that seemed to be roughly outlined by still more circles, only these circles were formed by small bare rounded stones. Ten circles, she counted, then added an eleventh circle in the center. A quick chill traced up her back. Perhaps it *was* a graveyard, an Indian graveyard, but then she recalled that most of the tribes that had once lived here, particularly the Conoyes, buried their dead in mounded cairns. The sudden notion struck her that she was the first person to set foot in this space in years, or decades, but then she laughed to herself when noticing several crushed beer cans. *So much for alien crop circles.* Then she noticed another path, narrow as the one she'd used to get here.

It ran in another straight line, farther east. Her doldrums were gone now as she immersed herself in the exploration. Fifty more yards of walking took her to another clearing, this one larger, and square rather than circular.

Found it, she thought.

A graveyard, a very old one, perimetered by an iron fence so decimated by rust it looked ready to crumble. Something smelled foul whenever the breeze shifted, but she knew it couldn't be from any of these age-old graves. Then:

Tabby mortar, Judy knew at once of the gravemarkers scattered about. *The headstones of the poor.* Crude pourings of the makeshift cement in which some mourner would scribe the decedent's name with a stick or finger. ELSBETH

CONNER, MAR. 1860–JULY 1880, one of them read. WALTER CAUDIL, MAY 1844–JULY 1880. Many other names pocked the solitary clearing. NORRIS, FITCH, POLTEN, read several other markers, and that's when Judy noticed the oddity. The dates of death.

Almost all of these people died in July 1880, she realized.

CRACK!

Judy shrieked as one foot sunk over a foot into the ground. Her eyes widened as she looked down. Shallow grave. Her foot had broken right through a coffin lid that couldn't have been more than three or four inches beneath the dirt. She slowly pulled her foot upward, surprised the sudden plunge hadn't sprained her ankle. *Oh my God, my foot's inside somebody's coffin!* Some rotten board came up with her foot, and when she'd gotten it all the way out, she could see she'd made quite a hole. Judy gulped.

The hole was big enough that she could see the old coffin's confines.

A natural but morbid curiosity lowered her to one knee to look in, and that's when she gulped again.

She plainly made out ribs, collarbones, and shoulder bones but—

No skull. No . . . head.

She pulled up more boards and earth. No, there was no skull in the coffin, and the bones of one arm and one leg were absent. The inscription read ALAN GOLDSBUROUGH, who'd died in July 1880.

"And I thought *I* had a bad day," she muttered to herself, stepped back, and—

CRACK!

"Damn it!"

She'd just collapsed another buried coffin lid, this one

belonging to someone named William Howeth. OCT. 1864–
JULY 1880. *Only sixteen years old,* Judy grimly figured when
she withdrew her foot. But then her stomach knotted
when she pulled up a few rotten lid-boards to discern that
young William Howeth's skeleton was intact, save for
legs. *They sure didn't bury their dead very deep,* she thought.

*Two people who died in July 1880, and both missing
limbs . . .*

What had happened back then? Hadn't Seth and
Asher Lowen mentioned something about a scourge of
Jewish settlers? But most of these grave markers had *crosses*
inscribed in them.

Then the most morbid question of all occurred to her:
*Is it possible that all these people died by some means of dis-
memberment?*

The idea made her shiver. She even thought of stamp-
ing a few more in to see, but then frowned at herself. *I
think I've trashed this graveyard enough.* "Alan, William,
sorry if I disturbed your repose," she halfheartedly apologized to the markers, then turned to leave.

There was no time to scream when the large hand
snapped out from the switchgrass and cracked her hard
across the temple. She staggered dizzily as thrashing
and chuckles surrounded her—and movement. Before
she could see straight again, two figures in stocking
masks—one thin and wiry, and one brawny—began to
molest her.

"Stop it! Just stop it!" she finally yelled.

Another smack across the head dizzied her worse, as
the thin one dragged her tank top right over her arms.

"How's that for some chest-fruit, huh?"

"Shee-it . . ."

"I've got—I've got money!" She tried to compose herself. "Just take it and go."

Chortling. "Oh, we want your money, honey, but not the way ya think," the brawny one said.

This is the real thing, she knew. She'd be crazy to think she could escape, and fighting back seemed just as senseless. *They wouldn't be wearing masks if they planned to kill me . . .*

She squealed, next, when the brawny one grabbed a handful of her hair to lift her up and force her to her knees. "You know the drill, Tits," he said, stepped right up, and opened his jeans.

Oh, my God.

"And if you even *think* about bitin'—"

He didn't need to finish the sentence, for his partner put a small pistol to her head and cocked it.

"And none of this spittin'-out shit."

Just do it, just do it, came the horrific thought, for she knew she had no choice. *Do it. Give them your money. Then they'll leave.* But in her mind she began to pray. She squeezed her eyes shut, took a breath, then . . .

"Not bad," said the big one.

At least he didn't take long, but he tasted as appalling as her dream last night. The thin one was worse; he'd clearly not washed in days.

"Yes, sir. That's some talent."

When she'd satisfied them, she doubled over.

"And don't ya dare puke. I like the idea of all that nut in your belly."

Her terror left her exhausted, her cheek pressed to the dirt. *Please, God, please. Just make them go away now . . .*

"Okay, Tits. Now it's time for *your* party." The big one's hand dragged her back up again.

"Ain't no big deal," chuckled the thin one. "Won't be the first time you've sucked dick for crack."

Judy's eyes bloomed at the remark. "What are you *talking* about?"

"Aw, now, don't jive us, Tits. We know all about it." A sheet of paper was flapped before her face.

"Internet, baby! The Internet!"

Judy stared at the archival printout. FSU THEOLOGY PROF BUSTED FOR CRACK, PROSTITUTION. *These animals backgrounded me!*

The answer to the obvious question came a moment later. "We gotta get you back where you belong," said the big one. He was finnicking with something in his fingers.

"For God's sake! What are you doing!" she wailed.

He was loading a crack pipe.

"Business, Tits. We read all about ya, and we know a good customer when we see one. All the money that rich loverboy of yours has?"

"You saw the article in the paper," Judy croaked. "I was mentioned, too. Then you ran my name through public records . . ."

"Um-hmm, and what a naughty girl you used to be. We mean ta get'cha good and naughty again. Figure it'll take— what's his name? Seth? Figure it'll take Seth months to figure you're back on the pipe, and by then you'll have drained half his bank account for rock. *Our* rock. There's nothin' better for business than a crackhead with a *rich* boyfriend."

This was obscene. *They premeditated the whole thing . . .*

"There's this buddy of ours?" The brawny one chuckled. "He calls it 'targeted marketing in free enterprise.'"

The thin one laughed, and had raised his stocking

mask enough to light a joint, showing facial hair. He handed the brawny one his cell phone.

"And here's why you *won't* tell loverboy what really happened." He showed Judy the phone's tiny display screen. *He took a picture while I was . . .*

"Cell phone camera, baby!" celebrated the thin one. "That's some technol-er-gee, huh?"

"So you go ahead'n tell him . . . and we'll email him this li'l pic of you smokin' our poles."

Now Judy just sat there, sullied, dirt-smudged, nauseous. The big one stuck the crackpipe in her mouth, then flicked a lighter.

"Fire up, Tits. We ain't got all day."

Judy spat the pipe out. "No."

The brawny one sighed. "What is it with folks these days? They're so fuckin' *rude*."

"Yeah, man. Rude."

He calmly picked up the pipe, offered it to her, and said, "Take the pipe and smoke the rock." The thin one put the cocked pistol back to her head.

Judy stared at the callused hand. "No. Fuck you. Go to hell."

The two masked men exchanged squished glances.

"Go ahead and blow my head off," she monotoned, "because I'd rather be dead."

The brawny one tapped a booted foot. "She got balls, ain't she?"

"Yeah. Balls bigger'n her hooters."

"All right, Tits. We're not gonna kill you. We're gonna kill that rich boyfriend of yours instead."

"Seth! Seth! Help me, Seth!" the thin one mocked in a distressed voice. "These bad men made me smoke crack!"

Both assailants honked laughter.

"We're gonna kill *him*, while we make you *watch*. And we're gonna do it real, real slow. We've used routers on people, honeybunch, and auger drills and band saws. Think I'm lyin'?"

Judy felt dead already. She took the pipe, lit the crack, and smoked it.

"Awright!" the thin one exclaimed, clapping.

"That's a good girl, a good dirty little ho." The brawny one looked down, muscular arms crossed. "And once loverboy finds out and dumps your ass, you'll be trickin' for us. Even old as ya are, you've got a couple years 'fore you're too wore out for the street. We'll have the scum bangin' ya bareback for twenty bucks a pop, get'cha all *full'a* the AIDS. And you won't care, Tits. All you'll care about by then is crack . . ."

Judy reeled as if on a roller coaster. The sickening and strangely metallic fumes caused a sudden endorphin dump that felt better than anything she'd ever known in her life. Her heart raced like a film on fast forward; her brain *squirmed*. When the glass pipe was empty, it was refilled and put back between her lips. This time Judy didn't need to be ordered to light it. Each time she sucked the fumes in, some of her soul was sucked out.

They made her smoke three more rocks, and when she was done she lay back in the graveyard dirt, quivering. Her massive euphoria seduced every nerve in her body as she simply lay there, riding the insane high.

The voice from above seemed fat, gaseous. "Now you're back in the saddle, Tits, just where ya belong."

"Once a crackwhore, always a crackwhore."

Something smacked her bare belly. "That should hold ya a day or two, but when ya need more . . . we'll be in touch."

Footsteps fading, more distorted chortles. "Pleasure doin' business with ya!"

When they were gone, Judy's face turned to retch, yet as she was doing so, she spied something disgusting piled just beyond the fence and recalled that foul odor.

Past the thicket of switchgrass lay several dead dogs heaped over one another, each dog headless. *Why would someone . . .*

Eventually her shuddering hand slid up to her abdomen and picked up what had been dropped there.

A big bag of crack.

IV

That afternoon, Seth fell right into his working groove, a blessed state for creative types, but something of a curse for those in relationships. The sequel's problem with new bitmap streams claimed his attention all day, with him being none the wiser as to the passage of time. Between trial and error, and near-constant conference calls with his technicians in Tampa, it was dark by the time they worked out the glitch. *That's what I call a day's work,* he thought when he finally left his office at nine P.M., but a sudden doubletake at the clock set off an alarm. *Holy shit! I worked the whole day away and totally forgot about Judy!* He snapped up his cell phone but didn't bother dialing when he saw her purse on the kitchen table. *She must've come home from her walk a long time ago, and she didn't want to disturb me.*

"Judy!" he called out. "Where are you?"

After receiving no answer, Seth took the stairs up two at a time, rushing into the bedroom. "Honey?"

There she was, sprawled across the bed, still dressed in what she'd worn for her walk. "Judy?"

She roused and slowly turned on the bedside lamp. "Hi, I—"

"I didn't hear you come home, and I was so caught up in work that I lost track of time. I meant to call you."

"That's all right. I didn't want to interrupt. I got back around two, I think. I figured I'd take a short nap but I guess I slept the rest of the day away."

Her voice sounded hoarse, and there were dark circles under her eyes. "You feeling all right? You look—"

"I must have the flu or something." She fell back onto the pillows and sighed. "Plus my period's coming. I just feel shitty."

"You must not have eaten all day. Let me get you something."

"No, no, my stomach's queasy, too. I just have to sleep this off."

Seth didn't like this, but what could he do? "I'll take you to a doctor tomorrow if you're not feeling better."

"I'll be all right," she said and seemed to groan. "It's just the flu or a cold." She coughed. "Did you fix the *House of Flesh II* glitch?"

"Yeah, took all day but I think we got it nailed. I also got a lock on the basement doors; the key's in the kitchen closet in case you ever need it. Oh, and I reported the Great Clay Robbery to the Somner's Cove police. Talked to a sergeant named Stein, seemed pretty on top of things. He said they'll have a car drive by regularly." Seth snorted a laugh. "I felt pretty silly telling him what got stolen."

"Yeah, I'll bet. Four barrels of old clay. Usually they steal televisions." She was trying to act like some modicum of her usually cheery self but it didn't work. She coughed again and winced.

I better leave her be, Seth realized. He came in and turned off the light. "You need cold medicine, aspirin? Some soup?"

"No, thanks, I just—"

"Get some sleep," he said and kissed her on the cheek. "I'll be downstairs if you need me."

"Mmmm . . ."

Seth left but before he closed the door—

"Seth?"

"I'm here."

"I . . . love you."

"I love you, too. Big-time. Now get a good night's sleep, hot stuff."

Seth went back down. Was he more worried than he let on? *Everybody gets sick sometimes.* He felt more negligent than anything. *Some boyfriend. She's gone all day, and I didn't even notice.* What if she'd gotten lost, or hurt herself? *Alcoholic to workaholic is no compromise. I better not ever take her for granted . . .*

Downstairs he poured a cup of decaf, then meandered out to the front porch. A cigarette would be good now, but . . . *No way,* he reminded himself. Better to breathe the warm night air and summer scents off the fields. At once, he was fascinated: the erratic green dots of light from fireflies could be seen hovering atop the endless plain of switchgrass; it occurred to Seth that he'd never in his life seen them before. Night sounds rose and fell. *Who needs Tampa? Who needs a big city when you've got peace and quiet and beauty like this?* He could've dozed off in the porch chair, staring out. *All mine,* he thought.

Eventually he stood up, peered farther out, and thought he saw a more defined light, not from fireflies but almost like lamplight. "What could that be?" he muttered. It was at least a half mile deep in the fields, off to the east.

Not a fire. Electric light.

What could it be at this hour? *A switchgrass field is no place for campers,* but then he thought a moment further and realized it must be some state workmen checking one of those irrigation stations Hovis had mentioned.

V

"—yeah, the guy who just bought the Lowen House," Stein was saying as he and his superior entered the Food Lion. "Said in the paper he made a shitload of money developing some computer game."

"And he was burglarized?" Rosh asked.

"Right, sometime yesterday when he and his girlfriend were out. They didn't break into his house, they broke into his *basement.*"

"And stole what?"

"Four barrels of clay."

Rosh shook his head as he eyed the bosom of one of the cashiers, then paused at a board boasting this week's sales. SPAM: 3 FOR $5! LACTOSE FREE MILK: 2 FOR 1! "Some whacky shit. Clay, huh?"

"I ain't kiddin', man."

Rosh scowled.

"Sorry. I ain't kiddin', *Captain.*"

"Acceptable." Rosh found the proper aisle and turned down. "We've got too much crime to fight to worry about shit like that. They guy's lucky he didn't get his car ripped off. We can't be everywhere, for shit's sake." He tapped Stein's uniform shirt. "Check this out, Sergeant." He picked up a box of Zip-Seal Mini-Bags, the one-by-one-inch size. "This has always killed me."

"What?"

"These little crack bags! A one-by-one zip-lock? You couldn't even put a grape in one of these things. All it's good for is crack or smack, nothing else. Yet some big Proctor and Gamble-like company makes 'em and sells them in grocery stores. Can you believe it? Look at this shit, Stein." Rosh pointed to the box. "A hundred mini zip-locks for a buck-fifty. The manufacturer knows damn well the *only* thing people buy these for are selling dope, and they make *money* selling them. But is it against the law? Hell no. It's just an innocent little plastic bag. Can't ban that, oh, no, not in a free country."

Stein stared. "That's your harp of the day?" And then he whispered, "Jesus, Captain, we use hundreds of those things every week bagging product!"

"That's my point. They should be against the law—like Sudafed—'cos they aid and abet drug dealers."

Stein let out a long, frustrated exhalation. "Captain, what the hell are we doing here?"

Rosh grabbed several boxes and gave Stein a cockeyed look. "We need more bags, man. Come on, get with it." And then he laughed all the way to the checkout.

The instant they got back in the cruiser, the radio squawked in exasperation, "Somner's Cove Unit Two, please come in."

"This is Unit Two," Rosh answered.

"I've been calling you for five minutes, Captain."

"Uh, we were . . . detained." He patted the a box of the mini zip-locks. "Police business."

"Respond to 705 Locust Street, for undesignated call."

"Roger," Rosh said and smirked when he hung up the mike. "Undesignated call—shit. Can't even buy crack bags without somebody interrupting us."

"Locust is right around the corner," Stein said, racing down the dark road.

Rosh said, "Shit," again, when they pulled up at the seedy, bungalow-like house. Three local cars, lights throbbing, already sat in wait, floodlights pointed at the porch. "I hate being the last car to respond in our own juris."

"Yeah, if we're not careful people'll start thinking we're bad cops."

"And what the fuck is County Technical Services doing here? We only see them when—"

"When there's a homicide," Stein finished and parked. "This looks like Pine Drive all over again . . ."

The sight—the lights, the shadows, the radio noise—funneled Rosh's focus. The cop at the door looked pallid, while others seemed poker-faced as they marked the crime scene. Both Rosh and Stein nearly reeled when they entered a cluttered room with holed carpet, half collapsed couches, and a television set with a shattered screen. Blood was everywhere: soaked up by the rug, splattered on the walls, even on the ceiling. A coffee table that had once been a cable spool left no doubt what had been going on here; there were lighters, glass pipes, and an ashtray full of pieces of crack.

"I can't believe what I'm seeing," Stein remarked queasily. "How many this time? Five, six?"

"Seven," corrected Cristo in his County Technical Services jumpsuit. "This is starting to look like a broken record sounds."

Name that tune, Rosh thought, but it was difficult to harbor his typical secret mirth looking at all that blood and death. One white male had his head twisted around so that he was on his belly but looking at the ceiling. Both legs had been wrenched off, and he'd been scalped.

"The perp or perps separated that guy's scalp from his skull," Cristo said tonelessly. His forceps pointed to the decedent's bare buttocks and stumps. "Then infixed the separated material into the excretory vault."

Rosh's lower lip drooped as he mentally translated the verbal hodgepodge. "You mean they tore his scalp off and shoved it up his ass?"

"Yes, sir."

"Then just say it, Cristo," Rosh spat, irked. This was hard enough. "Next time, just say, 'They tore his scalp off and shoved it up his ass.'"

Cristo smiled. "Yes, sir."

A black female sat backward on a couch, armless; and a haggard fiftyish woman, probably the "den mother," had somehow been pulled in half just below the ribs. Rosh didn't like the way the lower half had been arranged on the floor with the legs parted. *Almost like they . . . Aw, forget it.* Two more men had been de-armed, and it appeared that their heads had been somehow pressed against one another until their skulls had given way.

"Why'd she get so lucky?" Stein pointed to a half-attractive female junkie in jeans and a sparkly blouse. She had all her limbs, unlike any other victim.

"What's with her?" Rosh asked. "Looks like she's got all her parts."

"Not quite, Captain." Cristo lifted her right leg. No

foot existed below her ankle. "They torqued her foot off the talus socket, and . . ." He pointed the forceps to her throat. "You'll note the atypical distension?"

The girl's throat seemed thick. "She got the mumps?"

Cristo grinned. "To expound in terminology more to your liking, Captain, they tore her foot off and shoved it down her throat." And then the tech's gloved fingers pulled the girl's mouth open.

Rosh saw toes sticking out.

"Don't see that every day, huh?"

Rosh and Stein paled.

"We're out of here," Rosh said, confused as well as disgusted. "Crimes this severe are a *county* gig—it's all yours."

Cristo rose, wiping his hand on his pants. "Don't leave yet, Captain. Remember what I told you last time, at the Pine Drive sixty-four?"

"Oh, yeah. Something about—" Then he slowly looked to Stein.

"Clay," Stein said.

"Clay *residue*, Captain. Residuum," Cristo corrected. "I told you the lab verified it on the murder last spring, but yesterday they also verified it at the Pine Drive crime scene. Smears of clay on the victims. They also found clay residue, well . . ."

"Well, what?"

"Inside the vaginal barrels of some of the female victims." Now Cristo stooped over the bottom half of the older woman's body, and pointed to the pubis. "Just like this."

Some manner of grayish fluid had leaked from the vaginal fissure.

"That's *clay*?"

"In some kind of suspension, yes, sir."

Rosh couldn't imagine what had truly gone on here. He didn't *want* to know. "I said it before, I'll say it again. We're *out* of here." He and Stein turned and briskly left. Rosh remained silent when he got in the cruiser. "Drive," he told his subordinate. "This shit's giving me bad karma. It makes me feel *haunted*."

Stein spat out the window as if to expel a bad taste. He pulled the cruiser away. "Whoever the hitter is that D-Man and Nutjob hire—he did that."

"Yeah, and he did the others, too. Just can't believe *one guy* could do a job like *that*. Lazy Whitaker said Jary told her it was one guy. And now we got this, this—"

"Clay," Stein said. "What's the connection? The guy who bought the Lowen House says someone stole clay out of his basement, not to mention that we've got at least three murder scenes with traces of clay on the bodies."

Rosh's TracPhone rang, to divert him from his confusion. It was D-Man. "Hey, partner, we just left a crackhouse on Locust, and it's just like the job you did on Pine. You did *this* job, too, didn't you?"

"Yeah," D-Man acknowledged over static. "So what?"

Rosh began to break out in prickly heat. "I fuckin' paid you to bring me Jary Kapp. Alive. I didn't pay you to do a chop job on seven more crackheads."

"Hey, you didn't say we couldn't kill witnesses! You paid us to get the guy for you, so we did."

Rosh stalled. "What?"

"We got the guy."

"You've *got* Jary Kapp? Alive?"

"Yeah, man."

Rosh couldn't believe it. "That fast?"

"We *work* fast. I'm sittin' here with the asshole tied up and gagged in my van. That's why I called. We're at the place we usually meet. Come and get him. We're busy."

Rosh's jaw dropped.

"You there?" D-Man said.

"Yeah, yeah. We'll be right there." Rosh hung up, dizzy with bewilderment. "Fuck. He says he's got Jary Kapp. Alive."

"Quick work. It was only yesterday you paid him and gave him the Red Sox hat."

Rosh stared off into twilight. "Shit, man. Maybe it *is* voodoo . . ."

The moon shined so bright it hurt Rosh's eyes when he got out of the cruiser. Behind them, the woods stood silent, while the switchgrass beyond the clearing hissed. The black step van sat like a square hulk, its owners milling slowly about in the impromptu graveyard they'd made of this place. Nutjob lit a joint while he watched D-Man sway some sort of a pole back and forth over the ground.

"What's that he's got?" Rosh asked.

Stein squinted in the headlights. "Don't know. Golf club?"

Curiosity lured them from the cruiser. It looked like one of those metal detectors. "What the *hell* do you have a metal detector for?" Rosh asked.

"Ain't no metal detector, Captain," Nutjob wheezed through a toke. "It's a . . . it's a thingmajig that shoots these . . . thingmajiggy waves into the ground'n tells us where shit's at."

"Thanks for explaining," Rosh said as sarcastically as possible. "D-Man! What are you doing?"

"Mass-penetrating sonar, it's called. Just testin' 'er out," the bald man said. The machine beeped erratically as he swayed the pole back and forth. "Doesn't read for metal, reads objects in the ground more dense than the dirt or some shit. I'm just makin' sure it works."

"D-Man! I'll repeat! What are you doing?"

"Somethin' for the boss, Captain." D-Man seemed annoyed. "Ain't your concern. Nutjob buried one'a his old duckpin balls while I wasn't lookin'. Just need to know if—" The machine suddenly beeped manically. "This it?" he asked Nutjob.

"Bingo." Nutjob dug quickly with a spade and removed the small bowling ball.

"I've heard of Easter egg hunts," Stein said. "But *bowling ball* hunts?"

"The ball's about the size of the thing the boss wants us to look for," D-Man told him and put the detector in the van.

Rosh rubbed his face. *Don't ask. Why bother?* "So. Are you guys jiving me about Jary? I got this funny feeling you are, 'cos there *ain't no way* you could possibly snatch that asshole alive in *one day.*"

D-Man instructed, "Nutjob? Get the package for Rosh—er, I mean, *the Captain.*" He grinned insolently.

Nutjob walked to the rear of the bulky step van. After a moment, there was some shuffling. The van doors were reclosed, and Nutjob shoved a very subdued-looking Jary "Kapp" Robinson into their midst.

"Here's your cowboy," D-Man said.

The short but muscular black man stood erect in front of Nutjob. Jary wore baggy sweat pants, a Jaguars football shirt, and untied Nikes; he had an Afro like a sixties activist but with a shaved line at the part.

"Well, well, well," said Stein, calmly astonished.

UnFUCKINGbelievable. "Hi, Jary," Rosh greeted. "I paid a lot of money for your scumbag ass, and I can say it was a pleasure seeing your brother's severed head the other night." When Rosh spit in his face, the captive didn't flinch; he seemed devitalized, his eyes strangely worn out above the duct-tape gag, arms limp behind him, wrists tied.

"See, the only bigger scumbags than you and your brother . . . are us." Rosh grinned. "*Nobody* sells rock on our turf. *We're* the guys who turn Somner's Cove kids into crackheads and whores, not jive cowboys like you."

Jary just looked back with those big, exhausted eyes. He didn't even flinch when Rosh tore the duct tape off his mouth, taking some mustache.

"What's wrong with you, brother?" Rosh asked. Then, to D-Man: "What did you do, drug him? This guy looks brain-dead or something."

"Probably in shock," D-Man replied. "That happens a lot."

In shock? Rosh thought, bewildered. *From what?*

Stein chuckled. "Maybe they turned him into a zombie, with that *voodoo* stuff."

Neither D-Man nor Nutjob seemed amused by the remark.

"Take this hunk of shit to the car," Rosh ordered, and then Stein shoved Jary toward the cruiser.

"You drugged him, didn't you?" Rosh demanded of D-Man.

"No. All's we did was what you paid us for. Now we're leaving. I'll call ya when we got more crack to switch. Tomorrow or the next day maybe."

"No, no, no, partner." Rosh hurried and grabbed

D-Man's arm before he could go back to the van. "Don't you want to know why I paid so much for you to take him alive?"

D-Man shrugged. " 'Cos you're a sick fuck who wants to torture the living shit out of him is my guess."

Rosh was furious. " 'Cos he witnessed the party you pulled at Pine Drive. He *saw* your hitter! That's what I want to know about. I can't let it go, D-Man. I'm *curious*, you know? I want to know how you guys are pulling these jobs? *I want to see your guy!* "

The veins in D-Man's shaved head tensed. "Leave it, man! Just forget it. What difference does it make so long as you get what'cha want?"

Nutjob tittered through a toke of marijuana. "He wouldn't believe it if ya told him—"

clank!

Rosh stiffened at the sudden sound. His eyes drifted to the step van. The sound came *from* the van.

"What was that?"

"Nothin'," D-Man insisted.

"The guy's in the van, isn't he? Your *hitter's* in the van—"

"No! Just forget about it! Nutjob, let's go."

"I want to see him!" Rosh yelled so loud his face reddened. "I need to meet the guy who's pulled arms, legs, and heads off over a dozen people in the last week!" Rosh pulled his gun. "I don't believe in fuckin' voodoo, so no more bullshit! Show him to me!"

D-Man glared, disgusted. "You're really fucked up, Rosh."

"That's *Captain* Rosh!" Rosh screamed and raised his pistol. "Show him to me *now!*"

Nutjob tittered again. "Go ahead, D-Man. Show him."

He grinned with rotten teeth at Rosh. "I'll bet'cha pee your police pants, Captain."

D-Man stared, then very slowly smiled. "Sure. Why not?"

He casually took Rosh to the back of the vehicle, pulled open the van doors. He grabbed Rosh's flashlight and shined it inside.

Fast as a pin bursting a balloon, Rosh's spirit burst as well, and everything he understood to be right and wrong, or good and bad, or black and white, shriveled down into something impossible, insane, and unspeakable. Rosh took one look into the van, shrieked, vomited, then ran sobbing back to the cruiser. He also urinated spontaneously in his police slacks.

D-Man and Nutjob laughed out loud as they watched the cruiser roar away.

VI

Judy awoke glazed in sweat that felt tacky as pancake syrup; her side of the bed felt sopping wet. *Oh, God, oh, God,* she thought. The clock read two A.M. In spite of all the terror-rooted exhaustion the day had delivered, she couldn't sleep. All she could do was shake, and—

Think about crack.

She rolled off the bed and knelt, praying, *God give me strength, for I have faith in my redeemer.*

No strength, however, seemed forthcoming.

She felt disgusting in the cool, tacky sweat, yet she knew she couldn't go outside nude. She'd previously en-joyed Seth's comments about her in-house "nudism," but that was the furthest thing from her mind right now. *I can't tell Seth but . . . I must quit. I must, I must!*

Just not tonight.

She pulled on a robe and slipped out, leaving Seth asleep in bed. Her hands shook as her brain forcibly excluded realistic thoughts. Certainly, the two masked assailants were the same men who'd stolen the clay barrels. For what reason, she didn't care, nor did she care about the prospect of reentering the basement tonight. She only cared about what she'd stashed down there earlier in the evening when Seth had been in the shower.

Moonlight lit the edges of the kitchen's tranquil darkness. She retrieved the key from the closet and slipped outside.

Her brain felt like a heart beating frantically for more blood . . .

The warm mugginess outside sucked more sweat from her pores. *I can't get caught.* What would Seth say? What would he *do?* Judy knew she'd rather die than contemplate that. The moon shimmered on her as she padded barefoot down the short porch steps. She wasn't so much consciously walking to the side of the house as much as the side of the house—and the basement doors—was yanking her there as if by a tether.

She unlocked and opened the doors. *Quiet, quiet . . .* She moved down the steps, then grabbed the dry-cell flashlight she'd left here earlier. For some reason she thought of the dead dogs in the graveyard—*headless* dogs. *God!* But she still moved deeper into the basement, not even squeamish knowing that the strangely mummified hand—and probably much else—was buried in the hidden room. Her hands shook uncontrollably now; she reached between the two farthest barrels and snatched up the bag.

Only six rocks left, she saw with a desperate tear. At the graveyard, she'd smoked half the bag, and three more pieces during Seth's shower. *Three now,* she pleaded, *two tomorrow, then the last rock the day after. And after that . . .*

She would quit, no matter how hard it was.

That or I'll kill myself . . .

She loaded the pipe, turned off the flashlight, and fired her lighter. The diabolical bliss shot to her brain at once; she felt enraptured, however evilly. *Because that's what this is,* she knew. *Evil.* The lighter cast chopped shadows on the wood walls, shadows that moved like people lurking. A half hour later, her brain sparkled as she finished the third piece. Then she groaned to herself, helpless, and cried outright. She couldn't help it.

She smoked the last three pieces.

When she turned with the flashlight, a squashed, grinning face seemed to float before her eyes, and a big palm slapped across her mouth, muffling her scream. The flashlight clunked to the floor to shoot its light to the other corner. The hand was pressing her face against the back wall, the grin still floating.

It was the larger of her two rapists.

"Shhh! Shhh! Don't'cha make no noise or else I'll have to kill you *and* loverboy upstairs . . ."

She wheezed in a breath when the hand slid off. She shivered in place. "My, God! What are you *doing* here?"

"Saw the light when I was drivin' by, so I thought I'd drop in and see how you're doin'? So how *are* ya doin', Tits?"

No no no no please no . . . "Why are you here?" she sobbed.

"Figured a junkie with a jones hard as yours must be runnin' low on your supply. That so?"

Judy looked to the dirt floor. "It's all . . . gone."

A snorted laugh. "Dang, girl! You ain't missed a step, and that's good. Here." He offered a plastic baggie. "Here's five more rocks. Free. How's that?"

Her brain lit up again, just knowing the supply was there.

"And all's ya gotta do for it is this," the whisper sharpened. "So listen up. Make sure you'n loverboy *ain't here* tomorrow between noon and two. Got it?"

She whined, helpless. "How can I possibly guarantee—"

"Just do it." The voice was stone cold. "Use them college smarts of yours, think'a some way to get him out the house."

"But, but—why?"

"Don't matter," he replied and suddenly squeezed her throat till her tongue jutted. "No questions. Do like we say and everything'll be dandy. *Don't* do like we say—" Like a card trick, his cell phone snapped open, its tiny screen alight with the snapshot of Judy smoking crack in the graveyard. She hacked a sob when the next picture clicked on: Judy performing fellatio . . .

"I understand," she croaked.

"Good girl. I got somewhere ta be right now but . . . shit." The masked face looked at his watch. "Always time for love, right?" And then he hoisted her up on a barrel top, pushed her back, and opened her robe.

"For God's sake, please no . . ."

"One more noise out'cha and I'll walk upstairs right now and cut his face off . . ."

Judy believed it. She bit her lip till it split when her thighs were splayed and her robe dragged apart. Her eyes rolled back when he entered her; all she could do was shut her mind off and focus on the last of the crack high.

Her rapist humped her perfunctorily and machinelike, joggling her atop the barrels.

"There. That's the ticket," he said when he was done. He stepped away to refasten his jeans. "Just you do as you're told, then you and Sethie-poo'll be just fine."

Judy lay back limp across the barrels.

"And don't forget. Tomorrow, between noon and two. Don't be here. Got it?"

Judy nodded, staring upward.

"And leave them damn doors unlocked."

"I understand."

He pinched her cheek. "You do what I say, and there'll be twenty more rocks waitin' for ya tomorrow night."

His footsteps scuffed off, then tromped up the stairs. Judy remained where she lay, her legs hanging off the barrel. More nauseousness rose when he felt her assailant's semen run out of her sex. She felt like something rising from the dead when she got off the barrel. She looked at the bag of crack and wept.

And smoked two more pieces, then stashed the rest and ran out of the basement. The awful euphoria made her struggle to remember her instructions. *The doors. Leave unlocked.* Back outside, she quietly reclosed them, refixed the chain but left the padlock open. A muffled noise sunk through the fog of her high: a motor?

The moon fell across the road in front of the house, leaving light like luminous frost. A large black step van pulled slowly past, its headlights off.

It's him, she knew.

She expected it to drive on but instead, the lumbering vehicle turned left, onto the wide service path that cut a straight line into the field, the road she'd walked today.

The black van disappeared, yet in the distance, to the east, she was certain a blossom of light glowed amid the tall grass.

Where the hell is he going? she thought.

VII

D-Man stopped the van on the dark service path and peeled off the stocking mask. Now at least he'd learn what was going on, not that he cared much. He only cared about the money and staying in good graces.

Nutjob remained asleep in the van, snoring through his pot-sodden stupor. *Loser,* D-Man thought and got out. *Asshole don't know what he missed out on.* His groin tingled after the rape. Switchgrass brushing both shoulders, he turned into the narrower path east and followed the light at the end.

What was it he called it? Something about circles? Didn't matter, just more of their weird Jew hocus-pocus. D-Man tried not to think too hard about such conjectures, nor about the *thing* that remained dormant in the back of the van. *Just doin' my job . . .* The Gaon called it a *goilem,* but D-Man figured it didn't matter *what* he called it. To him, *monster* would do.

The lights grew brighter as he approached; eventually he entered the circular clearing. *Damn. What a show.* Several more dead dogs hung upside down on tripods, headless. He didn't know what they used the heads for, but what they used for the bodies was clear. Buckets sat beneath the neck stumps, filling with blood. Floodlights on more tripods lit the scene, bright as an artificial sunlight glowing within the field. At least ten members of the Kahal worked in tandem: several tending the buckets, others walking slowly about the clearing carrying more buckets, dribbling the stones with fresh dog blood. *The Circle of Ten Circles*, D-Man recalled now. Ten small circles of stones formed the main circle, with an eleventh in the middle. All the Kahal dressed as the Gaon did, black slacks, black shirts. One silhouette appeared before one of the floodlights, a cut-out shape of crisp darkness.

"Ah, my faithful friend. What do you have to tell me?"

D-Man stalled. "We just done tested the detector in one of the buryin' grounds, and it worked just fine."

"I'm pleased. And the woman? Is she sufficiently cowed?"

Cowed ain't the word. D-Man almost laughed. "She'll do anything we tell her. And it's all set for tomorrow 'tween noon and two. She's gettin' the dude out the house and leavin' the basement unlocked."

"Perfect," the Gaon whispered.

"But—but—"

"What's bothering you, my friend?"

D-Man simply had out with it. "These lights, fer one thing. It don't matter none we're half a mile in the field. Ya can see the lights from the road."

"No one," the Gaon clarified, "will see the lights. I know this to be true for I have *faith* that it is true. I hope that one day you learn such faith."

Best keep it shut, D-Man resigned. Why argue? The money was still green. He changed the subject by looking at the queer pebbled circles on the ground. "So's what's it for?"

"A temple of beseechment in death, D-Man. After all these decades, the sacred will of our ancestors will be fulfilled. I don't expect you to understand just how important this is to us."

And I don't care, D-Man thought, though even now he was beginning to feel ill at ease. These *people*, and their *magic*, and now these—these circles of bloody stones . . . The Gaon actually believed he was the reincarnation of some Jewish dude from over a hundred years ago. *This is a weird fuckin' crew I'm workin' for.*

"And how is the good Captain Rosh?" came the next question.

"He was none too happy about the delivery bein' delayed but once we did that snatch job for him, that settled him down."

"We had more important things to do," the Gaon said. "The proper mixing of the clay, but now that job is done. The next delivery should be ready in twenty-four hours."

"Oh, and, well . . . He saw it tonight."

"He saw . . ."

"You know. *It.* Had no choice but to show him."

"I see," the Gaon replied. "And his reaction?"

D-Man had to smile. "He was shit-scared. Took the sass right out of him."

The Gaon nodded. "Which can all be used for our gain. Just as the woman is cowed by drugs, the captain is cowed by cash, and now . . . by terror."

You got that right. D-Man hated to think what would happen if he ever got *out* of the Gaon's good graces.

"So tomorrow, between noon and two, you've arranged to access the basement?"

D-Man nodded. "If it's there, we'll find it."

"It's there. I know it is, for I've been foretold."

Whatever. "Shouldn't be a problem."

The Gaon gave D-Man a piece of paper. "And here's what you're going to be doing tomorrow *after* two o'clock. With any luck you'll be back by not much past midnight."

What the fuck? D-Man thought when he looked at the paper. And then the Gaon explained.

"You want us to do *what?*" D-Man asked, slack-jawed.

"You've never failed in the past. And it's better this way."

"But it's so risky! We could get caught so easy!"

When the Gaon turned in the light, his face was revealed—of course, the face of Asher Lowen. "You need more faith. Do you have faith?"

"Shit, I don't know!"

"Everything you *do* is risky, yet you've never been caught. Tell me, D-Man. Do you believe that you're just lucky, or do you believe that you're being protected?"

"Protected?" D-Man stared.

"Protected by the ideal that's protected us," Lowen finished. He put his arm on D-Man's shoulder and turned him back toward the path he'd entered from. "Don't worry, my friend. I have enough faith for both of us, and my faith . . . is *power.*"

VIII

A small-gauge chain—not a leather strap—comprised the tourniquet this time. The cricket chorus throbbed through the night; the river guttered. Stein stood chain in hand over the prone form of Jary Kapp, who lay on the ground, wrists and ankles still lashed.

"Hey, Captain," Stein called out. "You've wanted this guy for over a year, and you paid a lot of money to get him. So—here he is."

"I don't care anymore," Rosh muttered, fingering his chin. He sat against the cruiser's fender.

"What's with you tonight?"

"I don't know!" he blurted, but he did, he did. Rosh had seen it, Stein hadn't: that . . . *thing* in the van. Yes, he very much had wanted Kapp to question about the Pine Drive murders but now? No need.

Kapp himself lay with eyes squeezed shut, murmuring. Prayers? Rosh couldn't conceive of a drug dealer such as Kapp believing in God. But after seeing that thing? Who knew?

Rosh nudged him with the toe of his shoe. "What was that thing, Jary? It was the same thing from Pine Drive, wasn't it?"

Kapp just gulped. Was he still paralyzed by shock? *That's how I feel right now,* Rosh realized. He kicked Kapp harder when he didn't respond. "What *was* it!"

Kapp hacked, then grated, "Somethin' from hell, man."

Something from hell . . . Rosh believed it, even though he'd only seen it for a split second. Skeletally thin, and glistening, like bones covered with wet mud. Lipless, with rotten teeth showing; noseless, with a face more like a shit-caked skull. When it had looked at Rosh, it did so with empty eye sockets, yet it saw him just the same.

Rosh stared at Kapp, who was still murmuring to himself. "You're praying, aren't you?"

Finally, Kapp's eyes snapped open, and he smiled. "Ain't you?"

Rosh felt sick.

"Punch my ticket, you white piece of shit cop fuck," Kapp provoked. "Don't care how or how slow, ya know? I want out. Don't wanna be in this world no more, not with that thing in it."

Rosh stared. His eyes flicked to Stein. "Kill him."

Stein knelt, wrapped the chain around Kapp's head, ear-level. He inserted a crowbar through two links. "Ready to meet your maker, Jary?"

Kapp grinned. "Yeah."

Stein cranked down on the crowbar. As the gird of chain tightened, Kapp began to chuckle.

"Harder!" Rosh yelled.

Stein torqued the bar like a lever that wouldn't quite give. Kapp's white teeth showed through the beaming grin on his dark face, even as he convulsed from the pain. "An' remember, Cap'n. I'll be gone, but you'll still be here . . . with that thing." And then he shrieked laughter.

Furious, Rosh stooped to help Stein. "Crank it like you got a pair!" He put his hands over Stein's and *cranked* the bar.

Kapp continued to laugh, even for several moments after his skull buckled and collapsed.

"There, ya fuck!" Rosh yelled at the dead man.

Stein sighed as he uncranked the chain. "So much for the Cracksonville Boyz."

"Throw him in the water."

Kapp's head looked stepped-on now. Stein dragged him—still shuddering slightly—to the river bank and flopped him in with a splash.

Rosh went back to the car, took one of Stein's cigarettes from the pack. When Stein got behind the wheel, he frowned. "I thought you quit years ago."

Rosh inhaled, eyes fixed on nothing. "Just drive."

Stein pulled off the old boat road. "So, come on, Captain. What's all that jive you were talking with Kapp?"

"Just forget it."

Stein chuckled under his breath. "A thing, huh? You sound like Lazy Whittaker."

"Be quiet!"

"Captain, for God's sake. Who was the guy in the van?"

"It wasn't a guy! Now drive the damn car and shut up!" Rosh bellowed.

Chapter Seven

July 1880

I

The last day of the month.

Conner and his men stood at the crossroads when the wagon from Baltimore Armory pulled away. Norris stood at his employer's side, palm itching. The crates had been unloaded, and now the men were prying off the lids. *Fifty pistols. And powder'n balls*, Norris thought. "If'n we didn't get stole from, Mr. Conner, things'll change a right quick around here."

Conner seemed preoccupied. "We better not'a gotten stole from. The wagon pulled away faster than my liking." But just as the doubt had been expressed several of the men started whooping it up.

"Good gawd-*damn*, Mr. Conner!" one celebrated. "They'se all here, all fifty of 'em!"

Norris smiled in relief. The ax-hand rushed up with a tarpaper-covered parcel; he unwrapped it to reveal a thirty-six-caliber pistol slathered in packing grease. "You count 'em all, son?"

"Yes, *sir*, Mr. Norris, sir! Fifty!"

"What about powder, caps, and balls?" Conner asked.

Another man hooted from the spread of crates. He hefted one crate. "Powder, caps, and what looks here like *hunnerts*'a minie-balls, sir!"

"Thank God," Conner muttered.

Norris doubted that God would have any interest in this endeavor. But with fifty pistols and ammo, they could indeed wipe out Lowen and all his people. "Makes a man feel good in the heart ta know ya can still make an honest deal in America."

Conner seemed diverted, even after the successful delivery. *He'd been drinkin' that night*, Norris recalled. *Probably don't quite know what he seed*. *Two monsters*, he'd said. Killed his wife Bonnie, plus Jake Howeth and his wife and kid. *Lowen and his Jews!* Conner had bellowed the next day. *Called 'em up with their black magic!* Norris didn't believe it, of course. It was probably just two of Lowen's men making a raid. And it didn't matter now. Not with FIFTY brand-new shooting irons . . . "Get the crates loaded in the wagon, men," he ordered. "We'll go back to camp'n get 'em up and ready."

Conner walked over to the crates. "There should be one more," he said with some trepidation.

"More guns, sir?"

"Naw. Somethin' . . . *else* I paid fer."

"Might you be talkin' 'bout *this*, Mr. Conner?" another hide-tunicked young man enthused, and pointed to the last opened crate.

It was full of dynamite.

"What'cha fixin' to use that for, Mr. Conner?" Norris asked.

More of Conner's tension went out of him when he saw the explosives. "More'a my plan, Norris. See, with the pistols, we'se'll shoot dead every single Jew in Lowensport— every Jew but *one*." He pointed to the dynamite. "But fer Gavriel Lowen himself? I got somethin' *special* in mind for him."

Norris didn't ask, but whoever—or whatever—had killed Conner's wife, all that did was deepen the man's hatred. "So this plan'a yours? When do we do it?"

"I figure we'll wait a couple more days, get things all mapped out, assign squads, so's we can do it right, just like when it was in the War."

"A good idea, Mr. Conner."

The sound of horse hoofs snagged their attention; they looked down the road and saw two mounted riders approaching.

"It's John Reid and his boy," Norris recognized. "On their way back from Salisbury."

"Aw, yeah. I sent 'em there a week ago to pick up some more shovel heads. After we wipe out Lowen's people, we'se'll have a whole lotta buryin' to do."

"Right, but . . ." Norris squinted. John Reid's face was creased with concern when he dismounted his horse.

"Howdy, Mr. Conner, Mr. Norris."

Both men nodded. "You get them shovel heads, Reid?"

"No problem, sir. But . . ."

"What's on yer mind?" Norris asked. "Look like somethin's botherin' ya."

Reid hesitated. "Well, sir, see, when we picked up shovel heads at the smith's, the man—name was Hawberk—he tolt us his brother worked as a dock-hand at the harbor, this bein' after I mentioned our camp was near Lowensport, sir."

"Yeah?"

"And, see, when I said Lowensport, this fella Hawberk recognized the name, asked me if it was a Jew town like he'd heard, so's I said yes, it is, but we ourselves don't live there proper. I assured him we wasn't Jews."

"Get to the point, Reid," Norris snapped.

"Well, sir, it's Hawberk's brother, like I done said, who told us he knew the name 'cos recently a steamboat come in to Salisbury, and the captain—Irish fella—mentioned his last stop was Lowensport."

"A steamboat?" Norris asked.

"Yes, sir, a steamboat carryin' a shipment paid fer by Gavriel Lowen, so's that why I'm tellin' ya. Don't sound good if'n ya think about it."

No, it don't, Norris thought. "This man say what the shipment was?"

"No, sir, just some barrels'a somethin'."

"Could be guns," Conner muttered. "Could be Lowen's plannin' to do to us what we're fixin' to do to him." He wrung his hands. "When's that shipment due in Lowensport, Reid? You know?"

"Next week's what Hawberk said."

Norris took Conner aside. "Sir, this changes things. Sounds ta me like Lowen *does* have guns in that shipment."

Conner gave a grim nod. "Which means we gotta kill him and his people 'fore that shipment ever gets here." He looked right at Norris. "So we ain't even gonna wait a day. Get everyone together at the camp for a briefing."

"So's when we gonna do it, sir?"

"We do it tonight. We kill 'em *all*. Tonight."

II

The Present

At 11:30 the next morning, Judy had rushed Seth out of the house. "Come on!" she'd faked. "It'll be fun!"

"That's all right by me," Seth had said. "I'm just glad to see you're feeling better."

In truth, Judy felt worse; she felt rotten to the core of her spirit. *Once a crackwhore, always a crackwhore,* the words haunted her. But she *had* to get him out of the house by noon. "I'm dying for more of those Maryland crabs."

Actually she had no appetite at all, and it depressed her further to see how effectively she lied. That morning, before Seth had awoken, she sneaked to the basement and smoked the last of the crack. *Don't let on,* she pleaded with herself as Seth drove them to Somner's Cove. She knew she'd have to devote her entire attention to pulling off this act—this *lie*—with the man she loved.

The touristy watermen theme of the restaurant gave the place a comfortable feel, but no tourists could be seen, just local blue-collar workers sitting mainly at the bar.

"I'm glad you liked the crabs," Seth said, ordering a dozen from the waitress.

"There's a two-for-one special on Screwdrivers today," they were informed.

Seth laughed, relieved, and ordered two iced teas. Judy sat opposite in the veneered wooden booth, focusing hard on the task of seeming normal. But she nearly broke out in tears when Seth went on, "It's so refreshing for an ex-drunk like me to realize that I have no interest whatsoever in booze anymore, no craving, no desire, no nothing. Probably the same for you with drugs, huh?"

Judy faked a smile and nodded. *Talk! Sound normal!* "I never really cared for the Florida crabs we had in Tampa. Too much trouble and too expensive."

"I read somewhere that this town was the Blue Crab capital of the country at one time, and also the oyster

capital. Speaking of oysters, I'll order some of those, too."
He smiled leeringly. "You know what they say."

It took Judy a moment to even calculate what he'd in-
ferred. "Oh, yeah. An aphrodisiac. We can test its validity
later." But it crushed her to lie again, to admit to herself
that the resurgence of her crack habit erased her sex
drive. *I'll have to fake that, too.* "I'll be right back, got to
go—you know."

Seth pointed the way to the ladies' room.

Once in the bathroom, she nearly collapsed from a fit
of shaking. *My God, my God, my God!* How could she pull
this off? She steadied herself in the mirror, and saw that
the crack had already thinned her face. How much longer
until she reverted to the ninety-pound drug-waif she'd
been but two years ago? *I can't let it happen,* she prayed,
Please, God, don't let it happen! Give me strength . . . She
washed her face, let herself simmer down, but then she
resickened herself when she recalled the details of this
ruse. *Right now there are two rapists in our basement.* What
could they possibly want down there? The remaining barrels were as valueless as the ones they'd already stolen.
And I let them in . . . She knew that more crack would be
waiting for her when they returned after two. *That will be
the last of it,* she vowed. She touched the silver cross around
her neck, wondering how soon its dainty chain might turn
into a noose . . .

During lunch, Judy had deliberately eaten very slowly,
barely tasting the otherwise delicious shellfish. She
smiled and nodded through conversation, mostly Seth
describing future levels of the game sequel; any remarks
she made she had to struggle to form, for already she was

cringing for more drugs. When Seth eventually noticed, he asked, "You *are* feeling better, aren't you?"

"Just—just, well, yeah," she feigned. "But I've still got a touch of something. Probably just a little cold."

"Maybe we better go home so you can take a nap." He held her hand across the table. "Sleep is nature's balm, they say."

"Yeah, maybe that's a good idea." A glance to a nautical wall clock showed her it was past two P.M.

Seth paid, then they sauntered out, his arm around her. The beautiful day shimmered in heat and sun. A sudden worry flared when Seth was unlocking the Tahoe. *What if those guys aren't done in the basement? What if they're still there when we get home!* But then her eyes flicked up when a vehicle drove by: a large black step van.

The same one from last night, that her stocking-masked rapists had driven into the field. Stenciled paint on the side advertized produce of some sort. Her gut sunk when she considered who was in it, but then at least there was some satisfaction. *If they're in town now, that means they're finished at the house.* She squinted at the license plate but gave up when the van turned the corner. It seemed to be heading toward the city docks.

She never got a look at the driver.

III

Asher Lowen rose from his office chair at the sound of the van's surly motor; it was almost one in the morning now. Could it have been that for even a moment he feared they might've been caught?

No.

Asher knew that his god would protect him and all of his endeavors.

"Sorry we'se late, Asher," Nutjob said when they came in the back door of the House of Hope. "The damn ferry broke down, took a hour ta fix."

"That's fine, but did you—"

"We got the body," D-Man said, "no problem. But . . . we didn't get the skull."

Asher's face went blank.

"I tried callin' you on your cell just past two to tell ya, but—"

"I was at a prayer meeting," Asher said. "You checked everywhere in the basement?"

"Yeah."

"What about beneath the remaining barrels? Did you move them, did you—"

"We moved 'em, and we swept every square inch'a that basement with the detector," D-Man assured. "It ain't there."

But I know it's there, Asher thought. *I know it.* He glanced to one of the Dutch ovens, the fumes of whose contents had been expended. "My mances *tell me* that it is there. Therefore, it *must* be there."

D-Man slumped. "Then tell us where else ta look 'cos it *ain't there.*"

Asher stroked his chin. "Perhaps there's another basement we're not aware of."

"Well, maybe, but I don't think so. Ain't no other outside doors."

"A door *inside,* perhaps," Asher suggested. Then, "The girl. You could ask the girl, when she needs more crack.

Give her some more freebies in exchange for the information."

D-Man's frustration was plain. "All right," he sighed. "I'll ask her tomorrow."

"Good."

Nutjob stepped away from the door, an unpleasant frown on his scruffy face. "Here it comes . . ."

The thin, haggard shadow crossed the floor as the goilem entered the room, its shining, clay-caked face expressionless. Across its shoulder was slung a sheet-draped corpse. Asher looked on in marveling pride. *More proof of the power of the melech, S'mol. Over a hundred years old and it still serves us so well.*

"That thing still gives me the creeps," D-Man muttered.

"Please, you'll hurt our servant's feelings," Asher joked. He pointed to the table, whereupon the bone-thin figure set down the corpse. "You'd be surprised to know that this *thing* once had a name, D-Man. It was Yerby."

"Yerby," D-Man mouthed, looking away.

"Repose," Asher said to it. The thing trudged to its box, lay down in it, and closed the lid.

"It did all of the digging," D-Man added. "Saved us some elbow grease, that's for sure."

"It serves us well, just as it served my ancestors," Asher remarked. "But nothing lasts forever. It's old, but now . . ." He put his hand on the sheeted corpse, then pulled off the sheet. "This one will be even stronger, fresher, more vital, just as Gavriel Lowen intended. Our providence is nearly upon us, and you men have done very well."

Both D-Man and Nutjob gulped at the sight of the corpse, a shapely woman still in burial clothes. Even after so much time in the ground, it could almost have been mistaken for a woman asleep.

"Don't stink none at all," Nutjob said.

"And it still looks almost alive," D-Man added.

"The sorcery of the *new* age, men," Asher said. "Embalming. And come tomorrow night, it will be so much more than *almost* alive." He led them back down the hall to the cafeteria in which food had never been cooked. When they looked in, several addicts tended the flank of ovens, baking down base-cocaine into crack. The heating process actually caused a crackling sound, hence the name. But the other side of the room?

Asher extended his hand. "Behold *my* sorcery . . ."

Some of the clay from one of the pilfered barrels had by now been removed in chunks, each chunk added one by one to metal drums. Water was added in small amounts, the clay then pestled until sufficiently mixed; the process was repeated over and over. "The *hilna*, men, the blessedly cursed clay of the Vltava River. Gavriel Lowen didn't live long enough to receive the shipment but now . . . we've reclaimed his treasure, to finish his great work."

D-Man and Nutjob could scarcely comprehend the words. "Can we—can we—" D-Man began.

"You may leave now, my good friends," Asher said as several addicts slopped more clay into more metal drums. "Just remember that faith bids its proper rewards . . ."

IV

Judy awoke the next morning in more gelid sweat; she was shaking for crack, but at least had managed to not smoke any after they'd gotten back from the crabhouse. As her eyes clicked open, Seth was sitting on the bed's edge, talking into his cell phone: "You're kidding me! What the hell are we doing wrong?" A strained pause. "I know, damn it. Yeah, you're right. I'll catch the first plane down."

"What's wrong?" Judy asked when she ground herself to full wakefulness.

"I've got to go to Tampa—today. More quadratics problems." And then he rushed to the shower.

I look like such shit, she told her reflection. *Sooner or later he'll know I've got something more than a cold.*

"Why don't you come with me?" he asked, toweling off after the shower, then quickly dressing. "Don't know how long it'll take, but—"

"I'll stay here and hold down the fort," her id answered for her. "I'm still feeling kind of lousy, anyway."

He paused with a concerned look, touched her cheek. "Are you all right? Seriously."

"It's just a cold," she sluffed. "I'll be fine." Then she whisked out of the room. "I'll make you some coffee."

Downstairs, she clenched through the task, then loaded his laptop in its case for him. *I'll get it all out of my system while he's gone,* she vowed. She knew that twenty pieces of crack awaited her in the basement. *I'll crack it up, then quit when he comes home.* But this was just more of her id—and deep down she knew that. She'd made similar vows in the past and never honored them.

"Damn, this is really screwed up," he said once downstairs with his suitcase. "If we don't get this bug fixed we could miss the deadline for the sequel." He rushed a kiss, and said, "Sorry this is such short notice." He'd already grabbed his bags, and was heading for the door.

Judy, robe-clad, followed him in a daze: "Have a safe trip, and call me when you get there."

"I will, I will, and—damn it!" he exclaimed. "I have to take the Tahoe to the airport. You'll be stranded here."

"Don't worry," she assured him. "I'll have an excuse to ride my bike."

"Okay, bye—and keep the alarm on. Love you!" And then he was driving away.

I love you, too, she thought, her willpower already corroding. When the Tahoe could no longer be seen, a sickening trance took her back inside where she got the key, then came back out and opened the basement doors. But her curse made her cringe; she couldn't get down the steps fast enough.

She swayed the flashlight around, growing frantic as she hunted for what should've been left. There, in the gap between two barrels, the plastic bag glimmered. She snapped it up, stared, then yelled aloud, "That lying bastard!" The bag contained but three pieces of crack, not the twenty promised. Was she actually crying when she lit the first piece? For herself, or for knowing that the three meager pieces would scarcely last an hour? She shuddered as she inhaled, the fumes, first, seducing her with wondrous promises, but then leaving her short-changed by the effect. It was never good enough, never like the very first high, but it kept forcing you to do it, anyway. The corrupt euphoria seemed like a tongue licking her raw brain. *God, it's so good but so awful . . .* The second piece went as fast, leaving her to sit slumped on the dirt floor, buzzing for twenty minutes. *Save the last piece—DO it!* she screamed through the high. She put the bag and pipe in her pocket, shrieking at herself. She was about to bolt out when a thought surfaced through her glittering daze.

Those men. *What did they do? What did they need down here?* She looked around with the flashlight. *Did they take more of the barrels?* But a quick count showed her six remained.

But . . . something looked different, didn't it?

They've been moved.

She was sure of it at once. The barrels had been moved across the dank room. *Why?* she asked herself. *Why on earth . . .* The hidden door remained closed and unnoticeable. *They must not know about it.* She looked down closer in the beam of light and easily noted the footprints, and—*Great!* came the sarcasm—the tiniest end of a joint. She pushed dirt over it with her foot.

But why move the barrels? *Almost as if . . . they were checking for something beneath them . . .*

She sat upstairs and cried for an hour, then slept convulsively for two more. In and out of sleep, she prayed, but the prayers seemed feeble, insincere. *God, forgive me in my state of disgrace. My sins are horrendous but I know your mercy is infinite. Take this burden off me, I beg you.* But even as the words abated, she still cringed for that last piece of crack.

Eventually she forced herself to shower, then put on a sundress with nothing underneath; she didn't want to feel constricted. But . . . *What am I doing?* The craving for that last piece bit into her like bear-trap jaws. *I've already been around this block, and I can't do it again.* For the second time, she fantasized of killing herself; then, she thought:

If I don't quit, I'll do it, I will.

But how? There was no gun in the house, and no way to asphyxiate herself. She couldn't see herself cutting her throat, knew she didn't have the courage.

The basement. There was rope down there.

That's how I'll do it . . . IF I can't quit.

But there still remained that last piece in the bag. *That'll be the last piece I ever smoke, one way or another.* She decided she'd go out to the fields, smoke it there, then throw the pipe deep into the switchgrass.

She was out the door. Stalking across the front yard, then across the road. The wide service path in the field seemed to suck her into it just as she'd soon be sucking the smoke through the pipe. She walked hurriedly, blanking her mind. *The last piece, the last piece, the last piece.* She walked a quarter mile into the field without being conscious of it. The fingers of one hand rubbed her cross, the fingers of the other rubbed the crack bag. *Make sure there are no workers out here,* her paranoia finally told her. Now she walked with eyes peeled, and turned into the narrower foot path heading east. A few minutes later, she stopped. Her humanity flitted away; she opened the baggie, loaded the pipe. She stared at it, hating herself.

"No!" she suddenly shouted. She thought of her rapists, and what they'd done to her. She thought of the past and what she'd done to herself, and then she saw a picture of herself prowling sidewalks at night, hoping for a trick. She remembered the leering faces when she'd get into a stranger's car; she remembered the revolting smells and sickening tastes, and then, lastly, she saw herself hanging by the neck. "No!" she bellowed again and threw the loaded pipe as far as she could into the switchgrass. *I'm not going to be a junkie, and I'm not going to kill myself!* The glass pipe arced end over end in seeming slow motion, then irretrievably vanished.

Silence followed, like the silence after an explosion.

"I'm not going to smoke crack," she whispered. She stalked off, farther down the path, unaware that soon she'd be at that odd circular clearing, which was only a few hundred yards shy of the cemetery where she'd been orally raped. She walked quickly, nearly jogging, as if her addiction were in chase. Still barely cognizant of her actions, she stepped into the clearing—

—and almost shrieked.

A man stood there, turning at her entrance. Judy's heart slammed because for a moment she thought it must be one of the masked men . . .

"Oh, it's you, Miss . . . I'm sorry, I forgot your name."

"Judy Parker," she droned in the after-scare. "Seth Kohn's girlfriend. You're Mr. Croter, the Realtor who sold Seth the Lowen House."

"Yes, yes, nice to see you again," he said, but seemed distracted as he meandered around the clearing. "What brings you way out here?"

"I . . . was just taking a walk," she told him, trying to unclench herself. "I came out here the other day when Seth was working."

"Really? Well, let me ask you something. These circles of stones—when you were here earlier, were they . . . like this?"

Judy had to wrestle back her attention. *What's he talking about?* But then she looked down at the ten circles of stones in the dirt, which formed a large circle in all, and the eleventh circle in the center. She focused, and noticed that they were splotched with something, darkened, and semishiny.

"No, they weren't," she said slowly. "They were just bare stones. And is that . . ."

"I know, it looks like blood," Croter said. They both

stooped for closer inspection. *Could be paint*, she told herself, but then why would someone . . .

Croter explained, "I drove by here last night and saw lights in the field. Lights that seemed to be coming from this exact spot—"

And two nights ago, I saw lights out here, too, Judy remembered.

"—so I thought I'd come out here and have a look." His expression turned stolid. "Yes. Somebody poured blood on these rocks."

"Within the last two days," Judy added. What a strange thing. Was it really blood? But suddenly they both paled when a breeze shifted, and filled the clearing with a ghastly odor.

"Smells like something dead," Croter gasped. Wincing, he approached the wall of switchgrass and pushed aside an armful of stalks, then, "Holy shit!"

Judy held her breath and looked. Her stomach lurched. "Oh, gross!" she exclaimed of the pile of headless animal carcasses. It looked like five or six of them. *Just like in the* . . . "You're not going to believe this, but the other day I found an old graveyard not far from here, and there were dead dogs there, too. *Headless* dogs."

Croter urged her away, toward the entrance. "I guess that explains where they got the blood."

The strangeness—as well as the revulsion—at least diverted Judy's consciousness. Croter led her back down the path to the wider serviceway. "Mighty strange, mighty strange," he said. At the main path, he turned north, away from the Lowen House. "My car's right up here, I'll give you a ride back."

"Thank you," she muttered. As she walked away, she glanced over her shoulder, in the direction of where she'd thrown the crack pipe. *I'm going to quit! So don't think about it!* Croter's old blue Pontiac was parked just out of view on the path, behind an outcropping of switchgrass. Judy walked to the car, fingering her cross and trying to banish the anguish running through her nerves. *Thank God he didn't see me.*

"I guess we should call the police, I mean, about the dead dogs and the blood."

He let her in the car. "Not much point in that, not around here. The police aren't good for much. Anyway, enough of all that. How are you and Seth liking the house?"

"It's great," she said without much enthusiasm. "We had a break-in, though."

"What!"

"Yeah, that was pretty strange, too. Did you read the article in the paper about the old steamboat they found on Seth's property?"

"Oh, yes. Something about an earthquake decades ago, diverting the river. Was there anything of value on it?"

"Not really," Judy said. "There were old shipping barrels on it, so Seth paid some men to move them into our basement. Turned out to be a waste of time and money."

Croter pulled off, looking at her. His Star of David glimmered. "What was in the barrels?"

Judy laughed thinly. "Broken plates, broken marbles, and coal dust."

Croter's expression lengthened.

"Anyway," she went on, "a few nights later, somebody broke into our basement and took four of the barrels. Seth filed a police report."

"Why would somebody steal broken plates, marbles, and—"

"Oh, I forgot to add, there were also four barrels of clay."

"Clay?" Croter asked in a tone that quickly lowered.

"Yeah. Can you believe it?" In thought she continued, *And can you believe that I let the thieves back into the basement later?* "Those were the only barrels they stole. The ones full of clay. Between that and headless dogs and blood-spattered circles of stones, I think I've had enough strangeness for one week."

Croter drove out of the service path, offering no comment. Instead, he seemed deeply contemplative.

"Maybe it's some farmer's superstition or something," Judy added. "Good luck with the harvest?"

"The blood, you mean?"

"Yeah, sure. I can't think of any other reason why someone would cover a bunch of circles of stones in blood."

Croter stopped in front of the house. He didn't respond, just looked at her instead. For the merest moment, he seemed to be afraid of something.

"Well, thanks for the ride, Mr. Croter," she said and got out. He simply nodded, mouthed something in silence, and drove away.

What's with him? she wondered of his sudden weirdness. Weirder, of course, was the rest: headless dogs and bloody stones. She went into the house, but at least realized she'd set her mind not to do crack, had none, yet wasn't terrified of the prospect. *I know it's not that easy, though.* The oddities in the clearing had gotten her mind off it. Suddenly a distant phone rang. *My cell phone. I left it upstairs,* she recalled and raced up the steps. *It must be Seth.* Merely thinking his name made her happy. She plunged through the bedroom door—

The roughened hand slapped to her throat and squeezed off her scream. The lean stocking-masked face leaned an inch from hers as fingers dug into her throat. "No scream-in'or else I'll kill ya."

Her eyes bugged; she nodded, and then the fingers loosened.

"Guess that were Sethie-poo callin'," he said. Yes, the skinny one this time, the long-hair. *The stinker . . .* A straggly beard or goatee puffed out the chin of the stocking. "When's he comin' back?"

"In a few minutes," she choked, and then her eyes bugged again when the fingers dug back in. She couldn't breathe.

"Thing is we saw him this mornin' pullin' onto the turnpike fer Salisbury, so don't jive me. When's he comin' back?"

Her voice sounded like grating stones. "Tomorrow, maybe. Maybe a few days. He's in Tampa."

He threw her down on the bed. "Good. Plenty'a time fer us to have some fun." His wiry muscles bulged when he ripped her sundress off. "Naughty gal, no undies, no nothin'. I like that." He pronounced the word *like* as *lack*.

Judy sat shivering on the bed. Seth's words floated in her head. *Keep the alarm on . . .* How stupid could she be?

"Bet'chew were pissed when ya saw we only left ya three rocks."

"You said you'd leave twenty," she replied, even as ter-rified as she was.

He unfastened his belt. "We was a mite pissed our-selves. See, we didn't find what we was lookin' for."

"What on earth *are* you looking for?" she defied him again. "You already took the four barrels of clay—for what, I can't imagine. And I left the damn basement unlocked like your friend asked. Why did you move the barrels around? Were you looking for something *under* them?"

The squished face smiled. "Damn smart, honeypot. Yeah, we was. But it weren't there. We checked with a detector thing. So's I'll tell ya what we're lookin' for, so you can help us out."

I wish I had a gun, the thought popped in her head. *I wish I could kill him . . .*

"We're lookin' for a skull. It was buried a long time ago, and it's somewhere in the basement. But we swept every square inch'a the place and it ain't there."

A skull. "The skull of Gavriel Lowen," she remembered the macabre information. "Why?"

WHACK!

The callused hand cracked across her face.

"Never you mind. *I* ask the questions."

Half her face burned from the slap. "The skull's not here!" she shrieked. "It's supposed to be buried at the ruins of the old mill in town."

"You know a lot, but it *ain't.* Someone dug it up a long time ago and buried it here," he said.

Judy winced. "Why the hell would somebody—" But she bit her lip and reeled back the complaint.

"Ain't kiddin' now, ya shut up'n listen." He stepped brazenly closer, right between her parted knees as she sat on the edge of the bed. "There must be another basement here, ain't there?"

The hidden room! her thoughts fired. *He doesn't know about it! That mummified hand's buried there so the skull must be, too . . .* A crude instinct told her to reveal the information, that surely she'd be rewarded for it, but instead she said, "I don't know of any other basement in the house."

"So *look!*" he quickly yelled in a high pitch, and the whole house seemed to shake. "Maybe there's a inside door somewhere, or a trap door."

"Okay, okay," she blurted. "I'll look. That could be true. We've only lived here a week and haven't checked everything yet."

"And we'se also lookin' for a little wooden box with a piece'a paper in it—"

The mezuzah, she realized.

"—and some funky kinda candleholder and a wooden bowl . . ."

Now Judy knew something he didn't, and it was something he wanted. *Which only means he probably won't kill me* . . . "I'll look around."

"You do that"—he pointed into her face—"and find the shit, we'll give ya *fifty* pieces'a crack."

Even in her determination not to smoke, her addiction seemed to pant at the words.

"And I'll give ya this fer the meantime." He produced another baggie, what looked like at least ten pieces. He threw it on the bed. "Awright?"

"Yes."

"Good girl. But 'fore I leave, ya still got some toll to pay . . ."

God Almighty, not again. He pulled his jeans down to his knees, showing inordinately large genitals.

"Ain't no big deal to a whore no ways." He chuckled. "Now flip over on yer belly. My buddy got'cha in your cookie, now I'se gonna get'cha in your butt."

Judy froze. She sat and stared at the obscenity of it all, and the obscene genitals. Disconnected commands from her brain took her over; in a split second she'd lurched forward, got a testicle in her mouth, and—

He screamed like a gelded walrus.

—bit down on the testicle until she felt it divide between her teeth. His shriek pierced her ears. More brainless impulse hauled her knees back to her face, then fired her feet forward as hard as she could. Both bare heels rammed his forehead.

The man flew backward and crashed against the floor.

Don't stop! Don't let up! Judy was on him as he thrashed and yelled, a mad synchronicity sending one hand to his scrotum and the other to the dresser lamp.

"I'll kill ya, I'll kill ya!" he raged, dazed, but then the protestations turned into mewls as she squeezed his other testicle with all her might, her adrenalin affording her preposterous strength. He flopped and kicked as the small organ ruptured in her palm, then—

THWACK, THWACK, THWACK!

—her other hand stamped the lamp base repeatedly against his forehead.

The thwacking went on for some time.

When she was done—and the man was certainly dead—the impulses didn't stop. She dashed into the bathroom, thinking *fingerprints!* and snapped on a pair of rubber cleaning gloves, then tore a brand-new plastic wastebasket liner from its box. A second later, she'd hauled the bag over his head. Her fingers pulled a new stocking from the plastic-lined card, then she expertly wrapped it around his neck and knotted it tight.

There, she thought, collapsing back against the dresser. His head had landed a foot away from the throw rug; now he would bleed into the bag, not on the floor. Paper towels wiped up the little bit of blood that had spilled thus far. She pulled up his pants, stuffed the towels in them, and refastened his belt.

Silence, then.

She sat nude on the bed and looked at him. The plastic bag didn't move—no evidence of respiration. *Yes, he's dead, the fucker's dead.* Nevertheless she looked on, for many, many minutes. For one moment the bag puffed— and she screamed—but then she heard a muffled, wet clicking that stopped a moment later. *The death rattle*, she knew.

She screamed again and thought her heart would erupt at the next shrill sound, but spared a laugh when she realized it was her cell phone.

"Hi, honey," Seth said when she picked it up. "Just wanted to let you know I got to Tampa without a hitch."

"Oh, good, good," she said.

"I'm at the lab now and we're working away. Jimmy thinks he knows what the problem might be."

Judy had to struggle not to suck in breath. "Really? What?"

"The pixalization codes were misallocated for the new enemies. All we have to do is reallot them."

Sound normal, sound normal . . . "How long will it take?"

"At least a day, maybe two."

"Oh . . . But . . . I miss you."

"I miss you, too, but I've got to do this."

"I know . . ."

"But I'll call tonight, let you know how it's going. How are things at the house?"

Judy felt a hundred miles away. She looked down at the lean cadaver on the floor, a bag over its head. "Things are great here, honey."

"How are you feeling? You sound kind of . . . exerted."

I just killed a redneck in our bedroom—oh, and I bit one of his balls in half and popped the other one, she heard herself say. Instead, she replied, "I was bike riding."

"Then you must be feeling better."

She watched the plastic bag redden from the inside. "Yes, a lot better."

"Good, good. I'll call later, and have a good night."

"I love you!" she blurted.

"I love you, too," he chuckled. "And make sure you keep that alarm on!" And then they rang off.

"You can bet sure as *shit* I'm never leaving that *fucking* alarm off again," she muttered to herself. But her eyes never left the rag-tag corpse. What now? Call the police? No, she already knew she'd had no intention of that.

So what *was* she going to do?

I'll wait till late tonight, her thoughts croaked, *and I'll drag him deep deep deep into the fields where the son of a bitch can rot.* She lolled on the bed, imagining the ludicrous image: a woman lying naked with rubber gloves on and a redneck corpse on the floor with a bag on its head. *I'm not out of the woods yet, though,* she thought, curling into a fetal position. This one was dead but there was still the big bald one who raped her in the basement; he'd surely be calling on her soon. *It's not just me. They know about Seth, said they'd kill him, too . . .*

She nodded in satisfaction even as the cold sweat began to ooze. *When the big one comes looking for his buddy, I'll have to kill him too . . .*

But still . . . The problem wasn't solved, was it? Her id seemed to grab her by the ears and crank her gaze toward the pillow.

The bag of crack lay there.

She picked it up, stared at it, counting ten pieces. *Seth*

won't be home for a day or two. I can smoke this, then I'll call it quits . . .

But there she went again, with her patented crack-smoker's promise, the promise that was *always* a lie. She'd thrown out one piece today, along with the pipe, but now she was staring at *ten* pieces.

She sobbed in hitches as she dragged herself up and trudged downstairs to look for something that would suffice for a crack pipe . . .

CHAPTER EIGHT

July 31, 1880

I

Just like in the War, Conner reflected on that last night of the month as the first gunshots crackled in the distance. The raiding teams had already been dispatched, leaving only a guarding party back at the camp, and then Conner and Norris to infiltrate the mill. They crept through the thickets under a low moon, each lugging one end of the dynamite crate. "Get ready," Conner whispered, patting the Beal pistol at his hip. "Lowen might have some'a his Jews guardin' the mill."

Behind them, the sleepy town of Lowensport awoke in a tumult of screams.

Norris stopped them behind a storage shed, scanning the mill-front with binoculars. "One guy there, at the door. Looks like he's fixin' to leave on account of the gunshots."

"Don't let him leave," Conner ordered. "Kill him now so's we don't gotta fight him later."

Norris raised one of the clan's few long rifles, a Springfield Model 1842 .69 caliber "smoke pole." He knelt, jammed back the hammer, and sighted, then let out half a breath.

BAM!

Norris bucked in his firing position as the gun roared,

spewing sparks. The sound left their ears ringing. "Haven't lost my touch—took his head clean off."

"Fine shootin'! Let's go."

They regrabbed the crate's rope handles and stalked toward the darkened mill. By the time they'd made it to the door, the town behind them was a pandemonium of gunshots.

The mill stood quiet inside, its great saw blades still, its drive-belts idle. At least the sound of the river now drowned out the intensity of shots and screams beyond. *Sounds like they're killing ever-thang that moves*, Conner thought with a nervous smile. They set down the crate and lit a slurry lantern. "Over here," he said.

Norris dragged the dynamite to some short steps leading up to the stack-deck. "You think them things . . . have any sense?"

"I—shee-it. I reckon so. They know how ta rape'n kill."

"So they might know how ta read, too," Norris speculated, and pointed to the stenciled words DYNAMITE: HIGH EXPLOSIVES! He first hooked up the fuse-roll, then covered the crate with a tarp.

"Good thinkin'," Conner commended.

"Now let's just hope they can bring Lowen in alive."

Conner pulled his pistol out, a reflex. "They will. Corrigan, Pursey, Stoddard—they'se good men, was with me in the War." He opened a window shutter to peer out. More screams and rapid gunshots poured in. He could see a few fires now; they were burning the east end of town. *And burnin' a lot'a Jews, too, I hope . . .*

"Guess all we'se do now is wait."

Conner nodded. "And if I'm right, once they bring Lowen in here, those two *things*'ll follow."

They sat and waited, listening to the din of death outside. Conner's hands were shaking. He remembered what Reid had told them when he'd come back from Salisbury: *Yes, sir, a steamboat carryin' a shipment paid fer by Gavriel Lowen.* But why was he worrying now? "You sure that shipment Reid told of didn't come in today?"

"Positive, Mr. Conner. I've had men watchin' the docks constant. No steamboats, no nothin'. So there ain't no way it could'a got here early, whatever it is."

Whatever it is, Conner thought. *Probably guns, but they won't do him no good now. By time they get here, Lowen'n his whole town'll be in dead and in the ground.* "And did the fellas finish diggin' the grave-pit? What bodies don't get burned up, we'll have ta bury 'fore that boat comes. Can't leave a trace."

Norris nodded with a stiff lip. "We dug a pit big enough fer the whole town'n then some."

The idea pleased Conner; he could see the bodies piled up in that trench. *Then the town'll be ours . . .*

Outside, the screams and shots seemed denser, a nightwind of death. *But the things,* Conner wondered next. *What are those two things doin' whiles my men're wipin' out the town?*

Conner and Norris twirled, pistols drawn, when the haulage door to the mill banged open. A figure shambled in the entrance.

"Jesus God, Corrigan!" Conner yelled. "Ya scared the shit outta us!"

The hefty wood-cutter trudged in, bent by a weight on his back. "What's goin' on in town'd scare more'n that outta ya, Mr. Conner," the man huffed and came forward.

"Did ya get—"

"I got Gavriel Lowen right here, sir." Corrigan rolled the lean form off his shoulder and let it fall to the floor. "Alive, and it weren't easy."

Conner's heart leapt, not from fear but in celebration. The unconscious form that flopped to the ground was Gavriel Lowen, all right, gagged and tied.

"Good job, man."

Corrigan sat exhausted on the work deck. When more distant screams rose outside, he shrieked.

"Where's Pursey'n Stoddard?" Norris asked and held up a slurry lantern.

Corrigan's once strong, youthful face looked haggard now in the lamp light. His eyes were shattered, and the long dark hair seemed dusted gray. "They'se both dead, sir. That's why it took me so long gettin' here—I hadda drag Lowen here myself."

Conner stilled. "Was it—"

"It was them things, sir, just like you said." Corrigan's eyes widened in the light. "They ripped Pursey'n Stoddard apart like they was dolls. It's the grace'a God I got outta there alive myself . . ."

The grace of God, Conner thought. *Shee-it. I know I ain't a Godly man myself, but I ain't no devil worshiper.* And those things, those abominable *things* that killed his wife and the Howeths, they were surely things made by the devil.

"They ain't fast, Mr. Conner," Corrigan said, "but they'se likely followin' me. They saw me snatch Lowen."

"That's what we want!" Conner exclaimed and dragged Lowen over and lay him across the tarped dynamite crate. *And they're coming here. Now.* "Norris! Run the fuse!"

Norris unrolled the black-powder fuse from the box, then out the nearest window.

Lowen was coming to, trying to sit upright. His eyes burned up at Conner; muffled sounds leaked from the gag through his teeth.

"Ain't ya gonna give the man a last word, Mr. Conner?" Norris asked from the window.

"Hell no." Conner spat at the sorcerer. "Don't want ta hear his hocus-pocus—he'd likely put a curse on us."

"Bet he would, sir, bet he would."

Even with the gag in place, Lowen managed to smile.

CRACK! CRACK!

Conner brought the Springfield's butt down hard across Lowen's shins. The bones broke; Lowen mewled, pain crushing his face. "Can't have him crawlin' off the box. Corrigan, git outside'n wait with Norris."

"But, sir, what 'bout—"

"I'm waitin' in here till the last minute. Now do like I say!"

Corrigan slipped out the window, while Conner dragged Lowen to lie across the dynamite. Lowen's pain erupted through the gag as a gut-deep shriek. Conner checked his pistol again, then—

WHAM!

Something impacted a pair of wooden double doors in the corner; they'd been barred with a heavy plank.

Them things're here already . . .

Several more *whams!* caused the doors to splinter and burst wide. Conner felt petrified in place. Broken boards flew into the mill; an awkward shadow shifted from the corner.

"Light it when I say!" Conner shot a terrified whisper to

the window, and then moaned from his heart to snap out of the dreaded paralysis. He drew his gun, stepped forward.

"Come on, ya ungodly things!" his voice cracked. "I got what'cher lookin' fer!" He stepped on Lowen's broken shin bones, begetting more ripping shrieks. "The man that brung ya here from hell is right here with me! Come git him!"

The lantern flame flickered; in its dim light, Conner could see enough as the first of the things came close enough. It was bone-thin, shiny as if somehow sweating through the meager layer of clay that covered it. An equally thin layer covered its skinned face. It loped forward, faster than Conner imagined it capable.

"Come on! Both'a ya's! I'm ready fer ya!" But no second figure appeared from the corner. Hot dread spread in Conner's belly when he realized why: there *was* no second abomination. Only one had come to free its master.

Only terror charged him now; he fired several slapdash shots, saw at least one bullet hole appear in the thing's hideous chest, but was not surprised to see it had no effect. Its thin feet thudded on the dirt floor as it quickened its pace.

"Light it!" he yelled, fired two more shots, and leapt for the window . . .

II

The Present

D-Man felt as nauseous as he felt confounded. *So this . . . is how they do it?* No spotlights lit the circular clearing this night; instead, kerosene torches burned. In the sputtering light, he could still make out the blood previously spattered on the multiple circles of stones that formed the greater circle on the ground. Several of Asher's rabbi's—all dressed blackly—busied themselves with scrolls that appeared yellowed with age. Asher himself addressed D-Man.

"I don't *know* where he is, is what I'm sayin'," D-Man reported, uneasy. "He don't answer his cell."

"And the last time you saw him was . . . when?"

"This afternoon, when we were drivin' back to your place from Somner's Cove. I dropped him off at the Lowen House 'cos we knowed Kohn wasn't home."

Asher steepled his fingers, thinking. "And how did you know that?"

"'Cos we saw him this mornin'; we were killin' some time before we had to meet Rosh for the switch. Kohn's SUV was pullin' off on the exit to 413. No other place he could be goin' except Salisbury. The girl wasn't with him but we did see a suitcase in back so we figured he was on his way to the airport."

"And?"

"And then around one or two we make the switch with Rosh at the crabhouse'n head back to your place. When we'se drivin' past the Lowen House, Kohn's SUV still ain't there, so I dropped Nutjob off to have a little talk'n keep her in line. He was gonna push her for anything she might know 'bout another basement, or where the stuff might be."

"I know it's there," Asher said, fisting one hand in frustration. "The portents have *told* me."

D-Man didn't know what a portent was. "Uh, so anyway, he was supposed to call me when he was done so's I could pick him up."

"But you never heard back from him," Asher figured.

"Right. I left messages on his cell." D-Man scuffed his boots in the dirt. "Thought his phone battery probably went dead, so's he just walked back to town, but—"

"I see. That was hours ago."

D-Man nodded. "Figured he just went back to his place, then got stoned'n fell asleep, but I already checked. Shit, Asher. I don't know *where* he is."

Asher gazed away, into the torchlight. "Then maybe Kohn's love interest is more industrious than we think. Maybe she killed him."

"Cain't see that, Asher. She slipped back hard. I'se bet if I told her to stand on her head'n shit in her face, she would . . . for crack."

Asher pursed his lips at the vulgar allusion. Before he could say anything more, one of his acolytes approached and quietly told him, "We're ready, Gaon."

A distraction that seemed rapturous lit Asher's eyes. "Bring the corpse out, and the offering."

Several other dark-dressed figures carried the freshly exhumed cadaver from the van. D-Man stared woozily as it was lain over the center circle of bloody stones. Flame-flickers danced on the dead skin. *This is a fuckin' trip*, his thoughts moaned.

"So beautiful, even in death. She'll be pristine." Asher's eyes looked unfixed. "In 1880, my ancestors had to cut the flesh from the corpses in order to reduce the surface area enough to be covered. That's how very little clay they had access to."

D-Man's gut shrunk when he caught himself looking at the dead, blue-nippled bosom. *And after this, they're gonna cover her with—*

"It's obscene to think that the clay Gavriel Lowen had

purchased would never arrive," Asher went on. "It makes me think of the trials of Job. But now we've been bestowed with the privilege that Great Gaon Lowen was never granted." He looked to the sky. "I can only wonder why . . ."

These people are fuckin' cracked, D-Man thought.

The linen-wrapped parcel was placed in the Gaon's hands. He smiled at the corrupt bread as though it were a newborn. "Your work is cut out for you, my friend," Asher's voice fluttered. He seemed suddenly flushed, holding back a deep joy.

"Yeah. Guess I got no choice but to have another visit with the girl."

"Go in the morning. Give her time to need more product. Whatever happened to your associate is not nearly as important as what must be retrieved from that house. If you need to torture her . . . torture her."

D-Man's throat tightened. He nodded.

"Now go, with the blessings of our melech." Asher smiled from far away. "Samael . . ."

Even as D-Man turned, he could feel something thickening the air and tingling his skin. Suddenly the impulse to flee overwhelmed him. D-Man didn't want to be around when they commenced.

He got in the van and drove out of the clearing, out of the field, and away as fast as he could.

III

By nightfall, Judy's hands sang with pain, from the blisters she'd earned digging in the basement for hours. It was the crack—*so much crack*—that made her oblivious, even mindless in this arcane task. She knew she would never divulge the existence of the hidden room but she figured if she doled out its contents one item at a time, she'd be able to manipulate the scenario in her favor.

The big one, she knew, would be harder to kill.

And sooner than later . . . he'll be back.

All she'd found while digging were several more pieces of bones, in addition to the hand they'd found. A femur, a collarbone, part of a skeletal foot—all strangely caked by the thinnest layer of something she could only believe was clay. But no skull. These pieces she'd unearthed in the east end of the hidden area. So . . . where was the skull? The worse question was: What did they want it for? But it wouldn't matter, would it? Seth had called earlier and said he probably wouldn't be back for a week now— more glitches. *I have to be off this shit before he comes home.* She thought of the dwindling bag. Only a few rocks were left.

By midnight, the edgy buzz was dulling. There was still one more thing she had to do tonight, so she smoked one more piece and got to it.

The dead redneck's corpse, though slight of frame, seemed interminably weighty. *Damn, it's like dragging a floor safe!* The macabre bag remained secure over the head, and she was relieved to see that his bladder and bowels hadn't voided, or at least not enough to leave a mess. She grabbed it by the shirt-shoulders and dragged it cumbersomely down the stairs.

When she checked outside, it was hot but she was relieved to find the sky cloudy, the moon obscured. *Maybe God is with me,* she had to chuckle to herself. The long vantage point on either side of the road showed no headlights. She moved faster than she'd ever moved just then, when she dragged the corpse out the door, down the front steps, and across the road into the edge of the switch-grass.

Her adrenalin surged—*I'm dumping a dead body!*—and when she stopped thirty yards or so in the switchgrass rows, the reality of overexertion made her collapse. She tried to calm herself, flat on her back; her heart was beating funny. *Middle-aged crackheads die from sudden heart attacks and strokes all the time*, she reminded herself, but that prospect scarcely daunted her. If she died, she'd be relieved of the burden of quitting drugs again. When she settled down, though, she knew this wasn't deep enough. She needed the corpse deep, deep in the fields. By the time the grass was baled the summer heat would have reduced it to bones. There'd be nothing to link it to her.

She spent another twenty minutes dragging the body deeper.

A hundred yards at least, she thought, huffing in the darkness. She sat down to rest more, only then remembering Hovis's warning of snakes in the fields. *With my luck it won't be a harmless hognose, it'll be a copperhead . . .* She could thrash her way all the way back as she'd come or . . . The service path was probably only twenty yards east, she figured, and that would be much easier.

Sweat drenched her; it made her feel awful along with her self-disgust and knowing that she'd likely smoke the rest of her stash tonight. Flecks of grass and field dust caked her face and crept down her blouse. Even with her eyes adjusted to the darkness, she had to feel more than see as she cut across the field. *If I'm only ten degrees off track, I could wind up walking a mile in this stuff before I get to the path.* But so be it. At least she'd disposed of the body.

Thank you! she celebrated when the rows of stalks at last dumped her onto the service path. But—

Jesus . . .

Her heart seemed to split in her chest at the sudden clatter of engine noise that caused her to dive backward into the field and lay still. *Who the hell's driving here at this hour!*

She froze only a few feet deep behind the grass when headlights wavered on the accessway.

A vehicle roared by, causing Judy's teeth to chatter. She'd only had a glimpse but that was enough to discern the vehicle: the black step van.

And the other rapist was no doubt driving it.

She didn't allow herself to move for many minutes. *Why's he out here now? And where's he going?* Was he going to the house, to question her as to the whereabouts of his accomplice? *How good would that look if he sees me walking out of this field when his buddy's missing?* She waited minutes more until she finally stepped back out into the path. *Just walk slow and quiet, and keep your eyes and ears open.* But before she could embark to the house, something seemed to float in the air—the most distant sound.

She froze in place, straining her auditory powers. *Voices,* she determined. Then:

Silence.

She looked behind her and could barely make out the more narrow path that led to the odd clearing.

There'd been light back there two nights ago, bright ones, but now . . .

Only the faintest light could be detected, the dullest yellow radiance.

A minute later, that radiance seemed to turn blue.

I don't know what's going on, and I don't care. But then

her heart twisted in her chest yet again when, minutes later, she heard more motor noise. She dove back into the grass.

More headlights wavered, but this time two cars—a black four-door sedan and a station wagon—cruised by very slowly. Judy's frustration raged, even over her creeping withdrawal: *What are all these people doing in the middle of a friggin' switchgrass field in the middle of the friggin' night!* She couldn't imagine. Neither vehicle bore any state agriculture crests, so who were they?

Friends of the man in the black van?

Again she waited in the grass is case more came along. Half an hour later she crept back out and walked home. At the end of the path she was about to step across the front road when—

Not AGAIN!

Still one more vehicle intruded on her. This time she could only quickly step back into the rows to keep from being seen. It was a car on the main road, and it was slowing down.

It stopped right in front of the house. Its windows were up; she couldn't see the driver. A two-door sedan this time, and lighter in color.

She heard a dull clack. The car sat a moment, then slowly drove away.

Was that . . . Mr. Croter's car? she wondered, then wondered harder what it could've been doing. She skimmed quickly across the road, realizing that the unknown visitor had stopped directly in front of her mailbox. *Newspaper delivery?* But, no. They hadn't subscribed to any papers yet. Nevertheless, she opened the mailbox and found—

One envelope.

Can't a girl dump a dead body in peace? She hustled back

into the house, turned on the alarm, and rushed to the kitchen.

The bright lights comforted her at once. She turned the envelope over in her hand. Someone had scrawled on it: SETH & JUDY

She opened it and unfolded a single sheet.

DO YOU KNOW WHAT A GOLEM IS? more scrawl had been written.

Judy blinked. A golem . . .

GET OUT OF THE HOUSE AND DON'T COME BACK, the handwriting finished.

III

In the morning, Judy felt like she looked: on the edge of ruin. The mirror forced her to confront the truth. Dark circles could've passed for black eyes, lines going down her already visibly thinning face. She'd used a dented soda can with a hole in it as a makeshift crackpipe. The last piece was smoked by ten A.M.

She left the alarm off. She sat in the living room and simply waited for the specter she knew would come.

I won't kill him today, she resolved. The dissolution of her addiction had her thinking that she'd cop one or two more bags off him first. *Then* she would quit.

Indeed.

Arms wrapped about herself, she stared at the front door, but screamed when the hand came around from behind and clamped over her mouth.

"You expect me to come in the front?"

Her body arched back when he lifted her up.

His lips brushed her ear. "If it was up to me, I'd kill your ass, but I need to know where my buddy is." He shoved her away, where she fell with a squeal to the couch.

"What?"

The stocking mask compressed his face. "You had a visitor yesterday, didn't ya? Where is he?"

"Who, your partner in crime?" she defied. "How would I know where he went?"

The man held up a fist. "He was *here*, and don't act like he weren't."

"Wasn't," she corrected. "That's not a subjunctive mode."

WHAP!

This one hit harder than the man she'd killed, but the pain had been worth it. Judy blinked the sparkles from her vision, tears misting. "He left here about three."

"Where to?"

"How can I possibly know that!" Her outburst surprised the intruder. "I need more crack!"

"Nuh-uh." He walked slowly about the plush room, idly inspecting things. "No more freebies. You wanna *get*, you gotta *give*."

"What? *This!*" she spat, stood up, and opened her blouse. "You want to rape me again like your friend! Go ahead!"

He looked at her with no interest. "Ain't in the mood right now. I'm sick of ya already. I'm on a hot seat now, baby. What he tell ya when he was here?"

Think, think! Judy urged herself. *Then lie.* "He told me to look for an alternate basement; he said there's a skull buried in it and he wants the skull. He also said he wanted me to find a wooden mezuzah, a candleholder, and a wooden bowl." She looked him in the stocking-veiled eyes.

"He said if I found it, you guys would give me fifty pieces of crack." She reached under the couch where she'd previously put the golden menorah and bowl.

Behind the mask, the man's eyes turned astonished.

"Here's half of what you want," Judy said. "So give me half of the crack. Now. It'll take me a while longer to find the rest."

He picked up the items. "Well if that ain't . . ."

"I want twenty-five rocks now. A deal's a deal."

"When's loverboy come home?"

"Tomorrow night, maybe," she lied. "He's not sure."

"Well then you's better find the skull and the box by tomorrow *day.*"

Shit . . .

"But if'n ya find that wooden box, we'll be able to find the skull."

Her face screwed up at the comment. She knew full well that the parchment within the mezuzah contained no clues as to the whereabout of the skull. *What the hell is he thinking?* It was best to not ask, better to bide her time. "Fine. Give me twenty-five rocks—"

He tossed her a bag. "There's ten. Ya get the rest when *we* get the rest." He turned and began to walk away.

"What time are you coming tomorrow?"

"Any time I fuckin' want." He grinned through the sheer mask. "Maybe tonight, if I get horny." He went back through the kitchen. A moment later, the back door slammed.

At least I didn't get raped this time, she thought in a tense relief. She ground her teeth when she looked at the bag of crack, smoked a piece to buff off the edge, then let herself think.

She'd give him the mezuzah tomorrow or the next day, but for now she'd keep looking for the skull. She still couldn't imagine what he meant. *If he has the mezuzah, he can find the skull himself?* What did that mean?

Her thoughts slowed—

Wait a minute! She rushed to her office, skimmed the books there, mostly her philosophy and theosophic texts. She had one shelf, too, of books on Kabbala.

"Here it is . . ." She pulled down a volume entitled *The Golem of Prague & Other Rabbinic Legends.* Suddenly a piece of the puzzle had occurred to her: what the bald intruder had said, plus the bizarre note left in the mailbox last night. She felt strangely certain that the late-night messenger had been Mr. Croter, the Realtor. *I'm sure that was his car.* But of all the things to leave in the mailbox . . .

As a professor of theosophy—basically high-falutin' folklore—it was natural for Judy to know what golems were, for their mythology had a way of weaving in and out of Talmudic texts throughout the ages. An inanimate being crafted from mud or clay and given a false life through certain mystic rituals. But of course it was all myth. Judy stared at the book's chapter-opening definition:

GOLEM: n. *(pronounced* goilm*), in Jewish folklore, an artificially created being—most often bearing human shape—endowed with life by supernatural means.*

The mere definition rekindled her recollections from the history of Judaic myth. The most famous golem came from the narrative of one Rabbi Judah Loew, the Marahal of Prague. Loew, one of the most prominent sixteenth-century Jewish scholars, was said to have used Kabbalistic magic to create a golem in the spring of 1580. The creature was made of clay from the Vltava River, clay reputed to have been enchanted by angels before the time of Adam. Loew's golem repelled a massive military persecution of the Jews in the Prague ghettos and was so formidable in its bloody onslaught that the emperor quickly begged Loew to call off the monster, and in return promised protection for the Jews. Loew agreed, deactivating the creature but keeping it close at hand should it ever be needed again.

But that's just a story, Judy knew. *A fable.*

The coincidence irked her. *Loew,* she thought. *Lowen. Lowensport. And now a note in my mailbox about golems . . .*

She read further:

> *Though there are many methods of animating a golem, Loew's remains the most famous. On the golem's chest he inscribed the word "aemeath," (meaning "God's truth") just after performing a secret ritual. When time came to deactivate the creature, Loew merely rubbed out the first two letters of the holy word, leaving "maeth," (meaning "death"). More obscure methods predated Rabbi Loew's famous achievement, during the schism between the twelfth century Kabbalists and the Kischuphs (for more, see "Kischuph and Anti-Hasidic Sects"). Originally Kischuph existed as an even more severe variation of Kabbala, but later became disenchanted with God when their mysticism gravitated toward occultism. Whereas Kabbala worships the Ten Sefers, or Ten Books of God's Enlightenment, the Kischups are said to have—via use of black magic—discovered the Eleventh Sefer, or the Sefer Met (the Book of Darkness) whose secrets were overheard by S'mol (Samael, the Jewish heriarchal fallen angel) when God was teaching Kabbala to the angels;*

hence, the most extreme Kischuphites became to Judiasm what medieval satanists became to Catholicism and Orthodoxy. It was these sects in particular who would masquerade as Kabbalists while serving the devil in secret. It is further thought that S'mol granted the secrets of the Sefer Met to all who would turn against God, and one such secret was the engaging of golems for maleficent purposes. Kischuphites used blood rites to charge golems, often through an occultized verge or circination (a circle energized by magic, see "Magic Circles"). A torch was lit within the circle, to light the demon's way, and when that light turned blue, the Gaon knew that the rite had succeeded, for this signaled proximity to the nether regions, which actually shared space with the fringe of the circle. At this point, an offering was made, typically some corrupt item of food to be bestowed to the demon solicited. Cursed bread is widely referred to through the middle ages, produced by burying fresh bread in the grave of a corpse. (S'mol is reputed to be particularly fond of it.) In return for this offering the solicited demon would give false life to a golem properly prepared.

Judy's mind stalled.

For Kischuphites, an evil golem was best when made impure, by covering the corpse of a sinful person with the spectral clay of the Vltava River, the largest river in Czechoslovakia.

She blinked at the words.

Golems were also engaged by the Gaons of Kischuphites as diviners, to find secret treasure or procure

*icons and totems lost. Some archival narratives claim
that S'mol also bestowed the secret of premonition via
kathomancy—that is, beholding the future by inspecting
the steam of the baked head of an ass or mongrel dog.*

Now the coincidences snapped in Judy's mind. *The
baked head of a dog,* she thought very slowly, remembering
the headless dogs she'd seen at the graveyard and the
clearing. *Clay from Czechoslovakia,* and she knew too well
that that's exactly where the clay stolen from the basement had come from back in 1880. *Blood rites in a magic
circle,* and what else could the bloody stone circle in the
clearing be?

"But if'n ya find that wooden box, we'll be able to find
the skull," the bald intruder had said, and here she was
reading of the golem's power in divining—*finding* things.
And last night, hadn't she seen light in vicinity of the
clearing turn blue?

The last connection made her most ill at ease. She re-
read the passage aloud: "An evil golem was best when
made impure, by covering the corpse of a sinful
person . . ." And in the basement were human bones, she
knew. *Bones and mummified flesh . . . covered with clay . . .*

Her thoughts ticked along with the clock. *Kischuph,*
she thought. Such an obscurity, though she remembered
it fairly well from some of the classes she'd taught. Kabbalists used the emblem of the Magical Sign of Zohar: the top
triangle containing the face of man illuminated by God,
the bottom triangle showing the dark face, or the face of
man seeking that illumination. While the emblem of
Kischuph had *two* dark faces, the bottom face seeking the
blessings of the ungodly.

Asher Lowen has the Zohar in his house, she thought. It

was proof that he was a genuine Kabbalist, so why did Judy have suspicions about him? The similarity of the names Loew and Lowen? More reading told her this:

> It was these Kischuphites who honed the black art of golem-making to serve the most nefarious purposes; in fact, heretical Gaons and their Kahals were often highly respected scholars of the Kabbala, while meeting in secret at night to pursue their unholy craft, animating golems to rape and kill gentiles and Jews alike, all in homage to Samael. Riches were bestowed to them in remuneration.

Judy muttered the conjecture aloud, "So maybe Asher Lowen and *his* Kahal are really . . ." But then she severed the notion, thinking, *No, no, no, it's just myth!*

The next passage:

> Unlike the famous Rabbi Judah Loew, Kischuphs would animate their golems with special words contrary to God, generally the name S'mol or other higher demons, or merely with a word denoting the function desired, such as "tzahch" (murder), "nohv" (steal), "ahf" (rape, adultery), or any other word to execute the desired function.
>
> Aside from de-animation (erasure of the animating word on the creature's forehead or chest), it is thought that golems may only be destroyed by severe impact, dismemberment, or fire. Warding spells, prayers of exorcism, and Judaic icons are thought to keep golems at bay.

More unease, for she knew that the wooden mezuzah contained a prayer of *warding*. She rushed down to the basement, pushed open the door to the hidden room. Now the prayer cabinet contained only the mezuzah. She picked it up. *Why would a redneck rapist and drug dealer want this?*

She paused, wincing at the beckoning withdrawal, then ran out of the basement, taking the mezuzah with her. Upstairs, she found the proper address in the phone book. She pulled her bike from the closet and rode off down the road.

IV

Several of the crack girls had revitalized the old clay with warm water and trowels, mixing it into a perfect, tacky mash, and it was Ahron and Eli who carefully spread it out over the dead woman's body, a slow process for meticulousness was crucial. The Gaon watched, his eyes aglitter.

"How long's it take?" D-Man asked.

"Once the corpse is properly covered?" Asher replied. "Only as long as it takes me to write the melech's name on her chest."

Great, D-Man thought with some sarcasm. *Then we'll have two'a them things, and if we get that skull we'll have three . . .*

"You're gonna use the skull for the head of the next one, huh?" he remarked. "But what are you gonna use for a body?"

"It's my hope that we'll be able to use *Seth Kohn's* body," Asher answered. "I like the irony. The man who owns Gavriel's house—the house that rightfully *I* should own." He patted D-Man's shoulder. "If you like, you can be the one to cut off his head."

"Uh, well . . ."

"And you were wise not to torture or kill the girl,"

Asher said next. "That can come later, and perhaps we'll try out the new addition to our family for the task. But she did find the menorah and holy water bowl, so it's logical to give her a chance to find the mezuzah." Asher looked back to the table where the dead woman lay, her nude features still robust in death, the face remarkably intact. In darkness, she might even pass for a living woman. "Take care, Ahron, to spread the clay smoothly."

"Yes, Gaon."

"Once enlivened, her features cannot be changed. We want her to look *pristine*."

I could be throwing back a beer or watchin' a tit flick, D-Man thought. *Instead I'm watchin' a bunch'a rabbis spread wet clay over a dead chick.* "How come the one in the box hadda have its flesh all cut off 'fore they could put the clay on?"

Asher regarded the long box that housed the surviving 1880 golem. "To reduce the total surface area, my friend. You see, in the time of my great ancestor they had so little clay to work with, they were forced to strip the bodies down to the bone. The less body mass, the less clay required. Now, though, we needn't worry about that." He looked at the four barrels of clay pilfered from Kohn's basement. "The hilna of the Vltava." His eyes gleamed at D-Man. "It's *magic*."

D-Man gulped.

"Gavriel Lowen could've made a *platoon* of goilems with that much clay, but he died before he could receive it. Now we have what he so needed, and we'll follow in his footsteps. Last night's supplication went perfectly. I *know* it will work." Asher glanced to the steaming dog's head sitting in a pot. "I've foreseen it."

Shit, man, I just wanna sell drugs, D-Man thought. *I don't want nothin' to do with this black magic shit . . .* But it was too late, wasn't it? He was already neck-deep.

Was it an inner thought—or a premonition—that suddenly stole Asher's attention? Eyes narrowed, he walked to the fireplace and swung out the iron bracket that held the next metal pot. With tongs he removed the lid, and the simmering dog's head within gave off a plume of steam. Asher stared into that steam, then closed his eyes.

What the hell's he seein'? D-Man thought with a twinge.

"I sense quite clearly now that your partner is no longer among the living. It's no matter, though."

"No matter?" D-Man objected. "If he's dead then someone must'a killed him. Maybe it *was* the girl, like you said."

"No matter," Asher repeated. He seemed dazed but content by the vision he'd just been shown. "Something much more important has just been unveiled to me."

"Yeah?"

"It seems the girl has not only found the mezuzah, but she's also taken it out of the house."

"So then—"

Asher nodded. "That blasted hex has finally been removed from the gravesite of Gavriel Lowen. S'mol is with us, good servant." Asher's pendant—the Sign of the Eleventh Sefer—dangled about his neck. He smiled at D-Man. "Go now, and take care of that other problem I mentioned."

D-Man made a dark nod. "Should I take that thing with me?"

"No." He opened the back door for D-Man. "I have other plans for him."

When D-Man left, Asher moved to the long box on the floor. He removed the lid, and said one word:

"Rise . . ."

V

Croter lived in a small house a mile out of Lowensport, nestled back in the woods. Judy was all but there before the teeth of her addiction bit down. She pulled her bike off between some trees and smoked another piece of crack, then collapsed to the ground, cringing. *I hate myself, I hate . . .* But what good was that? There'd be no quitting before Seth got home; deep down she knew that.

All she could do was continue to lie to herself.

She lay there for a time, as the sun sank through the trees. Eventually, she was able to steel herself and make it to Croter's house.

The man looked harried when he opened the door to her knock. "Miss . . . *Parker?* What are you—"

"Doing here?" She took the mezuzah from the bag and held it up. "You know what this is, don't you?"

Croter was taken aback. "Uh—why, it's an old-style mezuzah, like people used to hang on their doors."

"And like Kabbalists used to use for prayers of exorcism and warding spells. It was in our basement, and I have reason to believe that the head of Gavriel Lowen is buried in our basement, too."

Croter tensed. "Really, miss, I don't know what you're talking about, and I'm busy right now, so—"

Next, Judy held up the note. "You put this in our mailbox last night. I want to know why."

Croter paled, stammering, "You're crazy! I never—"

"I *saw* you, Mr. Croter. You pulled up"—she pointed to the blue Pontiac in the gravel drive—"in *that* car. Last night. While some ritual was taking place in the clearing out in the fields."

Croter slumped. "I guess you better come in."

Judy followed him inside, immediately noticing several suitcases set out. "Going on a trip?"

"I'm leaving town," he said, and sat down hard on the couch. He sipped from a glass, next to which stood a tall bottle of whiskey. "I dropped my son off at my ex-wife's earlier today—they think I'm going to a Realtor convention. But what I'm really going to do is disappear." He looked up. "Where did you find the mezuzah?"

"It was in a hidden room in the basement, along with several bone fragments that are covered with *clay*. I've seen the clearing, the headless dogs, and opened graves of people dismembered. Tell me what's happening."

Croter's voice cracked. "I—God! I can't! It could mean my life . . ."

"Asher Lowen isn't really a Kabbalist, is he? He's part of a secret Kischuph sect."

Croter paused, "Yes. And originally . . . so was I . . ."

The words pulled Judy's gaze away.

"Just get out!" he cracked back. "That's what I'm doing! You've got no choice!"

"It was Asher Lowen who stole the clay, wasn't it? Clay from the Vltava River in Prague."

"Two of his grunt-workers, yes."

Judy pictured the physical characteristics of her two rapists. "A muscular bald man, and a skinny one with long hair and probably a beard or goatee?"

He seemed surprised. "D-Man and Nutjob's what they're called. I don't know their real names. They're drug dealers."

Tell me about it, Judy thought.

"How did you know?"

"They're the ones who wanted me to find the mezuzah," she said, "*and* the skull—so I figured they had to be the ones who stole the clay, too."

"That clay was originally purchased by Asher's ancestor, Gavriel Lowen—"

"A descendant of Judah Loew." Judy put the pieces together. "The rabbi who defended his town in 1580 by making a golem with clay from the same river. But Judah Loew was a Kabbalist, a benevolent scholar and man of God."

"Gavriel was the first of his descendants to turn heretic. He sold his soul to S'mol and became a sorcerer who mastered the blackest arts of the Kischup. And Asher Lowen is his direct heir." Croter looked hopelessly to the ceiling. "Everyone in Lowensport today is related to the handful of infant survivors from the slaughter of 1880, me included."

Judy finally sat down, to listen intently. "Tell me about the golems."

"In 1880, Gavriel made two golems by means of a Kischup rite, but his townspeople only had a small amount of clay, so they had to cut the flesh off the two bodies. He reasoned that these first two golems would suffice to fortify them against the Conner scourge until larger amounts of the clay arrived, but the earthquake prevented that from ever happening. Gavriel was killed when his lumber mill was dynamited. Two golems were *made* but only one was destroyed in the blast."

Judy's voice lowered to a fearful suboctave. "What happened to the second one?"

"It's here, in town, at Asher's Yeshiva. It's *always* been here. He's been using it to kill people, rival drug dealers mainly."

Judy winced. "Asher's a drug dealer, too?"

Croter nodded haggardly. "He's rich—S'mol grants riches upon the faithful, and protection as well. He originally bankrolled the local crack operation in Somner's Cove. He works with the police. Drug mules bring raw cocaine to the Cove in crabbing boats that Asher paid for. Then Asher's people convert the cocaine into crack, and the cops have it distributed. It all gets done at Asher's House of Hope."

Rehab center, my ass, Judy thought.

"He's a millionaire, and he's never been caught, and none of the others ever get caught, either, because we all swore an oath."

To S'mol, Judy's thoughts whispered.

Croter seemed jittery as he continued after another sip of liquor. "Asher's been waiting for this day more than any other. The goilem that survived is old, starting to fall apart now. It won't be able to serve him much longer—the goddamn thing's almost 130 years old. But now that he's got that consignment of clay—"

"He's making another one," Judy deduced. "I saw the lights in the clearing last night. That clearing is some sort of occult circle used for rituals, isn't it?"

"Yes," Croter nearly moaned. "With that much clay he can finally take up where Gavriel left off. Asher's a devil worshiper, a disciple of S'mol, and now that he has all the Vltava clay he needs, he can fulfill the prophecy. He can animate the most destructive—and the most *evil*—golems in history, with Kischuph sorcery."

Judy felt her perceptions warp as the words sunk in. *I can't possibly believe that, can I?* "So that's what was going on in the clearing last night. It was Asher—"

"And his Kahal. They're doing a test run, so to speak. They're making a new golem with a random body so they can see if the ritual really works. If it does, he can fulfill the prophecy that he's foreseen."

"What *is* the prophecy?" Judy asked next. "And why do they want Gavriel's *skull?*"

"You just answered your own questions," the haunted man replied. "Gavriel's skull *is* the prophecy. Asher will use that skull to form the head of the most horrendous golem yet—it will be a golem with Gavriel's own wisdom and power. It's just one more thing Asher foresaw in the fumes of his mances. In a sense he'll be bringing Gavriel Lowen back to life. That skull is in your basement somewhere."

"I don't think so, I've already dug around. Seth told me that the skull was buried at the ruins of the *mill*, not in the house."

Croter's lips pursed. "That's because I told him that, and it's a lie. The skull was originally buried at the mill, by the few survivors of the Conner clan. But several months later, a school of Kabbalist rabbis in Baltimore heard about the scourge. *They* retrieved the skull, *they* buried it in that room in your basement."

"And *they* must've been the ones who blessed the house and put the warding prayer in it."

"Yes," Croter admitted. "So that nothing evil could ever enter the house and retrieve that skull. That's the only reason Asher has never been able to go in to the house, and neither could his golem. Only nonbelievers, like those two rogues who work for him, could cross the threshold. The only thing I can speculate is that the skull is probably buried in the northwest corner of the room. Did you check the entire room?"

"No, just the end where we found the bone." *Northwest corner,* she pondered. *Same as a crossroads.* "I've got no choice but to try," she said. "I'll start digging again tonight."

Croter seemed alarmed. "You *mustn't* do that, not now."

"But you just said—"

"Now that you've removed the mezuzah"—he pointed to it on the coffee table.—"the warding spell has been removed."

"Oh, Jesus!" Judy exclaimed. "I didn't even think of that!"

Croter nodded. "And sooner or later, Asher will realize that. He and his Kahal will be able to enter the house themselves . . . or worse."

Or worse . . . Judy sat still in the moments of silence that followed. All the coincidences thus far were hard to deny but . . . could it actually be true? Her nerves were already beginning to wind up for more crack, but she staved it off by reminding herself of Seth. What could she possibly tell *him* about all of this?

Eventually she asked, "What now?"

"What now?" He laughed mirthlessly. "I leave town. I'd advise that you do the same." His terrified eyes found hers. "It's all true, Miss Parker."

She gazed back at him, thinking, then her heart almost stopped when a phone rang in another room.

"My ex-wife, I'm sure," Croter said and got up. "Calling to raise hell." He disappeared through a door behind him.

Judy bowed her head and rubbed her eyes. *God Almighty. What am I gonna do? I'm strung out on crack and I've got THIS to deal with . . .* She still had several more rocks with her. She prayed to God for the strength to throw them out. She could call Seth, admit to it all, but . . . would he believe anything she had to say about Asher Lowen and his diabolism? *Seth would think the crack has made me delusional.* If Croter was right, however, she and Seth would have to get away from here. But there was one thing she knew she must do first.

She looked at the wooden mezuzah. *I have to put this back in the basement before Asher finds out it's gone.*

Ten minutes passed, but Croter didn't return. *Did he leave out the back?* No, his luggage was still here. She sat fidgeting, rubbing imaginary crack-bugs on her thighs, then promptly got up. "Mr. Croter?" she called out. She put an ear to the door, heard no phone conversation on the other side. She waited a moment more, then pushed the door open.

"Mister—"

Croter lay convulsing and balloon-faced on the kitchen table as a bulky figure's biceps bulged; a stout rope had been wrapped around Croter's throat, each end in a ham-sized fist, both of which tightened the rope so firmly that it dug an inch deep into the meat of Croter's neck. He flopped several more times on the table, face darkening, tongue jutting, and then fell still.

Next, his murderer's face pitched up slowly at her call: two narrowed eyes set over a grin on a gleaming, shaved head.

"Hey, Tits. Fancy meetin' you here."

The muscular hulk was her surviving rapist, D-Man. Judy screamed, turning, but not fast enough for the lightning-quick hand that fired out and latched onto her hair. He dragged her across the floor, mauling her breasts for good measure. "Was on my way to your place after I took care'a him. Thanks fer savin' me a step."

Judy screamed until his meat-hook hand girded her throat and squeezed. The sudden pressure made her eyes bulge.

"I ain't askin' more'n once. Where's Nutjob?"

"Who?" she hacked.

"My bud. Don't bullshit me, bitch." He hoisted her up by the throat, then slammed her down atop Croter's corpse on the table. He squeezed harder.

Her heels pummeled the table. Without the stocking mask, the face was even more terrifying. She tried to hack out a response but couldn't until he lessened the choke-hold.

"I-I told you—" Her fading senses struggled to remember her lie. "He left around three yesterday—"

"You lyin' ta me?" he suddenly bellowed.

"No, no!" she wheezed. "I swear."

The tense hands paused.

"And I . . . I found the mezuzah," she got out with her next choke.

He released her and hauled her to her feet. "Gimme it'n I won't kill ya."

The breath whistled back into her lungs. When her vision cleared she took him to the front room. "There," she said, pointing to the coffee table.

"Well, shit my drawers," he whispered in his rough elation. He picked it up, examining the old, handcrafted wood. "So this is it. Without this thing in the house it don't matter where the skull is. We'se'll be able to find it sure as shit."

It was with no volition of her own that she grabbed the liquor bottle and shattered it against the corner of the table. *Oh, shit!* She hoped for the bottom to break off, leaving a large ring of razor-sharp edges; instead, the entire bottle smashed to pieces. All she was left with was the bottle neck.

D-Man guffawed when he realized her feeble move. "Guess I'll be killin' ya, anyway," he said, and snatched her hand, squeezing until the bottle neck fell. He muscled her to the floor as she screamed in his face.

He wrenched up her sundress and tore her panties off. "But I gotta git it one more time, see? Seems a waste not to." Her slapped her senseless. "And who knows? Maybe Asher'll make the next golem with *your* body . . ."

"I killed your asshole friend," she said through gritted teeth. *Oh, please, God, help me . . .* Was she trying to distract him, or just delay the inevitable? "And I left his fucking corpse in the field."

His ministrations slowed.

"I bit one of his balls in half and bashed his head in with a lamp."

D-Man stared down at her, but then—

He *howled.*

In the pause, Judy had snapped the cross off the pendant around her neck and jammed it in his eye. His hands flew up to the sudden wound, blood and humor showing between fingers.

"And now I'm gonna kill *you*, you sick piece of shit," she said, unconsciously finding the bottle neck and jabbing it broken side–first an inch to the side of his Adam's apple. This time the howl trebled. Judy jerked aside, missing a faceful of blood by a split second, and squirmed out from under him. On his knees, he arched his back. Blood flew out of the bottle neck, a stroke of luck guiding the glass directly into the jugular and carotid. Now he raged on the floor, and even when he removed the glass, blood continued to fly.

Judy just stood there and watched him shiver as he bled to death. "You look better with the stocking mask on," she muttered to him. When his tremors slowed, she pumped his upper chest with her foot, causing more blood to eddy out even after his heart had stopped. When the reality of what she'd done set in, she felt only dull and unimpressed. *I'm really tired of killing rednecks . . .*

Yuck. She pulled her cross out of his eyeball, wiped it off on his shirt, and reconnected it to the chain. *Maybe there really is a God,* she half joked. Next, she searched the corpse's pockets, took keys, a cell phone, and the pistol. Then she left the house.

Don't smoke the crack, don't smoke the crack, she pleaded with herself. Outside stood the large, ugly black step van. She felt the crack bag in her pocket, wincing. *Not yet, not yet!* she whined, climbing into the van.

CHAPTER NINE

July 31, 1880

I

The mill exploded behind them with a concussion they didn't expect. *We're gonna die!* Conner thought as he was thrown to the ground. The black sky lit up briefly, then came a rain of bricks and boards. Norris and Corrigan cried out along with Conner at the debris and cacophony. The three of them lay half dazed in the brush, until the destructive roar changed over to a gentle crackling.

"Still alive," Conner muttered. He dragged himself up. *And them, too, it looks like.* He helped the two others to shaky feet. Norris looked shell-shocked but intact and Corrigan, though bloody-faced from a flying board, finally roused to recover full senses.

"Jesus God," Norris murmured, gazing behind them. The mill was no more, just a pile of burning larch timbers.

"Ain't no way that thing survived an explosion like *that*," Corrigan grated. "And there probably ain't a speck of Lowen left either."

"Good job, men," Conner attempted, though his voice cracked from an after-fear.

Norris sighed against a tree. "Yer plan worked, Mr. Conner."

"Not all'a it," he reminded. "That second *thing's* still out there somewhere."

"We got damn near a hunnert men tearin' the town up," Norris felt sure. "Don't care how strong it is. It ain't gonna whup a hunnert men."

Let's hope not. Conner gazed toward the town. "Don't hear no more shootin'. The boys must be finished. Let's round 'em up."

Lit by moonlight and the fading mill fire, they crunched through the thicket and found the trail to Lowensport. When they arrived on the shell-paved Main Street, the town stood dark, still, and eerily silent. No more shots, no more screams. The fires at the east end had burned out. Dead bodies, mostly men and women clad in the austere black garments of the Jews, lay this way and that, littering the street, hanging out windows, collapsed in doorways. From several houses, babies could be heard squalling.

"Should we collect up the babies, sir?" Corrigan asked.

"Naw, let 'em sit in their own shit fer the night. We'll put 'em all in a boat in the morning," Conner said. "Whoever finds 'em can raise 'em." He rubbed his hands together in the seeming success. "We gotta bury all these dead Jews *tonight*. Norris, give a call."

"Conner clan!" yelled Norris with hands around his mouth. "Come on out! Front'n center!"

Conner meandered past several houses, looking into windows and doors. Only a few of his own men lay dead, but each and every house was occupied by a dead Jew. Most of them were killed by shots to the head. The more comely women and teenagers had been stripped and raped first. Conner liked the sight. *Yeah. My men did a damn fine job. They killed everything that moved.*

Five minutes later, though, no one had reported to the street.

"Conner clan!" Norris bellowed again. "Git out here! We got work ta do!"

After another few minutes, Conner began to feel a little ill.

"Maybe they all went back to camp after the killin' was done," Corrigan speculated.

"Maybe, but that weren't their orders," Norris replied.

"Let's look around," Conner said. "I only seen two or three'a our boys dead. Why ain't nobody comin' out?"

The answer awaited them around the next corner, in an alley between the general store and the blacksmith's.

"Holy God in heaven," Norris muttered.

Now Conner began to feel very ill.

They'd found the rest of the men—piles of them, heaped in the alley. It was as though they'd tried to converge on something from all sides but had been routed.

"They been . . . pulled apart," Corrigan whispered in shock.

Not one body of the dozens and dozens remained intact. Limbs had been torn from sockets, heads twisted off necks, rib cages cranked open like macabre cabinet doors, revealing glistening innards. Several skulls looked popped like gourds, and Conner had the awful notion that bare hands had done the popping.

Only now did Conner know true fear. "It was that goddamn thing."

"The second one," Corrigan added.

"Our boys killed every Jew in Lowensport," Norris moaned. "Then that thing killed every one'a *them* . . . "

"We gotta get back to the camp!" Conner suddenly exclaimed. "The women and children!"

They ran through the night, reloading their weapons. Several more dismembered bodies littered the way, men who'd obviously fled the town in terror, but then—

That thing caught up to 'em! Conner knew.

The worst that could be feared awaited them at the camp: another slaughter. The Sibley tents had been torn down, and the wooden shacks allotted for Conner's lieutenants ripped asunder. The few men left to guard it had been the first to go; a mound of their body parts greeted Conner on the trail, and a massive gush of blood still moving. Deeper in the camp were the women and children.

None had been spared in the nightmarish onslaught. More heads and limbs had been flung to all sides. Many women lay spread-legged in their death poses, obviously raped first or afterward. Bile rushed up as Conner thought, *How many women can that unholy thing rape in one night?* Norris collapsed to his knees when he found his wife armless and somehow eviscerated through her sex. Corrigan wept openly at the sight of his wife and two children, the children picked apart, and the woman pulled in half at the waist, swirls of intestines packed down her throat. Conner, Norris, and Corrigan trudged through the whole of the camp and found not one living soul. Whereas his men had at least spared the infants of Lowensport, that thing had not repaid the gesture in kind.

"What in God the Father's name are we gonna do now?" Norris croaked.

"Weren't no God the Father here tonight," Corrigan whispered.

"All we can do, men, is head for the hills," Conner said, hands numb from the horror he'd witnessed. He gazed out into the night. " 'Cos we know goddamn well that thing is still out there somewhere. We gotta high-tail it outta here now."

Norris looked at the litter of body parts. "Before it finds *us*."

II

The Present

It had taken Judy several minutes of gear jamming and bad language to reacquaint herself with stick shifts sufficiently enough to drive the beaten black step van. The beastly vehicle roared and rattled as she pulled away from Croter's house. Twilight seemed to press down on the road running along the field—either that or the van's headlights were unduly dim. She saw no cars either way. *Don't smoke the crack*, she kept telling herself. Instead she flooded her mind with the nightmare the day had brought. *Golems. Magic circles and dog-head divination. Asher Lowen not only a shadowed drug kingpin but a Kischuph warlock.* Then: *Seth!* She needed to call him right now, even though she had no idea what she would say. What? *Seth, honey? I have to put the mezuzah back in the basement to maintain the warding spell; otherwise Asher Lowen with be able to find Gavriel's skull, which, by the way, is buried in our basement. Oh, sure. He wants to make a golem out of him . . .*

That wouldn't wash, she knew. *I'll just call him up and tell him not to come home. I'll tell him I'm flying to Tampa tonight, and I'll explain later.* That probably wouldn't work, either, but she could think of nothing else. She whipped out her cell phone as she drove, then moaned when she saw that the battery was dead. *Shit!* She immediately thought she could call him on the redneck's phone, then moaned again when she realized Seth's number had been stored in her phone for so long, she'd forgotten the actual number. *I'll have to recharge the damn thing first.* The wall of switchgrass seemed to hiss as she drove faster down the road. Minutes later, she'd parked in front of the house and was rushing in.

Shit! she thought again when she flicked on a light switch and nothing happened. She flicked several more. Nothing. *You gotta be kidding me! Not a power failure! Not NOW!* She wouldn't be able to recharge her phone. But she knew she had a spare battery upstairs already in the charger. Up she went, huffing, and snapped it in. *Finally! Something goes right for me*, she thought when she saw she now had nearly a full charge. Before dialing Seth, though, she saw she had six missed calls.

She listened to the messages, all from Seth. The last one said, "Judy, damn it, I'm getting worried. You haven't called back. I know it's probably nothing, you probably went to bed early 'cos you weren't feeling well, but I'm coming home tonight. I have to know that you're okay . . ."

"Shit!" she yelled aloud this time. Tonight? *Tonight is now!* She called him at once, then wilted when she got his voice mail. Obviously he was already on the plane and had to turn his phone off during the flight. All she could do was leave a message: "Seth, I'm okay, but . . . *don't* come home! I need you to trust me on this. When you get in, don't leave the airport in Salisbury. I'm coming there right now and I'll meet you. Please, honey, I know it sounds crazy but don't come home!" At least he'd get the message when the plane landed. But for now—

thunk.

Judy froze. The noise had sounded deep, and it didn't help that the house was dark. Had it come from . . .

The basement?

Her sweat turned cold. Was Asher in the basement right now?

Or something even worse?

I should never have taken the mezuzah out of there, she thought too little, too late. She went back downstairs, convinced at first she'd simply leave, go to the airport, meet Seth. But . . .

All this time she'd been wondering if any of this was true, in spite of the astronomical coincidences, Croter's conviction—and murder—and then what D-Man had said when he'd been attempting to rape her again:

Maybe Asher'll make the next golem with your body . . .

If she didn't believe it, why should she be afraid?

Once and for all, she thought next, and went downstairs. She grabbed a flashlight. Then she got the pistol and the mezuzah from the van.

She walked around the side of the house.

Shit, she thought yet again.

The basement doors lay open.

She crept down, the flashlight glaring ahead. What shocked her worse than the noise she'd heard was seeing the hidden door pushed partway open. From within came a faster digging sound. When she stepped closer to the pitch-black maw—

The digging stopped. Then Judy screamed when an inhuman shriek shot out of the room and pierced her eardrums. *Something's in there,* she knew, but what?

The flayed shriek doubled after another step toward the doorway. Something impossible in her made her want to *see* it, and she suspected that the intruder's howls of rage had something to do with the presence of the mezuzah itself.

And its contents.

As Judy edged toward the hidden door, it flew open, and some impossibly thin figure lurched out. It glimmered as if wet. Her flashlight only caught a glimpse as it attempted to rush her, her own shock compressing her senses, but she made out empty sockets for eyes, a scrap of hair on its head, and a thin face like a muck-splotched skull. Judy blindly raised the mezuzah; the thing howled again, then flinched backward into the front corner. *It wants to get out of the basement,* she realized, *but it can't confront the mezuzah . . .*

The single glimpse of its face was all she could bear. Now its rack-skinny form huddled, its knobbed back to her, as it appeared to burrow into the floor's raw earth with skeletal hands webbed by clay. *It's trying to dig its way out.* She was staggered by the wetness of its thin clay skin whereas she'd have thought after over a century the material would've dried to dust. Just more proof of the validity of its occult existence. She thought of using the gun but then rejected the idea. *It's just bones covered with clay, internal organs long gone, no blood.* But she couldn't let it escape.

Could it really dig its way out?

She remembered what her text had said: "Warding spells, prayers of exorcism, and Judaic icons are thought to keep golems at bay." *At least that part works,* she thought. "Golems may only be destroyed by severe impact, dismemberment, or fire . . ."

She took another step closer and this time its shriek made her skin crawl. The closer the proximity between the thing and the parchment prayer, the more agony the thing felt. Beside her sat one of the barrels, the one that contained rusted sledgehammer heads. She set the mezuzah down to face the corner, then lifted out one of the heads. It probably weighed ten pounds. "Jesus!" she yelled when she heaved it forward.

The impact collapsed one side of the thing's rib cage. Judy collapsed the other with a similar blow. Now only a spine comprised the creature's back. "Fucker!" she shouted, heaving a third rusty head.

Fwack!

The blow cracked the thing's skull, sending a third of the cranial vault flying to bits. *This is getting easy*, she dared to think next. It continued to dig, however hopeless the effort; the damage from the blows of heavy iron reduced its progress to sluggishness. This time Judy grabbed another hammerhead and walked right up to the goilem.

Fwack, fwack, fwack!

She drove the metal block's butt down repeatedly into what was left of the thing's skull . . . until no skull remained at all.

Another blow from the side crushed its ancient spine, and separated the figure into two shivering pieces. Still, somehow, a supernatural impulse in its arms caused it to continue digging—

FWACK! FWACK!

—until the next two blows pulverized both shoulders and sent the broomstick-thin arms to the floor.

"You're done," she muttered. Two more blows—for the hell of it—snapped the clay-sheathed thigh bones. Judy dropped the iron block and sat down on a barrel to rest.

Some of the fragments jittered in the dirt, the skeletal hands especially. *I guess I believe it all now, hmm?* She even laughed to herself.

She took the flashlight into the hidden room, then

gasped at the northwest corner. *Just like Croter said . . .* Before Judy had intervened, the goilem had managed to disentrench a foot of earth. Half buried at the bottom sat a moldered skull.

That's where it would stay. *And here's where this will stay,* she thought when she placed the wooden mezuzah and its potent prayer back in the cabinet.

Once back in the main basement, she looked at the bag of crack, paused, and gulped. *Later!* she swore to herself. The yearning to smoke several pieces made her feel like something bending and about to break.

Not yet . . .

She rushed up the steps and slammed the double doors closed. Then she got in the van and drove away, and she knew she wouldn't stop until she got to the airport to meet Seth.

III

Seth parked a few minutes before midnight. The house stood dark, not a good sign, and when the sky rumbled he shirked at the mass of black clouds rushing to obscure almost all twilight. No doubt the storm was to blame for the BAD SIGNAL message every time he'd tried to call since getting off the plane in Salisbury.

What could be more fucked up? he fumed when he entered the foyer and found all the light switches dead. *No cell phones* and *no electricity . . .*

"Judy! I'm back!" he called out. The dark house seemed to suck up the words. *Please be upstairs asleep in bed,* he prayed, but when he burst into the bedroom, flashlight in hand, no Judy awaited him.

What is GOING ON?

His heart raced. He picked up the landline, got no dial tone, then hurled the phone across the room. *Can't even call the police 'cos there's NO PHONES!*

The answering machine blinked. *Backup battery,* he remembered. There was one message on the machine. Maybe Judy had left a message on the landline as well. *I wonder if it'll play the message on battery power.* He pressed the button.

"You have one message," came the generic voice, then: *BEEP!* "Uh, Mr. Kohn, I'm sorry to leave a message like this. I called the number on the finalization documents, and got your forwarded number. This is Mr. Karlswell, from the Schoenfeld Funeral Home. I, uh—oh, this is so strange. I'm afraid there's been a . . . misadventure at the cemetery, the most despicable sort of vandalism. I'm sorry to inform you, Mr. Kohn, that the plot where you buried your wife two years ago was . . . vandalized very recently. Believe me, the police are looking into it. You see, sir, your wife's body was . . . taken. Umm, I'm terribly sorry about this, Mr. Kohn. Please call me as soon as possible."

"End of message."

Seth stared at the machine, mouth agape. *What in the name of . . .* First, Judy gone, unreachable, and now . . .

Someone stole Helene's BODY?

Too much was piling up too fast. He had to find Judy, find out what had caused her to leave such a strange message herself.

He ran back downstairs and out, determined to drive to the police station. Approaching the truck, though, he paused, irked by something. The prestorm breeze caused the endless switchgrass to hiss, but secreted in that hiss, he swore he heard a woman's voice:

"Seth?"

He froze, peered across the road. The high grass swayed; the breeze disarrayed his hair. *Who is that? That's not—*

"Judy!" he yelled. "Is that you?"

But there *was* a figure, just a foot deep in the switch-grass. It seemed half hidden, timid as it looked right back at Seth. It was a woman, for sure, but it *wasn't* Judy.

"Who are you?" Seth demanded. He jogged across the road, then the figure pulled herself within the tall stalks.

"Wait!"

Seth barged right into the wall of grass, thrashing through. Rapid footfalls guided him. "Stop, damn it! I need to talk to you!" he shouted. More thrashing up ahead, then it stopped. *Probably one of the rehab girls from Asher's clinic*, Seth figured. *Fell off the wagon.* "Listen, I won't hurt you, I just need to know where my girlfriend is."

"Don't come closer, you wouldn't understand," came the soft, feminine flow of words.

This is crazy, he thought, but stood still. The corroding twilight and the stalks made her details almost impossible to see. Almost. The woman was stark naked standing only feet away from him. "How did you know my name?" he asked.

"Oh, Seth . . ."

Her voice sent a chill up his back. "Let me explain." And then the grass shivered as she shouldered through more high stalks. Seth made out the flat abdomen, curvaceous thighs, and firm, pert breasts. But she seemed *dark*. *She's all dirty*, Seth guessed. *Must've been living out here for a while.*

"Judy is waiting for us," the voice flowed.

"*What? Where?*"

"At Asher's." The grass hissed again. "But they need something in your house, in the basement."

"That makes no sense! Judy's at *Asher's?* Why?"

"That will be explained later. I'll take you to her now, but first you have to go into the basement and get the skull."

The skull. Seth stared.

"It could mean her life, and all of ours," she said, dark eyes fixed on him. "You must trust me. You'll understand it all once we're there. But you have to get the skull first."

It could mean her life? Seth could fathom none of this, but it seemed now there was only one way to find out what was happening. *Just get it,* he told himself. *And get Judy* . . . "All right," he said, and stomped out of the grass back to the house.

Crazy. The skull? She must mean Gavriel Lowen's. *And it's been in the basement all along? But what on earth—* Again, he severed the questions to prioritize the next step. He threw open the double doors, tromped down the steps, and grabbed a flashlight.

"Holy shit," he murmured at the disassembled skeleton on the floor. Was it the rest of what Judy had found in the hidden room? *Covered with clay,* he realized when he picked up a thigh bone. The clay was moist. *Stick to business. Then I'll get to the bottom of this.* The hidden larch door stood open; Seth walked right in. The hole dug in the other end couldn't have made it easier. There, half covered, was the browned skull. Seth pulled it the rest of the way out, then left the basement.

Now this kooky girl's got some explaining to do. He rose out of the stepwell, turned, then froze. The woman stood right there before him, brazenly naked but somehow *smeared* with something.

Clay? he had to wonder.

But he didn't have time to wonder about the strange, wet squiggles on her chest because at that same moment the skull fell out of his hand when he recognized the woman.

It was Helene, his dead wife.

"H-Helene?" the impossible word ground from his throat.

She was beautiful in spite of what sullied her. The luxurious contours he remembered so well, the erect bosom and jutting nipples . . . and the smile. It was all there, even though he *knew* he'd buried her two years ago. Then the cryptic message from the funeral director replayed in his head.

Whatever wet substance covered her, it caked her hair as well, and her pubic thatch. Her eyes gleamed at the skull on the ground, then back up to him.

"You have no idea how important that is," came her exuberant whisper.

"You're dead!" he screamed. "This is impossible!"

One bare foot took a step closer, then another. "Are you sure it's not a dream, Seth?"

The question stilled him. A *dream?* "No, it can't be . . ."

"Then how can I be standing here now?" Another step. "Because you're right. I'm dead."

The switchgrass hissed. Seth couldn't move as she came right up to him and stroked his face with cool, moist fingers. He was paralyzed by the impossibility. When she kissed him her dead tongue twirled in his mouth. Then—

He was instantly on his knees.

She'd shoved him down with uncanny strength. Now he was eye-level with her clay-mucked pubis.

"You always were my favorite lover, Seth," her voice eddied as her fingers laced behind his head. She pulled his mouth to her groin.

Seth performed the act she yearned for, revolted as he was. When his tongue laved upward, her darkened thighs clenched.

"I don't know why I ever cheated on you . . ."

His efforts stopped. "Wh—"

"My greatest regret, sweetheart. But you were so obsessed about developing that stupid *game*, you never made time for me." She pushed his face back, digging fingers so hard into the back of his neck, he was forced to continue. "The night I died, I *wasn't* driving back from the mall. I lied to you."

Seth tensed, but then the fingers bit back in.

"I was driving back from my lover's apartment. And goddamn you for asking me to turn around for fucking *cigarettes*." She pulled his face so close he could scarcely breathe. "Good, good, like that, like you used to," she cooed. "And I don't resent you for finding a new lover, honey. This . . . Judy. I look forward to pulling all of her organs out through her mouth with my bare hands . . ."

Seth was appalled but forced to carry on, his mind now a swamp of despair and heartsickness. When the abomination climaxed, Helene sighed, rising up on tiptoes.

She stroked his hair, leaving dainty streaks of clay. "That was lovely, darling. And soon we'll be together again forever." And then her hand smacked Seth hard across the temple. His vision snapped to a blur; the last thing he saw before he passed out was the cryptic word fingered across her bosom: S'MOL.

IV

"Step into the Circle of Ten Circles and see how the flame brightens as you near . . ."

The words sounded so distant, Seth could barely hear them as his consciousness slowly reformed. *Where am—* His blurred vision detected the flicker of torches and shadows of figures. Then, *Oh, God. Helene . . .* It couldn't be true, just an evil dream, but when he lifted his head from where he lay, he could *see* her, her body still somehow robust but smeared with wet clay. That word—S'MOL—seemed to quiver across her bosom. Her dead eyes stared off as the other figures seemed to shift.

The echoic voice returned. "Only faith can save us now, my holiest melech. Empower this night, as you so empowered my great ancestor." And then the figure raised the skull into the air.

Seth, even in his aching daze, recognized the voice. *Asher Lowen, and the other two . . .* He squinted. Ahron and Eli, the rabbis he'd met at Asher's house.

Seth lolled his head to both sides, realizing now that his ankles and wrists had been tied, and he'd been lain in a circular clearing walled around by switchgrass. *The fields,* he presumed. *That clearing Judy saw from the bedroom window.* He tried to focus closer, and found himself lying within an odd circular configuration—ten feet wide or so—yet the circle's border was composed of a ring of smaller circles made of stones. Did the stones glimmer red? Seth counted ten such circles just as Asher's ethereal voice proclaimed, "Ten circles for the Ten Hells, and the eleventh for the Eleventh Sefer—the glorious *Sefer Met*." Now Asher seemed to touch a strange pendant about his neck, two triangles sitting atop one another, in each a dark face. "Here we now pray for the vigor of the Zemu'im, the Secret Discipline from the time of Adam . . ."

A *ritual*, Seth realized, for he also realized that just beneath his back where he lay was an *eleventh* circle of bloody stones. *And I'm part of it.* So was the skull, it seemed, for it was set down beside his head.

"Worthy Ahron—"

"Yes, Gaon!"

"Kill this fodder so that it may have *un*life in S'mol's great glory."

Seth had no time to react when a knife was plunged into his chest. His scream bolted up into the night, and suddenly each frantic beat of his heart expelled blood. The wound left him shuddering in a chill even as his surroundings seemed to grow hotter. *I'm dying*, his fading thoughts murmured. *For what?* The expanding dampness spread across his shirt.

"We see now no longer with our human eyes but with the eyes of our Neptesh, our black souls . . ."

"S'mol be praised."

"Evil for evil, just as was written so long ago. The Zemu'im and the Calling of the Seals make it so."

Seth hacked blood, gasping.

"Now we will close our eyes and, embodied in faith, we step together into the Eleventh Circle. In reverence and glory we hold our eyes fast to the ground . . ."

The madness sucked down on top of Seth, heartbeat

slowing, less and less blood staying in his body. *I'll be dead soon*, he knew, *but what happens before then?*

And what was that other sound he thought he heard? Footsteps?

"And now we look up again," Asher's fading voice declared, "in grace from the power of S'mol and the Secrets God has whispered of but once . . ."

Ahron and Eli gasped, and so did Seth even in his death throes. The torches lit about the great circle now appeared to be hundreds of feet away. The round walls of switchgrass were no longer in evidence but replaced by walls of smoky murk. Shrieks and scuffling came to Seth's ears, and, yes, he was certain now: footsteps.

Then the light of the distant torches turned blue.

"Great S'mol," someone whispered.

More heat poured over Seth's quivering body—an unnatural heat that couldn't possibly exist even on a night hot as this. When Seth's dimming eyes could look again, the circle of torches seemed half a mile in diameter now, such that they could barely be seen.

Seth's retarding breaths began to rattle, for he saw something else now: the source of the footsteps.

They were figures, but they seemed scarlet-skinned and heinous-faced—inhuman. Then they all stopped, all but one, who kept approaching as a gaunt form with a mouth that took up most of its angular face and black orbs for eyes. The thing was smiling.

"Gaon!" whispered Eli in a sudden urgency. "The fodder for the rite—he isn't yet dead."

"It matters not, friend Eli. He will be once we cut his head off." Meanwhile, the most prominent of the macabre figures continued to approach.

"Great melech," Asher breathed in awe, falling to his

knees. "I bow down to you . . . and I beseech you, with this humble offering." His hands reached out, in them what looked like a loaf of bread. The spidery, three-fingered hands of the scarlet figure took the bread and brought it to its hole-punch nostrils. It breathed the scent of the bread, then smiled with black-crystal teeth.

The thing took a bite of the bread, then began to laugh, a sound more like a jackal than a man.

"Anoint this lowly sacrifant, great S'mol," Asher begged, still on his knees, "and this skull of your worthy servant, so that we may do your bidding." Asher glanced to Eli with a nod, and Eli knelt before Seth, raising a hatchet over his neck . . .

V

Judy drove back home through the black night, nervous tears dampening her cheeks. *He must not've gotten my message.* Which could only mean that he'd left the airport immediately after deboarding the plane. She kept trying to call him on the way back but now she couldn't even get his voice mail; the storm rolling in told her why. Each mile back brought more frets. *What am I going to tell him? And what if he goes into the basement?*

Relief surged when she parked the cumbersome step van and saw the Tahoe in front of the house. But the relief was false. She searched high and low but Seth was not inside. What now? Where would he have gone? She paced the front yard, thinking, but when thunder rumbled, she glanced aside and saw the basement door lying open. *Oh, my God, no . . .*

She crept down, calling his name but knowing she'd

get no answer. The flashlight was still there but in a different place. She roved its beam above the pieces of the dismantled golem, then grimly noted that the hidden door was open when she *knew* she'd closed it earlier. *He's been here. Who else could it have been?* The mezuzah remained where she'd left it, but . . .

More thunder rumbled when she pointed the light into the hole in the northwest corner. The skull was gone.

Blind impulse took over. She left the basement, then got D-Man's pistol from the van. What else could she do? The keys remained in the Tahoe, so she got in and took off. She turned it right onto the service path that cut through the switchgrass field. *They need the skull for a ritual*, she reasoned, *and the rituals take place at the clearing. The Circle of Ten Circles . . .*

She stopped well before the side trail and cut off the engine. *I was right.* Even from here she could see the torchlight filtering back through the high stalks. When she walked to the trail itself she noticed the black sedan she'd seen leaving here last night. Asher Lowen's car.

She soft-stepped all the way to the clearing, careful. She heard voices, and thought she made out the words, ". . . in grace from the power of S'mol and the Secrets God has whispered of but once . . ."

A *Kischuph rite*, she knew. God's secret overheard by S'mol before his ejection from Heaven. *The Sefer Met, the eleventh book of God's emanations, whose secrets would be exploited by God's enemies . . .*

Then she heard, "Great S'mol," and saw the sputtering lamplight turn blue. Judy peeked through the stalks and saw:

The clearing and its newly wetted circles. A figure lay

still in the circle's center, next to a skull. Judy couldn't see the prone man, for her view was blocked by someone dressed in black. But she *could see* Asher, dressed similarly, on the other side of the circle, and next to him, Ahron, his adjutant. Asher's face looked hot, his eyes keen in a vision. But then she saw . . .

What in the hell is . . . Standing off was a nude woman—nude yet smeared with what could only be clay. She glistened, and so did the word inscribed on her chest, S'MOL. *Another golem*, Judy admitted. And the more she looked at the thing, the sicker she felt until she fully realized who it was.

Helene. They dug her up and—and turned her into THAT . . .

But then her worst fear yet was realized, when the man blocking her view—Eli—lowered himself to the prone figure: Seth.

Eli raised an ax, clearly meaning to decapitate Seth.

VI

Seth's blood loss left him with no strength at all. His dim eyes watched the hatchet rise, while Asher and the scarlet-slimed thing looked on. Seth contemplated his death, hoping he'd be forgiven for his sins but could only feel outrage and wrath. *Why? What have I done to deserve this?*

Beyond him now, the hellish perimeter of walled smoke looked a mile deep. Seth thought of Judy, his love for her, and smiled, just as the hatchet reached the top of its arc and began to descend.

He thought he heard a loud snap which he didn't understand, nor did he understand why the hatchet dropped and Eli collapsed, howling with his hands to his head.

"No!" Asher bellowed.

Another sharp *snap!* like an echoic plip of water, and then Ahron fell as well, blood shooting from his Adam's apple as he convulsed in the mist.

"Tear her apart!" Asher yelled, and that's when Helene broke from her stance and rushed outward. Seth chugged in a great breath and blinked, only to reopen his eyes and find himself back in the clearing lit by the closely set torches. The last burst of his adrenalin gave him the strength to lean up, to look over . . .

Helene had dragged Judy out of the grass and was straddling her. Judy kicked and flailed her arms but all attempts to defend herself were meaningless. "When Seth becomes a goilem," Helene said in a black chuckle, "I'm going to watch him fuck your headless corpse." And then she grabbed Judy's head and began to *twist*.

Seth groaned, summoned one last fit of energy and grabbed the hatchet. He flung it at Helene.

But all it did was glance harmlessly off her shoulder.

Helene released Judy's head long enough to glance over at Seth and smile.

Then she flopped over and lay still.

What happened? Seth wondered. He crawled over to where Judy lay hacking and shaking off her daze. When he collapsed in her lap, she hugged him.

"My God, what did they do to you!"

"Knifed me," he sputtered. He stared over to where Helene lay surprisingly still. "How did you—" He saw that the word S'MOL had been wiped off her chest. Judy had replaced it with another incomprehensible word: MAETH.

"It means 'death,'" she told him. "When you distracted her with the hatchet, I changed the charging word of the spell."

Seth looked up at her. He didn't understand and didn't care. All that mattered was he was with Judy now.

"Don't move, I'm going to drag you back to the car," Judy hurried, "get you to the hospital—"

"No, no point . . ."

"Yes!" she yelled, and began to drag him down the trail.

"Did you see?" his voice grated. "They took me to a place—it wasn't the clearing, it was a place a mile wide and walled around by smoke."

"Seth, you were in the clearing the whole time. They were using you and that damn skull for a Kischuph ritual. Asher and his people aren't really Kabbalists, they're sorcerers. They practice the Judaic equivalent of black magic." She dragged him onward, her cross glittering.

"No, no, it changed. It was like a pit, a mile wide and these—these *things* came out of the smoke. I think they were *demons*. And one of them—" Seth coughed a faint trace of smoke. "One of them they called S'mol . . ."

Judy paused a moment, then kept dragging him. "Don't talk, honey, save your strength." She kept dragging him, her hands clenched to his shirt at the shoulders. Seth gazed upward, watching black clouds. He raised his hands to hers at his shoulder and said, "Judy?"

"Don't talk! Save your strength, we're almost to the car—"

"I love you," he whispered.

She kept dragging, ignoring exhaustion. When she got back to the Tahoe in the service path, she didn't realize he was dead.

"Seth?" She thumped to her knees. "Seth!" She moaned at the great stain of blood on his shirt. She felt for a pulse, then tried CPR for several minutes.

"Oh, Seth," she wept and let her face drop to his chest. She cried for a while, then sat up with a sigh. "Too late for the hospital," she croaked. She regained her breath, then got his body into the Tahoe.

Thunder rumbled overhead.

She pulled a rough U-turn in the path, crunching down a wedge of switchgrass. She didn't drive back to the house, nor did she turn right to go to the hospital in Somner's Cove. Instead, she turned left, to Lowensport.

CHAPTER TEN

September 1880

I

"Golemancy," the Maharal said. "Ancient evil—the blight of our original faith."

One of the other responding rabbis whispered, "Kischuph."

The Maharal sighed. His name was Benjamin Moreinu, the prelate rabbi of the entire Jewish community in Baltimore. Rumors that were more like pleas had sifted to his Yeshiva shortly after the earthquake here last month— the most ghastly stories of more murderous persecution of his people. The Maharal had immediately brought his delegation, along with a dozen strong male members of his Kahal, to investigate, and to bring aid.

They stood on the main streets of Lowensport, stifled by its desertion. The east end had burned down, but the rest remained intact and graveyard-silent. The other men he'd brought for labor stolidly loaded the carriages with, first, the decayed corpses of the slain Jews, and then the dismembered bodies of this horrendous Conner clan they'd heard about.

It's all true, the Maharal thought now.

It would take days to bury the dead in their respective places of interment. Evidently, here, most of the Jews were as evil as these Conner people, not real Jews at all but heretics. The Maharal walked slowly with his rabbis to survey the horrific aftermath. Only two Lowensport adults had survived the purge, one Amos Croter and his wife Derorah. They'd hidden themselves in the woods and had sent word to Baltimore. When the bloodshed had ended on the last night of July, Croter and his wife—never willing members of the Kischuph sect here—had seen to the care of the Lowensport infants who'd been spared. There were twenty-two such infants, one being the ten-month-old son of Gavriel Lowen himself. *Babies are innocent of evil*, the Maharal felt secure. *God has decreed it*. Here they would be raised in the remainder of the town that hadn't burned, and nursed back to the proper faith.

No one spoke much as they continued to walk through the dead town.

"Maharal!" one of the workers called out. "I believe we've found it!"

They moved quickly to the razed mill, now just ash and charred larch. Some of his men had been digging here for hours, to discern what other truths could be found of Amos Croter's claims. *They dynamited the mill, Maharal, and the only living man within before the blast was Gavriel Lowen.*

The Maharal knew well of this name, which sent a chill up his spine even now. *Sorcerer . . .* The digger showed him the skull that could be none other than Lowen's. Several other diggers had already found the parts of the goilem destroyed here as well.

"Take it all to this heretic's house," the Maharal instructed. "The rabbis there know what to do. Tell them I shall arrive later, before sundown, for the final intercessions and prayers of banishment . . . and give them this."

The Maharal handed over a wooden mezuzah vessel.

* * *

The slaughter of Lowensport had been ghastly enough, but now he and his delegation had proceeded to the camp of collapsed tents and demolished shacks that gave cover to Conner and his rogues. The slaughter here?

Much, much worse.

"Amos Croter said that *two* goilems were created," one rabbi remarked.

"Only one was destroyed in the mill, clearly . . ."

"And the other one . . . did *this.*"

The bodies lay everywhere, men, women, and children alike—all torn limb from limb. "S'mol is said to grant golemancy to those who turn from God," the Maharal said, his voice like smoke. "Riches and infernal power with which to serve darkness. S'mol mocks creation by mimicking God's breathing of life into Adam, who was made of mud."

"Amen," several men said.

A corruption *of God's creation*, thought the Maharal with the sickest heart.

"We must thank our Creator that the earthquake last month had sucked the steamboat down."

The Maharal nodded. "Surely, the arm of God sunk that boat. He was with us, indeed." *With that much Vltava clay, Gavriel would've perpetrated evil all throughout this secluded land.*

Another rabbi bid the question, "But where did he get the clay for the first two goilems?"

Still more of the notorious legend was obviously true. "Every member of the town brought it here themselves, from Prague, when they emigrated in 1840. There were barely more than a hundred of them, chased from their homeland and condemned as Kischuph. Each of them was able to secret several ounces apiece, brought over in jars and tobacco tins. Perhaps Gavriel Lowen *foresaw* the persecution that awaited. Evil, my friends, has many faces."

When he could bear no more witness to this noxious place of bodies and rot, he led his people past the outskirts, for the stench was stifling. Wild dogs had obviously fed well.

Then, men in the distance called out.

"Maharal! We've found some more!"

"It's Conner," he was told. "And those two there, his lieutenants."

"They were still wearing their ID tags leftover from the War."

Two other woodsmen lay pulled apart in the thicket. Flies buzzed en masse, and maggots rilled. Their faces—what hadn't been eaten off—hung in peeling rot, yet ghosts of their expressions remained: unutterable terror. The severed limbs had been gnawed—more wild dogs, no doubt—and their bellies emptied.

"This one here, Maharal," one of the men identified. "The one called Conner."

In spite of the atrocity, the Maharal saw a wretched justice laying before him. The goilem, charged by the wrath of S'mol, clearly had had some wits: the thing had chained Conner to a tree only yards from his ravaged comrades.

"So we see. When the dogs had had their fill of *dead* meat, they came for the *living* meat." It was all too clear that Conner had been fed upon while still alive.

Vengeance is mine, saith the Lord, thought the Maharal.

Later, as the sun began to sink, a horse and carriage took him and his rabbis down the sleepy road toward the house built by Gavriel Lowen. *Soon, God's will will be done, and then we can leave this accursed place.*

One of the rabbis beseeched him. "Maharal, if I may. We understand that the Kischuphite's first creature was killed in the mill—"

"Yes," the Maharal confirmed. "But remember, Lowen brought *two* to unlife, not just one. No doubt the second goilem slaughtered Conner and his wicked clan."

"The second goilem," the rabbi muttered.

"And I know what you ponder, good servant. Where is that second monster now?" The Maharal's gaze reached out to the darkening horizon. "I can only suppose that time will tell . . ."

II

The Present

"Come on, Captain," Stein complained from the coffee machine. "What gives? You haven't been yourself for days."

Rosh looked up from behind his desk, blanched. *What gives? Shit.* Since he'd looked into the back of that step van, his whole world had changed. Up was now down, white was now black. Everything he knew to be *right* was now undeniably and irretrievably wrong.

Stein smirked, fudging the night-shift operating report. "It's like you don't even want to sell crack anymore."

"Keep your voice down," Rosh grated, rubbing his eyes.

"We're the only ones on tonight, remember? Let's go bust up some whores or something, kill a few rummies.

Like you always say, they're bad for the economy." Stein laughed, hoping his superior would do the same.

"The only thing I honestly want to do," Rosh said, "is leave town, never come back."

"And give up your Scarface gig? Man, take a vacation."

Rosh flinched when the door swung open.

"The Mystery Man," Stein said. "We haven't seen you face-to-face in a long time."

Asher Lowen, looking harried and a little bit shocked, came in and closed the door. He locked it behind him.

"It's not a good idea for you to be seen here, Mr. Lowen," Rosh spoke up. "Rabbis don't hang out at police stations."

Asher sat down; he seemed exerted. "I need your help, Captain, and being that I've helped you quite a bit in the past, I'm sure you'll oblige."

"Where's D-Man and Nutjob? Usually they're the ones who deliver your messages."

Asher set down a small bag. "I have reason to believe they're both dead, and I came very close to being dead myself just a little while ago."

Rosh and Stein looked at each other. "You look pretty banged up, Mr. Lowen," Stein pointed out. "What happened? Some out-of-towners moving on your turf?"

"There was a mishap," Asher confessed very lightly. "Several of my men were killed. We were preparing something that's very important."

"What?" Rosh asked with a twinge in his gut.

Asher pulled a browned skull out of the bag. "You wouldn't understand even if I told you. And you wouldn't believe it."

Rosh cleared his throat to keep his voice from cracking. "After what I saw in the back of the van the other night, I'll believe anything."

Asher, even in his distress, managed to smile. "Such is the difference between faith and witness. Very rarely are we shown such signs and wonders."

Silence for a moment. Then Stein broke it with a chuckle. "The Captain's all shook up 'cos he says your hitter's a *monster*." He waited for an amused reply but Asher's face remained stolid.

"I need protection," the rabbi said.

"From what?" Rosh suddenly blurted out. "That thing?"

All three men jumped to their feet at the loud crash from the front lobby. The sound of breaking glass, hurled furniture, and thudding footsteps rose to a mad din.

"It's that *thing*, isn't it?" Rosh wailed.

"No," Asher whispered. "It's another one, but it's worse . . ."

Rosh's face reddened. "Stein! Get out there!"

Stein cocked his pistol, unlocked the door, and dashed out. Rosh closed the lock right behind him. Gunshots rang out in a quick staccato, then more thrashing. Stein's screams rose high, then plummeted to muffled mewls. Then . . .

More silence.

"Get me out of here, Rosh," Asher calmly ordered.

Rosh fumbled at the window, then yelped at the loud *bang!* Then another, then another. Something huge was impacting the locked door—a *metal* door in a *steel* frame—until the frame began to grind loose.

Rosh trembled in place, in tears now. He shakily raised his pistol and waited for the inevitability—

BANG!

The door and frame together were knocked out of the wall.

Rosh shrieked into his portable radio, "All channels, all units! Signal thirteen, signal thirteen, Somner's Cove HQ! Send help now—"

Dust and smoke hung in the imploded doorway.

Two human legs were thrown into the room. Then two arms.

Then Stein's head.

The assailant stepped through the threshold.

Rosh emptied half his magazine into its glistening, gray-brown chest. In his delirium, he noted the word wetly inscribed there—TZEDEK—which was a different word from what he'd seen written on the one in the van. But something else . . .

This one was broad, filled out, hulking whereas the other one had been nearly as thin as a skeleton. Dark hair sprouted from the top of its head and the open eyes, though clearly dead, looked right back at Rosh.

The cluster of bullet holes grouped in the center of the chest looked like hole-punches. Rosh desperately fired several more shots, lower, but to no effect. He fired the last shot—

bam!

—in the center of the thing's clay-smeared forehead.

Then the thing smiled.

Rosh screamed like a baby as he was thrown from wall to wall; then he barked, doglike, as his right arm was slowly torqued out of his shoulder. The thing's face pulled close, then its earthy fingers pried Rosh's jaw down until mandibular tendons tore.

First Rosh's right hand, then his entire arm was rammed down his throat.

He lived just long enough to feel his own fingers twitch in the pit of his belly.

Seven minutes later, three county cruisers and a state pursuit car squealed to a halt out front. Officers with automatic weapons covered one another as they infiltrated, first, the thrashed lobby, then assaulted the captain's office in the back.

How the inner office door and frame had been torn from its seat no one could guess, yet even more inexplicable was the man-sized hole seemingly blasted out of the cinder-block rear wall.

"You gotta be shitting me," someone said.

The mangled remains of two men in law enforcement uniforms were what seized the attentions of the respondents foremost. Blood shellacked the floor to show them scarlet mirror images of themselves. Eventually, the senior county evidence technician arrived—a man named Cristo—and his first verbal reaction was something akin to, "The hits just keep on comin'." In a short while he was able to ID the two decedents as Captain Rosh and Sergeant Stein, yet he could not account for the mode of extreme violence that certainly and obviously had led to their deaths. Somehow, though, he was not surprised by the equally unaccountable traces of clay that he found on the body parts.

Then a final mystery presented itself. Parked askew in the front lot was a dark late-model sedan registered to county resident Asher Lowen, yet Mr. Lowen could not be located on the premise, nor would he ever be seen again.

III

Judy supposed it was something premonitory which caused her to wait back at the Lowen House in the dead of night. The black clouds massed low, yet thus far no storm had broken. She waited and watched, not quite sure what she was waiting *for* . . .

After Seth had died, she'd elected not to take him to the hospital, instead, driving straight to Lowensport, and the specious House of Hope. The town looked abandoned, not a single light burned in any house. Following her hunch, she'd dragged Seth's body through a back door and found, initially, plastic buckets of crack cocaine, surely tens of thousands of dollars' worth, along with rows of conventional kitchen ovens that were evidently being used to "cook" cocaine base down to crack. In the same room, though, she found all four of the barrels stolen from their basement, the barrels marked HILNA. One had been opened; a quarter of its content was missing. Judy didn't have to wonder exactly what this clay had been used for.

It took her half an hour to sufficiently soften more of the clay with hot water and a trowel that had obviously been used for that purpose in the past. Once done, she covered Seth's body with the clay, packing it on extra thick, thinking, *The more clay, the more strength* . . .

Then she wrote on her dead love's chest the word TZEDEK, which was phonetic Hebrew for VENGEANCE.

Seth's muck-caked body rose, then walked out of the room.

Next, Judy drove back to the clearing, remembering the textbook. *Severe impact, dismemberment, and fire*. The hatchet in the Circle of Ten Circles was still there, and with it she emotionlessly dismembered the disenchanted golem that had been the corpse of Seth's wife.

By four thirty A.M., she was still waiting at the house, and that's when the hulking figure appeared from the switchgrass, bearing the unconscious body of Asher Lowen and a small bag. The thing did not acknowledge her as it descended into the basement. She winced at several ugly cracking sounds, and then howls of torment. Other less distinct noises reached her ears. A splashing sound? Wood abruptly splitting? Judy wasn't afraid when she slowly took the steps down and switched on the flashlight.

Asher Lowen lay cringing, his thighs and upper arms snapped like broomsticks. The two barrels of coal dust had been cracked open, their contents heaped liberally over Asher's form and around the inner walls. Gavriel's skull had been pulverized.

The splashing still resounded. The golem enlivened by the word for vengeance was upending the gasoline can on the pile of coal dust and splashing the larch wood walls. When the can was emptied, it clattered to the floor.

Then the thing that used to be Seth turned and looked at her.

"Oh, God," she sobbed. She knew what he wanted.

Judy touched her cigarette lighter to the edge of the gasoline stain. First the pile of dust ignited, slowly incinerating Asher Lowen, and then the larch walls turned to fire.

Judy stepped back, looking at Seth.

He stood in the middle of the rising gust of fire. His clay-sheathed arm extended. His finger pointed to the basement steps.

Sobbing, Judy rushed out just as the first wave of heat and smoke reached out for her.

She stood back in the yard for a time, watching the

basement doorway disgorge flames. She started to walk away but stopped.

From her pocket she withdrew the bag of crack. *Seven pieces left,* she saw, and halfheartedly she thought, *Seven. The perfect number.*

She threw the bag into the fiery doorway, jogged to the Tahoe, and drove south, for the airport.

There'd only been one thing she hadn't noticed. Earlier, when she'd returned from her first trip to the airport, she'd left the black step van parked in the front yard, but now it was no longer there.

EPILOGUE

Grassy fields and hardy farmland shimmered in green chaos, mile after mile after mile. First Maryland, then Virginia, then Kentucky . . . The black van clattered on, belching smoke, jamming gears, and squealing bearings. A typical person wouldn't dream of taking a vehicle this run-down on so arduous and indeterminate a road trip, yet Lydia Lowen, attired in her austere black dress, hardly qualified as typical.

S'mol protects the faithful, she knew. Perhaps Asher wasn't faithful enough, or perhaps, just as God worked in mysterious ways, so too did the devil.

Upon the failure of the last rite, the town had already disbanded—as it was written—and would reassemble no more, each individual venturing out as a beacon of darkness in a world of blessed turmoil. And as S'mol had given Lydia protection, he'd also given her the strength to singlehandedly roll the three and a half remaining barrels of Vltava clay up the ramp into the back of the van. When she'd found D-Man's formidable corpse at that traitor Croter's house, she'd hauled it up into the van as well.

She considered that Asher may have gotten too greedy. Pride and avarice were sins either way. *He'd lost sight of the wisdom of our melech,* she felt sure.

I will not.

So she drove and drove, content in her protector's embrace, and would go to wherever he guided her. *Just like Moses*, she thought with a quiet smile.

And she was sure that D-Man's body would make a fine goilem, and would be the first of many.

☐ **YES!**

Sign me up for the Leisure Horror Book Club and send my FREE BOOKS! If I choose to stay in the club, I will pay only $8.50* each month, a savings of $7.48!

NAME: _____

ADDRESS: _____

TELEPHONE: _____

EMAIL: _____

☐ I want to pay by credit card.

☐   ☐ MasterCard.   ☐ DISCOVER

ACCOUNT #: _____

EXPIRATION DATE: _____

SIGNATURE: _____

Mail this page along with $2.00 shipping and handling to:
Leisure Horror Book Club
PO Box 6640
Wayne, PA 19087
Or fax (must include credit card information) to:
610-995-9274
You can also sign up online at **www.dorchesterpub.com**.
*Plus $2.00 for shipping. Offer open to residents of the U.S. and Canada only.
Canadian residents please call 1-800-481-9191 for pricing information.
If under 18, a parent or guardian must sign. Terms, prices and conditions subject to
change. Subscription subject to acceptance. Dorchester Publishing reserves the right
to reject any order or cancel any subscription.